Walk the Red Road

Book Two in The Whisper Legacy

Kristina Circelli

What Amazon™ Readers Are Saying about <u>Beyond the Western Sun</u>

Cover Art by Kelly Hall

© 2011 by Kristina Circelli
ISBN: 0976372827
EAN-13: 9780976372820

First Edition

1 2 3 4 5 6 7 8 9 10

For My Husband, Seth
Together, We Forge Our Own Red Road

Character Guide for The Whisper Legacy

Whisper: Also known as *Kanegv*; the leader of the Land of the Dead, daughter of the Raven-Eater; led Ian Daivya into the spirit realm to save his son, Cole Daivya, in <u>Beyond the Western Sun</u>

Hunting Hawk: Whisper's mate, once served the Raven-Eater but helped Ian succeed in saving Cole in <u>Beyond the Western Sun</u>

Smoke Speaker: Whisper's grandfather and Blue Feather's father; a powerful Elder and Speaker

The Raven-Eater: The former leader of the Land of the Dead; Whisper's father

Blue Feather: Smoke Speaker's daughter and Whisper's mother; known as Gentle Heart in <u>Beyond the Western Sun</u>

Ian Daivya: Cole's father, traveled with Whisper to the Land of the Dead in <u>Beyond the Western Sun</u> to save Cole and end the Raven-Eater's reign

Cole Daivya: Ian Daivya's son, accepted to the Raven-Eater's hearth as a child in <u>Beyond the Western Sun</u>; known as Fighting Fox and Second Son in <u>Walk the Red Road</u>

Creator/Great Spirit: The leader of the Spirit World

Kamama: Whisper's spirit guide, also a prophet-type figure in the Land of the Dead

Earth Keeper: Creator's War Chief, sent to the Land of the Dead to stop the impending war

Dark Water: The leader of the Little Men; Whisper's ally

Sun Woman: The Sky Spirit, leader of the Sky Vault; mother to Blue Cloud

Blue Cloud: Sun Woman's daughter, trapped in Red Bird's body until she can be freed

Anya: The child

The Circle:
Red Water
Fast Bear
Gray Feather
Dark Moon
Earth Seer
Peacekeeper
Sight Keeper
Panther
Healer
Little Sky
Striker
Tall Bear
Smoke Speaker

The Little Men:
Dark Water
Second Son
Burning Wind
Star Seer
Dream Maker
Lifter
Earth Dancer

Whisper's Army:
The Little Men
Sun Woman
Brave Woman
Adagatiya

Creator's Army:
Splinter Foot Girl
Blue Corn Maiden
The Circle

Pronunciation Guide:

Vowels

A-"ah" as in "blah"

E-"ay" as in "hay"

I-"ee" as in "see"

O-"oh" as in "toe"

U-"oo" as in "boo"

Other Sounds:

GV-hard "guh"

TSA-"jah"

QUE/QUA/QUO/QUU-"kw" before vowel

TI-"di"

TSI-"gee"

Prologue

For many moons he had dreamed of this moment, imagining the day he would be welcomed back to the Land of the Dead and reunited with the ones he loved most—the daughter he left behind, and the granddaughter who had given up her life for destiny. Speaking to the smoke that wafted up from warm fires could only offer so much, and he longed to hold his daughter in his arms again, to greet his granddaughter with a bow of respect, as she now held a title much more powerful than his own. And now, alone in his hut with only the wind to wish him farewell, Elder Smoke Speaker welcomed the warm embrace of Death.

For ninety-seven years Smoke Speaker had followed the path set before him by his ancestors, and in death he looked forward to walking the Red Road with his family. He had been sick for awhile, and spoke of his illness to none. The last thing the Elder wanted was to be found and buried. No, only the animals would know of his passing, and only the animals would be responsible for his body. A journey into the Spirit World was not his chosen path; he wanted to be in the Land of the Dead, with Whisper and Blue Feather. To ensure his passing to that once forsaken land, he had sharpened his prized flint-tipped blade and dragged it across his wrist, letting his illness and his blood bring him into death.

It seemed so long ago that his granddaughter had given up her life so that Blue Feather could live, so long ago that Blue Feather decided to stay, and be with the daughter she never knew. It had saddened him when he learned that Whisper had sacrificed herself just for Blue Feather to remain in that dark land, but ultimately, it was the right decision. Now, mother and daughter ruled over the Land of the Dead side by side. And he was ready to join them.

"Great Spirit," the Elder whispered, closing his eyes for the final time, "let me walk in peace."

When his eyes opened, a gray curtain of mist and melancholy met his eyes. Smoke Speaker knew this place. He had traveled once to the Land of the Dead to save his daughter, and instead came back to the living world with Whisper. This was the land of Waiting, where all dead souls came to determine their eternal fate.

Smoke Speaker didn't waste any time. He was eager to see his family, and in death, his old, brittle bones let him move much faster. He headed quickly to the Bridge of the Dead, keeping his eyes down, his attention on his destination rather than the lost souls wandering aimlessly. They had forgotten where to go, who they were, and were now forced to live forever as decrepit spirits driven by hate and hopelessness. Only one attempted to cross the Elder's path, but a simple prayer had the dead soul moving on without conflict.

How long it took him to reach the Bridge of the Dead, Smoke Speaker couldn't say. To him it seemed like hours, but it could have very well been days. Eventually, he reached the Bridge, and the tower he would enter before crossing.

As it was the first time he crossed, the Bridge of the Dead was surrounded by dead souls cheering and cat-calling like drunken spectators. They dared not touch the grotesque gate constructed with the remains of the deceased—blood and rotting guts and foul bits of clothes. Tatters of cloth flapped in the breeze and a rancid stench wafted from the Bridge of the Dead, where blood, gore, and death coated the surface.

Taking in a brave breath and ignoring those who eagerly awaited his turn at the Bridge, Smoke Speaker squared his shoulders and entered the hut, ready to face the Watchmen.

The familiar stench of rotting corpses mixed with mud and stale air instantly offended his senses. Brown sludge dripped from the walls of the cramped hut, a single gray candle casting a menacing glow from the corner. On the other side of the room was the door that led to the Bridge of the Dead, a narrow, black door that seemed to form out of candle wax and brown muck. It looked so far away, an illusion of the Watchmen.

"*Speak...stranger...*" the voices of the Watchmen penetrated his ears. They spoke slowly and without care, yet in whispery tones tinted with desire for blood. "*Who seeks passage...across the Bridge of the Dead?*"

The old man held his head high. "I am Elder Spoke Speaker of the Panther Clan. I am a powerful medicine man, and plan to join my daughter and granddaughter in the Land of the Dead." A pit of dread formed in the back of his throat when the Watchmen appeared before him, their empty eye sockets strangely curious. Their bodies were translucent, woven together with wisps of wind, smoke, and dead souls. Death and despair radiated off of them.

"*You willingly pass...to the Land of the Dead.*" Now their voices were curious as well, for only one other had ever come to them with the intention of heading straight for the land where souls become lost and forgotten. "*State your purpose there.*"

"My family is there," Smoke Speaker answered calmly, honestly. "My granddaughter, *Kanegv.*"

The Watchmen drew back at that. They spared one another a glance before surrounding the Elder in a blur of spinning smoke. "*The half-breed,*" they rasped with both envy and hate, envy for all that she had accomplished, hate because she would not free them from their post. "*We were warned. . .about you.*"

That caught Smoke Speaker's attention. "Warned about me for what?"

"*They. . .are. . .waiting.*"

The door opened, and the Watchmen disappeared back into walls. Cautiously, the Elder crept back outside, where the dead souls had stepped back from the bone-crafted fence in awe. He turned his old eyes to see what they were seeing, a smile of hope and surprise crossing his wrinkled face.

The Watchmen were right. They were waiting for him.

But they were not the ones he was expecting.

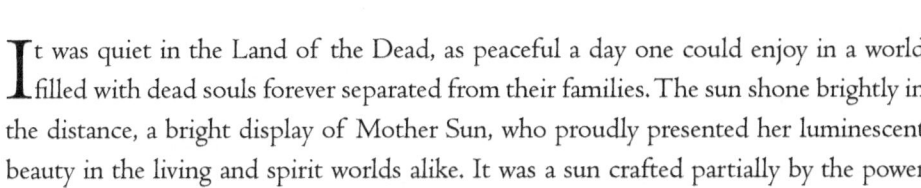

Chapter 1

It was quiet in the Land of the Dead, as peaceful a day one could enjoy in a world filled with dead souls forever separated from their families. The sun shone brightly in the distance, a bright display of Mother Sun, who proudly presented her luminescent beauty in the living and spirit worlds alike. It was a sun crafted partially by the power of the half-breed, the woman who brought brightness to a world of darkness, the heir to the Land of the Dead who looked for a fight and was always ready for war.

That woman now sat atop Eagle, soaring so high above her land that not even the whispers of her people could travel the wind to her ears. Having made her peace with Eagle, being granted forgiveness for murder as an act of treason against the Raven-Eater, the woman known as *Kanegv*, as Whisper, leaned over and rested her chin on her hands as she stared out at the Western Sun.

It seemed so long ago that she had passed through the Western Sun to meet her final death. And, in fact, it had been. Whisper had seen eighteen years since the Raven-Eater put an arrow through her chest, since taking the throne of the Land of the Dead, and still she looked the part of her twenty-three year-old self.

But her youth fooled none. Her haunting black eyes that had seen life and death, those skilled hands that could kill without hesitance, the power that swelled within her that surpassed a magic any had ever known before, all gave Whisper a hardened look of pure malevolence. Yet she could also be kind and compassionate, and it was her two sides that made her the leader the Land of the Dead needed.

"*Sanctuary,*" she whispered to Eagle, directing her companion to her own personal haven among the dead. As Eagle shifted, gently lifting his wings in the light breeze, Whisper looked down on her kingdom fondly.

She saw the Weeping Forest in the distance, with its black trees and heavy curtains of sticky thicket. She saw the plainspeople beyond that, relatively new villages populated by dead souls who had long since forgotten their names and former families. To her right were the Barren Plains, where Mole still reigned and brought deceit to any who dared to believe his words. On her left sat the Fire Mountains, hot and tall and treacherous. Beyond them, the Land of the Dead stretched for endless miles, covered with undergrowth and trees, spotted with small villages, and stalked by the creatures that preyed on the flesh of dead souls.

But there was also beauty in this world of shadows, a place that could never be the light of the Spirit World, but one that held its own charm and quirks nonetheless. It was not meant to be a land of hope and peace, and yet, it wasn't a place that instilled fear in any who spoke its name. Whisper had made it her own sort of safe haven for those unfortunate enough to enter into the realm where darkness met death.

Whisper sat up, tucking her legs just behind Eagle's wings and peering out at the land they were approaching. She adjusted the strap across her back that held a recently sharpened blade and made sure the belt around her waist, which included a small knife and medicine pouch, was tight. She wore a loose top that crisscrossed her shoulders and was torn at the hem, with baggy buckskin pants decorated with the marks of her ancestors.

Pieces leftover from the pants she had made with her own two hands had been braided and wrapped around her wrists and accented with black and red beads, black for the color of the West and red for the color of the East, the directions of death and life. Those beads mimicked the ones tied in her hair, painted blue for the North and white for the South. Her hair was held back with a thin string of what closely resembled hemp. Long ago she had been forced to give up her beloved boots that had seen her through her first trek through the Land of the Dead, and today she wore sandals that didn't do much more than protect the soles of her feet.

She was dressed for a day without worry of war, and planned on enjoying what free time she actually had to herself.

Eagle soared over the Fire Mountains, easily avoiding the drafts of searing heat that wafted up from the caverns and jagged peaks. Whisper ran a hand down his smooth feathers absently as she awaited their destination, thinking back to her days in the living realm, wondering what her grandfather was doing at that very moment. She thought of him often, and looked forward to their reunion.

As Eagle began his descent, she could hear the sounds of the waterfall, the churning rapids, of the rare songbirds as they called to the rising Mother Sun. When he was above the river, his shadow but a speck of reflection against the crystal-clear waters, Whisper rose and stood upon his back. She balanced perfectly, bracing herself for the long fall.

"*Wado,*" Whisper thanked him for the ride, then leapt.

Chapter 2

Smoke Speaker allowed his guides to lead him across what he could only describe as the most beautiful landscape he had ever dreamed. And he truly believed that's what it was—nothing but a dream granted to him by the love of his ancestors as he passed into the Land of the Dead.

Tall, majestic trees bearing luscious fruits lined the solid rock walkway, while colorful wildflowers saturated the scenery with vibrant reds and purples and yellows. The sky above was a bright white-blue that made his spirits soar, and the sun was so gorgeous that he wished he could simply stop and stare. The golden orb soothed his sorrow over death and warmed every last bit of him, as though welcoming him to the place where he was meant to be.

A soft breeze passed through the trees and lifted his long grayish-white hair from bony shoulders. It was a wind filled with nostalgic scents that brought him back to days spent watching the birds and deer with his father as they immersed themselves in the wonder of nature, one that made the air dance all around him. A smile crossed his wrinkled, rugged face as his deep chocolate eyes took in the beauty that surrounded his old body.

Yes, this was the place destined for him. He could feel that much in his bones. But still he was unsettled by the fact that the rules were being broken for him, that he was allowed into such a paradise after having taken his own life.

"Where are we going, my brothers?" he asked the two men walking just in front. They were dressed in spotless white frocks adorned with the symbols and images he had come to know and love throughout his long life, while their feet were bare yet didn't seem to mind walking across the terrain. Both had long, sleek black hair tied in thick braids by pieces of leather that trailed down their backs. Their skin was deeply tanned and bore the scripts of their people, tribal designs and markings that told tales of days in battle.

One of them turned slightly to address the Elder's question. "You have been chosen, Elder Smoke Speaker. Your death has new meaning now."

* * *

Her body turned in the air, freefalling to the earth gracefully as the wind whipped her hair into a frenzy and wrapped Whisper in a blanket of warmth. The voices of her people, the scents of her land, soared toward her and rammed into her ears while her arms stretched out to her sides so her fingers could play through the palpable strands of air. It was a fall that would have terrified others, would have been met with screams and pleas for mercy, but to Whisper, it was peace.

Here, in the air, she was free.

She smelled the water as her body hurled closer, and opened her eyes to take in the beautiful falls, the white-frothed peaks, the river that stretched on for miles. The faintest of smiles crossed her face as she twisted, lifting her arms above her head and setting her hands together. Just before she hit the water, she closed her eyes.

The rapids ripped Whisper in a full circle as soon as she broke through the surface, sending her body two dozen feet downriver across rocks smoothed by ages of running water. This was a ride she loved, feeling completely helpless as she was swept away, at the mercy of a river that didn't care about her life or death. The river didn't need her for guidance, or look to her for advice. The rapids didn't ask for forgiveness when they slammed her knee against a rock, or bow down to her out of fear. She was on her own.

Just when it looked like she would shoot up to the surface, the current jerked her body down. Whisper knew this ride, was familiar with the tug that rocketed her head-first further beneath the surface. Soon she was blind in a cocoon of black water that threatened to crush her as it sent her deeper into uncharted territory. Even with her eyes closed, she knew that all around her, waiting on the other side of the current, were translucent fish-like creatures with jagged teeth eager to tear her apart if only they could break through the rushing barrier. She could feel their want for blood, could hear the desire for flesh that pulsed through their nerves.

Soon, her chest began to burn and her lungs threatened to burst. Even in death, the heavy pressure of deep water affected bodies like they were still of the living, a mystery not even Whisper could solve. When the current slowed just enough so she could open her eyes, she lifted the blade from her belt and slashed out through the water, gaining her footing on the slippery rocks and spinning in a circle as she lifted her body out of the raging waters. She twisted and arched with her knife stretched out before her, water spraying from her loose hair and whipping around her in a thick red halo.

"Not this time," she whispered with a smirk as the dead scaled bodies plopped into the water and floated on the surface, pools of blood rippling throughout the cave. The first time she'd been to this place, this underwater cavern of darkness and destruction, one of them had taken a chunk from her side. They didn't respect her place as leader of the Land of the Dead, and she respected them for that, though not enough to spare their lives.

The others fled when the bodies of their fallen brothers and sisters hit the water, and so Whisper turned and trod through the pool to solid ground. The only light came from strange, worm-like creatures that clung to the stalactites of the cavern and emitted a beautiful blue glow. The light that cast around the cave revealed thick walls of wet rock smoothed down after years of water runoff. The ceiling was high, shouting echoes to all corners of the cavern with every step she took.

Whisper had discovered this place by accident, during a hunting trip at the river when she lost her footing. She'd been hunting a legendary beast in the Land of the Dead, one that had haunted her ancestors. *Ukenta* was known by many names to many tribes, and he lived here, in this river. It had only taken one rough bump of her makeshift raft to send her into the water, then the current had taken care of the rest.

She felt at home in this open, airy cavern with razor-toothed fish and no sunlight. She felt safe, relaxed, free. It was a place away from her real life, yet was also a space where she could keep an eye on her land without worrying about prying eyes.

Taking a seat on the only stone ledge, Whisper sheathed her knife and ran her hands through her wet hair, ringing out the water. She leaned forward and rested her elbows on a rock pillar that rose to her knees. In that pillar was a round basin filled with dark blue water. She never knew how that pillar arrived at its sacred resting place, and it was a story she hoped to one day learn. Sometime long ago, far before her time, far before the Raven-Eater's reign, some powerful leader or shaman had blessed this place and bestowed upon it an ancient magic. That magic allowed her to see things that normally would be veiled even with her own abilities.

"*Ududu*," she whispered, picturing her grandfather in her mind as she lightly grazed her fingers across the water and instructed it to reveal the events of the past few days in the Land of the Living. For a moment nothing happened, then the ripples came together to form an image that brought sadness to her heart.

Elder Smoke Speaker sat at his hearth, staring vacantly into the fire. All around him the birds sang to the morning while a light fog drifted across the ground. The sun was already shining, a bright blue sky welcoming the new day. Yet it was unable to soothe the Elder, for he knew his time had come.

It had been awhile since Whisper last looked in on her grandfather. She was able to watch some things from the Fire Tower with her own powers, but even she had her limits. Here, in this place, in this cavern she had named *Owenvsv*, Home, she could be right next to him, seeing what he saw, hearing what he heard, feeling what he felt. It was a connection stronger than any she had ever known before.

Right now, she felt his tiredness and the aches in his old bones. Smoke Speaker had let his body shut down, fasting until his final days. He was old and ready to move on, and by refusing his body food he was forsaking his place in the Spirit World so he could be with his daughter and granddaughter in the Land of the Dead. Whisper felt the pain in his belly in her own, and nearly gagged at the nausea. Her eyes were heavy, but she could bear his exhaustion better than he.

"Elder," she whispered sadly, hating to see him so frail, someone who had once been a steadfast beacon of strength now reduced to a visage of brittle bones and sorrow. She touched the water again to move the vision along, watching as he lay down on his straw bed, drew forth his knife, and closed his eyes for the last time after lowering the blade to his wrists. Whisper didn't cry, as her tears were saved only for those moments of deepest heartache, but her souls grieved as the last breath left his body and she felt a part of her die along with him.

Soon the vision took her to the Bridge of the Dead, where the Elder stood before the Watchmen, who delivered a message Whisper didn't understand. When he crossed the Bridge, the vision faded.

"*Ududu*," she said again, commanding the vision back, but nothing appeared save for a single ripple of water. Something, or someone, was blocking her sight.

Angered, Whisper rose and kicked the pillar, not moving it an inch. She paced the edge of the water, where the fish were eagerly awaiting her return. It didn't make any sense, as nothing had ever barred her vision before and certainly nothing had ever been stronger than her. Something was happening, and it infuriated her to know that she was caught unaware.

Her senses picked up a scent then, high above the cavern. She snarled to herself while her spirits began to soften at the same time. Whisper sighed, turned away from the water and pillar, and let out a shout of rage and frustration that echoed off the walls. She'd wanted to sit here in peace, reflect on things, not deal with the problems of the only person who knew where *Owenvsv* was located.

There was a small opening at the back of the cavern. It was there that Whisper headed, slipping back into the darkness. After a few steps the floor gave out and she freefell back into the water deep below the ground, where the current carried her to the surface.

Chapter 3

For too long Creator's people had walked the roads of the forgotten, disrespected for their beliefs in nature and harmony. For too long their traditions had been mocked, cast aside, ridiculed as they suffered at the hands of the non-believers. Now, they were being given a second chance, an opportunity to bring their heritage back to the Land of the Living and rejoice in the rebirth of a time where love, unconditional giving, and a deep value for culture were celebrated. And in restoring their place among the living, they would provide a safe haven for those passing into death.

The Raven-Eater had turned the Land of the Dead into a place of fear, and that evil had trickled into the Land of the Living, making it a world frightened of the old ways. He had corrupted their minds, his own people, to fight a personal war. And now, the Great Spirit was determined to put an end to that reign of fear and terror.

A new sun had finally risen. What was once a place where bringers of hate were renowned in order to fight in another's war would soon be a true sanctuary for the lost and beaten, no longer forgotten, no longer hurting. His mission was to ensure the ones who walked the Red Road were celebrated with respect, whether they made the long journey to the Spirit World or were not lucky enough to receive their proper burials.

It would take the greatest of minds, the greatest of powers, to bring this vision to fruition, which was why he had gathered the most supreme collection of spiritual leaders for his journey. With this last soul, his legion of leaders was complete, and together they could guide the spirit realms in a new direction.

"The time has come," a man said then, entering the room with a smile. He was bare-chested with a buffalo cape cloaking his shoulders, while loose buckskin pants decorated his legs. His torso was wide and heavily scarred, proving his status as a fierce War Chief. "The others are awaiting his arrival."

The collector of souls smiled as well, rising from his seat. He towered over the War Chief, nine feet of pure muscle and power, but the other man had no reason to fear him. "Good, Earth Keeper. Let us go and meet him."

Together, the two headed out of the massive palace of stone and earth and stepped out onto grass that cushioned each step. His greeting would be warm and inviting, and he hoped the Elder remembered that when he presented his mission.

Not all things could be as pleasant as this place, particularly when the future of all worlds were at stake.

Guilt tore at Elder Smoke Speaker as he patiently waited at the river's edge. His two companions had left him only moments ago, turning to head back to the Bridge of the Dead in order to collect more souls granted passage into the Spirit World. They hadn't explained their purpose, and so the Elder was still confused as to why he was here. He had let himself die. He had purposely starved his body of the nourishment it desperately needed, had let himself bleed instead of bandaging his wounds, and had passed knowing his final resting place was in the Land of the Dead.

And now he was standing but a boat ride away from the land of spirits given a second chance in death. The world behind him was beautiful, with air that sparkled, clean aqua waters, and tall luscious trees bearing savory fruit. Eventually, that land gave way to a more barren, desolate landscape that led the way back to the Bridge of the Dead. It was back there that he belonged, on the other side of the world where the lost resided, not here, where hope and happiness were waiting around every corner.

He had been promised any and everything by his companions, who made it their mission to convince Smoke Speaker that he was desperately needed.

"*The world is changing,*" one had said solemnly, arcing an arm across the sky. "*Only here are talents such as yours respected to their fullest.*"

They hadn't answered the Elder's many questions, so he'd given up asking them. Instead, he waited at the river and struggled with himself over actually passing into the Spirit World. For so many years he'd promised his daughter and granddaughter that one day he would meet them in the Land of the Dead. He'd told Whisper while training and preparing her for her death that she would never be left alone, that he'd always be at her side to help her handle all that the Land of the Dead tossed her way.

And now he was breaking that promise.

Was it worth it? Would Whisper and Blue Feather understand his reasons, or would they hate him for his decision? He guessed his daughter would come to terms with his choices, but Whisper was another story. He could not predict her reaction, and that scared him most of all.

"Your thoughts are deep, Elder," a voice said at his side. Smoke Speaker turned, startled to see that a young man had rowed up to the riverbank. "I am Earth Keeper. I will take you to the Great Spirit."

The Great Spirit. The name reverberated in the Elder's mind. For his entire life, Smoke Speaker had dreamed of one day meeting the Creator of Worlds, but had resigned himself to the fact that he would never greet the maker of his people. Knowing that he was about to be brought to such a spirit was almost too incredible to believe. Unable to speak, he climbed into the canoe and settled in as the warrior began to row down the river.

"Earth Keeper…you are of the Iroquois?" Smoke Speaker gestured to the man's tribal markings on his shoulder.

"Yes. I was a War Chief killed during a raid. Many women and children died. A neighboring tribe attacked our village, and an arrow pierced my heart when we fought back the next morning." He spared the Elder a single sad look. "My people were victorious, but I lost my life. Now, I assist Creator."

"A noble position," the Elder commented, more so to himself. "Perhaps you can tell me why the Great Spirit has taken me from my place in the Land of the Dead."

Earth Keeper hesitated, rowing steadily through the smooth waters. The sun was beginning to lower, creating an orange glow that lit up the mountains in the background. "You are a respected Elder, Smoke Speaker, one with great power. It has not gone unnoticed by Creator. He needs your assistance, Elder, for the preservation of our kind."

"What do you mean?"

"I can say no more, Elder. Only the Great Spirit can tell you the rest."

Smoke Speaker could respect that. Loyalty was not something he would ever question. "What about my family? They are still in the Land of the Dead."

"They must remain in the Land of the Dead. This is not their journey, Elder, but yours and yours alone. They must accept that."

Smoke Speaker doubted they would be so willing to accept, but didn't say so. Instead, he kept his eyes forward and let his mind wonder over what could be so important that Creator needed his help. He was but an old Elder who lived in the mountains. What could he possibly be needed for?

Chapter 4

Hunting Hawk was waiting for her when she rose from the water. He watched as she lifted herself in one smooth motion, a vision of fury and frustration and power dripping with the cold water of a merciless river. The former Navajo warrior admired her steadfast strength and unwavering courage. It was a confidence she needed to be leader of the Land of the Dead, one that had drawn him to her from the very beginning.

He remembered their first meeting clearly, when she was the enemy and he was the War Chief ordered to cut off her head and bring it back to the Raven-Eater. Even then, there'd been something about her that intrigued Hunting Hawk. That fearless walk, those mesmerizing eyes, the way she looked right through him as though he was but a speck of dust in the wind. And when she made her proposition—freedom in the Spirit World in exchange for him faking her capture—he knew he had to stick around to see just who and what this woman was. Forsaking eternity in the Spirit World was the best decision he'd ever made in life and in death, as he now had the woman he'd always dreamed of to call his own.

Even if that woman was currently glaring at him with impatience and disdain written across her face.

"What is it, Hunting Hawk?" Whisper asked as she approached, eyeing the man while wringing water out of her hair. She adjusted the blade strapped across her back. "I told you I would be back soon."

"I know, *Kanegv*, but there are more important matters at hand than your need to get sucked into an underwater cavern." There was derision and scorn in his voice, but his tone was light. He was the only one able to talk to her in such a way.

"Make your point, warrior." Hunting Hawk may be the man sharing her bed, but he was not above her wrath.

"The Elder has crossed the Bridge of the Dead. Our scouts lost him after that, said some kind of barrier forced them back." He noted the look that crossed her face, but didn't know it was caused by her own experience with that barrier. "I thought you would like to know, so you could await his arrival from the Fire Tower."

Whisper nodded and let out a shrill whistle that made Hunting Hawk's ears ache. Eagle appeared out of nowhere and landed gracefully just a few feet from his rider.

"Room for two?" He knew the answer before she turned by the squaring of her shoulders and tensing of her back. It irritated her simply to have the question asked, which was partly why he did so. For reasons unbeknownst to him, it annoyed his mate whenever anyone assumed they were welcome in her presence, and he supposed it was part arrogance and part detachment with the emotional side of a person that had her so unwilling to make a genuine connection with another. And yet, Hunting Hawk asked the questions that got under her skin because a reaction was guaranteed, usually one that amused him. There was no doubt as to what she was capable of doing when upset, but he enjoyed ruffling her feathers.

As expected, she turned slowly and glared at him with those deep black eyes. "Find your own road home," she replied, her voice low and rough. Consenting, the warrior spun around on his heel and started for the Fire Tower. An invisible wall struck against him on his fifth step, all but flattening his face against the air. Mildly annoyed, he faced Whisper again, who had taken her seat atop Eagle's back and was staring at him with a half-grin.

He seized the opportunity and hopped on behind Whisper, wrapping his thick, scarred arms around her and relishing the feeling when she leaned back against him and rested her head on his shoulder.

After a brief and relaxing flight with Hunting Hawk, Whisper was sitting atop the roof of the Fire Tower, staring in the distance at the Western Sun. Keeping watch over her world of dead souls for this long, Whisper knew every river, every forest, every village that developed within her land's boundaries. She knew which direction souls came from when passing through the Western Sun, how long it took to reach the Fire Tower. She was ready to meet her grandfather and show him the kingdom she had built since they last parted ways.

Now, Whisper was positioned in the stone chair that rested at the edge of the Fire Tower. One leg was slung across the armrest, the other was propped up on the low, jagged-tipped wall that wrapped around the roof. She absently twirled a feather through her fingers, chewing on the end as she watched the Western Sun, waiting impatiently. Her eyes, deeply black and reflecting all the death and devastation of the world, stared without blinking and her mouth was set in its almost permanent scowl. She was a beautiful woman, no one would deny, but her beauty was dark, powerful, frightening.

"He should be here by now."

Whisper slowly turned her eyes to the figure approaching from behind. She had sensed Blue Feather's presence long before she opened the heavy wooden door. "He is old," she replied. "Even in death old bones do not move as quickly."

"Still…perhaps we should meet him at the Western Sun."

"If you go near the Western Sun, you turn to ash."

Blue Feather chewed her bottom lip, having temporarily forgotten that part of her curse out of her excitement in seeing Smoke Speaker. For so many moons now she had lived among the dead, a beating heart amidst a sea of forgotten souls. The Raven-Eater, once a fierce tyrant bent on destruction and revenge, had stolen her from her home and brought her to this place of hate and darkness, cursing her with a magic so powerful that not even Whisper could break the spell. She would stay just four and twenty summers for the rest of her eternal life, a mother only a year older than her daughter, a living woman in the Land of the Dead.

Since Whisper had murdered the Raven-Eater, her father, atop the Fire Tower just inches from where she now sat, Blue Feather could enjoy peace in her pseudo-death. She was no longer ruled by fear and sorrow, but instead could sleep at night knowing she was reunited with the daughter she gave up so many years ago. Whisper may be the half-breed, a woman part evil and part good, part Raven-Eater and part Blue Feather, but she was still her daughter, and Blue Feather loved her with all her heart. At times, when the Raven-Eater's blood wasn't controlling her mind, she even suspected that Whisper loved her too.

"I suppose I'll wait here, then."

Whisper heard the regret in her mother's voice as she lowered herself to her knees and stared out at the sun. Regret was not something known to Whisper's heart, as her decisions were based on reason, which allowed only for logic, and desire, which did not allow for guilt. However, she did recognize the look on her mother's face and while she did not feel sympathy for the woman, she did care enough to please her. Blue Feather was, after all, the reason why she had survived the Raven-Eater and been trained by Smoke Speaker in the Land of the Living.

"I will go to him," Whisper said, disgust tinting her voice. She despised leaving the Fire Mountains. Even her place of sanctuary, her secret place of home, was nestled deep in the heart of the mountains. Crossing the Barren Plains was like abandoning her home altogether, leaving the Fire Tower defenseless against potential attacks. Not that she'd experienced any major battles since taking her place at the throne—very few dared to brave the wrath of the half-breed, a woman who could not be killed, but would slit the throat of her own husband without blinking should he betray her trust.

Stifling a bored sigh, Whisper rose and faced her mother. "I will bring him here myself, so that we may be reunited once again."

"Thank you, *Kanegv*," Blue Feather also rose as she spoke her daughter's true name. She reached out and ran her hand down Whisper's braided hair, not bothered by the fact that her daughter's eyes narrowed at the touch. Such was her way. "I'll prepare a feast for his arrival."

Chapter 5

They enjoyed a long yet beautiful and peaceful ride down the river, their boat finally touching the shores of paradise. For a moment, Smoke Speaker merely sat and took it all in. He'd only seen such splendor in his dreams, and never thought the magnificence of the Spirit World would ever meet his eyes.

The smooth blue waters of the river gave way to a sparkling shore lined with glistening white shells and tan sand that formed small dunes. Just beyond those dunes were rolling hills of lush green grass spotted with patches of colorful wildflowers surrounding thick tree trunks that reached up toward an azure sky. Fluffy white clouds wafted across the dome, the sun shining brightly and casting warmth down on the land that wrapped him in a loving embrace.

In the distance, the Elder could see villages filled with strong huts, wide pastures with grazing animals, and happy spirits that mingled with one another. There was laughter all around, spirits who were at peace with their eternal souls and had found homes with one another. The Elder reveled in the sounds of joy, closing his eyes and remembering his own happy times with family.

As he stepped from the boat and touched the welcoming shore, Smoke Speaker was filled with a sense of home he'd never known before. Suddenly, the mountains of North Carolina were but a distant memory and he knew that this place, the Spirit World, was where he was meant to be. Hope, love, happiness, elation, all filled his heart and rejuvenated his spirit as he followed the guards further into the land. He felt younger, stronger, smarter. He felt like he was being welcomed back to the land that had called to his spirits since the day he entered the living realm. Yes, this was his one true home after all.

"We will make way to the Great Spirit," Earth Keeper said, turning slightly to glance at the Elder. "He is waiting for you."

"Yes," Smoke Speaker said dreamily, looking around in wonder. "I am eager to hear his offer."

* * *

Whisper stood in the center of her room, her feet planted in the middle of a drawing etched into stone. She had carefully, painstakingly carved and painted the representation herself, letting her ancestors guide her hands as she mapped out the medicine wheel of her people. She used this wheel as strength and guidance whenever she needed to travel, as it kept her grounded and her feet walking the Red Road of those who walked it before her, rather than the path the Raven-Eater had blazed across the Land of the Dead with his hate and vengeance.

At times, she felt her father's strength tearing at her souls, calling to the parts of her that craved bloodbaths and sacrifices. And worse, those times were becoming more and more frequent, which meant the Raven-Eater was still a strong presence in her heart and mind. She fought against that influence frequently, keeping up a steady battle with the two parts of herself so that she did not become the spirit who brought fear to the Land of the Dead and rewarded those who supported her in murder and wickedness.

No, she had defeated that evil tyrant, the one who gave her life, the Cherokee chief who stole a woman from the Land of the Living to create the half-breed, a woman of half death, half life who couldn't be destroyed. She had defeated hate in its purest form, and in turn, parts of her spirit were freed that she never knew existed.

Once Whisper had recognized that gift granted to her by pure power, no one could stop her. Not even the fury of the Raven-Eater.

The longer she stood in the center of the stone medicine wheel, the more relaxed she felt. Power surged through her, starting from her toes and working its way up to the top of her head and down to the tips of her hair. She turned to face the West, her direction of travel, and whispered a quick prayer for a fast and plentiful journey. The West, the direction of death, answered her prayer with a warm breeze that gently lifted her black hair and sent vibrating tendrils through her veins.

She was ready.

Eagle took them to their waiting place, Whisper hopping off his back with ease and not bothering to watch as Hunting Hawk slid off behind her. She planted her feet firmly in the dry earth and waited. She could stand in one spot for as long as it took, a steadfast pillar of strength in a world threatened by constant chaos.

As the minutes passed, she turned her eyes up to the magnificent Western Sun, which never failed to inspire and amaze her.

The reds and purples swirled together smoothly, creating soft images that relaxed anyone who laid eyes upon the vision of beauty. It had been a long time since she'd seen the Western Sun so close, and even longer since she'd seen the other side, which was harsh and unforgiving as it thrived on the souls—and their eyes—who struggled to pass through. Once, long ago, the Sun had nearly stopped spinning as the Army of the Dead, the Raven-Eater's army, passed through and reached the outer edges of the Land of the Living. To do so would mean the end of her world and theirs as souls dead and alive passed through at their own free will.

For now, the Western Sun was safe. And she would wait here, on the right side, for her grandfather to join her.

Just a few steps behind, Hunting Hawk watched Whisper as she watched the Western Sun. The Sun was one of the few things that could hold her attention for long, and was the only force able to put her at peace with the world. He often wished he had that kind of power, the kind to comfort her, to instantly bring solace to her heart. They had been joined for many years, and trusted one another with the most important secrets and missions, but still she often held him at an arm's length. He supposed it was the blood of the Raven-Eater still pulsing through her that had Whisper so closed off, and he could only pray that one day he found a way to break through that barrier.

He was confident that eventually he would find the cracks in her tough exterior, but for now he would simply be the one to catch her when she fell. And he knew that day was coming. Not even the strongest of leaders could put up such a tough front forever, and with the arrival of Elder Smoke Speaker, he was sure her softer side was about to show as her family was put back together again.

So he took his place next to his mate and waited alongside her. He gently reached out and touched the small of her back, a gesture that had taken Whisper a long time to get used to. Once she had flinched and drawn her blade at the touch; now she inched closer to Hunting Hawk ever so slightly.

How many hours passed, they didn't know. Eventually, Whisper stood as close to the Western Sun as possible without scorching her flesh, staring at the inferno as though she were able to see through the flames.

"I do not understand," she said over her shoulder to Hunting Hawk. "He should be here by now. I saw him take his own life."

"Perhaps he got lost."

"He has been here before. He knows the way," she argued, squinting up at the Sun. "Something is wrong. Something—"

Whisper stopped mid-sentence when she sensed the approaching figure. In less than a second her bow and arrow were aimed at the dead soul coming their way.

The man froze in place, holding up his hands in defense. He was filthy, with matted hair that was once blonde now caked with dirt and dried blood. Streaks of grime ran down his cheeks and his clothes were in tatters, the result of his long race across the Bridge of the Dead against the cat he had run over as a teenager and never bothered to look back. He was young, early thirties perhaps, with a tall frame and sturdy build.

"Whoa," he said instantly at the sight of the arrow, and took a big step back. At first all he could see was the deadly tip, but then his eyes traveled to the woman behind the bow and he knew that this was the one he was searching for. They'd said she was beautiful in a dark, evil kind of way, and they were right. Those black eyes, the way that black hair whipped around a strong, sharp face, dark beauty was his very first impression.

But they had forgotten to mention how those eyes drew a person in, and he found himself wandering closer to the strange woman, eager to know more, before he could stop himself. "You're her," he said with reverence, aching to reach out and touch her but knowing she would likely slice his hand off with one swift arc of that blade at her belt. "You're the leader of the Land of the Dead. They said you would be here."

"They?" Hunting Hawk repeated as Whisper lowered her bow and glared at the man, who was clearly of no threat to her. "Who are you?"

"I...I'm Eli," the man said slowly, not daring to inch closer. "A man met me at the Bridge and said I had to find you because you would be waiting for someone."

"Who met you at the Bridge?"

"I don't know." Eli shook his head, fear pitting in his stomach when Whisper stalked over to him. "I swear, he didn't tell me his name. He wanted me to give you a message."

Whisper grabbed the man by the throat and slung him to the ground. Behind her, Hunting Hawk voiced his disagreement over her actions but she ignored him. "*What* message?"

Eli clutched his throat, feet kicking at the ground. In his panic he could barely register the fact that the woman was only holding on, not squeezing. "I...I...don't know...please...let me go."

"Tell me what was said."

Eli racked his brain, hating himself for forgetting the message in his moment of fear. The rage and distrust in the woman's eyes terrified him. "Um...something about an Elder. That they had him."

Whisper released Eli and straightened, pointing at the man with an arrow. "Give me the whole message."

Eli sucked in a deep breath and stood. "Okay...He said that an Elder... Smoke Speaker, I think? The Elder would not be traveling to the Land of the Dead, because he was needed elsewhere for an important journey. The man said they would take him, and he would be safe, but that you would never see him again. And that you shouldn't search for him, because it would be futile."

Fury and grief tore at Whisper, fury for the faceless, nameless man who dared to take the Elder and grief over possibly never seeing him again if she couldn't find out where he was taken. "Why...why have they taken him?"

"He wouldn't say. I asked, but he said it wasn't my concern. All I had to do was tell you the message and I'd be free. He said I could go to the Spirit World when I relayed the message."

Whisper sneered, cocking her head to the side as she listened to the doubt and hope radiating off the man's thoughts. He believed what was told to him, believed he was meant for greater things than the Land of the Dead. "You are in my land now, traveler. I decide where you live and die."

Hunting Hawk recognized that tone in her voice, but before he could react Whisper had shot the man straight through the heart with the arrow in her hand. Slightly disgusted, he stomped over to Eli and yanked the arrow from his chest, watching as the body turned into ash and disappeared in the wind.

"He was given a task, and he completed it," he snapped at Whisper, throwing the arrow at her feet. "Who are you to take his life for that?"

"Who am I?" she repeated, picking up the arrow and cleaning it. "I am *Kanegv*, leader of the Land of the Dead."

"You are not Creator."

Whisper stopped, looked up at Hunting Hawk with both curiosity and admiration for his bold remark. Never before had he shown any sort of admiration or creed in the Great Spirit, and he certainly had never compared her to the leader of the Spirit World.

"Creator has forsaken this land. He has no say in my actions. Nor do you." Turning away before she could inflict her rage on the only man who held her heart, Whisper began to walk off.

"Where are you going? The Fire Tower is the other way."

Stopping just long enough to answer, but not bothering to turn her head, Whisper replied, "To find out what happened to Smoke Speaker. Alone."

Chapter 6

There was only one who knew the true secrets of the Land of the Dead, one who was so old and wise that he was considered the faithful spirit of all that rested beyond the Western Sun. Even Whisper respected this spirit, this creature that represented her soul, for no matter her title as ruler of the Land of the Dead, *Kamama* had wisdom far beyond her years. *Kamama* had seen war, death, famine, hate, but also life, hope, victory, and compassion. He was unbiased but honest, all-knowing yet foreshadowing, clever yet childlike. And it was for those reasons that Whisper sought him out.

It was not a safe journey, but she feared little in her land. Most creatures her grandfather had told stories about lurked in the shadows and retreated further into the dark when she passed. Rumors of her long-ago battle with *Ustahli* in the Weeping Forest had spread from one edge of her land to the other, and none wished to have her wrath set upon them.

Because she wanted no other to know about her own personal advisor, Whisper made the trek alone. She walked without rest for two days and nights straight, keeping her eyes forward and her profile to the Western Sun as she headed into the blue light of the north. The messenger's words replayed in her head and she struggled to decipher their meaning. Smoke Speaker had been taken to another land, which could only be the Spirit World. Which meant, in her mind, that Creator wanted him. But for what purpose? And why would the Elder agree when his destiny was to be with his family in the Land of the Dead?

When she approached *Kamama*'s home, Whisper took a moment to collect herself and her thoughts. She stood at the opening of the cave, reflecting on her mission, deciding on the right questions to ask. There was always a sense of trepidation when entering the cavern, a worry in the back of her mind that she would be judged or cast aside by the one who truly understood all parts of her souls.

The gaping black hole buried in the side of the hill seemed to mock her for her hesitation, and with that sense of humiliation she marched in, removing her bow and quiver and setting them along the hard-packed dirt wall. *Kamama* was a gentle soul and did not approve of weapons, and would not speak to any creature bearing arms—even his Queen.

Whisper knew these walls, these narrow turns and stone barriers. She was familiar with each nook and cranny the cavern held, as she had spent a great deal of her early years as ruler within *Kamama*'s chambers. During her living years *Kamama* often came to her in visions and dreams, but here, in the Land of the Dead, she went to him. This was his home, and she was but a guest.

She reached out and let her fingers graze over the surfaces as she passed, taking in the scents of old age and wisdom, the dim glow lit by the pearl-white creatures that clung to the roof of the cave. Long ago she had discovered that when touched, these unique creatures lost their luminescence and tumbled to the floor to shrivel and die, and so out of respect she never let her hands reach past her head.

At *Kamama*'s chambers, Whisper didn't bother to knock. He had known she was coming before the cave was even in her sights. Such was his way. She placed her hand on the cold stone door, one side of her mouth shifting from its normal scowl into what could almost be mistaken for a half-smile, then pushed the heavy barrier open.

Kamama was waiting for her, as she had anticipated. She entered his lair and offered a single nod of recognition in his direction, stepping forward as she kept her eyes on the figure resting at the hearth in the center of the room. The fire cast an orange glow around the circular room, while the smoke wafted far up and escaped through the open rock ceiling as wide as she was tall. When she stopped before the fire, feet planted firmly in the etching of the medicine wheel, *Kamama* shifted and came into the light.

Whisper hadn't laid eyes on her spirit guide in what seemed like a lifetime, and her memory, for once, had failed her in his magnificence. *Kamama* stood tall and proud atop a pile of bright blue blankets, resting on graceful webbed feet tipped with pearl-white nails that gripped the edges of the blanket carefully. From those feet rose a slender body of plush gray hairs so smooth and fine that they could have been water rippling in a light breeze. His fur-like skin undulated with each deep breath as wings decorated with swirls of lavender and blue arced out in elegant heart-shaped beats. His wings were so fine they seemed to be made of silk, yet traces of color and ancient markings highlighted each line and fold that spun its way from body to air. Patches of purple were surrounded by thick lines of cobalt, with spots of white lining the edges of both wings to form a perfectly balanced pattern. And at the tips, ever so lightly, black lines blurred into lavender as though painted with an artist's touch.

With each light waft of wing, brilliant colors reflected in large black pools of eyes that saw all and missed none. His eyes were large and perfectly round, shifting with the movements that caught their interest. In tune with those shifts were thin, beaded antennae topped with feathery spheres that reached out to the visitor with interest.

This was *Kamama*, Butterfly, Whisper's spirit guide and advisor. Every part of him spoke of elegance, and every part of him demanded respect without commanding loyalty. He was on no side but that of enlightenment, spoke no harsh words except when justly deserved, and judged none even when his own souls were looked down upon. But even as a beacon of the unbiased, in his heart would always be a special place for the one who ruled the Land of the Dead.

"*Kanegv*," he welcomed, his voice a whispery tendril on a nonexistent wind. "My child and mother, you have returned to me."

As a rare sign of respect, Whisper bowed her head without lowering her eyes. "It has been too long, *Kamama*."

"Yes, but I am not the one who has stayed away. Why have you waited so long to regard me with those enchanting black eyes?"

A part of Whisper enjoyed hearing her eyes called enchanting, as all others feared her gaze. Only her guide could see past the surface, it seemed. "The demands of the kingdom have consumed me. The Land of the Dead was a wasteland, and I have worked hard to repair what the Raven—"

"Do not speak his name, *Kanegv*," *Kamama* ordered quickly, and Whisper relented with a mere nod. Her guide was superstitious, and believed that speaking the Raven-Eater's name would be giving power to the fallen tyrant.

"The Land of the Dead needed my attention more than I needed a friend," she said instead, a tug of sadness tearing at her spirit.

Kamama felt it too. Many nights they had sat at this fire, reflecting on Whisper's reign. She had sought him out after murdering her father and taking over the kingdom that was rightfully hers, seeking his advice, his guidance, what he knew of the past, present, and future. He was her spirit guide, assigned to her soul by Creator himself at her birth, and although he was sworn to treat all beings living or dead equally, Whisper would always be his favorite child.

In the past, he was always willing to offer his wisdom on how to build the Land of the Dead back to what it was truly meant to be. How to introduce light, how to make the people whole again, how to give souls of the dead a place of sanctuary rather than eternal terror. And Whisper had listened. In her short time as ruler she had transformed the land into a place worthy of the dead. She had shown that while the

Raven-Eater made up half of her souls, she could control which bloodline she choose to let rule her own self. She would not be defined by who she came from, but by the legacy she left behind.

But now *Kamama* feared for her control. She was a strong spirit in many ways, but at her core, she still had many years of growing and even more of learning. It was that growing and learning process that would test her strength, especially now. He knew what had been done, what must be done, and what path Whisper would likely take. He could advise, but only she could choose her destiny.

"Yes, I have not been needed much by you lately," he said sadly, his translucent wings dropping a bit as the fine hairs of his body shifted. "But now you have a new need of me. You have come about Elder Smoke Speaker."

"So you know he has been taken from me."

"Taken from you?" *Kamama* repeated, a hint of humor in his voice. "He never belonged to you, my child. Smoke Speaker was not taken, but guided to his true destiny."

"His destiny is *here*, in the Land of the Dead, with his family," Whisper insisted, hands curling into fists. Her words took on a dangerous tone. "That was our plan. He trained me to take over this land, free Blue Feather, and lead the people into a better afterlife. And when he passed, he would join us at the Fire Tower."

"Plans change, *Kanegv*. What once was, what once was believed, is no longer truth. You must learn to change with the present."

"This is not about changing, *Kamama*. This is about loyalty, and keeping one's word. My grandfather promised to take his place at the Fire Tower, and he is yet to fulfill that oath. Has he betrayed me for another calling? Did he make the choice to go on his own, or was he taken against his will?"

Kamama paused before answering, breathing deeply as he watched the young woman with so many years of death and shadows clouding her judgment. She was strong, a fearless leader who understood justice, but she was also just a girl who grew up never knowing the love of a mother and father. There were many things she could not comprehend, and many things she refused to see. The Elder's journey would not be acceptable to her, and he knew she would fight until the very end.

"I know why you have come to me, *Kanegv*," he said slowly, seriously, dipping his head slightly as his wings fluttered. The flames of the fire wafted in the breeze, sending a flickering orange glow around the dirt cavern. "You want to know why he was taken, where he was taken, and how you can get him back."

"You know all of this."

"Yes…but it is not my place to reveal such information." At the sudden flash of rage that crossed Whisper's face, he took a brief step forward, unafraid and insulted. "Do not look at me such ways, child. You may be my Queen, but I am still your guide." He nodded when Whisper dropped the expression reluctantly. "All I can tell you, child, is that Smoke Speaker is needed for a great quest by Creator. The Great Spirit has taken the first step on the path to a grand journey. He needs the Elder for his success."

This was the first time Whisper had heard news of a journey of any kind, let alone one led by Creator. She prided herself on knowing all about her land and the Spirit World, and she had spies in both to guarantee she was always made aware of anything out of the ordinary. The Great Spirit was up to something, and it involved her grandfather. And she knew nothing about it.

"What is this journey?"

Kamama only shook his head and retracted his wings. "I have said too much already, child. Creator's journey is his own, and Smoke Speaker is his pawn. It is up to you to learn more." He shifted, the subtle movement sending the flames into a soft dance of orange and yellow hues. Whisper watched as he turned, then lowered her head as he began to walk away.

She looked back up when he stopped suddenly, deep in thought. "And *Kanegv*…as you begin your quest for knowledge, you must remember who your true enemy is."

With that, the sparkling creature retreated into the shadows, leaving Whisper alone by the fire.

* * *

From her perch far above the Land of the Dead, an old woman watched. Despite her age, thick hair tumbled down her back in fiery crimson waves, held back partially by a thin leather band decorated with two blue feathers. Her eyes were black, surrounded by deep wrinkles that traced across her temples and forehead, while her nose was sharp and small above a full mouth lined with age. Her lips were pursed in disgust as she stared down at the wandering souls, her slightly gnarled hands clutching the hem of her buckskin shirt angrily as she rose.

She hated them, all of them. She hated the way they squinted their eyes and made faces when they looked in her direction, hated that people favored the moon and smiled at his arrival. Her hatred had once destroyed her soul, and she harbored her resentment still for the people who took her family away.

There was only one she accepted as worthy of her light, one who walked beneath her realm with pride and courage, one who could stare up at her visage through wide eyes that took in all the glory she had to offer.

It was this woman, in fact, who had brought the light back to the Land of the Dead since the Raven-Eater's reign. During that time, she had been forgotten, a distant memory people searched for in times of darkness. The people knew her by many names, and they called her what they willed during times of misfortune and hope alike, but she preferred Sun Woman.

And now, Sun Woman's time had come. She had known there was something different about this leader of the Land of the Dead from the very beginning, but there had never been an opportunity to use the new heir to her own advantage. But now Creator had taken someone dear to the half-breed, just as someone dear had been taken from Sun Woman.

So she would guide Whisper to the far reaches of the Land of the Dead, a place so old even the Raven-Eater once feared it. The Forgotten Lands were home to the men who would never again know the light for their crimes against Sun Woman, and she could use their hate and anger for revenge, just as she could use the half-breed to further her unspoken plans.

"Rise again, Little Men," she murmured as she cast her thoughts to the sleeping spirits. "You will soon have a visitor."

Chapter 7

Instead of being brought straight to the Great Spirit, Smoke Speaker was led to a small, picturesque meadow just inside a grand palace. Along the way, they had gone by several villages, and he hadn't been able to help himself as they passed, looking into windows, observing children laughing and playing. He'd been to the Land of the Dead and had been shocked by the depressing darkness, the listless souls, forgotten memories. But here there was family, there was hope. He wondered why he'd ever wanted to meet his granddaughter in the Land of the Dead only to spend eternity without light and happiness.

Just beyond the meadow, he could see what he guessed was the Great Spirit's private quarters, a spectacular structure crafted of hopes and dreams, life and love. The white castle sparkled in the sunlight, towers grasping for the clouds with crystal-like tips that radiated color and arced rainbows across the sky. The Elder could only pray that he one day would be able to explore the halls himself.

For now, he was positioned next to an old man with Shawnee markings. There were thirteen of them in all sitting in a circle around a stone hearth. A small fire had been lit, the flames a soft orange that formed images of animals with each flicker in the wind. It was fascinating to watch, and the Elder couldn't help but search the smoke for messages. The fire had once been his means of communication with the dead, with Whisper, but he didn't know how well his gifts worked in death.

The thirteen men sat silently, regarding one another with both suspicion and awe. It didn't take an explanation for the Elder to know that this was a gathering of powerful shaman, medicine men, and chiefs. They were men of all ages from different tribes, but gifted nonetheless. That he could tell simply from the wisdom and power that shone in their eyes. They had been brought together for something big; Smoke Speaker could feel it.

Before he could wonder any longer, a warm breeze passed through the meadow and suddenly, a figure appeared before them. If a man could be described as beautiful yet frightening, powerful yet gentle, the Elder thought, then this was him.

The Great Spirit stood before the gathering silently, hands clasped behind his back. He was tall, taller than any person Smoke Speaker had ever seen, bronzed skin accented with black tribal markings, sleek black hair tied back in a braid with white feathers, broad shoulders that led to muscular arms, and a strong face with chiseled features. His eyes were deep and black, with thick brows and a forehead lined with ages of tension, worry, and the stresses of leadership. His mouth was full and fierce, yet when he smiled, his face melted into softness and friendliness, as though he would lend a helping hand to even his worst enemy. He was dressed in all white, a pearl-colored tunic with leather ties that crisscrossed down the front, loose white pants, and leather moccasins. Wrapped around his shoulders was a cloak made of white buffalo fur, a sacred gift. And when he spoke, pure power radiated from his voice.

"Welcome to my hearth," he said in that deep voice, nodding at the men before him. "I know many of you have been waiting for this moment, until the time came for our last member to join." He glanced over at Smoke Speaker, giving another nod. The Elder was too nervous and touched to respond. "Red Water, Fast Bear, Gray Feather, Dark Moon, Earth Seer, Peacekeeper, Sight Keeper, Panther, Healer, Little Sky, Striker, Tall Bear, and Smoke Speaker." He looked at them individually as he spoke their names, introducing them to the others while welcoming them to his home.

"Our people are fading, lost in an eternal darkness from which there is no escape. They need our help to survive," Creator continued, staring down into the fire. Smoke Speaker didn't know what others were seeing, but he saw his people's history in seconds—the old ways before settlers came, the Trail of Tears, being forced to live on reservations in order to preserve just one small part of their culture. He saw massacres, alcoholism, men and women giving up their spirituality for a chance at a so-called normal life. He saw traditions being forgotten, crafts sold at shows for menial pay, mockery by those who would never understand what it was they abhorred. He saw despair, and the end of hope.

Then the vision changed, and he saw Whisper standing atop the Fire Tower, staring out at the Western Sun. Her expression was one of wanting, like she was expecting something. The Elder had a horrible feeling that she was waiting for something, or someone, that would never come.

Creator regarded the men firmly, knowing what each of them had seen. All thirteen faces around the fire were uncomfortable and sad, wishing life had turned out differently for their ancestors. Eight of the men had died before the time of the White Man, so they knew only what Creator had shown them of time after their passing, but their power was needed nonetheless and knew their love for their people would see them through his mission.

"For too long our people have been pushed aside and forgotten," the Great Spirit said as the images in the fire faded. "For too long they have been ignored, mocked, massacred. But now a new time has come. We have been given the opportunity to start anew, and replenish the Land of the Living." He paused to let his words sink in.

"How is this possible?"

Creator smiled and turned to look at the man who asked the question. "Gray Feather, much is possible in these times. I have gathered you because you thirteen are the keepers of the old ways. You have shown me your devotion to your people, and now I ask you to use your knowledge to save our ways. The journey begins here, in the spirit realms. With our influence in death, we can restore the ways of old in life.

"A child will be born," he told his gathering, lifting a hand and gliding it across the air. The breeze rippled, colors joining together. The thirteen Elders leaned forward eagerly, staring into the image. They watched a young man and woman as they held hands and walked along the beach. It was nighttime, the stars shining down on the water, cool waves lapping against their bare feet. They were a couple in love, looking forward to the miracles life had in store for them.

"Their child will be the savior of our people, a child born to lead a land according to the old ways," Creator said, lowering his hand. The image disappeared in the wind. "You have been chosen to lead this child into the future."

After a few moments of silence, Peacekeeper cleared his throat. During his time, he had been a fierce warrior that led hundreds of raids against his tribe's enemies—the Crow, the Lakota, and the White Man. Despite his name he'd prided himself on contributing to his people's warlike reputation, but after the treaties of the 1800s and diseases brought on by white settlers, he'd become his village's spokesman for peace. He'd always been a powerful warrior, strengthened by the favor of Creator, everyone always said, and in battle it seemed there was a greater force looking out for him. That same power followed him in negotiations with settlers, though eventually he had been betrayed.

"What is this child's purpose?" Peacekeeper asked, a bit concerned. "I have seen much war in my days, and we cannot send a child to fight the white man."

"No, Peacekeeper, the child is not meant to fight. The child is meant to enlighten." Creator shook his head and gestured towards his land, all of the Spirit World. "We are not starting a war with the white man, or their many religions. We are seeking to reintroduce our own, to take back the control stolen from us, and give our people their rightful place in the land that was, and always will be, their own."

The more the Great Spirit spoke, the more the men nodded in agreement, eager to be a part of Creator's calling. This was a day found only in their dreams, a time when they would stand at the forefront of their spirituality and claim their place as leaders in this world and the next. They wished to bring back the old ways just as much as Creator, and so their circle was nearly complete.

Only one was filled with hesitation, fearful of what Creator's plan may cause. The vision in the air had Smoke Speaker chilled to the bone. He feared what it meant, what Whisper would do once she discovered the plan. And she would find out, as she was powerful and most importantly, she was a born and bred Speaker. The Great Spirit would not be able to keep his plan from her, and when she learned of the mission, she would come looking for the Elder.

Smoke Speaker said a silent prayer, hoping his granddaughter would never witness what he had just seen.

Chapter 8

Whisper lay wide awake in bed, mulling over her visit with *Kamama* and the messenger's words. The more she thought about it, the angrier she became. It didn't matter to her why Creator wanted Smoke Speaker. The Great Spirit could plan his journeys and embark on quests all he liked, so long as she was left out of it. But what did matter was that he had stolen something from her, and she would not let such an offense go by without a response.

She was not bound by Creator's laws. If there was any lesson she learned from the Raven-Eater, it had been that one. Whisper acted by her own rules, and refused to give the Great Spirit any claim over her.

Frustrated, and wondering how she would avenge the slight against her, Whisper shifted and glanced over at Hunting Hawk, who lay sleeping beside her. Despite her anger, she nearly smiled, her face softening for the briefest of moments while she watched him in slumber. Hunting Hawk had a strange power over her, could calm her with a mere smile, make her feel whole with a simple touch. He was her shoulder to lean on, a source of wisdom, and most importantly, her one true friend. He had been by her side since the very beginning, declaring his love and vowing to always be her path back to the light when her bloodline threatened to drag her down to darkness. Whisper found it impossible to say the same words back, but some small part of her hoped he could read it in her eyes. If anyone could see through her, it was Hunting Hawk.

A quiet chirp distracted Whisper from her sleeping companion. She looked over to the windowsill to see a small redbird fluttering down. The bird interested her, as very few animals ever dared to get that close to the Fire Tower. Slowly, she rose from the bed, pushing back the fur-lined cover and barely registering the cold stone against her bare feet. She wore nothing but a buckskin robe, and instinctively she grabbed the dagger always kept strapped to the side of the bed. Her quarters were simple—large and clean, with a bed, makeshift wardrobe made of solid rock, and a trunk of weapons—but she always made sure she was protected.

The only light came from the three candles on the wall by the door. The candles were nearly burned down, white wax dripping down to the floor. By the time they went out, dawn would be approaching.

The redbird fluttered its wings as Whisper approached, as though it was nervous being so close to the leader of the Land of the Dead. "Brave little bird," she muttered, lifting her knife warily. The bird hopped along the sill at the sight of the dagger, then chirped when Whisper glanced out the window and lowered it after reassuring herself there were no awaiting intruders.

"It's just a bird, *Kanegv*," Hunting Hawk said sleepily from the bed. "Come back to me."

The request made her smile in the dark of night. She'd heard those words many times before from Hunting Hawk, as he spoke them any time the Raven-Eater's blood threatened to take over her soul. She supposed now they escaped his lips merely because he was half asleep.

"It is not just a bird," she answered, kneeling down so she was eye level with her feathered guest. "It is Redbird, daughter of Sun Woman."

"Sun Woman?" His voice was full of question and sleep as he lifted himself from the bed. He wore only a pair of loose buckskin pants, the shadows from the candlelight flicking across hard muscle adorned with black tattoos that symbolized his people, the life he once had. "Why is her daughter a bird?"

Whisper nearly rolled her eyes before she reminded herself that Sun Woman was a belief native to her own people, one Hunting Hawk had likely never been exposed to. She rose and turned to face him, leaning back against the stone windowsill. Redbird hopped to the side, chirping lightly.

"In the old days," Whisper said, letting Hunting Hawk put his arms around her waist as he approached, "Sun Woman lived on the far side of the Sky Vault, but her daughter lived in the middle. Sun Woman would visit her every day for dinner, in her daughter's home just above the earth. But Sun Woman hated the living because they could never look at her without scrunching up their faces, but they always smiled at the moon." Somewhat absently, Whisper glanced over at the pale white moon, which was lowering just beyond the horizon.

"Sun Woman vowed to kill the people of the earth by sending down harsh rays that gave them fevers and killed their crops, until they began to fear they would all die. So, the people went to the Little Men, who were practiced in dark magic. The Little Men changed two villagers into snakes, an adder and a copperhead, to kill Sun Woman when she visited her daughter. Adder tried first, but was blinded by her bright light and could only spit yellow slime."

"As he does today," Hunting Hawk murmured, lowering his face to breathe in the scent of Whisper's hair. She hardly noticed the gesture.

"Yes, and so they both left and the people continued to die. So the people tried again and the Little Men changed two villagers into a rattlesnake and the great *Ukenta*. *Ukenta* was horned and large to ensure Sun Woman was killed, but rattlesnake was eager for glory. He positioned himself outside Sun Woman's daughter's house and coiled up. When her daughter stepped outside, he struck without looking. The daughter died, and the snakes forgot to wait for Sun Woman. When she found her daughter, Sun Woman grieved and the people no longer died, but the world was dark forever."

When Whisper's voice trailed off, Hunting Hawk lifted his head. "And so she turned into a redbird?"

"No." Her tone was one of both amusement and annoyance. "But that is a story for another time." Unwinding herself from Hunting Hawk's embrace, she focused on the creature before her. "Why have you come, Redbird?"

The bird chirped in response and took a tentative step forward, then bowed her head. Her wings fluttered just a bit, as if impatient for the woman to understand. Whisper held out a hand, slowly extending just one finger. Cautiously, Hunting Hawk put a hand on her arm as though in warning, and at the same time Redbird leaned forward, baring the top of its head.

The moment the two touched, Whisper was shown the path to her future.

In a flash of red light, Whisper's mind was transported to a place far beyond her reaches. The sounds of anguish, whispers of the dead, piercing calls from splintered spirits, all grasped for her as she twisted and turned in a thick whirl of air. This was a place of emptiness, where she could not find her footing or make sense of what she saw.

Confusion suffocated the air, flashing orange lights blinded her, the sound of drums and flutes in the distance called to her while putting up a barrier that rejected her very being. But it was in that land she needed to be; she could feel it deep in her bones. Someone, or something, was there, waiting for her, pleading for her to discover the way.

Then, as quickly as it began, the wind faded and she was left to hang, her spiritual form suspended in the air. From somewhere high above she observed a different land, a desolate place where the sun dared not to shine. In the distance were campfires, and eerie music was carried on the breeze. Steady drumbeats mixed with flutes, a song that reminded the soul of its loneliness and sorrow.

From her place high in the sky, Whisper watched as the ground began to ripple and the clouds parted, letting in white rays of light that streamed down from the Sky Vault. Six beams spotted the dry earth, which rose to form small, disfigured spirits holding arrows and clubs. They twisted and turned within themselves as though being put back together again after years of being torn apart. But before they could complete the transformation they turned, staring up at the sky, directly at the intruder.

In unison with one another, and with the music reverberating off the air, they lifted their bows, arrows nocked. Before Whisper could react, they released.

* * *

Smoke Speaker awoke with a start, searching around his large stone room for the figures that haunted his dreams. He took a moment to slow his breathing when he realized he was alone, part of his racing mind marveling over the fact that nightmares were still present in the Spirit World.

He'd dreamed of a barren wasteland ruled by fire and fear. In his nightmare, he was chased by a feathered beast that circled high in a dark red and purple sky, screeching down its hate and thirst for blood. The Elder had raced across a ground scattered with potholes and fallen trees, stumbling over his own feet, sweat pouring into his eyes.

This was a place few knew about, a place he had only heard horror stories of during his first journey into the Land of the Dead. No one who ventured there ever came back, as the creatures that inhabited the lands were ruled by revenge and a lust for destruction. Their power was beyond the Elder's comprehension, and they practiced dark magics that had led to their exile so long ago.

The Raven-Eater had spoken of them only once to Hunting Hawk, in private, as Smoke Speaker stood just outside the door in hopes of figuring out a way of freeing his daughter from the evil tyrant's grasp. The ruler had mentioned his desire to explore this area and ensure the creatures' place as soldiers in his Army of the Dead. But the Raven-Eater never made it there, as even he feared what they were capable of. The Elder had heard rumors that he'd sent messengers to that forsaken forest, but none had ever made their way back to the Fire Tower.

And now Whisper was headed there, blind to the horrors she faced. Something, or someone, had reached out to her, showing her the way to the one place that could suck out her soul and leave it for the beasts that roamed the Land of the Dead. She would go in unwittingly, thinking the solution to the Elder's disappearance would be found there, and instead would be faced with the ones who had been sought for allegiance with the Raven-Eater.

Smoke Speaker could only pray that Hunting Hawk was at her side. Without her constant companion, she may succumb to the darkness that spread from all corners of that world. Without her mate to bring her back to the light, she would revel in the darkness that hid in the deepest depths of her heart.

Without Hunting Hawk, Whisper would be lost in the Forgotten Lands.

* * *

The young woman stared up at her lover adoringly, wondering how she could be so lucky to have such an amazing man looking down at her with that look of warmth and tenderness in his eyes. His gaze wrapped her in love, filling her heart with happiness as she allowed herself to open her soul to everything he had to offer. Sickness and health, good times and bad, he was her own, and she was his.

He didn't always have that look, as there were times when a strange gloom showed through his handsome face like he was remembering traumatic times in his past. But he could never fully recall those memories that were just beyond the brink of recognition, the ones that adulterated his dreams and sent him into fits of terrors until he shot awake in the night.

And yet, whenever he looked at her it was with love, unconditional love that took away all the bad things he never knew but suffered from nonetheless. Never did he allow those things he ran from in the night to cloud what he felt for her. But despite the terrors that followed him from his child to adult years, he was not an unhappy man. Rather, he was content knowing his nightmares were part of his life and choose to find joy in the things that made him happy.

She was one of those things, the woman that completed him, the one that filled his heart with hope and happiness and reminded him that he too could have the loving marriage his parents still enjoyed so many years later. He had taken the first step tonight, surprising his beloved with the ring that symbolized their union. He wanted her to be his wife, his lover, his best friend, until death did them part.

And in taking that first step, he had unknowingly set in motion all the tricks that death had in store for him.

Chapter 9

"You don't have to do this, *Kanegv*."

Blue Feather wrung her hands together nervously as she watched her daughter. Whisper ignored the comment, tightly rolling a pair of pants and setting it at the bottom of her pack, covering it with an extra shirt, a pouch of medicinal herbs, and what weapons she couldn't fit on her belt. She didn't need much to travel, as she knew how to rely on the land and was welcome in any villager's home. Besides, if her journey was to take her where she believed it would, she wouldn't be staying long.

Outsiders weren't welcome in the Forgotten Lands.

Whisper may have been relatively new to the Land of the Dead, but she knew the stories. The Forgotten Lands were home to the Little Men, spirits banished long before the Raven-Eater's time for their crimes against Sun Woman. And if the redbird had shown her the path, then she could only assume that Sun Woman was requesting an audience with her. Only the Little Men knew how to reach the sky spirit, and so Whisper was ready to face some of the most feared and mysterious creatures if it meant furthering her cause.

If anyone knew what was happening, and willing to tell her the truth, it was Sun Woman. She had a vengeance against Creator, as well as the entire living world. For Whisper, there was no better person to have on her side.

"*Kanegv*, listen to—"

"You have no say in this, Blue Feather," Whisper snapped, swinging the pack over her shoulders. "Creator is up to something, and I must learn the truth."

"Some things are not meant for you to know."

Her eyes narrowed as she faced her mother. "Do not question me, Blue Feather. If you have lost faith in my ways, you are free to join your father."

Leaving her mother fighting back tears, Whisper stalked through the Fire Tower, feeling heat pulse across her back as her markings came alive within the familiar walls and led her with each step. She no longer needed the inkings to tell her where to go, but they were part of her now and connected her to the Fire Tower.

Soon she came out at the horse stalls located just outside the southern wing. As requested, her stallion had been prepared and was ready for travel. She stopped short when she saw Hunting Hawk saddling his own horse.

"I am traveling alone."

Hunting Hawk hardly glanced up. "You are traveling with a companion. It is not up for debate."

Whisper felt the rage building in her chest at his words. She took a deep breath, her hands clenching into fists as she fought the feeling. A tightness formed in her chest, gripping her bones, spreading across her face as her thoughts raced and formed images of what she could do to the man for daring to disregard her command.

Seeing the reaction, Hunting Hawk straightened and walked over to Whisper, taking her by the chin with his rough, scarred hands and staring down at her intently. "Do not let him win. Come back to me, *Kanegv.*"

As she stared into the warmth of his soulful brown eyes, a warmth that shone through his usual hard warrior glare, Whisper was captured by his gentle affection. His deep voice soothed her soul, reached the part of her that craved and longed for his touch. She smiled a rare smile, allowing him to kiss her softly on the cheek. "You may accompany me, Hunting Hawk," she agreed, leading them to the stallions. Together they swung up on their horses, then set off for what was promising to be their most perilous journey yet.

Sun Woman watched from above as Whisper and her companion mounted their horses and set off across the Barren Plains. She noted with pleasure that they rode without hesitation, the hooves of *Soquili* pounding the dirt without care for the creatures of deceit that dwelled beneath the ground.

It gave Sun Woman a strange kind of satisfaction to know that Whisper feared no one and no creature. It was rare to see such vigor and confidence in a spirit that resided in the Land of the Dead, let alone one that attempted to restore order and peace in a formerly forsaken land. The Raven-Eater had once displayed that same kind of arrogance, and it led to his downfall. The child of his blood believed herself to be invincible of his mistakes. Perhaps she was, or perhaps she was so blinded by her own sense of self-worth that deception would be easy for the sky spirit.

Without hesitation, the half-breed would gladly accept her offer and walk blindly into Sun Woman's plan without a care for what ulterior motives lurked behind the curtains of deceit.

* * *

It was early morning when Smoke Speaker woke, the sun gently lighting his spacious room in an orange glow. Before he rose for the day, he lifted himself to his elbows and took a moment to glance around his new quarters. It was a beautiful sight, one that he welcomed after a lifetime of living among the woods in a small hut filled with only his most prized possessions.

Polished white floors spread from wall to wall, with smoky silver pillars rising up at the corners. The walls were a beautiful pearl hue, lightly textured with gentle waves that rose up to a domed ceiling that was sprinkled with white, starry glints of lights reflected from the morning sun. A long window on the east side sparkled with the sights of a vast blue ocean set below towing verdant cliffs.

He was deep in *Owenvsv*, the home of the Creator. Smoke Speaker had heard mention of a place nicknamed *Oway* at powwows in the past, but never would he have guessed that meant home for the Great Spirit. The other twelve elders were in rooms identical to his own among their wing of the palatial estate, given all the comforts they could ever possibly request in preparation for their new journey.

It was that journey the Elder feared, for he was close to this task. His heart ached for what he was being asked to do, not because he didn't believe in its cause, but because there was still a great part of him that longed for his family. It wasn't right, breaking his promise to join them in the Land of the Dead, and while he was honored to be chosen by Creator for this task he knew in his heart that the Spirit World was too great a place for his own eternity.

Knowing that, he rose from the bed and marveled when his old bones didn't crack and moan. While he showed his age still, he felt like a young man again as he dressed and began the walk through *Oway* to find the Great Spirit.

Before long, voices began to travel down the white, naturally lit corridor. Creator's voice, speaking to a man the Elder identified as Earth Keeper. They were speaking quietly and quickly, and it was obvious it was a conversation meant only for them. Though he knew it was wrong, curiosity got the better of him and he stopped just outside the room.

"How do you feel about our chosen Circle, Earth Keeper?" the Great Spirit asked, his voice reverberating off the pearly walls despite his quiet tone. "Do you feel they are able to lead this child to our future?"

"The spirit realms will benefit from the child's presence, and the child will lead the way with the Circle's guidance," the other man commented, and Smoke Speaker heard him set something heavy down on a table. "I suspect the Elder Smoke Speaker will be the one to guide our counsel."

"Yes," Creator agreed thoughtfully. "Smoke Speaker has shown himself to be a strong leader and shaman. His skill in guiding his apprentice to walk the Red Road despite her bloodline is impressive. I trust he will bring that same knowledge and power in guiding this child as well."

Pride swelled up inside Smoke Speaker. They were talking about Whisper, and his hard work in defeating the Raven-Eater's influence over her souls. Creator was proud of him, and that honored the Elder more than any other personal success he could name. Not needing to hear more, and not wanting to spoil that feeling with his own thoughts of hesitation, Smoke Speaker turned and silently made his way back to his room.

Just as the Elder was turning the corner, Earth Keeper let out a heavy breath. "We have not heard word from *Kanegv* since the Elder's arrival into the Spirit World. She was sent a messenger, but not even our spies have reported back as to her reaction."

"Yes, that is troubling," Creator agreed. "I had expected a retaliation of some kind by now. I fear that our messenger not returning *is* evidence of her reaction. That is why I must ask you to do something for me."

Inside the small room, lit only by a dim, white-flamed candle, Earth Keeper narrowed his black eyes and crossed his arms. "You wish for me to travel to the Land of the Dead?"

"Yes," the Great Spirit said again, gently touching the man on the shoulder. "I know it will be hard for you, but I need someone I can trust. You will find the half-breed and gain her trust, and make sure she stays away from the Spirit World so this child can be born and raised with our guidance. She must not learn of the child. She will never understand our mission."

Though every part of him dreaded experiencing that place of fire and evil, Earth Keeper nodded. "As you wish, Great Spirit." He bowed his head, then took his leave. When he stepped outside of the room, he turned to stare down the hallway Smoke Speaker had just exited, a knowing grin crossing his rugged, weathered face.

He would go to the Land of the Dead and find Whisper. The rest was yet to be foretold.

Chapter 10

They rode for thirteen nights straight, stopping only to study their maps and readjust their course with the ever-changing landscape that made up the Land of the Dead. Their stallions raced across barren lands, through thick and thorny brambles, around lost souls wandering and searching for their final resting place in death. Black blood in the shape of hooves left a trail in their wake, bringing forth the creatures that hid in the dark forests or deep within the ground, watching the ruler of the Land of the Dead in her journey to the Forgotten Lands. So far, none had dared to cross their paths, fearing the power of their leader, but the closer they got to their destination, the less those creatures were concerned about meeting their fate by daring to defy their guardian.

And that was what Whisper wanted. She was depending on their indifference, banking on their hate, and planning to use their evil nature to her own advantage.

Just as the sun began to lower on their fourteenth day of travel, the earth started to change from smooth and cool to a fevered landscape of cracks, holes, and deep caverns. Thickets of thin, gnarled trees rose up from the ground, a thick layer of black leaves canopying the air in darkness. Scattered around the earth were thorny bushes with limbs that arched out in wild twists and circles, grasping at their flesh as they passed by slowly and cautiously.

This was no place for a horse, and so the two riders dismounted and removed their packs. Whisper gave the stallions a quick order to stay in the area, weaved a protection spell around them so that no lurking creature could feast on her animals, then looked over at her companion. "Are you prepared, Hunting Hawk? This is not a forest that takes kindly to strangers."

"As ready as you are, *Kanegv*." Hunting Hawk shouldered his pack and adjusted the dagger at his belt. "Do not let your thoughts stray."

She ignored what could have been considered an insult. He was insinuating that here, in this dark and depressing place, she could be overcome by her father's bloodline, that she was powerless to control herself. It was true that she was known to lose herself in thought and often times make herself oblivious to the world around her, just as it was true that Hunting Hawk was always ready to command her back to consciousness. But, such was his way, and she would let his comment slide because he was the one who brought her back from the depths.

Instead of fighting back, she led the way into the forest. The air thickened the moment they stepped in amongst the trees, heavy with the scent of death and despair. The trees were slick with yellow sweat, sap running down the bark and pooling at the base in sticky puddles that clung to their boots. Every step echoed off each trunk, sending their own sounds back to them as a warning against going any further. The sky above was dark, lit only by a few gray stars scattered among gray clouds.

"So, perhaps now is a good time to tell me why I'm following you to the Forgotten Lands."

Whisper huffed, only slightly amused. "I did not ask you to accompany me."

"What kind of War Chief would I be to let you travel alone?"

"A smart one?"

He conceded to her on that point. "What kind of man would I be to let my mate travel to unknown lands without my protection?"

At that, Whisper softened and nearly smiled. In that look, Hunting Hawk knew he had won. "We are traveling to the Little Men. They are creatures even the Raven-Eater once feared."

"And if these creatures would not partner with the Raven-Eater, what makes you think they will join with you? Why are they of any use to you?"

"Because unlike the Raven-Eater, I know what they want in exchange for their alliance. And because they can get me to Sun Woman, who alone can tell me what plans Creator has for my grandfather." Whisper stepped over a fallen tree, staring ahead into the darkness. She didn't know where exactly their home rested among the Forgotten Lands, but suspected they would arrive only when her hosts wanted them to. They had a special kind of dark magic, one that allowed them to manipulate their landscape and hide themselves from the world. They could ensure Whisper and Hunting Hawk were lost for years among the trees, or invite them into their home at the next step.

"Sun Woman? Why would she be on your side?"

"Sun Woman has long been on the side of the one who opposes Creator and the living," Whisper answered, sending a thoughtful glance up toward the sky as though hoping for a response.

"So tell me her story."

There were few things Whisper enjoyed more than sharing the stories of her people. It pleased her even more that Hunting Hawk was always willing to listen.

"I have already told you the story of how Sun Woman's daughter was killed, and what part the Little Men played in her death. But you have not heard of what happened next." Whisper's voice took on a softer tone, as it usually did when she was telling a story. It was a welcome change from its usual hard and angry resonance.

"When Sun Woman discovered her daughter's death, the Land of the Living was cast into darkness, a reflection of her depression. So the people went to the Little Men and asked for a solution, to bring her daughter back from the Spirit World. Some say that the Little Men chose a small gathering of men to do their bidding for them, though others state that they traveled after Sun Woman's daughter themselves to right their wrongdoing. I believe that the Little Men went themselves, preparing to travel to the ghost world with a box and rods as long as their arms.

"They journeyed to the ghost world and arrived after seven days, to a realm where all the souls were dancing. When they found Sun Woman's daughter, they struck her with the rods until she fell to the ground, so they could put her in the box. They had been instructed to not open the box until they returned to Sun Woman."

Whisper paused to take a breath, shaking her head when she felt her words suddenly mix and mingle with one another as though getting lost in a storm of thoughts. For a moment, she could have sworn she heard a chanting voice, words urging her toward another path. She focused her mind just as a sudden warm breeze blew through the trees. Hunting Hawk lifted his eyes to the sky somewhat warily, knowing they were being watched.

"On their way back to the Sky Vault, the girl woke and begged to be released. She pleaded for food and water, but they ignored her until she said she was suffocating. They were close to home so they let her continue to beg, but then she stopped speaking. The men were concerned she was dying, and thought it would be safe to check since they were so close to the Little Men's home. As soon as they lifted the lid, a redbird flew out of the box and into the bushes, so when they arrived the box was empty. Because they did not do as ordered, it is said that was when people were no longer able to bring back lost souls from the Spirit World or Land of the Dead."

Hunting Hawk spared her a sarcastic glance. "Says the woman who sent two dead souls back to the Land of the Living."

"There are ways around the rules." Whisper shrugged off the comment, knowing that in sending Ian and Cole Daivya back to the Land of the Living so many years ago she had contributed to whatever imbalance was shifting between the two worlds.

"So what happened next?"

"Sun Woman was devastated that her daughter escaped, and cried so much that her tears flooded the earth. The people got together and decided to send their finest men and women to dance and perform for her, so that she would be happy again. Eventually, a drummer played a song that filled her soul with peace and Sun Woman smiled again. She forgot her grief, but did not forgive. To this day she blames the Little Men for not only killing her daughter, but for failing to return her from the Spirit World. And because Creator forbid the return of dead souls from the ghost worlds, and refused to find her daughter lost in an unknown spirit realm, he too lost her loyalty."

Hunting Hawk took a moment to let the words sink in, imagining how he would react to his daughter's death, should he ever have a child. He too would forsake those who not only killed her, but failed to bring her back.

"So you believe that Sun Woman will work with you to bring the Elder back?"

"I do not know what she will do, Hunting Hawk. But, I do know that she will tell me what I need to know. And the Little Men will take me to her."

From deep within his cavernous home, *Kamama* watched Whisper on her journey to the Forgotten Lands. He had tried once to guide her away from that path when she was explaining Sun Woman's wrath to Hunting Hawk, hoping to make her forget, but she had brushed off his subconscious nudge with a mental shrug and set her course with more determination than ever.

Although he was her guide, not even *Kamama* could stop her from traveling to see the Little Men. But because they were forever connected, he was able to see what she desired, perhaps even before she did. And now, she desired revenge, a blind revenge that she did not even understand in its entirety.

Unlike her return trip to the Land of the Dead, which was fueled by a lifetime of training for a pre-ordained fate, this undertaking was for a revenge he feared would lead to her downfall. He had known from the beginning that she would succeed in killing the Raven-Eater and taking her rightful place as leader of the Land of the Dead. It had been a mission set forth by destiny itself. But this time was different; she was taking on the Great Spirit, and no one had ever attempted such a feat.

Kamama feared for her safety, and for his own. If Whisper was defeated, if the Great Spirit found a way to destroy her, then he too would discover what horrible lands awaited those unfortunate enough to encounter their second death in the ghost worlds.

* * *

She had never experienced a feeling quite like this, a love so deep and ador-ing that she knew it was meant to last forever. When he looked at her, she felt like the heroine from one of her favorite romance novels, a woman who had been given a second chance at life and love, perfectly matched to her one special someone.

She hadn't had an easy life, born to parents who considered alcohol and gam-bling more important than raising their daughter. And while he had enjoyed a child-hood of luxury, he was nonetheless haunted by nightmares of a trauma he could never quite understand. They were blessed to find one another, able to encourage and help each other see past the darkness and create a path of light.

Together, they were walking that road. The aisle was paved before them with hope and good intentions, and everyone around them couldn't wait for the two to be wed. Just weeks had passed since their engagement, but it felt like years. They wanted to be married now, to start their new life together as man and wife, a union of two lost souls who found one another at last.

And while they planned their wedding, they kept just one secret to themselves. As they slept beneath a full moon, wrapped around one another and enjoying peaceful dreams in their new home, a child was waiting to be welcomed into the world.

Chapter 11

They walked for hours, breathlessly climbing over fallen trees, shoving their way through thick underbrush, pulling their booted feet from grimy pits of muck with almost every step. Behind her, Whisper could hear Hunting Hawk muttering curses in his native tongue, obviously not happy to be wandering among the nighttime forest while coated in mud and wetness.

"We will arrive soon," she assured him, stopping for a break. She looked around, attempting to get her bearings, but in this rainy forest direction was not something easily discovered.

"How do you know?"

Whisper pointed to the sky. "The light is changing."

Hunting Hawk followed her finger, looking up toward the night sky. It was true, the light had changed. Gone were the red and purple lights that streaked across the Land of the Dead's sky, and in their place were strange golden orbs that pulsed in tune with a nonexistent song. It was a beautiful if not eerie sight, one that haunted him almost as much as his first look into Whisper's unfathomable visage.

Just as he was going to ask what those lights meant, a strange crackling sound echoed throughout the forest, the sound of breaking limbs and falling trees nearly deafening them. The thunderous noise worked its way in a circle around them, then gales of strangely scented air blew in from the south. The trees arched and bowed in response, shifting in the ground as though having grown legs of bark that walked across the spongy earth. The canopy seemed to moan as it swayed in the breeze, pointing in the direction the travelers were to head.

Whisper stood in place, watching the trees, then turned her head when the shifting stopped. A clear, dry path was spread before them, leading to a large clearing not far ahead. Setting her shoulders, she stalked confidently in the direction provided for her by the forest spirits, not waiting to see if Hunting Hawk followed.

It was a quick walk to the clearing, and they both stopped short at the edge to take in the eerie sight. Seven huts that reached no higher than their hips were set in a semi-circle along the clearing's edge. They were made of something black and sticky, crudely constructed with splintered logs that were anchored together by thin, sinewy strips of plant-like material. Each hut was surrounded by a rough fence topped with barbed spikes, warning any intruders of certain torture and death.

As they stepped closer, Whisper and Hunting Hawk saw that the huts were built around a large hearth glowing with orange embers that shone brightly even in this world of grays and colorless figures. It was constructed of enormous gray boulders stacked three high, and filled with thick logs blacked with soot. In the center, a clearing big enough for an average-sized person had been carved out, the space surrounded by stones to protect from the scalding flames. Whisper wondered why anyone would need to lie within the fire, and why anyone would trust the Little Men to keep them alive.

"Is anyone here?" Hunting Hawk asked, taking another step forward. His footsteps ricocheted off the rocks scattered throughout the clearing. Warily, he eyed the huts, then turned to the hearth. It was oddly big compared to the dwellings. "Why would such small creatures need a fire this size?"

"Perhaps their sacrifices are large."

She said it with such approval in her voice that Hunting Hawk looked over his shoulder in surprise. Whisper was staring at the coals as though imagining what had been burned above them, edging her way closer in hope of seeing what remains may be lying inside. "Then we will avoid being their next."

Before she could respond, a fierce wind blew throughout the clearing, throwing hot ashes into their faces. Cursing, the two leapt back and wiped at their skin, then stared through blurred eyes as dark creatures appeared in the doorways of all but one hut.

A man from the center hut emerged first, no taller than Hunting Hawk's knee. Seconds later the others appeared on either side, save for the last dwelling on the end. At first glance they appeared to be identical, but upon closer inspection Whisper saw that there were subtleties in their appearance that marked them as individuals. A slight cleft in the farthest one's chin, a leaner build on the third, fuller lips accenting the center brother's scowl.

That center figure was dressed elaborately, clearly the leader among his clan. His broad shoulders were cloaked in thick buffalo fur that draped down is bare chest, which was covered with intricate black markings. The buffalo cloak was decorated with white bone beads and thin feathers, while his throat was similarly adorned with seven bone necklaces that hung down in varying lengths. Around his waist was a wide leather strap that held strange-looking metal and wooden tools.

The buffalo cloak matched his pants, which were a dark tanned material with fur lining the seams. Animal prints were stitched from waist to ankle, and around both thighs were sharp blades strapped with leather. His feet were wrapped in hides, anchored to his ankles and legs by crisscrossing strips of sticky leather. The same strips kept his long, thick hair tied back in braids, though strands had worked their way loose in the breeze and blew around his soot-smudged face, which was hidden behind a black fur hood. In his left hand was a gnarled walking stick that dug into the ground as he took a step forward, and rose.

Both Whisper and Hunting Hawk's eyes widened just a bit as the six men started to grow, rising higher and higher, muscle thickening and bone stretching. As they walked closer in unison, the leader just a step ahead, their bodies lengthened, widened, until they were just inches taller than Hunting Hawk.

It took only moments for them to transform, their strange clothes and furs growing along with them. It happened so quickly, so seamlessly and easily, that Hunting Hawk wondered if they had imagined the entire event. Now full-grown men, the six stared at their guests with black eyes that were surrounded by rugged lines of age and lifelong weariness. Their mouths were set in snarls, cheekbones tattooed with circles, the sharp facial angles and strange symbols only adding to their mystery and dark auras.

For a moment they simply stared, then the leader nodded in Whisper's direction. "You have traveled far, half-breed. Not even your father would dare to enter our lands."

"The Raven-Eater was a coward," Whisper answered coolly. "I would prefer not to be compared to him."

The man considered the comment, sizing Whisper up with a lingering gaze from head to toe. She looked nothing like the Raven-Eater, but for the same smug, arrogant sneer that he had so often worn. She even stood like him, straight yet relaxed, perfectly composed yet braced for a fight. She was not a woman of mercy, he knew, and had heard stories of her lust for blood, something he could appreciate. But she was also a good ruler of the Land of the Dead, and for that he would not slay her on the spot.

"I am Dark Water," he said, then gestured to the others behind him. "These are my men, my brothers. Welcome to the Forgotten Lands."

"I thought there were seven."

Dark Water regarded Hunting Hawk with disdain. "Our seventh brother was lost long before your time. We were never evil beings who craved the solitude of this forest, and he could not handle being banished to the Forgotten Lands only to let them corrupt him, as he knew we would be corrupted. And so he left after Sun Woman cursed us within these lands, and in these bodies. We await the day he is reborn, and brought back to us."

"What happens then?"

"We are free."

The answer confused Whisper, as only Sun Woman could free the Little Men, but she accepted it nonetheless. It was not her place to question Sun Woman's curse, and she didn't care what they would do with their freedom. "Perhaps I can help."

The man laughed then, a threatening sound that didn't echo like others did. It was eerily hollow and empty. "You? The half-breed? Your kind forsook mine a long time ago." He started to circle her, tapping his walking stick on the ground while the remaining five men spread out as though preparing for battle. "Did you come here hoping for allegiance? We told the Raven-Eater we would never swear loyalty to his kind, and you are no better an ally than him."

She could have been offended, but Whisper decided not to waste the energy. The Little Men, little though they no longer were, had reason to be filled with hate and retribution. And she was there to break through that barrier. "I am not here to ask for allegiance," she replied, moving a hand to her knife just in case. "I am here to ask for help."

"Help?" one of the brothers asked scornfully. "You, asking us for help?"

"Silence, Burning Wind." Dark Water stopped circling after casting a glance back at his men. "And what could we possibly do for you?"

"Get me to Sun Woman."

He had not been expecting that, and it showed in his eyes. Fear, mixed with shock, mixed with suspicion. "Sun Woman is the spirit that cast us here. She is the reason for our curse. She is a blight on our very kind. And you would expect us to bring you to her? Why?"

The answer was simple. "Because you are the only ones who know how."

She spoke the truth, and the fact that she knew that only irritated him. The half-breed was not supposed to know their secrets. It made her dangerous, untrustworthy, having such information without them revealing it to her. "It is true. We are the only creatures able to make the connection. Sun Woman gave us such knowledge knowing no one would ever dare to ask. It seems she was wrong."

He gave the idea thought for a moment, consulting with his men silently. Hunting Hawk risked a sidelong glance at Whisper to see that she was waiting impatiently, but trying not to let boredom and irritation show on her face.

Finally, Dark Water shook his head. "You have given us no reason to trust you, half-breed. We have not heard word from you since you took over. Why are we to help you now, when you have done nothing for us?"

She had been expecting their lack of cooperation. "Because I can get you the one thing you want most."

"And what is that?"

"Your seventh brother."

* * *

Her plan was being set into motion so flawlessly that she knew fate itself was on her side. Sun Woman watched eagerly as Whisper spoke with the Little Men, and while she turned her nose up at the beasts responsible for her daughter's death, she needed them to complete this part of her plan.

Once Whisper was with her in the sky, Sun Woman could set the stage for her plan and deceive the leader of the Land of the Dead into allying herself with the sky spirit. Sun Woman knew that when she was aligned with the half-breed, power would finally be hers.

She could only pray that Whisper was so blinded by hate and revenge that she never saw what Sun Woman truly wanted.

Chapter 12

It was early morning, and the Great Spirit stood on the balcony smiling at the rising sun. Mother Sun was most glorious in the morning, when she peeked out above the horizons in pinks and purples, soft hues that gently woke his people in songs of color. There was peace in his land, and beauty, and those he would not trade for anything.

And so it bothered him greatly when his morning ritual was interrupted by the sound of heavy footsteps in the hall. He knew those steps, as Earth Keeper had never been one to tread lightly, and he knew when those steps were made in haste. His consort had something to tell him, and it likely was not good news.

Earth Keeper knocked and the door opened slowly, closing behind the man as he entered. Creator turned but did not leave the balcony. Instead, he gestured to the other man, his white robes swaying in the faint breeze.

"It is a beautiful morning, Earth Keeper," he greeted. "And yet I fear you have come to spoil the moment."

"I have, Great Spirit. I have news of the half-breed."

Creator looked over at the man with a frown. "So she has gotten word of her grandfather, I presume? We expected she would not take the news lightly."

Earth Keeper hesitated, wording his thoughts carefully. "Yes, but we did not expect this reaction. My spy tells me that *Kanegv* has gone to the Forgotten Lands, to find the Little Men."

Although he had been wondering if she would seek out the exiled, it worried Creator nonetheless. The Forgotten Lands were not to be brushed aside, and the fact that the half-breed willingly entered told him that she knew he was up to something. "The Little Men do not serve anyone but themselves. The chances of them assisting her are unlikely. The chances of her returning from the Forgotten Lands are even slimmer."

"And if she does?"

Creator turned to the man. "Then she will have more knowledge and power than I can trust. That is why we must go now."

Earth Keeper bowed his head slightly, eager for the chance to serve. "As I promised before, Great Spirit, I will do what you ask of me. Tell me what I must do."

The Great Spirit turned his deep, thoughtful eyes back to the morning sky. In the Spirit World, the sun rose in the south, bringing unity and peace to his people. "I will get you to the Land of the Dead, but from there you must remain strong. You will be crossing over into a place of melancholy, and that feeling will try to strip you of the light. You must fight it, and move on. Once you are in the Land of the Dead, you must become one of the half-breed's advisers. Gain her trust, convince her that the Elder was never of importance to her, that he used her for his own selfish gain. Make her see that she does not truly love or want him. When you are not around the half-breed, you must speak with her men, convince them that they serve the wrong leader. And, as always, report to me of her actions."

Though he was eager to serve, the request frightened him. The Land of the Dead was not a place where deceit and treachery were welcomed. He'd heard the stories of what happened to the ones who attempted to cross the half-breed, the merciless.

"As you wish, Creator." Earth Keeper sucked in a breath and clasped his hands behind his back. "I will prepare to leave as soon as possible."

"And Earth Keeper," Creator called over his shoulder just as he reached the door. Earth Keeper stopped, waiting for his orders. The Great Spirit turned, his voice casual but his eyes filled with dread. "If the half-breed gets too close, and refuses to leave the Elder in my care, you know what to do." His face darkened then. "Take the ones who matter most."

The Great Spirit brought Earth Keeper to a place few had ever heard of, an open land where the air smelled stale and nothing dared to grow or exist. It was a desolate place for the Spirit World, one-of-a-kind in its strangeness. It gave Earth Keeper a sad, sorrowful feeling deep in his gut, like he was leaving behind his home and venturing forth into death.

"This is not the time to have doubts, Earth Keeper," Creator said, placing a hand on the man's shoulder. "Go forth into the Land of the Dead with courage, and remember your mission."

He swallowed hard. "I will, Great Spirit. I will not disappoint you." Earth Keeper looked over his shoulder, nodding when Creator offered an encouraging smile.

"Walk in peace, Earth Keeper."

Squaring his shoulders, the spirit flexed his grip on the dagger Creator had provided, then stepped forward into the fissure in the air.

Instantly, everything changed.

The sky, once a brilliant blue and filled with fluffy white clouds, was heavy with red and purple lights that clung to grayness. The air, once sweet and soul-satisfying, was thick with the scent of blood and mortality. As far as his eye could see there was a vast nothingness that emptied his spirit of light. At the same time, a horrific sense of doubt filled him, clouding his judgment, masking his confidence. He'd known the Land of the Dead was a realm where even the strongest perished, but he hadn't been expecting this kind of feeling.

As part of the Spirit World, a place where souls were guarded against the dark, Earth Keeper was overcome by melancholy and gloom. It consumed him, grabbed hold of his souls and feasted on the light within him. As he dropped to his knees, gasping out in aching pain, he swore he could hear voices in that dreariness, encouraging him to give up, relishing in his weaknesses.

He desperately reached out to the stones at his feet, arranging them in a protective wheel in hopes of casting out the shadows. The Great Spirit hadn't prepared him for this, the unrelenting fingers of misery that devoured him from the inside out.

Unable to find the strength to fight, Earth Keeper gave in to the darkness.

Chapter 13

Dark Water stared at Whisper suspiciously. "What you say is not possible. Our brother is gone." He took a step closer and eyed the stranger. He was impressed by her lack of fear, the way she stared him down without worry, but he was also wary of her words. He knew of the half-breed and her skill in twisting truths. She could lie without speaking deceit, and make anyone believe what she had to say.

"No one knows where our brother is, or why he left," he continued. "There is only one spirit who would know the path to his journey, but you have no way of reaching her."

"Yes, but you do." Whisper closed the gap between them and gave him her signature soul-clutching glare. "You send me to Sun Woman, and in return I will find your brother. You have my word."

They made preparations quickly, much to Hunting Hawks' protests. Dark Water tied golden feathers into Whisper's hair and painted matching lines down her shoulders and arms, sweeping the color across her collarbones. He wrapped her wrists in blue bone beads, then tied a white sash around her waist, "to keep you grounded," he said. Whisper knew what he meant—while her soul may travel to the sky spirits, her body needed to remain tied to the earth. She allowed him to reach around her, draping the fabric across her hipbones, not noticing when his hands lingered at the knot, although Hunting Hawk did.

After preparations were made, Dark Water led Whisper to the center of the hearth. There was just enough room for her to lie down, the rocks surrounding her form to protect her from the fire. She fit perfectly, as if the spot were made just for her.

Safe in her cocoon, prepped for the ceremony, Whisper folded her arms across her chest, dagger in hand. She needed the Little Men for her journey, but she didn't trust them and it made her feel better knowing Hunting Hawk was keeping an eye out for danger. She stared up at the night sky, eyes scanning the wispy clouds as they floated across glittering stars. Soon she would join them, and make the first move in her plan to take down the Great Spirit.

The Little Men surrounded the fire soundlessly, Dark Water lifting a hand and pointing toward the stone structure. Flames erupted from the coals, surrounding

Whisper in a fiery haze. Hunting Hawk jumped at the orange blaze, racing to the pit only to be shoved aside by Star Seer, one of the brothers. Furious, he nearly stabbed the man before he saw Whisper lying safely in the center, her bronzed skin reflecting the light with a thick sheen of sweat. Her eyes were closed, but her hand was steady on her blade. He knew she was listening, waiting for an attack.

"*Unitsi*," Dark Water called to the Mother, holding out his arms and tipping back his head. His voice echoed throughout the clearing, wafting up to the sky along the tendrils of smoke. Then he began to chant. He spoke in a language Hunting Hawk didn't understand, one Whisper recognized as an ancient tongue known only by the first Elders that once made up the Great Spirit's council. Not even she knew those words. How Dark Water knew was a question she would save for later.

The more he spoke, the more his words began to take on a musical tone. The Little Men lifted their instruments, wooden flutes and stringed pieces and odd objects crafted by the bark found solely in the Forgotten Lands. They began to play as they slowly circled the fire, only Dark Water standing still. From his place outside of the Circle, Hunting Hawk crossed his arms and watched, entranced, when the music floated up toward the sky in visible strands of air that crisscrossed through the fire. Streaks of orange and red twisted around the stones, surrounding the Little Men, dancing as they danced, vibrating each time their feet struck the earth.

It was an eerie tune they played, rhythmic in its haunting melody, a slow, whispery song that brought time itself to a standstill. The Little Men continued their dance, eyes closed as they played their instruments. Dark Water, the leader, standing frozen as a statue with his arms lifted to greet Sun Woman. Star Seer, the hunter, moved in a rhythm that mimicked a man stalking his prey. Burning Wind, the healer, beat his hands on a worn drum while whispering words meant to cure. Dream Maker, the artist, played an eerie tune on an elegant and ornate flute crafted by his own hands. Lifter, the shaman, brought forth sparks of white light every time he placed a foot on the earth. And Earth Dancer, the dreamer, created an air of mystery and magic through simple yet patterned movements that matched his brothers' songs.

Then, as the air thickened and the music began to thunder across the skies, the dancing stopped.

The Little Men lowered themselves to their knees and leaned back, baring their faces to their ruler. Dark Water joined them and together they began a new chant, their words mixing with the music, bringing Hunting Hawk to his knees as well as the tune filled his eyes with tears he could not explain. Instead of fighting it, he watched as the flickers of fire that danced throughout the circle turned their attention to Whisper.

The music's pace quickened then and the wind picked up, blowing into the blazing flames gently as it lifted Whisper's body. But not her body, Hunting Hawk realized. It was not her true form slowly circling into the sky before him, but her spirit, a thinly veiled spirit that represented her very life-force in the Land of the Dead.

As he watched, Whisper's spirit rose into the sky, the flames reaching up with fiery tips licking at her heels. Her head had fallen back, long black hair swaying in the breeze, and her hands were relaxed in a way he had never seen before. Soon, she was but a star in the sky.

Dark Water lifted his staff high above his head, staring straight into the fire and Whisper's still body. Then, with a force that shook the trees, he slammed it down into the ground, cracking the earth as a wave of blue light washed over them. Whisper disappeared in a flash of white, completing the ceremony.

Chapter 14

She felt like she was wrapped in a cocoon of water, slowly suffocating to death. Her body was bound by heaviness, crushing down on her chest as she struggled to free herself from invisible chains.

Then, just as rage filled her heart at being trapped, Whisper burst through the wall and surfaced into brightness. Instantly she was blind, the fierce whiteness cloaking her eyes as she crawled to her hands and knees. She was soaking wet, water dripping from her hair and chilling her spine as it trickled down her back. Her clothes felt unusually heavy, and as her eyes adjusted to the bright light Whisper saw, through a hazy white fog, that she was wearing a ceremonial dress that clung to her body.

The dress fell nearly to the ground, with a slit up the side that stretched nearly to her waist to allow for easier movement and agility. The buckskin arched low across her chest, and was tied together at the back with thin straps that allowed her black tattoos to show through—a map of the Land of the Dead that had served as her guide many years ago when she saved the dead son of Ian Daivya.

A thick belt was tied around her hips, decorated with animal images and symbols. Whisper let the end trail through her fingers as she picked at the fringes that fell from her shoulders and down her arms, wondering what she was wearing and where it had come from.

"The leader of the Land of the Dead deserves to wear only the best," a voice said from behind. It was a voice filled with thunder and lightning, yet was somehow welcoming and friendly at the same time. "Do you not agree?"

Whisper turned, pleased that she was still gripping her knife. The woman sitting before her didn't look threatening, but she knew better than to trust appearances alone. "Sun Woman," she said, half in awe of meeting the spirit that controlled the skies. She was more beautiful than Whisper had imagined, an older woman who radiated from the inside out, a golden glow around her that sparkled with each movement.

Sun Woman was tall, with soft curves and an elegant face. Her eyes were the color of the sun, almond-shaped and deep, accented by thin lines at the corners. When she smiled, her full, rose-colored lips pulled up into a grin that suggested both friendliness and danger. It was an elegant face, but also one that had seen grief, war, death, destruction. The spirit's long black hair lifted in the gentle breeze, framing her face in shadows as she rose gracefully from her seat.

"I've been waiting for you."

"The Forgotten Lands are not easy to navigate." Whisper stood in place, eyeing Sun Woman cautiously. "Why did you show me the path here?"

Sun Woman laughed, her voice echoing off the delicate clouds that cloaked their feet. "You never were a subtle woman, *Kanegv*. It is part of your charm." She gestured to the fire, which crackled softly in the morning light. "Join me, and we will discuss your reasons for being here."

It amused her to be called charming, and while she knew Sun Woman was merely being polite, Whisper nonetheless sheathed her blade as a show of trust. She took a seat next to the spirit, her face emotionless. "Why am I wet?"

"I suspect the Little Men were having a bit of fun with you," Sun Woman answered. She waved a hand in front of Whisper, who felt a blast of warmth encase her body. Looking down, she saw that she was completely dry. "Better?"

"Yes." Comfortable now, even in the dress, Whisper allowed herself to relax slightly. She nearly hesitated before speaking, but decided she wanted to get the visit over with as quickly as possible. "You know where Elder Smoke Speaker is, and why he has been taken from the Land of the Dead."

"I do." Sun Woman nodded. "And I know what Creator wants from him."

Whisper waited, but the spirit seemed finished. She lifted a brow impatiently. "And?"

Sun Woman smirked. "Do you think I would give up such information with nothing in return?" When the other woman gave merely a half-smile of understanding, she lifted a box. "Do you know what this is?"

Whisper eyed the golden box, taking it in her own hands when Sun Woman offered. She ran her fingers over the intricate carvings, taking in the detailed trees, the flowing river. The lid was slightly ajar, and she opened the box just enough to see the plush interior lining, glowing and soft with one lone red feather. "I do." Then she realized what the spirit desired. "You want me to return your daughter to you."

Sun Woman's eyes darkened then. "There were seven Little Men entrusted to bring my daughter back from the Land of the Dead. Only six remain. I did not learn until after his exile that it was the seventh brother I needed, and by then it was too late. I want my daughter back, *Kanegv*, in return for telling you why the Great Spirit wants your grandfather. And in exchange for telling you how to get your revenge, I want something else."

The promise of vengeance weighed on Whisper's heart and filled it with lust and greed. "Name your price, Sun Woman."

Chapter 15

Whisper considered the offer, running her fingers through her hair as she processed Sun Woman's bargain. It was fair, in the simplest definition of the word, and relatively easy on her part. Almost too easy, in her opinion.

She knew there was more to the offer than the spirit was letting on; there always was. But for now, she would let it go to get the information she needed. What Sun Woman lusted for, what Whisper could hear on the unspoken words radiating from her mind, was beyond her ability to do. That would be a battle for another time, and when such a time did come, she would have to decide which side she would rather be on. Sun Woman was powerful, and demanded even more powerful things of her realm and the people below it. Whisper would let the sky spirit believe that she was capable of such great feats if it meant getting what she wanted.

"I accept your terms," she told Sun Woman, handing her back the box that once held her daughter's soul. "Now, tell me what I need to know."

Sun Woman took a few steps forward, her dress swishing around her ankles and her moccasin-clad feet sending up delicate clouds into the sky. She lifted a hand, bone bracelets accented with yellow beads dangling from her wrist, and drew it across the air. A wavering image appeared, sparkling and pristine, picturesque and dream-like.

"The Spirit World," Whisper said quietly, both disgust and awe tingeing her voice. It was a place she had only dreamed of, one she would likely never see, one that called to her yet pushed her away. She had no place in the Spirit World, but there would always be a small sense of regret for what she could not have.

The image shifted then, revealing a circle of men sitting around a fire. They were looking at something intently, pointing and drawing in the sand, writing with excited hands on parchment paper.

"What do you see?" she whispered, leaning closer toward the vision. Then she drew back when she took in the familiar face. "Smoke Speaker." The Elder was there, sitting among the thirteen, his face a mix of wonder and anticipation. He was happy, a fact that burned Whisper to the core. He didn't seem to be sad at all, wasn't tormented by the fact that he was torn apart from his daughter and granddaughter. No, he wasn't affected in the least.

She had expected Smoke Speaker to put on a front, to pretend to be pleased with his calling. She'd expected to see the truth in his eyes, that he was secretly waiting for the day he would be reunited with his loved ones. Whisper could read the Elder better than anyone, and right now she could clearly read now that he was happy to be there, acting as though he was with friends, old comrades he was excited to be with in his death. He lied, she thought, when he said he would join them in the Land of the Dead. Or at the very least, he had no qualms in going against his promise.

"Creator is planning a new beginning," Sun Woman said from behind, her voice gentle. She knew that look on Whisper's face, one of masked grief and fierce rage. It was a look she had seen all too often staring back at her in her own reflection. "He has waited for many moons to collect your grandfather's soul, and now his Circle is complete."

"...Complete for what?"

"For the rebirth."

Whisper thought about it, but the ancient spirit's words didn't make sense. "In what way?"

Sun Woman cast Whisper a long, sad glance. "*Kanegv*...it is no secret that our people have been cast into the shadows to make room for...Western culture." She waved a dismissive hand. "Our people once ruled the land, respected it, believed in it. Now they are forced into cages, mere reflections of a culture that once was. Languages are lost, spiritualities are forgotten, our Mother Earth is destroyed. And Creator seeks to change this."

It was a noble cause, one Whisper could respect. She too had often felt that burn of rejection. But still, something about this mission didn't sit well with her. "Creator simply cannot force our traditions onto the Land of the Living. That would make us no better than the ones who stole our ways."

"He does not wish to force our ways on the living, but to bring our spiritualities back to comfort those who have passed. And in restoring our ways on the dead, he will be able to influence the living."

"How? What does he need with the Elder?"

The spirit pointed to the vision in the air. The thirteen Elders were discussing something, nodding and smiling and looking eager to begin whatever quest they had been assigned. "Some things I cannot see, *Kanegv*, but I do know this. The Great Spirit has put a plan in motion. He has reached out to the living, and is using them for his benefit. He is clever, Creator, and is casting a fog over even my own vision. But," she said with a knowing smile when Whisper sighed and crossed her arm in frustration, "I have my ways."

Intrigued, Whisper moved closer, her feet silently gliding over the cushioned ground. The fire in the hearth flickered as she passed, a shadow cloaking the bright orange flames in the darkness that followed the woman who ruled the Land of the Dead. "And what have your ways revealed, Sun Woman?"

For just the briefest of moments, the same darkness passed through Sun Woman's eyes. "There is a child," she answered. "Not yet born, but conceived. The Great Spirit is interested in this child, but I do not know why. He has tasked the Elders with watching the child, guiding it."

"For what purpose?"

"I do not know," she said again. "The child is important, the most important being Creator has ever encountered. And yet, its purpose is clouded. That, you must discover on your own."

"And you know how I will accomplish this." It wasn't a question, because Whisper already knew the answer. She wouldn't be here if Sun Woman didn't know what she needed to hear.

Lifting her hand again, Sun Woman touched the vision and it changed. The Elders vanished, replaced by a strange vision of desolate land surrounded by barren landscapes and craggy holes cut deep into the earth. Even in the vision she could feel the emptiness and a sense of impending doom.

"What is this land?" Whisper asked, peering into the air and searching her memories for tales of such a destination.

"It is a place without a name," Sun Woman answered, her voice taking on a haunting tone. "It is a place the Great Spirit created out of fear, during a time when rebellion threatened his realm, and has kept hidden for his own protection." When Whisper merely stared at her, the spirit nodded toward the nameless place. "This is where you must go. The Great Spirit built a bridge here, a place where only the one who rules the Land of the Dead can cross over into the Spirit World for consult."

Jealousy and confusion built up inside Whisper. "Why was I never told of this place?"

Sun Woman shrugged indifferently. "Not many know of its existence, and those who do fear Creator too much to dare cross into his realm. You will not be welcomed, *Kanegv*. He will fight."

"And so will I."

"Yes." Sun Woman eyed the other woman curiously. She had heard stories of Whisper, of her tendency to leap without looking, act without thought, kill without hesitation. She was unpredictable, at times irrational.

She was perfect for accomplishing Sun Woman's vision.

"I will show you the way. And in return, I expect you to fulfill your promise."

Whisper turned at that, her eyes narrowing. "As I expect you to do, Sun Woman."

"Agreed." Sun Woman held out her hand. "And as a token of our agreement, I offer you this." She made an offering of peace and agreement, one that Whisper inspected carefully.

"A feather?"

"Not just any feather." Sun Woman held it out until Whisper took hold, turning it over in her fingers. "A golden feather, offered by the Great Eagle himself before the Raven-Eater cast him into the darkness. If you ever find yourself in need of an escape, light this feather and you will find sanctuary." Whisper accepted the offering, tying the feather to the bone beads already attached to her hair. "And *Kanegv*. As you embark on this journey, you must remember who your true enemy is."

The words struck a chord in Whisper, eerily similar to those that *Kamama* had spoken not long ago. But she didn't address them. Now wasn't the time. "Send me back, Sun Woman, and you will have your revenge."

Sun Woman opened her hand, a small fire burning in her palm. "As will you."

Chapter 16

Creator watched his Circle of Elders as they studied the Land of the Living, taking in the souls who would change the course of his people. The two, a young man and woman, had no idea what destiny had in store for them, but the Great Spirit was eager for fate to take hold.

For many, many years he had waited for this moment, and now his Circle was complete. These thirteen men would walk the Red Road set before them and lead the child into a new age, where their people were no longer forgotten, cast aside, ignored. But it was more than that, *he* wanted more than that. This child would be—

The Great Spirit frowned and turned, startled by the sudden intrusion into his world. It was slight, but it was there, a rippling in the air, a shadow in his heart. Someone, or something, was trying to gain access into the Spirit World. Worse, that someone or thing was succeeding.

But he knew this feeling, recognized the darkness, the hate, the subtle call for vengeance by a grieving mother. "Sun Woman," he whispered, casting a glance up to the bright blue sky. He was on friendly terms with the sky spirit, enough for her to shed light on his realm, but not enough to earn her forgiveness. "What do you want, old woman?"

She was gone before he got an answer, and he doubted she even detected his question. Curious, he walked over to the Elders and observed their work, eager to see what Sun Woman had seen when she stole a glance into his realm. The vision worried him.

The Elders were watching as the young couple celebrated the new life they were bringing into the world. The woman was just starting to show, glowing with the light of an expectant mother. The man adored her, excited to be a father. So Sun Woman knew of his plan, but the Great Spirit wasn't so naïve as to believe that she was looking just for herself. No, Sun Woman wouldn't risk the Sky Vault just out of curiosity. She was getting something out of her intrusion, and he knew just who she was working for.

"You are not the only one with a secret weapon," he whispered, backing away from the Elders after giving an approving nod. "Do not start what you cannot finish, half-breed."

In the privacy of his room, Creator prepared to call the one spirit who would have the power to stop the half-breed as she prepared for battle. Or if not stop her completely, then delay her even if just for a day's time. Once a free spirit, then a prisoner, and now forever torn between two worlds while settling among them, she was a beautiful woman wanted by powerful men who would wage war for her heart. And in this history of battle, she came to understand warfare and learned to never hesitate when releasing the bowstring. Above all, she cared the safety of her people, and was the first to fight when those she loved were in peril.

But she was also just, and fair, and knew what was best for her kind. And so Creator would use her, bring her to his side, let her be part of a new era for her people. With her leadership and skill, the half-breed would know what struggles she faced should she decide to fight back. It would be power against power, old magic against that yet to be truly discovered, two forces that would forever stand at opposites ends of the spectrum.

Standing in the center of his room, robed in white buffalo hides and painted with the markings of his people, the Great Spirit called to Blue Corn Maiden.

* * *

From deep in her slumbered sleep, the spirit stirred. She stretched her long, tanned body, eyes fluttering open to see the bright sky through the small opening of her hut. At the sight of the sparkling sunlight, she frowned, looking up curiously for a moment before rising. She knew that light, that humid scent in the air. Summer was smiling into her hut.

But it was winter she woke for, winter she was forever destined to greet as she awoke from her deep sleep. Winter was when she was summoned to fulfill the promise she had made to regain her freedom, and to wake early could only mean something was brewing in the Spirit World.

"I feel you, Creator," she murmured sleepily as she rose from the straw bed, pushing her tangled black hair from her dark eyes. She could sense his urgency, however masked by the forced calm it was. He needed her, and needed her now. She acknowledged his silent message with her own communication sent on the air currents, then lifted her small frame from the bed. She slipped on her worn moccasins, tied a frayed buffalo hide around her shoulders, then stepped outside.

The brightness stung her eyes, which were so accustomed to the grays of snow and ice. She blinked to clear the tears that formed, then tipped her head back to take in the sky she had once longed to see, and had long since forgotten even in her dreams. The blues were more beautiful than she remembered, the warmth more pleasant than her skin recalled, the clouds more peaceful than any tranquility her souls could summon now. It was a beautiful day, and it saddened her deeply.

The spirit sighed, lowering her stare to the forest of trees and lakes that stretched out before her home. She sucked in a deep breath, releasing it slowly in a misty haze as her eyes took on a stormy, gray glow. The leaves begin to wither, the branches frosting with ice.

"Winter comes early for you, *Kanegv*," she whispered, her breath a misty cloud before her eyes. "I pray you are prepared."

Then, with a final regretful glance up towards the sunny sky, Blue Corn Maiden turned and walked back into the warm safety of her hut.

Chapter 17

Whisper didn't make the trek to the no-name land alone. Hunting Hawk followed, as did the six Little Men, who walked in a straight line behind her, silent and focused. They had refused to let her travel alone, and she knew that was because they didn't trust her to follow through on her promise. But she couldn't take offense, as deceit lay behind every one of their words as well.

It was a short journey to their destination, which Whisper didn't think was a coincidence. Sun Woman had banished the Little Men to the Forgotten Lands for a reason—they were exiled and unable to return to any kind of civilization, yet were in range to defend the Land of the Dead should any spirit ever attempt to cross over uninvited.

And now, Whisper was going to do just that.

She was armed for a fight, if it came to that. She wasn't sure what to expect from the Great Spirit, but she knew better than to go in unprepared. Her trusted bow was strapped across her back, pointed arrows secure in their quiver. She had sharpened her favorite knife, one taken from the Raven-Eater's own dead body, and tied the sheath to her belt. Her long black hair was in a tight braid to keep loose strands from her eyes.

From behind, Hunting Hawk kept his eyes on Whisper as they approached the nameless place of crossing. He was suspicious of her motives, and of what was said between her and Sun Woman that she was refusing to reveal. He knew better than to ask too many questions, but something wasn't right. She had been gone too long, and came back too pleased, for him to believe that they had merely talked. No, they had struck a deal, one that would likely end in disaster for one or both of the spirit realms.

Lost in thought, Hunting Hawk nearly stumbled into Whisper when she stopped short, hand instantly going to her knife. He put his own hands on her shoulders to steady himself, peering around to see what had caused her surprise. The Little Men did the same, forming a semi-circle around the sight and waiting for instruction.

Pausing just long enough to unsheathe her blade, Whisper slowly approached the unconscious man lying in the center of a medicine wheel that looked as though it had been marked in haste by shaking hands. Her deep black eyes narrowed, her mouth set in a thin line as she pondered over who this stranger might be, lying in the center of a no-name land.

She nudged his shoulder with a booted foot, taking in his rugged, tanned face as he turned over onto his back. He was young, not much older than her in his living life, but had a face that told stories of war and hardship, with faint scars across his jaw and an intriguing mark above his left eyebrow. His hair was decorated with braids and white beads, along with a blue-striped feather at the end of each knot. His clothing was strange to her, a pale tunic decorated with markings of a foreign tribe and pants made of a soft material she couldn't identify. His feet were bare, but not marked by calluses. Wherever he was from, the earth was soft and plush.

"Is he from the Spirit World?" she asked quietly, kneeling down and poking him in the shoulder with the tip of her knife. "How did he get here?"

Hunting Hawk squatted down next to her. "And more importantly, *why* is he here?"

"He is indeed from the Spirit World," a voice said from behind. The two rose and turned to face Dark Water, who was pointing at the man with his spear. "He is a servant of the Great Spirit."

Whisper stared at the man suspiciously. "And how do you know this?"

"He wears only the finest clothing." Dark Water gestured to the stranger's pants. "That material is made from the hide of Spirit World buffalo, and is saved only for those who serve Creator." Then he frowned and took a step closer. "But to have been sent to the Land of the Dead, he must have angered the Great Spirit greatly."

Whisper turned her attention back to the dead soul. "Or he is a traitor," she replied quietly, thoughtfully, then nudged him harder with her foot. "Maybe he is here without Creator's consent." She considered kicking him, but Hunting Hawk grabbed her arm and pulled her back a few steps when he began to stir.

The first thing he felt was pain, excruciating pain behind his eyes when he opened them to a strange red and purple light. It took his eyes a few moments to adjust and his head even longer to stop throbbing. When he was able to concentrate, he then felt fear, the fear of a man in an unknown world surrounded by dark figures clutching knives and sharp spears.

A bit shaky, he rose to his hands and knees, rubbing his eyes with the heels of his hands, then slowly got to his feet. He stood before the figures, attempting to appear confident and strong as he observed the woman who stood just a few steps in front of the others, a look of disdain spread across her face.

"You're her," he said, his voice rough and full of awe. "You're the half-breed."

"Yes," Whisper said slowly, observing the stranger. "And you are?"

The man took a step closer, only to take two back when Hunting Hawk started forward. He held up his hands as a peace offering. "I am Earth Keeper," he answered. "I was the War Chief for the Great Spirit."

"Then why are you in the Land of the Dead?"

The man was silent for a moment, fidgeting with the edges of his tunic. "It would appear I spoke without thinking first of the consequences."

"Meaning what?" Whisper pushed, at the same time Hunting Hawk asking, "What did you say?"

"I did not agree with Creator's plans, and spoke of my feelings," Earth Keeper admitted. "He cast me out in punishment, so I found the crossing and passed through. But...something overcame me. Something dark. I do not know what happened."

Interested, Whisper moved until she was nearly toe-to-toe with Earth Keeper. She stared into his eyes, taking in their thoughtful depth, letting her gaze trail across his face. He stared back at her hesitantly, nearly lifting his hand to her own cheek as her stare started to mesmerize him. Then, unexpectedly, she shoved him hard and sent him tumbling back to the ground. She pounced on him immediately, shoving her blade to his throat before he could protest.

"A servant of the Great Spirit appears in my realm on the day I travel to the crossover place?" she snarled, her angry glare frightening the man to his very core. "A man accepted into Creator's good graces is suddenly exiled just after I find out about the Elder? It seems to perfect to be true. Too convenient. So why am I to believe you?"

"*Kanegv*," Hunting Hawk said quietly from behind, in a tone he often used to combat her rage. "Let him speak."

After a moment, Whisper backed off, allowing Earth Keeper to stand. Though he was embarrassed, fury flared in his eyes. "You have no reason to trust me," he replied, wiping the blood from his throat, "but you will." When Whisper merely crossed her arms, he gestured to the sky as though the Great Spirit were hovering just above. "I have served Creator since I first crossed into the Spirit World. I was known to my people as a great leader and War Chief, and Creator wanted me as his own. I have done his bidding from the beginning, but in his age he has gone beyond what I am comfortable doing."

"A War Chief with morals?" Whisper scoffed. "What could be so terrible for you to refuse?"

"The child," Earth Keeper said, and his words caught Whisper's attention, as well as the others'. "It began as a dream, a wish to give our people back the respect they once had. But now it is personal, and I fear the Great Spirit has made a mistake."

"A mistake in what way?"

Earth Keeper looked over to Dark Water, who had asked the question with no small amount of skepticism. "This child is not our savior, and taking it from the Land of the Living will only cast the Spirit World into darkness. To take a living child and force its spirit into a world of death, that is not our way. It's——" He caught himself, but Whisper knew what he was going to say.

"It is our way," she finished, knowing by the way he turned his eyes to the ground that she was right. "Taking a living child makes the Creator like us, like the Land of the Dead...Like the Raven-Eater. I can only imagine he did not appreciate being compared to such despicable souls such as ourselves."

He heard the sarcasm in her voice, but thought it best not to address it. Instead, he merely nodded. "I shared my thoughts, and out of anger he exiled me. He said it would be my burden to bear, forced to live in the world I would dare to compare him to."

Whisper thought about his words, fingers tapping on the hilt of her blade as his confession echoed in her mind. She spared a glance over to Hunting Hawk, who wore the same wary expression as she did.

"So what are we to do with you, Earth Keeper?" she asked. "Send you to your second death, or believe your words?"

He worded his reply carefully, knowing it could be the last thing he ever said. "I know the Great Spirit through and through, and I know every part of his home. He exiled me here. I no longer have any loyalty to him."

Earth Keeper concentrated on the ground as he struggled to hear what was being said about him. He pretended to be fascinated by the patterns in the dirt and tried not to feel threatened by the five men who stood guard around him in a circle while Whisper, Hunting Hawk, and Dark Water discussed what was to be done with him. At times he heard Whisper's voice rise angrily, only to be hushed by her mate. He wasn't sure if she was on his side or not, though, and that worried him. To be on the half-breed's bad side was to be directly in the line of fire, and now that he was here, able to see the beauty that was the feared leader of the Land of the Dead, he knew he wanted nothing more than to be on her good side.

He was sent to this dreadful land to be a spy for the Great Spirit. To lie, to deceive, to make sure Whisper stayed in her own realm. But now, seeing the passion that filled her, the haunting darkness that deepened her black eyes, the strength that fueled her every move, he was finding himself more and more entranced. He realized, with some amount of incredulity, that he was jealous every time Hunting Hawk touched her, every time she looked at her companion with affection rather than hate.

Earth Keeper shook his head to clear it of such foolish thoughts, and to remember what he had come here for. Just as he was settling his expression back into one of wary boredom, the trio turned and walked back to him.

"You will tell us how to breach Creator's walls," Whisper said, pointing at him with her knife.

"It would be much wiser to stay here," he answered hesitantly. "The Great Spirit does not take kindly to strangers who mean him or his people harm."

"I do not plan on harming him. I want to find the Elder, and I know he is with Creator." Whisper crossed her arms, planting her feet firmly in a stance even Dark Water now recognized as combative and threatening. "This is not a matter for discussion, stranger. You will tell me how to reach Creator, or I will send you to the depths of your second death."

He believed her, and that terrified him.

Despite his mission, despite the Great Spirit's words echoing in his mind, Earth Keeper found himself telling her how to find what she was seeking, and how to slip in unnoticed. He knew every inch of *Oway*, and knew it well. He spoke as though in a trance, captivated by the half-breed's dark aura, unable to stop the rush of words as they poured from his mouth. With his help, whether willing or not, the half-breed would find herself in the middle of the Circle's sanctuary ready to face Creator.

While he spoke, Whisper didn't move a muscle. She stared at him, listening intently and unnerving him with that dedicated if not dangerous glare. It was only when he finished that she shifted, looking over to Dark Water.

"You will come with me. Hunting Hawk, stay with him. He is to be considered our prisoner until I know for sure he is not a liar."

Hunting Hawk looked like he wanted to protest, but knew better. He merely nodded and took his place next to the prisoner. Earth Keeper sighed and hoped Whisper would come back unharmed, or else he knew the man would literally have his scalp.

The sun was starting to lower by the time Whisper and Dark Water positioned themselves along the line Earth Keeper had drawn in the sand. An invisible barrier, he had explained, the crossover between one realm and the next. But to pass through, one had to imagine themselves on the other side, and be prepared for a welcoming, and not let the mind wander lest it take the spirit to a dark place trapped between worlds.

Whisper didn't know what *Oway* looked like, so instead she imagined her grandfather. Smoke Speaker smiled in her vision, beckoning her forward. Taking in a deep breath, Dark Water mimicking her actions, she stepped forward into the crossover.

Chapter 18

Elder Smoke Speaker sat back and sipped the mug of warm tea a servant had just brought him. It had been a tiring day, pooling his gifts together with the rest of the Circle to begin to carve out the Red Road for Creator's chosen child.

The child was developing, not yet aware but very much alive, the parents thrilled over their miracle. Mother was nurturing, father was kind, and both were looking forward to the future despite suspicions of doubt that tugged in the corners of the man's mind. He doubted his ability to provide for his child, doubted his ability to guide, but the love was there nonetheless.

It was fascinating to the Elder being able to touch a mind not yet formed, to speak to a conscious being not yet aware. The child heard their prayers, understood their instruction, and still was unable to acknowledge even its own existence. The Circle had been tasked with a groundbreaking mission, and it would take every one of them to ensure the child was able to take her rightful place in the spirit realm.

Smoke Speaker slid down the bench to make room for Elder Tall Bear as he approached. True to his name, Tall Bear was a hulking man that towered over them all, with long, thick limbs and broad shoulders able to carry the weight of an entire tribe. He had been a respected Ojibwa healer in his time, one gifted with a unique ability to speak to animals as though they were his most trusted friends. He had lost his life defending his village from raiders, and still wore the beautiful ceremonial robes his family dressed him in for burial.

"Do you wonder what this is all for, Elder?" Tall Bear asked after a moment's silence. He turned his weather-worn face to Smoke Speaker, eyes nearly hidden behind folds and wrinkles. His black hair was tied back into a tight bun, tucked at the nape of his neck with a blue pin. "I am not one to question the Great Spirit, but even I wonder what makes this child so unique."

Smoke Speaker hesitated. He had an idea of why Creator wanted the child, and why the child was important, but it wasn't his place to reveal such information. In fact, he guessed that one reason why the Great Spirit wanted him in the Circle was because of what he knew, although he hadn't yet said anything to confirm his suspicions.

Still, Tall Bear was his friend and a member of the Circle, and they all deserved to know what they were up against. If their leadership guided the child, and subsequently, the Circle, to the place he had dreamed of, then they all needed to be prepared.

"Perhaps Creator—" Smoke Speaker started to share his thoughts, but stopped when he felt a sudden change in the air. He looked over to Tall Bear and set down his cup. "Did you sense that?"

Tall Bear rose. "Yes. A rippling in the wind." He had barely put his hand on his knife when two figures appeared, one already aiming an arrow at his heart. The Elder froze, staring at the hauntingly sinister and armed woman and her strangely dressed companion while the remaining Circle raced in, already having sensed the intrusion. He could only guess that the Great Spirit was not far behind.

From his spot next to Tall Bear, Smoke Speaker took a cautious step forward with his hand held out as a peace offering. Whisper didn't notice, and he hadn't expected her too. He knew that look of concentration and fury in her eyes, the one she got when she felt threatened, when someone held a weapon in her direction. It was one she often got when she hunted, seeking out her prey with confidence, and without mercy. She would stare her opponent down until he backed away, or died.

"*Kanegv,*" he said quietly, speaking to his granddaughter, not the half-breed. "*Kanegv,* look at me."

The voice startled her out of her glare, and Whisper shifted her attention to the Elder next to Tall Bear. When she saw him, she lowered the bow. "Smoke Speaker."

He wasn't sure if it was relief, surprise, or anger in her voice, or a combination of all three. "It is wonderful to see you, my dear."

For a rare moment, Whisper was speechless. A strange mix of emotions raced through her as she stared at the Elder. It had been nineteen long years since she'd last seen that face before her own eyes, and she marveled over how old he was. Of course, he'd been old even during her time, but now those wrinkles were cut deeper, his hair was whiter, and his body thinner than she'd ever known it to be before.

But there was still that twinkle in his eye, that aura of power surrounding his very being. He hadn't lost any of the special traits that made him Elder Smoke Speaker.

The sight stirred something deep in her, but she couldn't place the feeling. She enjoyed seeing the familiar face, enjoyed the memories that came flooding back as he met her stare with a knowing smile, but at the same time, rage surged through her as her head began to pound behind her eyes.

There he was, smiling at her, welcoming her. There he was, content in his disloyalty.

Before she could respond to his words, the Circle simultaneously shifted attention to something to her right. Whisper followed their gaze to see the Great Spirit standing on the steps leading down to the room. Disillusionment instantly filled her. She didn't know what she had been expecting, but this...this was not it.

The Great Spirit was a tall man, but not so large as to seem intimidating. He had a friendly if not rugged face, deeply tanned and accented with sharp lines and black tattoos along his jaw. His hair hung down perfectly straight, an elaborate braid on one side decorated with white feathers that matched the stark white of his peculiar, if not captivating, tunic. He was barefoot, she noted with a frown, finding it odd. A leader should always be prepared for battle, and it appeared this ruler thought he had nothing to fear.

Like the Elder, he too exuded an aura of power, but Creator's was much, much more. Not only power, but confidence, hope, life, a magnetic energy that almost made her wish she could be held in his strong arms.

A trickster force, she thought, clearing her mind of such foolishness. Instead, she turned her attention briefly to allow herself a few seconds to glance over her surroundings. The light was harsh enough to sting her eyes, but she could stand it. The sun was different here, brighter, warmer, and illuminated the Spirit World in brilliant color that practically sparkled. The trees rising up in the center of *Oway* glittered in green, swaying in a light breeze as though dancing with one another. In the distance she could hear birds singing, children laughing, and even rivers gently gliding over smooth rocks. It was peaceful, it was happy, it was life manifested in death.

And it was revolting.

Whisper's mouth worked up into a sneer as she faced the Great Spirit once again. To live in such brightness, happiness, she knew it was all a false face, a cover for something darker that lay beneath the surface. Creator merely stared back at her calmly, waiting for her to speak as he clasped his hands behind his back. He had known this moment would come, and felt she had the right to talk.

"I have come to collect the Elder," Whisper said, her voice low and threatening. "He is not yours to take."

"*Kanegv*—"

Smoke Speaker was cut off by Creator lifting an arm to silence him. "Nor is he mine to keep," the Great Spirit agreed. "It is true that I took him from you, but I have never held him here against his will. I need him here, where he truly belongs."

"He belongs with his family."

"We are his family."

Whisper shook her head, taking a step closer to the Great Spirit. Behind her, Dark Water had unsheathed his knife and was prepared to fight. "This is not a matter of discussion."

"No, half-breed, but it is a matter of choice." Whisper was a bit taken aback by the sudden change in his tone, the dark inflections in his voice. She was even more surprised by his chosen title for her. Creator took advantage of her silence to address the Elder. "Smoke Speaker, the choice is yours."

The Elder had known it would come to this, having to make his own decision to stay or go, just as he had known what his answer would be from the beginning. At the heart of the matter, it was an easy choice, doing what was best and not allowing himself to consider the opinions of others. His choice could not be influenced by his granddaughter, by Blue Feather, by the Great Spirit. Only he could know what was best for him and the offer made to him.

Swallowing his fear, squaring his shoulders, he made his decision.

"I am staying."

Confusion spread across Whisper's face. "I...I do not understand."

The Elder sighed, genuinely sad. "*Kanegv*, things have changed. What I am doing here, what the Great Spirit asks of me, this is bigger than you and me. This is about our people, not just about us."

She barely heard his words. "I died for you," she accused, stalking over to him, not noticing the black trail of ash that followed in her wake, turning the crisp green grass to a dead path of nothingness. "You raised me to die for you, for your daughter, with the promise that one day you would join us. And now you turn your back on your family? On Blue Feather?"

He chose his words carefully. "I think Blue Feather would understand what I am doing."

"Oh yes, the precious child," Whisper snarled, pleased by the look of shock in his eyes. "Did you think I was unaware of the child, Elder?" Smoke Speaker stayed silent, afraid that the knife she had suddenly gripped was meant for him. "Any skilled

Elder can guide a child, Smoke Speaker. But only one can fulfill the promise made to a girl who slit her own wrists for your vision."

"And look at what that vision brought you, *Kanegv*," Smoke Speaker snapped, suddenly defensive. "You died not just for me, or for Blue Feather, but for your kingdom, to take your place as the rightful heir of the Land of the Dead. It was not my choice alone, and I will not take the blame for your actions."

"Half-breed."

Whisper spun on her heel at the intrusion. Creator was staring at her from the same place, his arms crossed and his feet set in a firm stance. "You cannot stay here. You must leave." He pointed to her feet, where a circle of black was slowly creeping along the edges of the earth. The same black ash trailed behind Dark Water as well. "The longer you are here, the longer you taint the Spirit World. You must go, either willingly or by force."

She considered her options. Leaving peacefully would give the Great Spirit and his followers reason to believe she was weak, but being removed from the Spirit World by force only threatened her image. She chose the lesser of two harms, taking one final look back to the Elder. The look of contemplation and finality chilled him to the core. "You have made your choice, Elder?"

He nodded slowly. "I have."

"Then you have chosen the death of the Spirit World."

* * *

Whisper left Hunting Hawk at the place of crossover, too furious and hurt to speak. The man had taken only a single look to know that she was not one for conversation, and even Earth Keeper was wise enough to remain silent. Instead, he allowed Hunting Hawk to tie his hands behind his back, and acted like he wasn't terrified when the other man told the half-breed he would take him back to the Fire Tower and await further instruction. Dark Water gave his men orders to return to the Forgotten Lands, and he would accompany Hunting Hawk to the Fire Tower as well.

When she was far enough away, Whisper silently called for her winged companion. In just moments Eagle appeared, swooping low to the ground and slowing just long enough for her to leap on his back. He knew where to go before she asked, feeling the tension in her body, the emotion pulsing through her body, seeing the visible rage that radiated from her flesh. They flew silently to her sanctuary while her mind raced with the events that took place in the Spirit World.

He would rather stay with Creator, and the Circle, than be with family. His real family. He would rather betray Blue Feather and break his word than come home. She had died for him, for his daughter, for the Land of the Dead. Did she have the right to be angry, considering the title the Elder had helped her earn, her kingdom? Was it the betrayal that hurt, or something else? Or was it simply the blood of the Raven-Eater that made her see only resentment when the Red Road didn't go in the direction she wanted?

She had no answers to her questions, and didn't want any. She didn't need answers. She needed vengeance, blood, truth. She needed to find peace before she acted without thinking, and made irrational decisions.

When Eagle glided over the river that led to Sanctuary, Whisper calmed herself long enough to thank her companion, then leapt from his back. She welcomed the rush of cold air that blew against her face as she fell, the icy water that stung her skin as she tumbled through the strong underwater currents, and even the sharp, painful bite of jagged teeth that bit into her hip as she surfaced too slowly, distracted.

Escaping further injury, Whisper sliced at the fish and made her way to the altar, holding her bleeding hip with one hand as she stared into the fresh pool of water in the stone podium. At first she saw nothing, then the water rippled and formed the Fire Tower. She saw Blue Feather standing at the edge of the gates, hands grasping one another as she eagerly awaited the approach of the figures in the distance. The closer they got, the more of her smile disappeared as she realized that the Elder wasn't with them, and neither was her daughter.

When tears formed in her mother's eyes, Whisper slammed a hand into the water, destroying the image. She felt an unfamiliar emotion bubbling up inside her, one that made her nauseous, dizzy, angry, sad. She felt ready to kill at a moment's notice, yet wanted nothing more than to draw her knees to her chest and weep. She gripped the sides of the podium, knuckles white and arms shaking from the effort it took to restrain her thoughts from exploding from her head in a maelstrom of terror.

Not knowing what else to do, not able to shake the sensation, not feeling the strange shift in the air that crackled with each pulse of her heart, Whisper released the pent-up rage and pain in one long, furious, guttural scream that echoed off the walls and rippled across the water, sending the carnivorous fish scrambling for their underwater caverns. The scream reached down somewhere deep and unknown, and she felt the tremor in her own bones when something responded, awakening from the depths. Then, as quickly as she felt it, the sensation was gone.

Her energy spent, Whisper slid to the cavern floor, her hands coated in her own blood and her eyes wet. Startled, she lifted her fingers to her face, momentarily pleased that she hadn't shed a tear. She couldn't cry, didn't know how to cry, wouldn't cry. Not for Smoke Speaker.

Not anymore.

Chapter 19

It was dark when she returned to the Fire Tower, Father Moon shining down to cast a white glow around the mountains. At night, those rock towers put off a faint orange glow, just enough to light the way, although she didn't need any to get her home. She was the half-breed, and darkness was no different to her than sunshine. She could smell her way home if she had to, but tonight, she was driven by something else, something dark and dangerous.

Her thoughts kept taking her back to what both Sun Woman and *Kamama* had said to her, words she had thought strange at the time but now understood. "Know who your true enemy is," she muttered, turning the phrase over and over in her mind. "Not Creator...Smoke Speaker." The one man who had for so long been her only ally, was now her true enemy. It was the only conclusion she could reach, the only one that made sense during a time when her thoughts were chaotic and confusing. She wasn't sure how to feel about such an end, and prayed she was wrong while knowing she must be right.

She didn't stop to find Hunting Hawk or Blue Feather when she entered the Fire Tower, didn't stop to breathe in the familiar smells she loved most. Instead, she kept walking, climbing, turning, twisting, letting the years-old map tattooed into her back guide her as she stalked to the roof.

There, as predicted, was Earth Keeper, strung up on the altar where the Raven-Eater had died nearly nineteen years ago. She had blindsided him under the guise of sacrificing her own mother, waiting for that perfect moment when Ian Daivya had crossed back over into the Land of the Living with a lock of the tyrant's hair to make him freshly mortal.

Hunting Hawk had placed Earth Keeper in a tight hold, his arms out to his sides and tied down onto the stone pillars, his legs lashed together and knotted to a hook in the floor. Around his waist was a thin band secured to the back of the altar with a strong chain that clattered with every breath Earth Keeper took.

When Whisper approached, he looked up. Already his face was haggard and fear was in his eyes. "Why are you keeping me here?" he asked, his voice rough with lack of water. "I have done nothing to you."

"One can never be too sure," she replied, squatting down in front of her captive. "I will release you, if you tell me everything I want to know about the child."

That was not part of the plan, not why the Great Spirit had sent him here. "I told you what I know."

Whisper's mouth curled up into a sneer. She squatted down, cocking her head to the side and staring in a way that nearly made Earth Keeper sick to his stomach. "Do you think I cannot detect a lie?" she asked, her question quiet yet echoing in his mind. "Do you think I do not know who and what you are?"

Earth Keeper frowned, confused. "I do not understand. I told you why I'm here, why the Great Spirit banished me. He exiled me before I could learn of anything else he was planning."

With a sigh, Whisper rose and began to pace. She contemplated her choices—killing him now, or seeing what truth time would bring. She knew he knew more, and that he was as loyal to Creator as he claimed to be disloyal. He wouldn't talk unless he was scared, and he wasn't nearly scared enough. A few more days on top of the Fire Tower would cure him of that.

"You should reconsider your loyalties, Earth Keeper," she said somewhat distantly as she stared out at her kingdom. "I am not a merciful leader, and I care nothing for your existence."

"That is not much incentive for me to answer your questions then, *Kanegv*. Especially when you have given me no justification for holding me captive."

She scoffed his comment. "Your incentive is your life, Earth Keeper. Join with me, and be on the other side of the battlefield. Stay with Creator, and spend your days here. The choice is yours." Earth Keeper didn't answer, but merely snarled in her direction. She shrugged. "It seems we are both hiding something then, Earth Keeper. You tell me what I want to know, and I will tell you why you are now my prisoner. I will return when you have made the right choice."

Hunting Hawk was waiting for her in their shared room, standing by the window, watching the moon. He didn't turn when she entered, and waited until she had hung up her bow and quiver before speaking.

"What happens next?"

"He dies."

He turned at the sudden, sharp retort, frowning at her harsh tone. "For what crime?"

"For being a liar." Whisper stalked to the window, crossing her arms angrily. "Let him sit at the altar until he is ready to speak. Once I know what he knows, we slit his throat."

Hunting Hawk shifted, cupping Whisper's face in his hands in an all-too-familiar way. That troubled, dark look in her eyes worried him, as it always did. "*Kanegv*," he whispered, tipping his head down until their foreheads were touching. "Come back to me." He kissed her cheek, letting the anger surge through her, relieved when she controlled it and allowed herself to listen to his words.

Then she sighed. "Fine…We will wait for the moon to rise three times, make him speak, then decide what should be done with him." She pulled away from Hunting Hawk's grasp and crossed her arms again, taking her place at the window. For a moment she simply stared out at her land, chewing on her lower lip while lost in thought. "These times are troubling, Hunting Hawk. The Red Road is not always so easy to navigate."

The confession surprised him. "You are not alone, *Kanegv*. No matter where the Red Road leads you, there is help along the way." He lifted a hand to her hair. "This is your time to discover who and what you are, and use that knowledge. Smoke Speaker and Creator have given you this opportunity to learn what you are capable of doing. The Red Road may be difficult to travel, but it is still your destiny."

She let the words sink in, knowing he was right. This was the first time since taking reign in the land of the Dead that she had come face-to-face with her enemies, and she would be tested for all she was worth. She could let the fates consume her, or she could thrive, and conquer.

Whisper started to ask Hunting Hawk what he thought of Earth Keeper, but the words caught in her throat at the sudden brisk wind that blew in, and the white flakes along with it.

Whisper turned to Hunting Hawk, holding up her hand with a questioning expression at the white power that quickly melted. They both looked outside to see the metal ridge along the window frame turn to ice and the night clouds turn a strange gray color.

"What is this?" Her breath came out in a misty cloud. She knew what snow was, had faced it every year during her time in the living world amongst the North Carolina mountains, but never had the Land of the Dead seen snow.

"Blue Corn Maiden has come," a voice said from the doorway. The pair turned to see Blue Feather standing at the entrance of their room, a blanket wrapped around her shoulders. "She has been testing the waters since you left, and now that you have returned, has brought winter upon us like a plaque."

The name wasn't familiar to Whisper. "Blue Corn Maiden?" she repeated. "How have we angered her?"

Blue Feather entered the room and headed to the window. She frowned over the frost that was already starting to coat the land. "My guess is that she has allied herself with the Great Spirit, and he is sending you a message, *Kanegv*. The Land of the Dead is not a place meant for eternal winter."

"I know this," Whisper replied testily. "Who is Blue Corn Maiden?"

Blue Feather let her thoughts fill with memories of a story told to her long ago. Not by her father, Smoke Speaker, but by a young man she met at a powwow as a child. She had been enraptured with him, enthralled by his strange, foreign accent, fascinated by his tribal markings. He was not Cherokee, but had been welcomed by her family and the Elders as a trusted Trader. He had told her a story once, only to her, and it stuck with her ever since.

"Blue Corn Maiden is of the Acoma," she told her daughter, resting at the foot of the bed. Whisper kept her place by the window, Hunting Hawk putting his arms around her bare shoulders to keep them warm. "She was known as the most beautiful of corn maidens, and was loved for her gentle nature, and the blue corn she provided each season. She brought the people good food and peace, and they cherished her for it.

"One day during winter, she went to gather firewood and came across Winter Katsina, the spirit who brought winter every year and was recognized by his blue-and-white mask. Like the other people of the Pueblos, he loved Blue Corn Maiden as soon as he saw her.

"He invited her to his home, and once she was there, he covered the windows and doors with ice so she could not escape." As she spoke, a thin layer of ice began to form in the open window space. With a snarl, Whisper slammed a hand through the ice, blood dripping when a shard cut into her palm. Lost in her story, Blue Feather continued without noticing.

"Winter Katsina loved Blue Corn Maiden, but she was always sad and missed her friends and family, and growing the blue corn that made her people so happy. And so, one day while Winter Katsina was away from their home, she managed to escape. She gathered yucca blades and brought them back, then started a fire to prepare her food. Once the fire started to burn, Summer Katsina entered with fresh corn for her to prepare, and she welcomed her old friend.

"However, Winter Katsina came home at that moment, and threatened to kill Summer Katsina with a knife made of ice. They fought with the elements, and soon Summer Katsina's warm breezes melted the knife and Winter Katsina knew he would lose, so he decided a truce was in order.

"Along with Blue Corn Maiden, they decided to return her to her people, but to only allow her to harvest corn for half of the year. This way, Summer Katsina would have her for part of the year, and she would live with Winter Katsina when the snow fell. Winter Katsina was not pleased with this arrangement, and still sends winter to the people even when spring has set, to show his anger over being defeated.

"Now, Blue Corn Maiden is the symbol of springtime to her people. In the Spirit World, she has the powers of both." Blue Feather stood then, a look of dread crossing her young, pretty face. "I fear that the Great Spirit is using her to punish you for entering the Spirit World. If Blue Corn Maiden's full powers are released, then the people of the Land of the Dead will suffer in a freezing winter for the rest of our time."

Chapter 20

It took him awhile to gather his wits enough to knock on the Great Spirit's door. Creator had been secluding himself within the walls of *Oway* for three evenings now, ever since Whisper's unexpected visit. He had avoided the black spots she and Dark Water created with their dead-souled presence, ordering the Circle to attempt a cleansing magic and purify the area before resuming leadership for the child.

Now that the Circle was finished, green grass struggling to break through the black, tarry earth, the Elder knew it was time to speak his mind.

The door opened just as he lifted his hand to knock. Sucking in a deep breath for courage, the Elder squared his shoulders and entered, stopping in the center of the room. The Great Spirit was standing at the window, hands clasped behind his back. He turned to face Smoke Speaker, a gentle smile crossing his face.

"I knew you would come to see me soon, Elder. The half-breed's visit must have unnerved you."

"I raised her, Great Spirit. I am used to her strange ways."

Creator chuckled at his admission. "Of that I am sure. But her words and ways were not what I was referring to." He lifted a hand, creating a portal in the air that revealed the living world to Smoke Speaker. He saw the young couple as they shopped for baby clothes and looked over a selection of toys. The woman was round with child, one hand on her stomach as she held out a pink blanket.

"A baby girl," Smoke Speaker whispered, remembering his granddaughter as a child. He had never seen her as an infant or even a toddler, but he held the memories of her young face close to his heart. Her eyes had always been clouded with the darkness that the Raven-Eater's blood brought to her soul, but in her younger years she had smiled more, and even laughed on occasion.

Shaking himself from his thoughts to find the Great Spirit watching him curiously, a half-smile playing at the corners of his kind mouth, the Elder gestured to the vision. "You brought me here because of them."

"Of course. I thought that was clear. I needed my Circle to be complete."

"No," Smoke Speaker shook his head, "I mean because of our connection." When the half-smile fell, he continued. "You threaten *Kanegv* with eternal winter and sent Earth Keeper to contain her in the Land of the Dead, and yet expect me to betray her for your cause."

A strange shadow flickered in the Great Spirit's eyes. The air thickened in the large room and a chill caused the Elder to shudder. "Do you accuse me of being unjust, Elder? Are you suggesting that I am wrong in my quest?"

"Not at all," Smoke Speaker said hurriedly, holding up a defensive hand and inwardly breathing a sigh of relief when the fire left Creator's eyes. "I simply think it is unfair to punish *Kanegv* for being angry with me, when the entire reason I am here is because she choose to die in my stead. Would you have chosen me, Great Spirit, if not for what I already knew?"

Creator considered his answer thoughtfully. The vision in the air slowly faded. "It is true that your knowledge will greatly help us, and that is one reason why I brought you here. But you are also a Speaker, Elder, and a powerful one. You will be able to reach the child. You were able to reach the half-breed even when she was being manipulated by the Raven-Eater's bloodline. It stands to reason that you can also connect with this child." With that, he patted the Elder on the shoulder and gently guided him to the door. "Do not fret, Smoke Speaker. She will see that you are here for the right reasons, and give up this quest for vengeance."

"You don't know *Kanegv*," the Elder replied, both sarcasm and fear tainting his voice. "She does not go quietly into the night."

"Then she will perish with the rising sun," Creator answered, smiling at his favored Elder. "Do not fear, Smoke Speaker. I have no desire to fight her. Perhaps we can even work together in our mission. But for now, I must view the half-breed as a threat, and so must you."

Smoke Speaker stared at the door for a few moments after the Great Spirit closed it. "Her name is *Kanegv*," he whispered, a cold, painful longing suddenly gripping his heart. His souls heavy with loneliness and the desire to be with his family, his mind knowing he must stay, the Elder began the long walk back to his room.

* * *

He watched her sleep, the steady rise and fall of her chest, the way her eyelids flickered slightly as she dreamed. His hand on her swollen belly, he felt his child kick occasionally, signs of life that made him smile despite the trouble brewing in his heart.

He loved his unborn baby, couldn't wait to meet her, cherish her, spoil her, but something scared him. Something was taunting him in his dreams, haunting him, the same faces and voices his nightmares had been filled with as a child. Always out of reach, always just beyond his memory when he awoke, but still they were there. His dreams had faded some as a teenager and adult, but ever since he learned he was to become a father, the nightmares had returned to torment him.

He feared passing along those night terrors to his little one, watching her suffer from restless sleeps and endless days wondering what her dreams were trying to tell her. But while he feared what he was, what he experienced, he also knew that, like him, his daughter would find peace with the one that held her heart. He looked at that beacon of hope and light now, smiling softly as his eyes grazed over her beautiful face, her peaceful smile of sleep.

She made him whole, made the world right. And she would do the same for their child.

Chapter 21

Dark Water wasn't happy, and he wasn't afraid of voicing his opinion. Unlike the others who cowered at her feet, he wasn't afraid of Whisper, wasn't afraid of what she might say or do. He knew she needed him, and they had an agreement. He'd upheld his end of the bargain, and now it was her turn.

He caught her at the stairwell before she could head back up to the roof. She was dressed for the storm, a thick coat over her shoulders with a fur-lined hood made from a creature he likely didn't know the name of. Her feet were wrapped in leather boots and her normal pants had been replaced with thick material and heavy stitching. She had the means within her to stay warm without the layers, but doing so took precious energy she couldn't afford to waste. Winter had been set upon them in full force and was showing no signs of relief.

Blue Corn Maiden was doing her job, and doing it well.

"*Kanegv,*" he said quickly, catching her attention. She stopped, irritated by the distraction. "We had an agreement."

Whisper stifled a sigh, wishing she could brush the man off and knowing that had it of been anyone else, she would have. But Dark Water was right, they had an agreement, and he likely wanted to get back to his brothers.

"Yes, we did, Dark Water," she agreed, sheathing her knife. "I promised you your seventh brother for leading me to Sun Woman, and I intend to honor that."

"When?"

"After I deal with Earth Keeper. I have found the one meant to be your brother, Dark Water. He will not be as you remember, but it appears Sun Woman played a hand in that."

"What are you saying?"

Whisper considered her words carefully. "Your brother's spirit was sent to the Land of the Living. He still has his roots here, and has even returned once, but was not able to reach his brothers."

Dark Water frowned, not understanding. There was a message in her words, but he wasn't following. "If he is in the Land of the Living, then how will he come back?"

Whisper sneered her half-grin of deceit and maliciousness, one that Dark Water found both intriguing and sly. "He will not have a choice, Dark Water."

After promising to fulfill her contract soon, Whisper left Dark Water at the base of the stairs and began her ascent to the traitor. While she climbed, she thought about the seventh brother. She told the truth about Sun Woman's actions, and had been astonished to learn just where his spirit had landed. But then, she knew that she shouldn't be surprised, for destiny had led her along this path before, and it only made sense for such paths to be crossed again.

But that wasn't the real reason why she was so eager to fulfill her promise. No, once she learned the dwelling place of the seventh brother's spirit, a strange kind of cold cruelty had filled her. It was so fitting, so perfectly unjust and undeserved, and yet, was the only being the spirit could possibly possess. The reincarnation was so poetic that Whisper almost regretted the tragic ending for the man who had no idea he was on his deathbed.

Pleased with the thought of completing her contract with Dark Water, Whisper made her way to the roof, bracing herself for the harsh winter winds. Blue Corn Woman had certainly made her presence known, sending icy winds, bitter gales, and heavy sheets of snow that coated the Land of the Dead in an unforgiving white blanket.

Still, she could handle the cold. She was the half-breed, filled with a power even she was yet to fully understand. That power warmed her as she stepped onto the roof, keeping her blood flowing and her body movements fluid despite the breath that clouded before her eyes.

Earth Keeper, on the other hand, showed the effects of exposure to the elements. His body hung from the ropes, head down, long hair coated in ice. He was shivering uncontrollably, which amused Whisper, as it always amused her to discover the body could still react to things even in death.

Her feet crunched over ice as she stalked to the altar, squatting down to his level. She pulled her knife from the sheath at her belt and placed the tip beneath his chin, lifting his head. It was a knife once held by the Raven-Eater's own hands, one he had threatened her with during their final battle. She relished the fact that she had stripped it from him, while utilizing the power still contained within the bone and metal for her own personal gain. At times, she could even imagine that the stench of death was still upon it, evidence of her triumph over the Raven-Eater.

When the blade bit deeper into his skin, Earth Keeper slowly opened his eyes, his breath shuddering out of him. He was paler than she remembered him being three days ago, his deep brown eyes dull, his lips cracked.

"Have you reconsidered, Earth Keeper?" she asked quietly. "Or shall I leave you to suffer in the cold?"

It was a few moments before he replied. "I owe you no words, half-breed," he rasped out, his mouth dry, his throat aching. He would have spit on her if he could muster up the saliva. "You are holding me captive with no just cause. I gave you no reason to distrust me."

"Oh, but you did, Earth Keeper." She rested back on her heels, running her slender fingers over the sharp blade. "You labeled yourself a liar in the very beginning."

"...How?"

Whisper huffed at the man's ignorance. "You said Creator made a mistake with the child."

He waited for more, but she seemed to be finished. "So?"

She shoved the man hard, slamming him against the freezing stone altar, chains rattling. He cried out in pain, and she could smell the blood that seeped down his skin from fresh wounds. "Creator does not make mistakes," she snarled, pointing at him with her knife. "He is the Great Spirit, your leader. He does not *make* mistakes," she repeated for emphasis. "He walks the Red Road, and his actions determine the fate of the world around him. They are not mistakes. They are destiny. A devoted servant would know this, and only a devoted servant attempting to trick the half-breed would be foolish enough to use such meaningless words."

Her own words confused his exhausted mind, but he understood her enough to know he had made a mistake, possibly a fatal error, in the first moments he entered the Land of the Dead. "Why didn't you just kill me then?"

"What would be the purpose?"

Earth Keeper sagged against the stone. "I am not on your side, half-breed. You knew that from the beginning, even when I attempted to deceive you. Why would you show weakness and let me live?"

Whisper placed a hand on the man's throat, fingers digging into flesh. "What is weakness, Earth Keeper? Stringing a liar up to suffer the elements, or showing mercy by sending him to his second death?"

His throat constricted, sending waves of pain down his back. He didn't want to play this game anymore. "I do not care about your ego, half-breed. I will not sit here and feed your need for self-worth. Either kill me or leave me in peace."

"You will not get peace, until I get the answers that I want." Whisper waited, but when it was clear he was still unwilling to talk, she drove a second small knife into the cracks between the stones far out of his reach and straightened. "Very well. I leave you to Blue Corn Maiden. It does not appear she cares for mercy either." She turned, watching out of the corner of her eye as Earth Keeper wrestled with his head and his heart, weighing the price of words versus the pain that ransacked his every limb. She saw him make a feeble and pathetic attempt for the knife sticking out of stone, then sigh when he realized that the only reason she had placed it there was to taunt him.

She had reached the door when he called out. "It's the child!" he cried, coughing roughly. "It was always the child."

She turned slowly. "What about the child?"

Earth Keeper cleared his throat, hating himself for what he was about to say. But the cold, the cold was too much. It had reached down deep into his soul, confusing him, turning him against the one who sent him to the Land of the Dead and let him suffer at the hands of his own secret weapon. "The Great Spirit wants the child as a ruler. He is using the Circle to meld her mind and soul before they are developed, to make her one of us. One of our people."

Interested, Whisper took a step closer. "Why does he want a ruler? And to rule what?"

"He wants a child shaped by his own hand, one he can use to bring our people back to the land. The Circle is to train the child as she grows up with them."

"With them?" Whisper walked back over to Earth Keeper. "Creator is taking her from the living world?"

"Yes. When she is born."

Interesting, Whisper thought, idly taping the knife blade against her leg. Snow started to fall, sending her captive into a fit of coughs. Then another thought struck her. "Why this child? What makes her so important than any other?"

This was the question he had been waiting for, and it was one he was actually happy to answer. He hoped it would throw her off-guard, and make her so angry that she would rush into battle without thought or planning, and fail before she could release the first arrow.

"The child is special," he said slowly, drawing in painful breaths. "Her mother has native blood in her. Creek, I believe, but not much. But it is the father whose bloodline that truly matters."

"Is he native?"

"Not by blood." Whisper crossed her arms as he sucked in another deep breath in hopes of warming himself against the cold. "But he has a connection to our people that no other living person will ever have, and that connection is a power that was passed down to his offspring."

"What kind of connection?"

This was the moment of truth, and for the briefest of seconds Earth Keeper's eyes flashed knowingly. "He is the boy accepted into the hearth of the Raven-Eater."

It only took her the blink of an eye to understand his words. Her question was shaky when she asked, "You mean the father is…"

"Yes," Earth Keeper said. "The father is Cole Daivya."

* * *

The Great Spirit smiled lovingly as he watched the vision in the air. Lately he had been creating this vision more often, looking in on the young couple and the child growing each and every day. He felt a deep love for the girl, despite never having met her, never having spoken to her while she grew in her mother's womb. It pained him to know that he was taking the child from her mother before she would ever know the woman's touch, but at the same time, he was doing what was necessary for the Spirit World, his people, and for himself.

He yearned for a child of his own, but it was a wish never to be fulfilled as the leader of the Spirit World. His destiny was to watch over those who had once been sons and daughters, mothers and fathers, grandparents and cousins. The people who made up his world came from family, while he had never known such love.

This was his chance to have some semblance of that life he watched over, an existence not meant for him. But it was also his chance to make sure the blood of the Raven-Eater no longer tainted any souls in the Land of the Living. Cole Daivya had been accepted as the tyrant's own child, and that acceptance affected the boy more than anyone had known, including the half-breed. To have that bloodline spreading throughout the living world was something he could not accept. He was saving both the living and Spirit World from darkness. Let the half-breed figure out her own world, until it was too late for her to realize that it was being taken away from her.

Longing filled him as the mother ran her hands over her belly, just weeks away from delivering. He wished he could be there for the birth, to see her daughter into the world. But soon, the child would join him in the spirit realms, and he would have everything he desired.

Chapter 22

"She is letting him take over."

Hunting Hawk shook his head, clasping his hands behind his back as he paced across the floor. Blue Feather watched him sadly from the high-backed chair by the window. Her daughter's mate was faithful and had high hopes, but some things were obvious to a mother.

"Too much of him runs in her blood."

"No," Hunting Hawk disagreed, his face twisted into angry denial. "She may be the half-breed, but she is not evil. The Raven-Eater was pure evil and hate. He saw nothing but darkness. I have served them both and can see the clear differences between them. *Kanegv* may have his blood, but she is not blind to his influence."

"Then why is she determined to fight the Great Spirit? Why can't she accept that Smoke Speaker has chosen to stay? Do not forget, Hunting Hawk, I was the Raven-Eater's prisoner. I think I know him just as well as you, if not better. And I can see him in my daughter, too, too much of him."

He stopped pacing then, staring at Blue Feather incredulously. Sometimes he forgot that she was so young, her life stolen from her, forced to live in the Land of the Dead while never aging. Whisper had far surpassed her mother in wisdom, and it was strange to think Blue Feather was trying to be a mother while never having the chance to see her daughter grow. "Have you forgotten that your daughter gave up her life for his dream? So that he could save you from the Raven-Eater? That he promised to join her here, and instead chose to abandon her?"

"I have not forgotten," Blue Feather sighed. "But things have changed. He has been called upon by the Great Spirit. He cannot give up such an honor."

"Is it an honor, Blue Feather?" he challenged. "Is it an honor to be ripped away from your family, to go back on your word, to abandon your daughter and grand-daughter?"

"You don't understand, Hunting Hawk." Blue Feather rose and patted the man on the shoulder almost sympathetically. "This is beyond you, beyond me, beyond *Kanegv*. This is beyond friend and family. The Great Spirit has called upon him, Hunting Hawk. He cannot turn his back on that." Then she smiled, and he saw the pity in her eyes. "You are her husband, and so you must stand beside her."

"And you? What must you do as her mother?"

His biting tone turned her smile to ice. "It is my calling to help her walk the Red Road, wherever it may lead."

A strange, unspeakable anger filled him as he heard her words, saw that she actually believed what she said. To avoid saying something he may later regret, he simply nodded and stalked to the door. Once he got to the hall, he turned just long enough to say, "*Kanegv* needs no one to walk her down the Red Road. Let us hope you do not become an obstacle in her path."

He stood alone in his shared room, fuming over Blue Feather's words. He'd always thought the woman to be flighty and immature, but never once would he have labeled her as foolish. But now, he couldn't believe what he had just heard.

Whisper's own mother, turned against her, refusing to believe in her, acting as though she knew what was best for a land she didn't control. These were times of hardship and grief, and potentially of war, and Blue Feather seemed to think that she could handle them better than Whisper. Better than the half-breed, the heir to the Fire Tower. Hunting Hawk could only pray that Whisper never heard such words from her mother for herself.

The more he mulled over Blue Feather's comments, the more Hunting Hawk realized why he was so upset. For too long now the woman had been making those subtle jabs at her daughter, hinting over her lack of control, suggesting the Raven-Eater's blood was too strong. And for too long Whisper had been struggling with herself, trying to be true to who and what she was without causing harm.

She was suffocating on her own identity, he thought, thinking back to all the times when Whisper had to step back and fight with herself, when he had to call her back to him before she was lost in the void. Was he part of the problem? Was he to blame for her struggles, always being the one to rein her back in but never helping her use what power she had been given?

Thoughtfully, Hunting Hawk walked over to the medicine wheel, the one Whisper had built with her own two hands. It meant so much to her, this circle of stone, a kind of sanctuary crafted from her own heart and soul. The Land of the Dead meant even more. She loved her land and her people, in her own way, and didn't need anyone accusing her of not being able to handle her own power.

And in that knowledge, Hunting Hawk was suddenly aware of what he had to do. Reining Whisper back in from the void was only part of his task. He had to help her realize both parts of herself and bring them together, before the power fighting to be free burned her from the inside out. She couldn't be one or the other, Whisper against the half-breed. She had to make the choice to become one with herself, or the struggle would defeat her.

But he was terrified of what may come of that union. When Whisper and the half-breed truly joined as one, nothing would ever be the same. She could become the strong, powerful, courageous woman he knew she was striving to be, or he could lose her forever.

Chapter 23

For one of the few times in her life, Whisper was procrastinating, sharpening blades in her weapons room to avoid having to face those who sought her attention. Normally, she knew exactly what she wanted, and went after it. No hesitation, no apologies, no second thoughts. But now she was up against a larger adversary, one who could be her greatest ally, or her biggest enemy.

She had to make Sun Woman happy. She was stronger and more powerful than the spirit in many ways, though lesser in some, and could handle her own, but she needed the ruler of the skies nonetheless. But how was she going to explain this catastrophe? How was she going to present the change in their contract without angering Sun Woman?

It seemed she didn't have long to consider her thoughts. Just as she was contemplating a way out of her meeting, she felt the change in the air. Whisper turned to the window, where Sun Woman stood with an orange aura that shimmered against the sunset.

"I cannot stay long," the older woman said, her husky voice impatient. "I am here to ask why my daughter has not yet been returned. We had an agreement, *Kanegv*."

"The sun still shines in the Spirit World," Whisper said quietly, turning away from Sun Woman and pulling out her knife, wiping the blade with a strip of cloth.

"The sun will lower when my daughter is home safely."

"The terms of our agreement have changed," Whisper replied, now facing the spirit. "I have new information regarding Creator, and it is not information that benefits either one of us."

Sun Woman frowned, crossing her thin, tanned arms. "What do you mean?"

Whisper sighed and sheathed the knife at her waist. At a distance yet not feeling safe, Sun Woman wondered why the woman was always ready for a fight. "Because the man I promised you for your daughter is the same man who fathered the child Creator has planned for himself." She let the words sink in, watching as Sun Woman's face changed from wary to confused to angrily understanding.

"Taking the boy changes everything. Doing so will have direct impact on the child and its mother, and if anything happens to the child, Creator will send everything he has to destroy the land of the Dead." Whisper picked up another knife, channeling her frustration into cleaning it. "The risk is greater now, Sun Woman, on my part."

"The Great Spirit is using the boy." It was a statement and a question in one, but the sky spirit already knew the answer. "He turned his back on the Land of the Dead, except for when it was convenient for him to pay attention."

Whisper nodded, approaching Sun Woman and lowering her voice. "So then you understand what you must do, in order to see your daughter again?"

Sun Woman's eyes darkened to a frightening color, a strange mix of blazing orange and deathly black. Her head lowered slowly into a slight nod just as her body began to waver. Her time away from the Sky Vault was nearly over.

Before she left, Sun Woman looked over her shoulder at the only person who had ever taken the time to help, or even to care. "Find my daughter, *Kanegv*, tell me how to get her home, and I vow the sun will never shine in the Spirit World again."

* * *

The cold bit deep into his bones, grabbing hold of his muscles and sending Earth Keeper's body into fits of terrified spasms. The snow continued to fall, building around his thighs, the wind nipping at his bare flesh without care. His breath was white and frosted, and his eyes were nearly iced shut.

She had forgotten about him, Earth Keeper thought bitterly. She had locked him on this altar, pulled information out of him, and left him here to die without a second thought. Her actions only proved that the stories about her were true after all. The half-breed was evil, a woman focused only on her own wants and needs, a spirit who dominated with a heavy hand and greedy ambition. She didn't care for her people or her land; she cared only for blood and vengeance.

The Great Spirit was right, he now knew for sure. There were times when he had doubted Creator's plan, wondered if it would work, if it was even possible, but he had followed without question because that was his role. And now there was no doubt in his mind as to what had to happen.

Luckily for him, he had hidden that part of the plan from the half-breed. This was so much more than simply bringing a child into the Spirit World, and by the time she realized that, it would be too late.

Chapter 24

In the early morning light, Whisper made her way across the Barren Plains on foot. She didn't have far to go, and she enjoyed the walk through her land as life began to stir. She felt Grandfather Mole beneath her feet, trailing along under the earth, both welcoming her presence and attempting to scare her away. He recognized her scent, otherwise he would have surfaced by now and tried to work his deceitful ways on her, as he did with all others who got too close to the Fire Tower.

Just beyond the Barren Plains stood the Weeping Forest. Birds had nested along the edges, and started to sing sweet melodies as the sun rose. They hadn't always shared their songs with the Land of the Dead, but had once hidden away in fear of being ripped to mere feathers by the Raven-Eater. Now that they knew their new leader welcomed their calls, they enjoyed singing to her presence.

Whisper tipped her head up and glanced at the nests as she passed by. Blue-bird heads peeked out from the edges, greeting her shyly with high-pitched chirps. She offered a welcoming nod and a whisper of pleasantries on the wind before slipping into the trees.

She decided to make this trip alone, but was prepared for her journey through the Weeping Forest. She had knives, and her favorite weapon, her bow. Hunting Hawk would have been her greatest ally, but she needed him at the Fire Tower keeping watch over her captive. Besides, the spirit she was going to see lived in a camp of women, and men weren't always welcome.

The trek took no longer than half a day, and by the time she reached the edges of the small village her pants were soaked up to the thigh. Whisper had used her magics to blaze a path through the snow so she could walk on solid ground, but that hadn't saved her from the wet earth and falling flakes. But she wasn't cold; she was able to keep herself warm, although it annoyed her that she hadn't thought to protect her clothing from Blue Corn Maiden's curse. She was further irritated that keeping herself warm drained her of energy that she wasn't comfortable exerting in potentially threatening forests.

Her aggravation must have shown on her face, because when she stepped into the camp, the women gathered in the center around a table of rotting plants rose and stepped back hesitantly. Some clutched their hands together nervously, others shuffled their feet and kept their stares on the dirt. Only one stood her ground, hesitant yet refusing to show worry, and that was the one she wanted.

"Brave Woman," Whisper greeted, approaching the wary woman, who met her gaze with defiance in her deep brown eyes. "I have come to speak with you."

"Perhaps you can tell us why our crops are dying, why Mother Sun cannot melt the snow, why we are being punished with winter." Whisper smiled at the harsh tone, and had the woman of known better, she wouldn't have mistaken the grin for amusement. "Do you find this funny, stranger?"

The smile dropped, and Whisper was no longer impressed by her bravery. "Stranger?" she repeated coolly, a hand on the hilt of her blade. "If anything, you are the stranger in this realm, Brave Woman. This is my land." She waited for the words to sink in, and saw the moment the other woman realized who she was talking to. "I would like to speak with you."

"Oh. Of…of course." Brave Woman turned and led the way to her hut, not daring to look over at the others, who had huddled together at a safe distance. She forced herself to not wring her hands together, a knot forming in the pit of her stomach as her mind raced with all the things the half-breed could do to her for showing such insolence. Silently, she cursed herself for speaking without thinking.

"Have you lost your touch, Brave Woman?" Whisper asked as she stepped inside the hut, noting the nerves. She cast a glance down at the woman's clenched hands. Brave Woman saw the gaze and immediately relaxed her fingers. "You are useless to me if you are full of fear."

Insult filled her. "I am Brave Woman," she answered, her voice haughty. "I conquer fear."

"Good. Then we have business to discuss."

As she settled down to propose her plan, Whisper let her mind wander a bit while she spoke. She took in the plainness of the hut, not surprised by how bare it was. Brave Woman was a spirit of simple tastes, as she had been in life. She had been the pride of her people, a woman who never took a husband because the only man she'd ever loved was killed in battle to save her.

Whisper had heard stories of this woman from Elders at powwows and other gatherings as a child. She wasn't Cherokee, but came from the Lakota. The old storytellers at their annual powwows told great tales of the spirit, their eyes shining brightly as they reminisced her feats as though they had witnessed each battle themselves. She had been born to a skilled and feared war chief, the storytellers said, and was known for her beauty, and her pride. Her brothers had been killed in battle, leaving just Brave Woman to defend her family's honor. In the beginning she had been known by a different name, her given name, but in her quest to avenge her brothers' deaths earned her new title.

"Tell me how you got your name," Whisper said after she finished outlining her plan.

Brave Woman, thrown off track the sudden change in topic, hesitated before answering. She took a moment to consider the half-breed's offer, and what she would want in return. And instantly, she knew the answer, as it had everything to do with how she earned her name.

"My father wanted me to marry," she started, her voiced tinged with bitterness. "Red Horn came with enough gifts to please my father, and they began to plan our union. There was another, Little Eagle, but he was shy, and I did not know of his love until it was too late. But I told my father I would not marry until my brothers' deaths were avenged. My mission was to count coup on the Crows for each of them.

"The Crow were stealing our land, so we organized a war party to chase them away. I rode out with Red Horn and Little Eagle wearing my finest white buckskin dress. Only the best for my brothers," she added when Whisper merely lifted a brow. "My father did not want me to go, but he understood, and saw me off with his war bonnet and horse to show his support. 'Go,' he said, 'and never look back.'"

Her eyes took on a faraway expression as though she was seeing the battle again, reliving the fear, the excitement, the courage. There was a sudden blast of heat in the air that warmed the cold hut. One that, Whisper realized, came from the spirit's own soul as she brought herself back to that day, telling her tale with animation and excitement.

"We came upon the enemy quietly, but there were too many of them. So many Crow covering the earth in a blanket of hate and peril." Then Brave Woman smiled and her eyes focused on Whisper for only a moment. "And we charged them anyway."

"I sent Red Horn to count coup for my eldest brother using his lance and shield. Little Eagle counted coup using my second oldest brother's bow and arrows. A younger warrior took my littlest brother's war club. And I carried my father's war stick, giving my men courage as I sang to them the old war songs.

"Eventually we were driven back, and my men lost their courage. So I finished the battle for them. I drove my horse straight into the enemy, counting coup with every touch and inspiring the Lakota to fight, and fight hard." As she spoke, her hand struck out just inches from Whisper's face. Whisper didn't move, didn't flinch, but instead watched the woman who was enraptured with her story.

Brave Woman's voice changed then, tinged with sadness. "My horse was hit as my people were driven back. We went down, and I had no way to escape the Crow. Red Horn rode past me, leaving me to the enemy. But Little Eagle gave me his horse, and despite my pleas to travel with me, made his last stand on foot. I gathered my people for another attack, and we drove back the Crow, but Little Eagle was lost to the war.

"I mourned him as I would have mourned a husband, and never stopped. He was the one I was meant to marry." She lifted her hand to her hair absently, running her fingers through the ends as though remembering the time when it was cut short, as her people did when in mourning. Her arms held the scars of deep lacerations when her blood was sacrificed to the earth for her fallen love. Then she sighed and dropped her hands into her lap.

"I was once called *Makhta*," she told Whisper. "But now I am known as Brave Woman, the Lakota who counted coup against the Crow." Her dreamy expression settled into the hard face of battle. "And I will fight for you."

Whisper nodded, accepting Brave Woman into her army. "And what do you wish in return?" She knew the answer, but wanted to hear the confirmation.

Brave Woman smiled sadly. "To be with Little Eagle. I was sent to the Land of the Dead after falling in battle against the enemy, who did not honor me with the proper burial of my people. Give us the life together that was stripped away before it began, *Kanegv*, and I will be the first to ride into battle against the Great Spirit."

* * *

Smoke Speaker awoke from a troubled sleep, the blankets wrapped around his legs as evidence of his thrashing and unsettling slumber. He lay in bed staring at the ceiling before rising, contemplating his dreams.

In sleep, he was trapped in darkness, surrounded by cold and fear and sadness. He searched the land for light, lost in a world without warmth, without Mother Sun smiling down on him. Calling out for his daughter, the Elder had stumbled across a barren earth, desperate for life, any kind of life.

But there was nothing. The world had shut down, retreated into itself to preserve what earth it could save until the plague of darkness had passed. He was alone, no living creature left to soothe his aching heart.

That sensation followed him even when he opened his eyes to the soft morning light. Golden rays poured in through the open, stone-framed window, and birds chirped happily just outside.

But still, something was stirring, Smoke Speaker thought as he rose from the soft bed and pulled on a robe. He wanted to spend some time in front of the fire reading the wisps of smoke, hoping for a message from some spirit who knew what might be happening. Surely someone, somewhere, had the answers he sought, and could soothe his troubled mind and let him sleep in peace in the Spirit World.

His heart sank just a bit when he saw Tall Bear sitting at the fire. In his hands was a steaming cup of tea specially brewed from herbs that grew only in the Spirit World. His eyes were sleepy, and the Elder wondered if he too had a restless night's sleep. The thought worried him, as the Spirit World was meant to be a place without such nightmares, and if they were to lead a living being to be a child of the light, then they would need their own souls to be free of such gloom.

Even though he wanted to be alone, Smoke Speaker sat on a cushioned bench adjacent to Tall Bear. "Do your dreams haunt you too, friend?" he asked quietly, tucking his white hair back behind his ear. Suddenly he felt his age.

Tall Bear smiled somewhat sadly. "I suppose so, Elder. I dreamed of my family, as I once knew them. And in my dream, I knew I would never see them again. It was...dark," he pondered, trying to hold on to what bits he could still remember. "I was lost, trying to find them, trying to find Mother Sun. But no matter how fast I ran, she kept retreating into the distance."

"It sounds like our dreams were connected, then." Smoke Speaker sighed and accepted the second cup of tea Tall Bear handed to him. "I fear for what is to come."

"What do you suspect?"

Smoke Speaker tipped his head back and took in the sight of the magnificent morning sun. Mother Sun was rising higher in the sky, smiling down on them. There was nothing in the air that warned him of danger, but he couldn't shake the feeling of dread he'd once felt as a child when he heard the legend of Grandmother Spider.

"There are stories of darkness," he said quietly, warming his hands around the mug as a chill passed through his body. "A time in the beginning where light was just a dream. It was said that Fox knew of a place where light shined down on the people all the time, filling their lives with hope and happiness, but these people were selfish and refused to share. So the men and women living in the blackness sent Opossum to steal the light from them, and hide it in the fur of his tail.

"But they did not know that the light burned, and when he hid it in his tail the fur burned off, and as punishment he was forced to live his days with a bare tail that spoke of this thievery. The people tried again, sending the Great Buzzard to steal the light. Buzzard flew into the center of the sun and set the light atop his head, but burned off his feathers. He too was punished by the Great Spirit."

As if on cue, the Great Spirit himself appeared at the hearth, listening intently to the Elder's story. He had heard it before, had spoken all the stories before and given life to the words that were now called mere legends, but even as the Creator of Stories he knew that when Smoke Speaker repeated one of them, there was reason to listen. He nodded at the Elder and smiled, encouraging him to continue.

Smoke Speaker straightened, his voice taking on an ancient, thoughtful tone as both pride and fear swelled inside him. Pride for becoming a storyteller to the Great Spirit, fear for what that narrative may mean.

"The people were devastated, and worried they had been defeated by the light and were exiled into a life of darkness. Then Grandmother Spider appeared, and said that she had a solution. Before she left, she molded a pot out of clay, then spun a silk web that reached to the far side of the world. She was so small, and her web so crystal clear, that no one saw her coming, and no one saw her steal some of the light and seal it in her clay pot.

"But when she returned, she discovered that the clay pot was hard, and that the light had turned the clay into something the people could use for food and water. The people rejoiced in this discovery, as they now not only had light, but also fire and pottery. And so Grandmother Spider was celebrated as the one who brought light to our people, and they flourished with her gifts."

After a moment of silence, Tall Bear cleared his throat. "This is what you dreamed of, Elder?"

Smoke Speaker nodded and rose to his feet. "I dreamt of darkness, of a world that light had forgotten. My father told me stories of Grandmother Spider, of times when Sun Woman asked her for help, and the light was stolen from the people. An eclipse, some tried to explain it, but it is much more than that."

"What is on your mind, Elder Smoke Speaker?" Creator asked gently, touching the man on the shoulder softly.

"I dreamt of the light stolen from me," the Elder answered, rubbing his hands up and down his thin arms. "I dreamt of the shadows that grew deeper and darker with each passing moment." As he spoke, those shadows began to form. Light at first, then darkening, turning black as the golden sun began to fade. "I dreamt of Mother Sun being wrapped in darkness as the world watched in fear."

The three raised their eyes to the sky, watching as the thin strands of black began to wind around the sun. One after the other, a constant web that spun faster and faster, blocking out the light, trapping in the warmth. Strands so tiny they couldn't be seen until they were stacked upon one another, woven together so intricately that only Grandmother Spider herself could ever remove them without destroying the sun.

"*Kanegv,*" Smoke Speaker whispered, just before the shadows overtook the earth. "What have you done?"

Chapter 25

Whisper was a powerful spirit, a half-breed bestowed with more magic than any creature had ever known, but now she was at her breaking point.

Blue Corn Maiden had done her job well. The snow fell without mercy, and the temperatures continued to drop. The natural heat that radiated off the Fire Tower kept the snow banks at bay around the mountains and across parts of the Barren Plains, melting the ice to slush as it fell, but the rest of her land suffered far worse. By this point, many villagers and forest creatures had moved closer to the Fire Mountains, making camp as close as they dared to keep warm and survive. And though she despised any spirit being so close to her home, Whisper let them stay.

She was starting to feel her energy drain as she kept her body a constant temperature, and kept the Fire Tower warm so her mother and mate didn't suffer along with the others. But now, the eternal winter was starting to fill her with infuriating rage every waking second.

Home after her visit with the warrior spirit, Whisper stalked through the Fire Tower, wrapping a fur-lined cloak around her toned shoulders. Her footsteps were heavy and echoed off the stone stairwell as she quickly ascended them. Hunting Hawk was waiting for her in their quarters, slowly running a stone over the edge of a blade.

"Where were you?" he asked, glancing up from the knife he was sharpening. "How am I supposed to protect you if all you leave behind is a letter telling me you will be gone for a day?"

Whisper shrugged and picked up one of the blades he had recently fashioned. He did nice work, she had to admit, better than her. Her specialty was in arrows, but Hunting Hawk made the best knives she had ever seen. It was no wonder the Raven-Eater had wanted him as his War Chief.

"I secured us an ally," she answered, setting the blade back onto the table. "Brave Woman."

"And what did you promise her?"

Whisper cast him a sidelong glance at the sarcastic tone in his voice. "No one works for free, Hunting Hawk, and I would not ask them to." She took her favorite place at the window and stared out at the white blanket that covered the Land of the Dead. Her breath came out in a frosted huff. "There must be a way to defeat this," she said quietly, looking up at the sky. Sun Woman was already burning night and day, trying to melt the snow and keep her people as warm as possible. By this time, Grand-mother Spider should have taken the light from the Spirit World, so Whisper knew it was only a matter of time before Creator's next attack.

"There may be a way to counter Blue Corn Maiden," Hunting Hawk said from behind. He stopped sharpening long enough to tip his head at the floor. "There were stories about these mountains that my men used to tell. Stories of a creature that lived below the Fire Mountains, a creature that the Raven-Eater had forced into sub-mission and planned to use during his war against the living. I never took much interest in their words since they had no proof, and never found any, but with the rising snow I think it might be to our benefit to search for their source. We never tried very hard as the mountains were off-limits to us, but times have changed."

Whisper frowned, then walked over to Hunting Hawk when he held out a hand. She stifled a grin when he grabbed her by the arm and pulled her onto his lap. Hunting Hawk wrapped his strong arms around her waist. "I will tell you what I know, but I do not work for free."

She huffed, knowing there was a catch. "Name your terms." She listened when he lowered his head and whispered in her ear, then slapped his arm. "No one will ever question your worth as a man, Hunting Hawk," she said, amused. "Fine. I accept your terms. Now tell me what you know."

Hunting Hawk thought back to those days he was forced to work under the Raven-Eater. His men had spent many hours talking quietly amongst themselves, afraid of what wrath the Raven-Eater might bestow upon them. He had never paid much attention to their conspiracies, had chalked them up to the ramblings of cowards, but he did recall one story that had captured his interest.

"There was a story among the Caddo," he told Whisper, resting his chin on her shoulder as he remembered the legend, "about a plentiful forest filled with life. Birds, flowers, gentle creatures of the earth that lived among the rolling hills and mountains. The creatures and people lived peacefully together for many moons, until a dragon cursed the land with fire and brimstone, and for the first time the land was introduced to famine, disease, fear, and pain.

"The people went to the Great Spirit and begged for help, pleaded for his assistance in defeating the dragon. Creator took pity on the people and sent down his wrath upon the dragon, banishing him deep into the mountains. But by then it was too late. The dragon had already scorched the earth, and no trees would grow, no creatures could live, no people could make their villages among the destroyed land. And so they moved, but still the Great Spirit took pity on what was lost. To show that the dragon would not destroy what was once a beautiful land, he created a river of pure, healing water, a place that could be shared by one and all as a river to heal. Creator made the dragon a guardian, made to watch over the river and those who call it home."

Hunting Hawk sighed then and felt Whisper tense. "That place of healing waters was corrupted by the Raven-Eater, hidden away so that no one would know of its powers. Because of its corruption, a new creature found its way there, a beast known as *Ukenta*. It seems only fitting, then, that you would be the one to find it next." He smiled when Whisper turned, her brow furrowed. "Yes, *Kanegv*, your place of sanctuary is a land sanctioned by the Great Spirit."

"And destroyed by the Raven-Eater."

"But restored by your presence. The Fire Mountains were once a land where life thrived. The dragon took that away, the Raven-Eater relished in the destruction and built his home on forsaken grounds, and you have made a new claim on the land."

"And the dragon still lives beneath the Fire Mountains," she finished. "The fires that once scorched this land and drove out the villagers were never extinguished by the Raven-Eater. He simply found a way to control the dragon."

"Or contain it," Hunting Hawk guessed, wondering what kind of contraption the beast was forced into, allowing him to heat the mountains but never leave his lair. "If we could find the dragon, and free him, then he could potentially defeat Blue Corn Maiden."

Whisper grinned her evil half-smile then and lifted herself from his lap. "Then we should go find him. And I am sure he will be hungry, so we should bring him a meal."

And she had the perfect person in mind.

* * *

Whisper shoved the door open to the rooftop, Hunting Hawk right on her heels. She stalked across the roof, slush soaking her boots. "It would seem we have a use for you after—"

Her voice trailed off as shock consumed her. The altar was empty. Where Earth Keeper once sat was now only empty air filled with wafting snowflakes. In disbelief, Whisper stalked to the altar and grabbed at the ropes, inspecting them with clenched fists. It was impossible. There was no way to escape her altar, not with the power she had wrapped around the stone, not with Hunting Hawk's knot-tying skills.

Then she saw that the ropes had been cut, and cut recently. She looked over her shoulder to see that the knife she had taunted the man with was gone. But how? It was too far out of reach for him, and the ropes were too tightly bound.

Earth Keeper had help.

Rage swelled within her, blinding her, deafening her, strengthening her. Her fingers tightened on the rope, and the power within her bled through her pores and seared the sinewy fabrics to ash.

Her eyes were black as night, pupils dilated, when she turned to Hunting Hawk. He froze. He knew that look, knew better than to make a movement. This was the half-breed, the Raven-Eater's daughter. This was not Whisper, but the creature of fury that dwelled deep within her.

"*Kanegv*," he whispered, never taking his eyes off her face, which was slowly darkening in a shadow that cloaked only her. "*Kanegv*, come back to me." But she was beyond the point of salvation, and he could only pray she broke through the barrier that drove her away from the light.

"Where…is…he?" The question came out slowly, in a low, raspy tone that chilled the man to the bone. "*Where?*"

"I do not know," Hunting Hawk answered quickly, shaking his head. "He was there last night. I checked on him myself."

Whisper felt the internal struggle within herself, her two sides fighting to overcome the other. One part could have ripped Hunting Hawk in half; the other was willing to hear his side. "Did you…free him?"

He heard the strain in her voice. "No. On my honor, *Kanegv*, I promise you that I did not free him."

The words filled her, but she had trouble accepting them. She swallowed hard and struggled to get out the next words. "Blue Feather?"

He shook his head again. "She had gone to see *Kamama* about the snow. She was looking to help you battle Blue Corn Maiden," he said quickly when Whisper's head snapped back to look at him. "The people are scared, the land is ill. We need help with this war."

Whisper considered it, and found her anger lessening. Her mother had gone to *Kamama*. That was brave, especially for Blue Feather. Not many ventured to see the spirit, and her mother traveling that far spoke of her love and devotion to Whisper, not Smoke Speaker.

"*Kanegv.*" Daring the touch, Hunting Hawk reached out and stroked a hand down her arm. He felt a streak of heat flash through him, vibrating from her flesh.

It took effort, but she managed to unclench her fists. Ash fell to the rooftop. "Find out where he is, Hunting Hawk." She lifted her face to his. "Find him, and rip out his throat."

* * *

It had been many years since he had seen the Land of the Dead in person, but it was almost every night that Cole Daivya saw it in his nightmares. But as always, he faced the same problem. He couldn't remember where he was.

He'd been just a boy when the Raven-Eater snatched his soul from the living world, and had almost lost that part of himself while living at the Fire Tower. Smoke Speaker's powerful magic had made it easier to forget the harrowing ordeal upon his return, a magic he hadn't expected as it wiped the child's memories clean from the forefront of his mind. So he walked the foreign yet familiar land alone, battled faceless demons, fought his way back home while never knowing that this place had once been his.

It was those dreams that haunted him even while he was awake, what had prompted his father to seek therapy for him as a boy, but never be willing to listen to the tales himself. It was as though his father was just as afraid, though they never spoke of the strange distance between them. And now, Cole was bringing new life into this world and could only plead to the God he wasn't sure he believed in that what lurked in his dreams didn't follow his little girl in life.

Chapter 26

In just a short time, Grandmother Spider's magic had taken its toll on the dead souls, and the land around them. The Spirit World was lit only by the fires people could build among the shadows, cast into a darkness they could not survive. Just as the Land of the Dead would perish in an eternal winter, so too would Creator's people suffer from a lifetime without light.

The Great Spirit was pondering this when Smoke Speaker came to his side, his gnarled old hands grasping the end of a torch. In the firelight, his wrinkled face looked both timeless and troubled.

"Something concerns you, Elder?" Creator asked as he stared out at the Spirit World, taking in the dots of firelight, the strange silence. A hush had fallen over his realm, his people spooked, waiting to see what would happen next. They had great faith in their leader, but with each passing hour that trust waned ever slightly, until eventually there would be nothing left but trepidation and bitterness.

The Elder sighed, setting the torch down in a holder anchored into the wall. He was too worried to fear about speaking frankly. "This is a dangerous game you are playing, Great Spirit. I fear you underestimate my granddaughter. She is capable of great things, many of them dark and unnatural."

Creator waited a few moments before responding, comparing himself to the half-breed and imagining what a war between them would be like, should it come to that. "Do you doubt my abilities, Elder? Do you think I too do not have dark and unnatural capabilities?"

"No, Great Spirit," Smoke Speaker said quickly. "I just..." He hated himself for what he was about to say, and thought less of himself for doing so. "*Kanegv* is deceitful, and at times dishonorable. In life she was honest and fair, but in death, she allows the Raven-Eater to invade her souls when it suits her purpose. And that makes her more dangerous than any of us know. She will not fight this war fairly, Creator, and will not stop until she gets what she wants. There is no truce for her."

"Then what do you suggest?"

He didn't have all the answers, but he did have an idea on how to bring light back to the Spirit World. It pained him to reveal his plans, as he would be going against the woman who had died so that his daughter would be free, but he would do what he must to prevent a war. There was a way to make his granddaughter see her faults, even if it meant betraying her trust to do so.

"Play her game, Great Spirit. Become the master of deceit, and lure her in. It is the only way to bring her down."

* * *

Once again, she made the journey without Hunting Hawk, leaving him to track down Earth Keeper and bring his head back to the Fire Tower. Her mate's skills were needed above the earth, where he could watch over the land in her stead and rule should something happen to her. She trusted no other with her kingdom, which meant he could not make this trek with her.

Instead, Whisper traveled with Dark Water, calling on his unique magics and abilities to be by her side as she traveled to a part of her land she had never even known existed. She had intended on taking this day to complete her agreement with the sky spirit, and find the lost daughter that would be her final bargaining chip. But before she journeyed to the place where Sun Woman's daughter danced her eternal dance, she had her people to think about.

The duo made their way to Whisper's place of sanctuary quickly, riding atop Eagle as he soared through the bits of falling snow. Rather than leaping off his back, Whisper waited until he had landed safely at the base of the river, then turned to Dark Water.

"I cannot guarantee what we will find in here. I have always traveled downriver, not up," she warned, gesturing to the narrow cavern just down shore where the crystal-clear water flowed out smoothly. "And I cannot guarantee your safety against the beasts that may lurk in the waters."

Dark Water nodded, gripping his spear firmly. He would protect himself, and his ruler, with everything that he was. He admired her bravery in heading into the unknown, and was willing to fight for such courage. "I am ready."

Together, they stepped into the water, fighting the current, searching their sides for potential ripples indicating an enemy presence, making their way into the narrow crevice. Cold water flowed over them as it tumbled from the rocks, and they took their time climbing up the slippery slope. Dark Water went first, scoping the area for potential danger, then helping Whisper up when her foot slipped on one of the rocks.

Once inside, their path was lit only by the torch Whisper held out in front of them, casting an orange glow around the wet stone walls. The further they walked, the shallower the river became, and soon they were sloshing through ankle-deep water, each step echoing off the walls. It was strangely loud in the cavern, the sounds of running water mixed with a kind of rushing noise neither could identify. It came from somewhere deep within the stone, calling to them.

Turning a sharp corner, Whisper came to a sudden stop when she nearly ran into a wall. Puzzled, she reached out and touched the stone, feeling cold water cascade down her hand. She looked up, seeing the beginning of the waterfall far above her head. They had reached a dead end.

Without a word, Dark Water lowered himself with his knee bent, hands waiting to take her foot. Whisper set her foot down and used his force to leverage herself against the wall. After taking a quick look around, she reached down and helped Dark Water find his footing and hoist himself up. Then together, they slowly walked through the wet, slick tunnel glowing with orange light. They no longer needed the torch, and so Whisper doused it and tucked the handle into her pack.

She'd thought they were close, but soon found herself ambling down corridor after winding corridor, always following the light, staying out of the shadowed halls where she could sense the company of beasts waiting for blood. Dark Water was always at her heels, watching her back, offering his own guidance when she seemed to hesitate. They worked together as though having done so all their life, hoisting one another onto high shelves with narrow channels when the pathway ended and shoving themselves back when the stone dropped out from under their feet unexpectedly.

As they hiked, Dark Water thought he saw a different side of the half-breed, one that he liked. Here, surrounded by stone walls and orange light, she wasn't the vicious, merciless half-breed that everyone feared. She was curious, inquisitive, fascinated by the maze and muttering to herself about making maps while reaching out to touch the designs carved into rock. He found himself watching her with interest, wondering what would catch her eye next, how she would react to it, and what he would learn about her and her realm the few times she spoke about the Land of the Dead.

"Do you hear that?"

Her question snapped him back to attention. Lifting his spear, Dark Water came to her side and listened carefully. "It sounds like...breathing?"

Whisper nodded. "Something is there." She pointed far down the long, straight passageway that angled downward sharply. They were already far beneath the earth, the weight of the world crushing down on them, and it appeared they had farther to go still.

Adjusting the pack on her shoulders, Whisper started down the path. It was a long walk, and as they neared the end, they could see a bright light flashing from a narrow opening. At that opening they stopped, hesitated. The two looked at one another, wondering who would dare to go first, imaging what they would find on the other side of the stone walls. Then Whisper shook her head at her own cowardice and stepped through.

There, in the center of the cavern with ceilings higher than Whisper could see, was a creature that could have stopped her heart were she of the living.

Beastly in its grand size, majestic in its beauty, the dragon lay across a marbled floor. Its arched back reached up toward the high ceiling, spiked with dark brown plates that protected against enemies. Glittering scales coated the creature's body, glorious mixes of greens and golds and reds that flickered in firelight spread in a ring around the cavern. The dragon was trim but muscular, each of its four limbs wrapped in thick layers of bulky muscle that rippled with every movement. Talons as long as Whisper's body tipped the back legs, while the front legs were smaller, more hand-like in appearance.

The creature's neck was long and elegant, leading to a head that wouldn't even have fit inside the doors of the Fire Tower. Its snout was narrow, and tips of razor-sharp teeth peeked out from strong jaws. This was a beast meant for war, for destruction, and yet, for simply the beauty of being.

Just in front of the dragon was a hearth, with a strong fire burning in the center. That fire was wrapped all around them, offering a much-welcomed warmth from the bitter cold. There was no wood though, which told Whisper that this was a powerful being, a spirit she must respect and fear all the same.

For a moment Whisper wondered why the creature was merely staring at them with those sparkling ebony eyes, looking somewhat sad and wary, then her gaze traveled to the dragon's tail, where four thick metal spikes were driven through the flesh, anchoring him to the cavern floor. She looked closer, and saw what she had missed in her initial wonder.

The dragon was clamped at every limb, each shackle held together by a thick rod. From those shackles trailed heavy chains secured to the stone. They were binding chains meant to prevent escape by even the largest of fiends, and this dragon was no exception. But Whisper suspected that were it not for the spikes through the tail, as well as those through each leg, that this creature would have escaped long ago before becoming weak and filled with hopelessness.

"The Raven-Eater," she whispered, suppressing a shudder. She turned to Dark Water. "We must free him." He didn't argue, though he looked hesitant. He could see that the creature was weak after so many years of imprisonment, forgotten about in a lonely existence. They had no immediate threat to worry about, though danger was always in the back of his mind.

Slowly, Whisper approached the dragon, reaching out with a hesitant hand to touch the glistening scales. She paused before making contact when the creature began to tremble, sending a gentle message out on the air that she knew was heard by the subtle change in breathing. Gathering her courage, she placed her hand down. He flinched instinctively, causing Whisper to do the same, but hardly moved. Instead, the beast sighed, a huff of smoke escaping his lips.

"*Adagatiya*," she said quietly. "Guardian of the sacred waters. We are here to help. And we hope that you will assist us, as we assist you. We are not servants of the Raven-Eater. We wish to free you from your chains."

She took the shifting of his eyes to the hearth as an approval of her actions. Nodding to Dark Water, they moved to his tail and eyed the metal spikes. Power radiated from the steel, too strong for *Adagatiya* to break the hold on his own. It was a deep magic that even Whisper didn't quite understand. But, she didn't need to understand it. She had the power to break it.

Gripping one of the spikes, she let her body feel the magic that swelled within her, felt her blood singing with rage and a bit of fear for what she was doing. She could be releasing a blight on her people, a devastation to the land, but it was worth the risk. This battle was worth it. A rumble echoed through the cave, starting within her body and thrusting outward, small rocks tumbling from the walls. The roar that burst from her reverberated all around them, slamming against the three spirits and sending their thoughts into a chaotic frenzy before settling down.

She had never felt a power quite like that, channeled by thoughts of bloodlust and vengeance, and she enjoyed it. She craved more just as the first spike disintegrated in her hands. The other three, loosened by whatever strange power had erupted from her, slid easily out of the ground as the two pulled them free. The Raven-Eater's lingering power weakened, they made quick work of the remaining spikes and unclamped the shackles.

His tail and limbs free, the dragon turned slightly, facing his two visitors with an interested expression. He was perfectly balanced on four wide, taloned feet, thick muscle rippling with every breath as he stretched out his magnificent wings. Blood oozed from his wounds. She felt Dark Water instinctively shift into a fighting stance, but Whisper stood her ground.

"I apologize for not freeing you sooner, *Adagatiya*," she said quietly. "I did not know you were here. It seems there is still a lot to learn about my land."

The majestic creature lowered its head in a nod, moving until he was face-to-face with Whisper. She set her jaw firmly, refusing to show any amount of fear when the jagged teeth inched closer to her throat. Then she heard a voice in her head, his eyes staring deep into her very self as though judging her worth. He could have destroyed them both with a single fiery breath, but out of respect he would ask this one question.

"*What do you ask in return for my freedom?*"

Whisper smiled then, a look Hunting Hawk would have feared. "How far do your fires reach?"

"*For what purpose?*"

"Does it matter?"

He was silent for a moment, assessing the situation. Then he relented. "*To the ends of the earth and back, if I so choose.*"

"Good." Whisper nodded, casting a glance back at Dark Water, who was staring at her with a confused frown. He couldn't hear the dragon's words, and to him it appeared as though she was talking to herself.

"My people are suffering from Blue Corn Woman's curse," Whisper told him, though she suspected he already knew. "I want you to warm the land, melt the snow. Free the Land of the Dead from this plague. Whether you send your fires through the bowels of the earth or fly above the land, I do not care. Save my people from this eternal winter. All I ask is that you do not burn the villages, the forests, or the people. Only the snow."

He showed his consent with another single nod. "*Anything else, my queen?*"

"Yes. You are an old creature, *Adagatiya*. You have seen much of what this land and the Spirit World have to offer. And I suspect you know where to find the one woman I need most." She narrowed her eyes then, leaning in close to the scaled beast. "Take me to Sun Woman's daughter."

"Just you?"

Dark Water's voice startled her out of her thoughts. Whisper spun around and faced the man, who was glaring at her suspiciously. She knew he was afraid she was abandoning him.

"Just me," she agreed, taking a step closer to him. "You, Dark Water, are needed elsewhere."

He eyed the leader of the Land of the Dead. "To do what?"

Whisper lifted a hand, fingered the golden feather in her hair while in thought. "It is time we send our own message to Creator. Take your men back to the place of crossing and enter the Spirit World. Find *Oway*, and the Circle."

"And then?"

Whisper's black eyes deepened, sending the cave into shadows that the dragon shied away from. "Find the Circle, and destroy them. But leave Smoke Speaker to me."

Chapter 27

Dark Water stood with his men at the place of crossing, gripping a recently sharp-ened spear that glinted in the moonlight. Around him, his five brothers stood anxiously, their faces painted black, their long sleek hair tied back with eagle feathers. They were dressed for battle, their usual furs tucked away in their huts and replaced with thick leather hides that wrapped around their chests and backs, their legs pro-tected by triple-stitched pants tucked into boots that reached up to their knees.

Burning Wind, Star Seer, and Lifter held long, double-edged knives, their scarred hands gripping the handles tightly. The remaining brothers, Dream Maker and Earth Dancer, chose spears and arrows, quivers strapped to their backs along with newly fashioned bows.

Their leader had already explained the mission, and it was simple. In response to Blue Corn Maiden's invasion into the Land of the Dead and Smoke Speaker's betrayal, Whisper wanted the Circle destroyed. And that was what they would do. The request came as a shock to the Little Men, and it wasn't one they were pleased to carry out as they did not consider themselves to be particularly violent beings, but they had made a deal with the half-breed. This was what had to happen in order to get their lost brother back, and so they would take up arms against the Great Spirit, committing an act that would never be forgiven.

Wordlessly, united by their journey and driven by the promise made to them, the men stepped into the crossover.

In the next step, they were in the clearing Dark Water had once stood in with Whisper. It was empty, the benches vacant and the one stone table bare of any signs of life. Leaves blew across their feet in a light breeze, the moon casting a faint white glow around the room.

The men didn't need light for their job. They had lived in the Forgotten Lands for longer than their memories could recall, and were accustomed to the night. It took only seconds for their eyes to adjust, and Dark Water glanced at his men in silent com-munication, telling them where to go. They had drawn out a map in the dirt before, the same map Earth Keeper had provided in his desperate and pathetic attempts to fool the half-breed, and they all knew where to go.

Silently, they broke free of their group, only the sound of their light footsteps resonating in the night. Their faces were void of expression, but their eyes were black pits mixed with malevolence and sadness that sought out their targets with single-minded missions. They knew what they wanted, what would come of their service, and would not stop until the Circle was destroyed.

As they stalked through *Oway*, they left in their wake black earth that curdled and oozed across the ground, trailing behind them in an infested smear of darkness. It misted around them, clouding the men in their own blanket of security as they passed through the hallways silently, undetected. Those black stains slowly festered and spread, contaminating the palace while the intruders sought out their marks.

Star Seer found Tall Bear first, sleeping soundly in a large bed made of compressed feathers. Without a word, an eerie deadness spread across his face, he lifted the spear and sent it into the man's throat. In the next room over, Earth Dancer came upon Striker and Dark Moon of the Circle. Their beds were at opposite ends of the room, but he knocked two arrows in the bow anyway, aiming precisely and releasing. The arrows twisted to the sides and found their marks directly in the center of each man's heart before they could even realize they were in any danger.

One by one, the Little Men silently murdered the Circle members while they slept, never needing to spend more than mere seconds in each room. They barely noticed the blood that splattered across their chests and faces, but the slightest bit of remorse showed in the tightness of their mouths. It was only when they reached the room that housed Smoke Speaker that they stopped, looking to Dark Water for guidance.

Dark Water knew this man belonged to Whisper, but he couldn't resist a look. Some part of him longed to see the last member of the Circle left standing, see that look in his eyes when he realized that his betrayal was all for nothing.

He threw the door open, expecting to see the Elder sleeping soundly in his bed of righteousness. What he saw instead had him stepping back, quickly closing the door and clutching his blade even tighter.

"It is time we return to the Land of the Dead," he told his men, keeping his voice even. Quickly they headed back to the place of crossing and passed over, where Dark Water parted with the others to find Whisper.

What happened next was up to her.

* * *

She arrived in a burst of flames, tumbling out of the fiery sphere smoking and snarling. When *Adagatiya* said he would send her to Sun Woman's daughter the fast way, he had failed to mention that way meant blowing a wall of fire that wrapped around her body and sent it cascading to the depths of a world Whisper had never known existed.

Her body burned and smoldered, her hair smoked, and her flesh was coated in ash, but the blood of the half-breed protected her from harm. For a few brief moments she felt suspended in the air, surrounded by an ocean of fire, then the bottom dropped out from under her and she was released from the hold with a hard jerk that left her head spinning. It was a journey Dark Water or Hunting Hawk couldn't have survived, and was meant only for her.

Rising to her feet, Whisper brushed at the soot covering her skin and clothes, relenting to the fact that it wasn't coming off and instead taking a few moments to get her bearings. Wherever the dragon had sent her, it was not a world she had seen before, and doubted the Great Spirit himself would venture here.

All around her, the earth rose up in spiraling mounds of packed dirt, reaching up toward the black sky that hung low as it threatened to suffocate the land with thick, murky clouds and foul-smelling drops of rancid rain. The ground was littered with deep cracks and crevices, narrow pathways carved of stone leading to a forest just in front of where she stood. The air was stale and thick with the scent of death, and the only light came from a faint orange glow flickering through the trees.

Stepping carefully, Whisper made her way toward that light, thankful that the farther she walked, the less the sky dropped down on her. As she neared she heard the sound of steady drumbeats. Out of precaution she unsheathed her favorite blade and held it in her left hand, her right hand brushing back thorned branches as she headed deeper into the woods. The thorns cut into her palm, but she hardly noticed the pain. Her blood dripped down and mixed with the dirt, trailing behind her in small, thick drops that rippled with each drumbeat.

Finally the woods opened up to a clearing, and in that clearing was her target. For a moment Whisper merely stood at the edge of the forest and stared, taking in the scene in awe.

In the center of the clearing burned an inferno as wide as at least two grown men, burning logs stacked against one another in a triangle, bright orange flames grasping for the black clouds in a starless sky. The hearth was surrounded by rough stones that formed a perfect circle, white sand spread before them that had been trampled by thousands of feet. And around that fire, people danced.

They spun in dizzying circles, sometimes clasping hands, sometimes dancing on their own, spinning around the fire in elaborate moves that celebrated their cultures and told the stories of their people. Whisper could tell from their various markings and apparel that they came from many tribes, and yet were all mysteriously here at this one gathering. Some wore long headdresses lined with frayed feathers that reached down to their ankles, others wrapped their throats in twine that held together the teeth from a fresh kill. Others still dressed in plain tunics sashed at the waist, while a handful of men were bare-chested with only a leather belt and hide to cover them. One wore an elaborate ceremonial gown of white leather, cut in a V at the throat and laced together with thick strands of hide dyed to match the ornately stitched pattern wrapped around narrow shoulders.

Curious, and not wanting to waste time, Whisper crept forth from the edge of the forest and made her way down to the sand. No one paid her attention, and not a single soul even realized her presence as she entered into the dance, her walk steadfast and determined. All around her spirits whirled and twirled, feet stomping to the beat of drums she could not see, smoke rising up toward the black sky in vibrations of air that wrapped around the trees.

And then she saw her, Sun Woman's daughter. The woman was young, barely matured into her adult body, and had her mother's beautiful and nearly overpowering aura. Sleek black hair was tucked back in a loose braid, decorated with blazing white beads and blue feathers, symbols of her heritage—blue for the north, where her people lived, white for the south, and all the earth that the sun touched below. She danced with her eyes closed, her face set in an expression of both relaxation and concentration. She knew this dance, performed it well, and was familiar with the moves. But there was something behind that tranquility that suggested discontent and wariness, as though she was merely performing the dance and not truly living it.

Eyes on her prey, Whisper slithered through the crowd, her gaze accented by the glowing orange blaze just to her right. She reached out to grasp the woman's arm, then stumbled when her hand passed right through.

Dumbfounded, Whisper stood frozen to her spot in the sand, staring as the dance continued around her, the spirits passing through her without a moment's hesitation or care. They didn't even know she was there, Whisper realized, couldn't see her, hear her, sense her.

"What is going on?" she asked herself quietly, stepping out of the circle and watching from the outside as they stomped and danced rhythmically, without break.

She sunk down to the sand, drawing her legs up to her chest and resting her arms on her knees as she watched them thoughtfully. "Where am I?"

"In the land where souls gather," a voice said from her side. Whisper looked over her shoulder but saw no one. Her brow furrowed and wariness filled her frown. Then her gaze fell to the branch at her side, where a small blue butterfly was perched. She scowled at the thought of being watched and followed, and suddenly the large voice reverberated from the tiny creature. "I have been waiting for you, my child."

"*Kamama*? What are you doing here?" Her voice couldn't contain her surprise. She had never seen her guide at such a small size, let alone outside of his cave in the Land of the Dead. Here, he seemed innocent, natural, a creature not of the other, but of the everyday.

"You have come seeking Sun Woman's daughter," he answered. "I have come to tell you how."

"But…why? I thought you were neutral. Why would you help me?"

The butterfly fluttered then, flying up and perching on her knee. "Have you forgotten who I am, *Kanegv*?"

"The keeper of secret desires," she whispered. "The creature that transcends worlds and restores the balance of nature. The only being able to travel to the Creator and make wishes come true." No, she hadn't forgotten. "And do you know my secret desire, *Kamama*?"

"Do you?"

She didn't answer, but instead turned her head and stared at her strange surroundings. "What is this place?"

"The land where memories gather."

"The land…is this the place of second death? Where souls go when they die in a spirit realm?" She felt a chill running up her back, but fought it.

"No," *Kamama* answered in a hollow, resounding tone, turning until he was watching the fire dance. "This is a world not many ever get to see. It is a sacred place, a land made not of souls, but of memories."

Whisper's brow furrowed as she tried to make sense of his words. "A land of memories," she repeated, curious. "The memories of our people?"

"Of all people. These memories are what keep us alive, *Kanegv*. They are what let us remember who we are, and where we came from. They are what let us have a future where our people are not forgotten. All the cultures of the world have this place, created from their own ways and their own beliefs. Without these recollections of truth, we would be lost in an empty void where identity is but a dream."

A world of recollections, a place where souls gathered. A distant realm unique to each culture of the world. The concept was nearly too great for Whisper to grasp in its entirety. But suddenly she understood, in some part. "And because they are memories, they cannot be reached. They are untouchable."

"Yes."

"Then...where does this land exist?"

"Somewhere between realms, my child. It exists because we believe. It thrives inside us, around us, and feeds on our memories. Without us, it would cease to be."

Whisper frowned, watching the dancers before her. "So then how are we here?"

"We are here because we believe in our people, and because the memories of our ancestors have been passed on to us, whether we remember them or not."

"So I am here because I have the memories of my people. But I do not have the memories of Sun Woman's daughter, *Kamama*. How do I reach her?"

Kamama opened his wings then and took flight, hovering just before her face. "You must find the one whose memories drive her."

"And who is that?"

"The seventh brother. You can only reach Sun Woman's daughter when the lost brother of the Little Men has returned to the Land of the Dead."

* * *

She returned to the Fire Tower instantly, and wasted no time in preparations. No one, not Dark Water, her mother, or even Hunting Hawk, would know of this journey.

Using the gift of her bloodline, she cast a strong lock around the door and then performed a cleansing ritual, lighting a bowl of sage and taking no time to savor the sweet scent. She made her offerings to the sacred directions, then purified her souls with the smoke before laying in the center of her medicine wheel, feet poised on the southernmost point to keep her grounded in the Land of the Dead while her spirit traveled.

And then, she left her world for that of the living.

Chapter 28

Cole Daivya spent the day in a fog. His sleep had been tormented with images of a shadowed woman with haunting black eyes, watching somewhat amusedly as he struggled to free himself of her stare. In his dream, he had been running through the forest, sticky black tar clinging to his skin, a horde of faceless zombies at his back. There was a foulness to the air, a sense of impending doom. It was the same nightmare he'd had many times as a child, but this time it was different.

This time, there was the woman.

Thinking back on it, he couldn't quite picture her face. It was like looking through water at a blurred image of some strange creature staring down at him sadly, if not impatiently. He didn't know who she was, but he did know she wasn't there to help him. She was there for something far more sinister.

Then he had reached a lake, the shores lapping against his bare feet and ankles. His clothes were torn to shreds, and his flesh was covered in fresh bloody scratches. And there, on the other side of the lake, was the woman. Watching him, judging him, drawing him in even as he fought to back away.

"*The chosen one returns,*" she had sneered, her voice carrying across the water. "*You have a new calling now.*"

"Who are you?" he asked in return, shivering in the moonlight. "How do you know me?"

"*You are the one who escaped. You are the one who must return. Until we meet again, chosen son of the Raven-Eater.*"

He had called after her, but she turned and disappeared into the forest. Moments later he awoke to find himself covered in sweat, his beloved fiancée asking if he was alright. Later, after struggling through work and unable to concentrate, he had gone to his father, seeking advice.

He would never forget that look of fear in his father's eyes when he spoke of his dream—the forest, the lake, the woman. And he would never forget the urgency in his voice when Ian Daivya ordered his son to never again speak to, or speak of, the stranger by the lake. Cole had questioned his father, but the man closed up, retreating into his office and refusing further company.

And so now here he was, on his way home after an impromptu trip to the grocery store to buy ice cream for his love, and their unborn child. Their little girl was getting bigger by the day, his one source of comfort from his dreams. Lost in thought, smiling at visions of his daughter as a bouncy child, Cole stepped to the edge of the curb and waited for the light to change.

Then she appeared, an apparition in the park just beyond the road. She wasn't whole, just a vision in the wind, and he wasn't even sure he saw her. But he wanted to. He wanted to see her, know her, speak to her. He had to know who she was, and why his father was so afraid of the woman who haunted his son's dreams. All thoughts of care and caution left his mind, and, keeping his eyes on the woman who glared back at him with a knowing smirk, stepped off the curb.

When the truck horn blared, he never considered the fact that he might die. Some part of him knew the vehicle was coming, unstoppable, directly in his path, but he didn't care. Instead, he only thought that he had seen that woman once before, during a dream where he perished beneath raging river rapids.

* * *

When Whisper returned home, the men were waiting for her.

She saw them from a distance, saw their stiff stances, their crossed arms, and even the tension set in their jaws. Something was wrong, and she doubted it was because of Cole Daivya. Not enough time had passed for them to know of his death just yet. So as she rode atop Eagle's back, letting the wind blow back her hair and the stench of the living world along with it, she pondered over what could possibly have Hunting Hawk and Dark Water so worried.

Eagle swooped down low, gliding just above the rooftop of the Fire Tower. Whisper leapt off his back, landing gracefully and effortlessly at Hunting Hawk's feet. She kept her face free of expression, but the glint in her eyes told him that she had been up to no good.

"Where have you been?" His tone was accusing, and instantly had Whisper's back up. Her half-lighthearted gaze turned hard and cold as it shifted to him. "Something has happened."

"What?"

He knew that voice, a low, raspy sound mixed with a power he would never fully understand. It vibrated around them, filling their bodies and grabbing hold of their minds. She saw them both as a threat, but one she couldn't yet kill. *"Kanegv,"* he said in that strict tone she had come to know as one guiding her back to the Red Road. Her eyes lost the faraway gaze, and so he stepped forward and gestured to Dark Water. "We have news."

Slightly worried at having seen even the briefest of insights into the half-breed's fury, Dark Water cleared his throat. "The attack on *Oway* was successful. My men and I did as you ordered, and the Circle has been destroyed."

"And Smoke Speaker?"

Dark Water hesitated, prompting Whisper to take a step forward. Part of him longed to comfort her, but the other half of him knew better than to provoke the untamable. "He lives," he said quickly. "We left him for you…but it appears the Great Spirit has other plans for him as well."

He told her then what he had already told Hunting Hawk. With each word, Whisper's expression darkened and her eyes narrowed, and when he was finished, she had become the half-breed in its purest form. Not even Hunting Hawk could bring her back from that place.

Nor would he even try.

She didn't need to think about what to do next. "Dark Water, you will find what you seek at the Bridge of the Dead. You have fulfilled your end of our deal, and so I will fulfill mine."

Dark Water knew a dismissal when he heard one, and so he took his leave, if not regretfully. He was eager to see what he would find at the Bridge of the Dead, although he was curious to know what Whisper had planned now that their agreement had come to an end. And so he turned quickly, finding his own way out of the Fire Tower.

When he was gone, Whisper turned back to Hunting Hawk. Those haunting eyes and equally haunting voice wrapped around him like a death song, and he didn't have a choice but to follow her orders.

"Tonight, we visit Creator," she told him, gripping the bone handle of her favorite blade. "We shall see what game he is playing."

* * *

From her all-seeing view in the Sky Vault, Sun Woman watched the lost soul enter the land of Waiting. She had once watched the boy, now a man, on his first journey to the Land of the Dead, led by the Raven-Eater's guards beyond the Western Sun.

She later witnessed his daring escape, gripped at his father's shoulder as the Army of the Dead chased at their heels.

It was an event that no spirit realm had ever seen before, and was yet to see again. The destruction of an evil tyrant, the rebirth of a new leader, the shifting of balances in the living and dead worlds when two spirits crossed back over.

It was that shifted balance Sun Woman was hoping to use to her own advantage. The half-breed had marched into the Land of the Dead with her head held high, revenge driving her forward, arrogance blinding her. She had thought that in sending the boy, a spirit stolen before his time, back to the living realm that she had restored the balance of nature, but Whisper didn't know that there was still the slightest of imbalances that left both worlds vulnerable.

Sun Woman couldn't repair the imbalance, but she could use it. And the newest arrival into the spirit realm would help her do just that. It wouldn't be easy, as she was not the only one determined to bring him home. But it was more than that.

This was not just one spirit in one body. This was the arrival of a host, and only time would tell which spiritual life-force was strongest.

Once Sun Woman knew who she was dealing with, she would stake her claim in the land above the earth, and rule the realm as the sole spirit of the Sky Vault.

Chapter 29

They made quick work of their journey, calling on Eagle to get them to the place of crossing and passing through without a moment's hesitation. Whisper led the way, equipped with her handcrafted bow strapped across her back and newly sharpened blade in her left hand. She had her sights set on *Oway*, and dropped into the clearing gracefully, Hunting Hawk just a step behind.

Once through the crossover, immersed in a world of black lit only by flickering firelight and a pale white glow settled around the edges of the ground, she noted the black stains that fanned out in an even pattern—the mark of the Little Men as they broke apart to find the Circle members and fulfill their oath to the leader of the Land of the Dead. There was a heavy, suffocating feel to the air, one of despair and sorrow, a sense of grieving that was struggling not to become hate, but instead forgiveness. And it wasn't a forgiveness that would come easily. Whisper knew it would require action on her part that she wasn't willing to do. Not yet, and not without a price. She wondered why Creator hadn't just restored the light using his own power, a temporary magic until Grandmother Spider returned the sun, and decided that this was a time of mourning where the Great Spirit would not allow any form of light out of respect for the lost Circle.

She could have felt guilty, regretful, touched, but instead, she pushed the sensations of grief and tears and confusion aside and followed the one path she knew would take her to see the last remaining Elder. How she knew where he was being held she couldn't say, but something drew her to that room, blocked off by a heavy wooden door.

She let Hunting Hawk kick it down, and her eyes took a moment to adjust to the complete darkness. She could tell by the change in the air that they had stepped into a large space, the walls cold and made of stone, the floor packed with hard dirt. The ceiling was high, and she couldn't sense just how far above her head it stretched. There were no lights, but she saw the outline of a torch on the wall just by the door, and directed her companion to set it ablaze.

The sudden harsh orange light that flared up blinded them both for a few seconds. The fire caught on a narrow trench in the wall and circled the room in a square, the flames flickering in their specially crafted holders. Someone had wanted this room lit this way, Whisper thought, and when she saw the figure at the back wall, she knew why.

The chains rattled slightly when she took a step forward, her eyes on the man who had been the only person she ever looked up to and admired. The man once so strong and steadfast, now so thin and frail and chained to a stone wall by the wrists, ankles, and waist. Around his stomach was a thick metal band that matched those on his wrists, from which hung broad links strapped into the wall. Smoke Speaker dangled limply, barely enough room for him to sit against the stone to give his legs some amount of relief. Even from the distance, she could see the scabs on his skin from the biting chains, the bones protruding from his chafed and pale flesh, the hollowness of his eyes from nights without rest.

She crossed the room in a few quick strides, dropping to her knees and lifting a hand to his face. "What has he done to you?" she whispered, gently turning his head so that he was looking into his eyes. "What has happened?"

The Elder looked up slowly, taking in the sight of his granddaughter, surprised by the concern written across her face. "They came in the night," he croaked through his dry throat. "The Elders were not prepared…They left me alive."

"I know that," Whisper answered softly. "I meant what happened to you. Why are you in chains?"

Smoke Speaker wheezed a bit. "The crossover…you and Dark Water. The Great Spirit…he thought I was working with you. That I told you how to reach us."

Whisper was silent for a moment before replying, feeling rage building in her chest. "He does not kill traitors?" she asked, both curious and angry. "What is his purpose in leaving you here?"

"To end this," a voice said from behind.

Whisper spun around to see Hunting Hawk already posed with his bow and arrow pointing at the man known as the Great Spirit. He didn't seem concerned about the arrow, and was staring straight at Whisper with no care to the War Chief. She noted that he was one of the few who actually ever dared to do so, and she had a small amount of respect for him for that, but for that alone.

"To end what?" she addressed his response, closing the gap between them.

Creator looked down at her, his eyes both firm and gentle. "Your men came and tainted this world with their evil, and murdered my Circle members in their sleep. This is not the Land of the Dead, half-breed. This is the Spirit World, a place of peace and comfort. You and your kind are not welcome here. We cannot undo the damage you

144

have already done," he gestured to the black marks around them oozing into the earth, "but we can ensure it never enters this world again."

She considered his words, knowing he was right. She didn't belong in the Spirit World, not as a visitor, not as a resident. She was an outsider, and respected the Spirit World enough to recognize when she needed to leave. Her goal was not to taint the realm and take away what made it magnificent, as not even she would dare to disrupt that balance between the spirit worlds. They needed one another, survived as polar opposites.

"What do you want, Creator?"

"As I said, to end this." He looked over her shoulder at Smoke Speaker, who was sagging against the stone, then back at the half-breed. "I know you and your ways, half-breed. I am not an old fool. You would not leave the Elder Smoke Speaker alive if you still considered him a traitor. I know you will not leave my land or call off your men until you get what you want. And I am prepared to give it to you."

Whisper glanced over her own shoulder then, frowning when the Elder winced as a sudden movement had the chains clanging against his frail back. Sadness crossed her expression, her gaze long and almost heartrending for the Great Spirit to witness. It wasn't right, what they had done to her grandfather, chaining him to the wall like a prisoner when he had been called to this place by Creator himself. It was unfair, and Whisper couldn't stand for such injustice.

Finally, she nodded at the Creator and gestured to Hunting Hawk to lower the bow. "You give me what I want, Creator, and you will never see me again."

Relief washed over the Great Spirit's face. He made a signal, and three men entered the room, rushing past Whisper, careful not to touch her, to unchain the Elder. They supported him out of the room and she followed, crossing her arms when they sat him down at the edge of the crossover barrier. They all stood in place for a moment until Creator turned to her expectantly, and her frown only deepened, one eyebrow lifting.

"What?"

Creator nodded to the Elder. "I have given you what you want. Now it is time for you to leave."

Whisper shifted, one hand on the blade handle at her waist and the other at her chin, one finger tapping her lips. She turned her back slightly on her grandfather to face the Great Spirit.

"When I arrived, Smoke Speaker told me my men came in the night, and that you had punished him for working with me." Her voice was quiet, accusing, and Creator knew better than to interrupt. "If I no longer considered him a traitor, then would my men have not simply unchained him and brought him back to the Land of the Dead? Why would I leave him here?" Now she saw the fear creep into his eyes and heard Smoke Speaker's breath quicken behind her. "I also am not a fool, Creator. I know when I am being lied to, and this was not a well thought-out lie. I would have expected better from you."

"You seem to have many unfounded expectations of others, half-breed." He wasn't going to play these games with her any longer. She was right, and he hadn't expected her to tie everything together. The Great Spirit had been hoping she would think the Elder was taken captive before the attack because of his suspicions, not because of any tricks he had up his sleeve.

Whisper knew she had gotten the better of him, and almost laughed. "I have to ask, Creator. How did you know I would come? Or that anyone would come, and that chaining Smoke Speaker would even be worth the effort?"

"We knew you would come back for the Elder, and that it was only a matter of time," he answered carefully, annoyed. "It was a gamble we were willing to take. Someone of your creation could never resist the temptation to cross over and take what is not rightfully yours. What we did not suspect was that you would be so malicious as to kill the innocent."

"I see." Whisper didn't bother to feel offended, as she had already won the exchange. "And what do you hope to accomplish now?"

Although he had been expecting some kind of battle after the arrival of Grandmother Spider, the Little Men's invasion had come as a surprise to the Great Spirit. The loss of the Circle troubled and saddened him greatly, and the only hope he'd taken from the deaths was that Smoke Speaker's false imprisonment had been set up by then, so the intruders could take the message back to their leader. He wanted to lure Whisper here and put an end to the impending war, and had resorted to her own kind of antics to get what he wanted.

But, deceit or not, they had made a deal. "This is not a matter for discussion. We had an arrangement. I give you what you want, and you leave the Spirit World behind, forever."

"Yes," she agreed, still amused at having caught Creator in his lies, and in his discomfort. "But I never said I wanted the Elder."

She nearly smiled at the expression that crossed the Great Spirit's face. The men at his side shared the same look of shock, and even Hunting Hawk seemed confused. As well he should be, since she hadn't told him of her plans.

"Then what do you want?"

"I want the child."

Creator held up a hand, mouth tightening into a thin line. "That was not the agreement."

"The agreement was that I would be given what I wanted."

"The agreement was for the Elder Smoke Speaker."

Whisper shook her head, never losing the satisfied smirk. "Then you should have specified that, Creator. You set the terms. Our contract is that I receive what I want, and I leave the Spirit World for good. I want the child."

The air thickened then with a palpable darkness, testament to his power. "You cannot have her."

She was ready for this, had been hoping for it. "Because of your plans for her, Creator? Do you think I do not have plans of my own?" She started to pace then, stalking her way around the three guards and Spirit World ruler in a circle. They followed her only with their eyes, ready to attack if need be. "I can see what you hope to come of this child. You wanted a child as a daughter, as your own." She knew she was right when she saw the change in his eyes. "And you wanted her as an heir. But not to this world."

The surprise in his face told her she was right, and he wouldn't bother to deny it now. "The Land of the Dead does not belong to you, half-breed. Just as it never belonged to the Raven-Eater."

"It is mine more than it will ever be yours. I fought for my kingdom, Creator, and I will fight to keep it. When did you fight for the Land of the Dead?" She took a step forward, her words biting at him. "When did you risk your life to defeat him? Or was it easier to let another take the fall, an enemy you hoped would be easier to defeat?" She had him caught, and reveled in his discomfort.

It took the Great Spirit but a moment to regain composure. He held his head high. "I have given you time to prove yourself, half-breed. The Land of the Dead is still a world of evil and corruption. It is a place without life or hope. It still reeks of the Raven-Eater's stench. You have not done it justice."

"And your child will?"

"Now is the time to empower our people, half-breed. We must remember our culture, our traditions of giving and love, and not let other influences destroy our spirit realms. With the proper training and guidance, she will be the leader the Land of the Dead needs—"

"She will *never* be the leader the Land of the Dead needs!" Whisper shouted then, throwing out her arm in a sign of fury. A column to her right crumbled from the force that erupted from her hand. Her face took on a distorted look of uncontrollable rage, and in that expression he saw the creature she had defeated but still allowed to live somewhere deep within her.

And suddenly, he feared for his life and the very existence of his realm.

Whisper sneered, pulling out her knife and dragging the tip along the edge of a stone bench as she continued to pace. "No child raised by the Creator could ever survive the Land of the Dead. With your white pillars, green meadows, chirping song-birds…what makes you think a child of the Spirit World could rule my land?" Her voice was critical and full of disdain. "The Land of the Dead would strip her of any light and happiness that lived within her, and she would wither away into nothing. The land would perish. And without my world, yours will fall."

The Great Spirit swallowed hard, taking a moment to gather his thoughts while she collected hers. "And you believe you can raise a child in the Land of the Dead to be your own rightful heir? You will destroy her. I will not allow that."

"The child is what I want, Creator."

"You cannot have her."

Whisper cast a single glance at Smoke Speaker, the last she would ever give him before facing him in combat, then at Hunting Hawk, who nodded and took his place at the crossing.

"Then I will see you in battle, Creator," she said icily, taking a few steps back to the barrier. "We are now at war."

* * *

The snow was melted, the air warm on their walk back from the crossing. Slush coated the earth and the sky rained down with white flakes, but they were gone before they ever touched the ground.

Adagatiya had done his job, and done it well. The land was heating, the earth heating up in a web of warmth with the Fire Tower as its center. The air was still thin and bitter, biting at their lungs with each deep breath, but at least their bodies were warm and comfortable.

They didn't speak during the walk back, Whisper plotting her next move and Hunting Hawk contemplating the ramifications of what his leader had just done. War with the Great Spirit, the Land of the Dead versus the Spirit World. This was not a war ever meant to be fought.

When he heard Whisper sigh with irritation, he looked up and saw Blue Feather standing in the entrance of the Fire Tower. Her hands were clutched together at her stomach, her own way of showing nerves and fear. She was a timid woman at heart and didn't like change, so he knew that they were in for more bad news.

"What have you done?" Blue Feather accused in a biting tone as soon as they were in earshot. Her hand came out, finger pointing at her daughter. "You said you were going for Smoke Speaker, but you did something far worse than that."

Whisper barely looked at her mother as she passed. "I did what I had to do."

"What you did was wrong."

Now she did look. "How do you know what I did? Or why I did it? You know nothing, woman. This is bigger than what you think you know."

Blue Feather hesitated, then regained her composure. She couldn't back down all the time, and certainly not to her daughter. "I know that you angered Creator. He is the Great Spirit, *Kanegv*. You do not want him as your enemy."

Whisper scoffed and turned, lifting a single brow. "No, Blue Feather. He does not want *me* as *his* enemy."

She left her mother standing speechless in the hallway, stalking the halls to her stone room. When she reached the doorway she nearly stumbled to a stop. Her eyes widened, her lips parting slightly in surprise as she took in the horrendous sight.

Her bed, her personal belongings, her weapons, they were all untouched. But there, in the center of the adjacent room, was an upheaval of stone that left her medicine wheel completely desecrated. In its place was an emptiness, a vast open void of sorrow.

Her place of comfort, the circle where she gathered her thoughts and strengths and balance, was gone, destroyed. Red and black stone tumbled together with yellow and white and blue, a palate of colors where all meaning was lost. She had created the medicine wheel from her own sweat and blood, calling on her ancestors to guide her hand and put their power into each stroke.

And now it was gone.

"I told you, *Kanegv*. You angered the Great Spirit, and this is your punishment."

The voice was quiet, but something inside Whisper snapped. She spun around, knife in hand, but a strong arm grabbed her before she could reach her mother. Hunting Hawk threw her onto the bed, then wrapped himself around her when she launched herself back up.

"I will end you for this, woman," she snarled, struggling against his hold. "I will *end you* for what you have done."

"This was not my doing!" Blue Feather protested, holding up a hand. "I heard it in the middle of the night. I came to your room. It was like an invisible army was tearing up the stone. I couldn't stop it from happening! All I knew was that something had happened between you and the Great Spirit, and whatever it was, you had angered him. He would never destroy such a sacred place without just reason."

"You cannot blame her for Creator's actions," Hunting Hawk said into Whisper's ear. He had grabbed hold of her hair and directed her head in his direction. "Let go of the half-breed. Come back to me, *Kanegv*."

It took everything she had, her teeth grinding together and her limbs shaking from the effort it took to not strike out. After a few moments, Whisper felt her hand unclench, and the knife fell to the stone. She was a bit shaky, but forced her breath to stay even.

Calmer now, she walked over to the destroyed medicine wheel, kneeling down to pick up a piece of stone. She would rebuild it, however long it took. From east to west, north to south, above to below, and to the center, she would make it her own once more.

"Send Brave Woman a message," she ordered to whoever was listening. "It is time we gather our army."

Chapter 30

The trek through the Weeping Forest was longer than Dark Water remembered. The land had grown since Sun Woman banished him and his brothers to the Forgotten Lands, and he was uncomfortable walking through such unfamiliar territory. He was on edge, whipping around at every suspicious sound, gripping his spear tightly. The long walk annoyed him, and also gave him time to think back on his days with the half-breed.

Whisper wasn't what he had been expecting. He had imagined a beastly woman, gnarled and twisted and corrupted by her disposition, a spirit that could send a man to his second death by her appearance alone. But the half-breed was more, so much more than that, and he wanted to learn everything about her. He remembered a time before the Raven-Eater, when the Land of the Dead was an empty place where spirits roamed, forgotten and forsaken. Then the tyrant had taken over, ruling the realm with a bloodlust that turned it into a place of fear. There was always talk of the half-breed returning, but no one ever knew if the prophecy was true.

Dark Water and his men ignored the Land of the Dead for as long as they could, refusing the Raven-Eater passage when he attempted to infiltrate the Forgotten Lands. They hadn't always been known for their practices in dark magic, but rather for their loyalty and peaceful ways. Banishment had corrupted them, and those who lived in darkness now sought them out for their own purposes. Even still, the Little Men rejected the Raven-Eater's request for their service, as they were for themselves, and themselves alone. Murdering the Circle members was not an act Dark Water and his brothers would ever pride themselves on, but it had been necessary in order to restore their family. And now he found himself considering an alliance with the new leader of the land, the beautiful queen who wanted for nothing and was capable of anything.

He was drawn to that power and intensity. Dark Water wanted to fight by her side, gain her trust, take the place he knew deep down was rightfully his. Whisper needed strength and old magic as her right hand. Hunting Hawk was but a stand-in for the one who truly understood the half-breed for who she was, and what she was capable of doing. And after he ensured her part of the bargain was held up, he would make her realize who her eternal companion truly should be.

By the time he emerged on the other side of the forest and approached the river, he was covered in sticky black goo and laced with tiny scratches from the needle-sharp thorns covering each branch in the thicket. He was thankful he had decided to leave his brothers at home to set up in preparation for their newest resident. It would have been harder, and much slower, to navigate six men through the brush.

Dark Water stalked the shoreline until he found the RiverKeeper, an old yet burly man who had been stationed to his post for the past eighteen years. Penance for serving the Raven-Eater, Dark Water had heard rumored throughout the land. The man was yet to show the signs of his eternal punishment physically, but the hollowness in his eyes told the tale of a spirit beaten into submission. The job was a kind of cruelty bestowed upon those who didn't deserve peace in death, although the last River-Keeper had taken the burden upon his shoulders willingly in order to serve the half-breed should she ever return to the Land of the Dead. And for that, she had set him free.

He bribed his way across the river, offering a trinket of value that the River-Keeper would never be able to use unless he was freed of his post. Perhaps the man held out hope that one day he would be free, Dark Water figured, or perhaps his mind was too far gone to know his offer was useless. No matter the reason, he rowed the man to the other side without a word.

Excitement built in his stomach as he continued his march across the barren land. He passed through the Western Sun without a second's hesitation, not stopping to let his eyes adjust. He had to arrive at the Bridge of the Dead in time.

But when he got there, someone else was waiting for him.

If he was surprised, Sun Woman thought, he didn't let it show on his face. There was a moment he took to square his shoulders and set his face in an expression that told her he wasn't looking forward to a conversation, but his stride was even and confident.

"Dark Water," she greeted, amusement in her rich, husky voice. "I don't image you expected to see me."

Dark Water hesitated before answering. He hadn't seen Sun Woman since she banished him and his men long ago for failing to return her daughter, since the day they lost their seventh brother, who had chosen to forsake his life for the chance to live another.

She looked the same now as she did then, aged yet timeless, thick hair that seemed to radiate with warmth, and an aura that glowed orange and yellow in the darkness. He wasn't sure how to feel about her presence, a mix of hate and fear and awe wrestling with one another in his souls. He wanted to despise her for what she'd done, but the guilt of having lost her daughter still filled him and he found that he couldn't fault her for their exile.

"You don't seem surprised to see me."

Sun Woman huffed and turned her eyes to the Bridge of the Dead looming before them. They were on the side not all spirits reached, watching those who attempted to cross as they faced the creatures they had wronged in the Land of the Living. "Surely you know the half-breed speaks only deceit. We got what we wanted from one another, but it is only natural for her to play both sides of the stone. I knew she had recruited you as an ally, and what better way to ensure your loyalty than by offering you the one thing you want most?"

His brother, Dark Water thought, slightly annoyed that he hadn't caught on to Whisper's game earlier. And in working with Sun Woman, she too had been promised what she wanted—her daughter, and the only way to bring her daughter back was with his lost brother's memories. She had used them both to get to the Spirit World, and left it up to them to determine who would get the brother in the end.

"We both used her as well, Dark Water," Sun Woman said as though reading his thoughts. "She gave us what she promised, even if it is one and the same. And I intend on taking what is mine."

Now he understood her intentions as well. "And I intend on bringing my brother home. The one you allowed to leave this world out of spite."

"He made his choice then, just as he will make it now." She turned her eyes to Dark Water, who had crossed his muscular arms and was glaring back at her with detestation in his black eyes. "He is not a child anymore, forced into the Land of the Dead. He is a man who has come of his own free will. He must choose, or else it is not his life. You have my word, Dark Water, that if he chooses my offer, he will be returned to you once I am through."

"Why should I trust you?" he sneered, taking a daring step closer. "You *banished* me to the Forgotten Lands."

"A curse for a curse, Dark Water." Sun Woman replied coolly. "Now, let us greet him together."

* * *

He was confused, frightened, and yet, not lost. The land around him was dark and bleak, desolate landscapes with cracks and craters threatening to swallow him whole. Strange figures draped in tattered clothing wandered all around him, sometimes bumping into him, other times not appearing to see him at all. But he felt like he had seen them before. In a dream, in another life.

One time or another, Cole Daivya knew he had been here before.

But where was here? Where was this familiar yet strange place? Try as he might, he couldn't remember how he had arrived. He recalled sunshine, the scent of stale air as he walked, then a sensation that someone was watching him. A woman, a face that flashed into his mind. One he had known long ago, perhaps, or only in a dream. He wanted to talk to her, and...then what?

The next thing he could remember, he was waking up on hard ground in a world of grays and blacks. Something was pulling him west, and so he let himself be guided. The longer he walked, the further he entered this land of the lost, the less he could remember of that old life where he knew he had left someone behind, but the name and face were forgotten. He struggled to hold onto that feeling of warmth and comfort, but with each step, the less he could sense that stranger's touch.

By the time he reached the Bridge of the Dead, he knew he was where he belonged.

The dismal contraption loomed before him, haunting in its elegance, sickening in its foulness. Silence fell over the gawking crowd when Cole approached, sensing something dark and different about him. It was enough to make him hesitate, tipping back his head to take in the sights of ragged tatters blowing in the wind, splintered wood crisscrossing every which way to connect a bridge that spanned a deep gorge. He could hear screams wafting up on the vines of hot air as lost souls tumbled to the place that welcomed the ones who never made it to the other side. Then he saw the ramshackle hut at the forefront of the bridge, drawing him in.

Confidently, if not arrogantly, he strode into the hut and faced down the Watchmen. Something about the way they moved, smelled, looked, was familiar, but he pushed those thoughts to the back of his mind as they swarmed him, judged him. He closed his eyes when he felt their sneaky tendrils worming their way through his thoughts, then draw back rapidly. When he opened his eyes, he saw that they were staring back curiously.

"*The prodigal son...returns,*" they rasped in unison. "*The half-breed...calls you back.*"

"The who? The what?" he asked, confused. "What are you talking about?"

But they didn't answer. Instead, they simply moved aside and let him pass. On the other side, he approached the bridge, dread curling in his gut. Then a happy, excited barking put a smile on his face.

"Whisper." He knelt down and grabbed the perky black lab in a hug. "I've missed you." Of all the things he was forgetting, he still remembered her bright as day. His parents had brought home a wriggling ball of fur when he was eight, and he insisted on naming her Whisper for a reason he still couldn't explain. And she stayed by his side until he was nineteen, passing away of old age and cancer. She'd been a loyal pet, a good friend, and seeing her again brought tears to his eyes.

"Okay girl, let's do this."

Cole knew what would happen next. His father always seemed nervous when it came to death and religion, but one thing he had shared was the Bridge of the Dead. Be kind to animals, his father had told him. Never harm a creature of the earth in hate or anger or spite, and always be thankful for the lives given up for your own. Cole had stayed true to those words, but also knew that if he was at the Bridge, then whatever he wasn't remembering from his past no longer mattered, because he had entered a life after death.

His father's lessons paid off, and he crossed the bridge with only the trouble caused by unhappy insects and a bird he'd once struck on accident while driving. And when he reached the other side, a man and woman were there to greet him.

"Welcome back, Fighting Fox," Sun Woman greeted, smiling warmly. She would not use his living name, but instead the one bestowed upon him by the Raven-Eater, the one given to him as a child, the one the Land of the Dead would welcome.

"You look well, Second Son," Dark Water said right after, determined not to let Sun Woman sink her deceitful claws into his lost sibling. And he truly was his lost brother, the second born of the Little Men. He didn't know how it was possible, how it had been done, but the man standing before him was a replica of the spirit Second Son had once been. The only differences that he could note were the blue eyes and sandy blonde hair. But the face, the build, even the voice, were those once belonging to his brother. It was a reincarnation he never would have thought possible, one so unfortunate that Dark Water nearly felt bad for the man who never stood a chance at life.

"Fighting Fox? Second Son? Who are you talking about? My name is…." Then Cole realized he didn't know, so he took a different approach. "Who are you?"

Sun Woman cut Dark Water off before he could respond. "We are family," she answered softly, her glowing eyes captivating the man. She knew it wouldn't take much to win him over. Already his mind was faltering, far more rapidly than most who entered the Land of the Dead. She supposed that was because he had been here before, and his mind was torn between both worlds. "And we are here to propose an offer to you. If you accept our offer, you will live peacefully in this land with your new wife and brothers."

Dark Water stayed silent, interested in where she was going with her proposition. But Cole wasn't so easy to convince. Something was triggered inside him. "Wife..." he said quietly, a face forming in his mind. "My fiancée...my daughter...I have a family. I have a family," he repeated, louder this time. "You've taken me away from them!"

"We did no such thing," Dark Water stepped in, sensing the man's sudden anger, but Sun Woman placed a calming hand on his arm.

"You stepped in front of the vehicle, ending your own life," she replied. "You have been sent to the Land of the Dead for your actions."

"What?" Cole shook his head. "I didn't kill myself. There...there was a woman. An Indian woman. I...I saw her in my dreams. Then she..." His hands gripped his dirty hair as he struggled to remember. Why was everything so fuzzy? Why couldn't he bring those memories to his mind? "What's going to happen to me?"

"You're going to come with me," Sun Woman answered, extending her hand. "Come with me and fulfill your destiny. Everything you desire will be waiting for you."

"My fiancée? My daughter?"

"Come with me, Fighting Fox. You are home now."

"Or come home with me," Dark Water cut in urgently, "and be with your brothers."

Unfazed, Sun Woman merely smiled again. "The choice is yours. Whatever you choose, you are safe with us."

Dark Water watched anxiously as Cole struggled between his head and his heart. The man fought to hold on to touches of his past life; the parts of him that once belonged to the Raven-Eater couldn't wait to be part of the Land of the Dead once again. Like Whisper, he was made up of two halves that formed an unequal whole, but he was yet to learn how to control it. And until he did, the light that once shone in his bright blue eyes would start to fade.

But unlike Whisper, there was a third force struggling to complete his being, one that recognized the scent of the Land of the Dead and longed to be free. Cole couldn't comprehend the many voices swarming around his thoughts.

Just as Dark Water was starting to lose hope, Cole lifted his arm and slowly reached out to Sun Woman. Their hands touched, and she wrapped her fingers around him with a warm smile. Then she drew him closer into a gentle hug, a light beginning to brighten around them. Dark Water held up a hand to shield his vision from the brightness, realizing that she was taking his brother away from him.

But before he could even think to be angry or sense betrayal of any kind, Sun Woman sent him a smile over Cole's shoulder. And in that smile, Dark Water saw the deceit she had planned for the man, the treachery set on the road before him, and knew that by the end of it, they both would get what they wanted out of Cole Daivya's return.

Chapter 31

It wasn't an easy feat, but with each passing night Whisper came that much closer to building her army. Since taking her place as leader of the Land of the Dead she had recruited lost souls and renowned spirits, sending out her own men to gather their loyalties and join her side. From the Army of the Dead that once served the Raven-Eater to her own gathering of forces, her warriors would one day be known as the greatest army any spirit realm had ever seen.

She stood on the edge of the Fire Mountains, looking out over her land as a small troop of figures headed her way, the newest recruits. Whisper recognized those faces, and prided herself in having earned their service. These soldiers would be sent into training immediately, taught by Hunting Hawk himself as he prepared them for what was soon to come. She enjoyed watching him train what fighters they already had, his hard muscles flexing with each movement, tanned body glistening in the gold and orange of Mother Sun. He was the master of his trade, a War Chief who took no prisoners, and the pull she felt toward Hunting Hawk when he was in his truest element was almost primal. His deep, growling voice reached her even in her sleep, awakening some primitive part of her that craved the touch of the man who made his living shedding blood.

While Hunting Hawk trained the beginnings of her army, and while Whisper used her influence to gather new troops, the Army of the Dead awaited orders, resting beneath the Barren Plains for the next war that called upon them. They needed no training, not even by her War Chief, as they fought on vengeance and bloodlust alone. They fought with the wrath of the Raven-Eater, and that was all Whisper needed from them.

When she was through training these men and women, these spirits of the forgotten dead, she would have the greatest army the Land of the Dead had ever seen. And then, when the time was right, she would release them all to do her bidding in the Spirit World.

As Whisper gathered her forces from the Fire Tower, Hunting Hawk stepped out onto the Barren Plains. His bare chest and shoulders were streaked with dirt and blood, evidence of a day of training. He was tired and irritable, and what he had to do next only annoyed him further.

Eyeing the Barren Plains, Hunting Hawk sneered at the mounds of dirt that streaked across the earth. He knew all creatures had their place in the Land of the Dead, but some of them he could have done without. *Utlva* was one of those creatures.

Nonetheless, he had his orders, and so he mimicked Whisper's own actions when calling the beast. He drove his hand into the center of a mound and pulled back a few handfuls of dirt, then waited.

It didn't take long. Hunting Hawk felt the earth trembling, then the large ball of scruffy brown fur popped out of the hole. Seconds later, another appeared, four eyes staring at him as claws clicked together greedily.

How may we serve you, mate of our mighty leader, they asked in unison, their voices earnest but the glint in their eyes revealing their deception. Hunting Hawk, like Whisper, knew their game, even when others didn't.

"*Kanegv* wishes for you to give Brave Woman a message. Her services are no longer needed, and she is to stay away from the Fire Tower." He could have sworn he saw them sneer.

As you wish, mate of our mighty leader. Together, they disappeared back into the earth. Hunting Hawk watched the dirt trail speed away from the Barren Plains and into the Weeping Forest. In time, Brave Woman would come, and then Whisper's plan would be put into action.

Chapter 32

The spirit was born in a way no one had ever seen before, a way that could not be explained but was revered and feared as a miracle brought forth by Creator himself. It took but one scratch from the thorny brush against a weary leg, and when the swelling had stretched the skin to its breaking point, a child came forth into the world.

The people loved this child, the one they named Splinter Foot Girl, fashioning her a dress made of elk teeth she was proud to call her own. To congratulate the people on their new daughter and to follow traditions, Bone Bull, a lone buffalo, sent a messenger to ask for her hand in marriage. The people refused, and so Bone Bull enlisted the help of his favored bird. It was only the creature with a reddish head and wings who could persuade them to relent.

And so the child married Bone Bull, and lived with him for many years. She wore his own beautiful painted buffalo robe, and was a dutiful wife. But she missed the men who had seen her into this world, as they mourned for her, and so Blackbird told the men they must seek out Mole and Badger to return what was lost.

Together, the cunning creatures burrowed into Bone Bull's home, and gave Splinter Foot Girl the arrows she would need for her escape. Then she left with them, until they reached the lone cottonwood tree, who ordered them to run around its trunk four times. Only then did the tree allow them to climb, and when they reached the top, they lay in wait for Bone Bull to find them.

Bone Bull followed their trail, but it was when Splinter Foot Girl spat a mouthful of blood onto the ground after accidentally biting her cheek that he was able to detect her scent. He gathered his herd to fight, and the cottonwood tree gave him the chance to fight for what was his.

"Let them break off their horns," the tree said when the younger calves rammed into the trunk. "Let them tire themselves, while I stand tall."

Enraged, Bone Bull attacked the tree from all seven sacred directions—north, south, east, west, above, below, and center—but in his final charge, he became stuck.

With their enemy secured, the young men who had come to save Splinter Foot Girl shot him down, covering him with the bits of bark knocked off by bull horns.

Their victory meant that Bone Bull had been defeated, and with his death, all buffalo could now be hunted by man.

The people rejoiced, but their happiness was short-lived. Round Rock now wanted Splinter Foot Girl for himself, sending Hummingbird to order her hand in marriage. The men refused, and to save them from losing their daughter again, Hummingbird told them that again they would need Mole and Badger. Splinter Foot Girl went to Round Rock, but her companions helped her escape, covering Round Rock in the earth.

Home again, she and her fathers fled, outwitting Round Rock and sending him tumbling over the edge of a cliff. Tired of running, Splinter Foot Girl fashioned a ball and kicked it high into the air. One of her fathers rose with it.

"We are done running," she told them, kicking the ball again. "We will live in a safe place now, where the others will not trouble us any longer. I will care for you all, and we will be together."

One by one they rose into the sky, safe from the perils of the earth, where they remain even today.

Creator knew the young Arapaho spirit well, had granted her sanctuary away from the beasts of the world, allowing her and her fathers to remain in a place of hiding where they could live and be happy.

In all their many moons, they had become a strong hunting family, the fathers teaching their daughter well. Now she was a fine huntress, a fierce warrior, and a loyal woman to those who had done her right. And the Great Spirit was one she owed her very survival to.

He found her in the tent, tending to the fire. Meat was cooking on a spit just above the flames. She rose quickly when he entered, dipping her head slightly in a show of respect. "Great Spirit. I wasn't expecting you."

"I told no one I was coming," he replied, patting her on the shoulder. He had a soft spot for Splinter Foot Girl, a beautiful woman with soft sable hair kept loose and straight, wide black eyes, and a gentle smile with deep and charming dimples at the corners. She had been through many pains, came from a remarkable birth, and still sought out new ways to learn to improve her world. "I must speak with you."

Quickly, but in detail, he told her what had happened in the Spirit World, and what he feared would come from the half-breed's war. When he was through, Splinter

Foot Girl's eyes glowed with anger and a look Creator recognized as pure loyalty to the one who had granted her a life free of marriage to beasts and stones.

"Tell me what I must do, Great Spirit."

"Lead them into battle against the half-breed. Show her that she does not rule my land, and has no power over anyone or thing, not even the Land of the Dead."

"As you wish, Great Spirit." Splinter Foot Girl drew forth her beloved hunting knife and ran the blade across her finger. This knife had seen her through many hunts, feeding her family and sustaining her life-force for another day.

Only this time, she wouldn't be hunting game. This time, she would be after something that was neither human nor animal.

* * *

Grief had struck her down, surrounding her heart in black chains of sorrow. It was hard to even get out of bed, and she ate only for the health of her unborn daughter. Life itself no longer made sense, each day ran into the next with no beginning or end, and her dreams were filled with images of what could have been, and what will never be.

Suicide, they said. Stepped right out into the path of an oncoming truck with a smile on his face. She didn't want to believe them, but she knew how hard it had been for Cole. His dreams haunted him even while awake, and he had spoken of a faceless woman who taunted him.

In fact, she too had begun to dream those dreams, perhaps because she now feared whatever nameless, faceless being he had been so afraid of all his life. Her nights were tormented, filled with visions of an empty, barren land, and yet other times she dreamed of peace, a place of love and light. It was as though she was being pulled in two different directions by two worlds who both wanted her soul.

Was this what her love had experienced for so many years? Was this the pain he always tried to hide from her? Had he taken matters into his own hands, and stepped out into the road hoping to put an end to a lifetime of nightmares?

The thought brought forth a fresh set of tears as she remembered Cole's funeral. His mother sat in the front, clutching her father's arm. His grandparents had been devastated, but sat solemnly, holding it together for the sake of their daughter. But his father, Ian, stood apart from the crowd, hands shoved in his pockets, head hung low. When she approached, offering what she could, he had merely shaken his head and muttered what she thought to be, "I should have told him the truth."

What truth? What did the Daivya family have to hide, and did it affect her unborn child?

Under other circumstances, she would have pressed the issue, but now she couldn't seem to care. If there was a secret, it didn't matter anymore. All that did matter was that she had lost the love of her life, and that he would never get to meet the daughter he already loved with all his heart.

He had wanted to name her Anya. Grace, he said it meant. Merciful. She hadn't been sure of the name in the beginning, wondering why he would favor a name suggesting a need for mercy, but now, she would give him this one wish.

"Baby Anya," she whispered, rubbing a hand over her stomach as she rose from the bed. "We will live for your father, and we will move on together."

Chapter 33

He arrived in a fit of fury, stalking across the Barren Plains as *Utlva* followed behind, eagerly awaiting a glimpse of battle, a taste of bloodshed. Dark Water ignored the mound of dirt rising at his heels, his glare focused on the Fire Tower instead.

She knew he was coming; she always did. So he wasn't surprised when the large metal door creaked open and she was standing just inside, her bronzed skin glowing in the light of the torches that lined the walls.

"You lied to me," he accused, pointing at her with his dagger. "You said you would return my brother to me."

"I did as I promised," Whisper replied, crossing her arms.

"He is now with Sun Woman. *Not* in the Forgotten Lands with his brothers."

"Returning Second Son to the Forgotten Lands was not part of the agreement."

Dark Water paused, considering. When he went over their deal in his head and realized she was right, he silently cursed them both—Whisper for her sly deception, and himself for falling for the trap.

"Sun Woman will return your brother," she said then, stepping outside and gesturing for him to follow. "She has need of him for only one purpose, then she will dispose of him and he will be yours."

He wanted to argue, but deep down knew nothing could be done. The half-breed had fulfilled her promise and brought Second Son back to him. And now, he had to wait for his brother to return back to him yet again.

"You knew all along," he said, thinking back to their earlier conversations. "You knew Second Son was Fighting Fox. But how?"

He was disappointed, perhaps even heartbroken, and so Whisper would give him that little bit of information. "Your brother chose to spend his eternity in the Land of the Living, but he was not settled. He went from body to body, reincarnating himself many times. But the Raven-Eater wanted him. He could not draw you in to serve with his Army, so he planned to steal Second Son's soul as ransom. He tried to steal the children from the forest that held Second Son's spirit, but your brother was smart and separated himself before it was too late. I was tasked to seek out the children the Raven-Eater attempted to lure into death and save them before it was too late. But then Second Son found the boy, and the Raven-Eater took him before he could escape. Before I could find him."

"But Cole returned to the Land of the Living. Second Son could have left then."

"No." Whisper shook her head. "He followed the boy into the Land of the Dead. They died together, and they were reborn together. He is now forever trapped in the boy's body."

He didn't like it, but there was nothing he could do about it now other than wait. Second Son and Cole Daivya were one, and he had to accept it. Accepting it, though, didn't mean he would forgive his ruler, no matter how he felt about her. He had to distance himself from Whisper before his regret soiled his view of her, and needed time to come to terms with her actions.

Before he could speak his thoughts, the air changed suddenly, a chill frosting through the land as the sky darkened, clouds parting and releasing sheets of freezing rain. The wind picked up, throwing dirt in their faces and howling with the voices of the dead. Beneath their feet, the earth rumbled, shifting and cracking in places.

When the sun disappeared behind a black cloud and ice dropped down from the sky, Dark Water smiled. Now she would see what happened when the one she needed most at her side was gone. "It seems your actions have caught up with you, *Kanegv.* Enjoy fighting your own battles."

Leaving Whisper standing in a warrior's pose, her fingers gripping her blade and her eyes narrowed against his words, he turned on his heel and walked away, leaving the half-breed to clean up her own messes.

Whisper didn't bother to watch Dark Water walk away. He had his reasons for turning his back, and she would allow him his moment of rejection, knowing he would be back in the end. No one looked at her like he did and stayed away long. Her attention instead went to the sky, eyes squinting as the wind bore down on her and sent freezing hail across her vision. She could hear voices in that wind, and she cocked her head ever so slightly to listen to the whispers threatening to rip her apart. They interested her, fascinated her as she pondered who had such anger toward her and why they were brave enough to step foot in the Land the Dead.

Turning, she raced back inside the Fire Tower, stumbling slightly when the earth released a deep shudder, her feet pounding on the stone stairs as she shouted for

Hunting Hawk. She nearly ran into him when she turned the corner into her room and he exited, already holding her bow and arrow.

"It seems Creator is sending us a message," he said sternly, a glint of excitement in his eyes. If nothing else, the former War Chief loved a good battle.

"Then we will send one back," she all but spat out, yanking her weapons from his grip. She stalked down the hall, slamming a palm into Blue Feather's chest when the woman stepped out from her room with a questioning expression. "You stay here. This is not your fight."

But she knew whose fight it was—Blue Corn Maiden. Only one spirit was known for the coming of winter, and this was her work at its finest. Whisper had never known the spirit personally, and she silently chastised herself for not thinking of recruiting spirits such as Blue Corn Maiden for herself.

Rather than go outside, Whisper raced to the rooftop, bursting outside to see that already mounds of snow covered the Land of the Dead. It fell too fast for the dragon's fires to keep up, coating every bit of earth. If she couldn't get to the Barren Plains, then she couldn't raise the army she had just begun to build, and Blue Corn Maiden seemed to know that. She couldn't see the spirit—and wouldn't, with her emitting this much power she was likely tucked away in some safe place—but she was all around, searching for the weak links, looking for that perfect place to strike her down.

Whisper didn't worry about the cold. The blood that coursed through her warmed her from the inside out, melting the snow at her feet as she peered into the distance. She saw them coming, twelve men, some young, some old, marching across the open land with their hands gripping blades and their mouths set in grim lines of anger and determination. Some of them dripped black blood from their necks, others had gaping holes in their chests.

The Circle. Dark Water and his men had done their job well, murdering the men in their sleep. And instead of sending them to their second death in that place no one knew truly existed or not, Creator had found a way to keep them in his own Spirit World, if for no other purpose than revenge.

For now, Whisper thought snidely.

But they weren't alone. In front of the Circle marched a woman, young but ferocious. And lined up on either side of her were grown men built with the years of hunting and farming.

"Splinter Foot Girl," Whisper muttered, her eyes narrowing into slits. She knew of the Arapaho spirit, the one who lived in between worlds, once married to

Buffalo and Round Rock. She was said to be quiet in demeanor, but fiercely loyal to those she loved.

And the half-breed was not someone she loved.

A corner of Whisper's mouth pulled up into a half-smile, an expression anyone would recognize as looking forward to the ensuing bloodshed. She nocked an arrow, pointed it in their direction, and released what she knew would be taken as the sign needed to attack. She watched the arrow in flight, her eyes following its downward spiral until it landed right at Splinter Foot Girl's feet.

As soon as the arrow pierced the earth, Whisper ran. She raced across the rooftop, booted feet slamming against stone, her left hand gripping her bone-handled blade while her right secured the bow across her back.

And when she reached the edge, she leapt.

Momentarily startled by the arrow that nearly struck her down, Splinter Foot Girl paused just before crossing the barrier into the Fire Mountains. Then she saw the half-breed running across the rooftop, leaping into the air, and followed suit. She and her men met Whisper just as she landed solidly onto the ground on one foot and knee, bracing herself with her free hand as the earth cracked around her. When she looked up, her black hair falling across those infinite, haunting eyes, Splinter Foot Girl felt the slightest of chills.

"You cannot defeat me, half-breed," she spoke first, lowering herself into a fighting stance as her men did the same. "I was not born of man and woman. I cannot be killed."

"No," Whisper sneered as the two began to circle one another. "But I can take off your head, and send your remains back to Creator while your spirit wanders lost in the Land of the Dead."

"You are welcome to try."

With that, Splinter Foot Girl launched into attack, her blade sparking against Whisper's. She threw her arm forward toward her chest, but Whisper blocked the move, lowering herself to the ground and swiping a leg that brought Splinter Foot Girl to her back.

The others attacked then, the fathers that would defend their daughter to the death and the Circle brought down by her order. The freezing wind surrounded them, frosting in their hair, the black clouds letting in only enough light to help the men see their enemy. Not even the Fire Mountains were a match for this cold.

Knowing they would follow, Whisper began to back up into her preferred territory, dodging the arrows released from the Great Spirit's council. Only one hit its mark, burying itself deep into her right forearm. Snarling, she ripped the arrow from her flesh and threw it at her enemies just as Hunting Hawk and his men rushed past her, throwing themselves into the middle of the fight. Hunting Hawk went after the fathers first, grabbing hold of one and using him as a shield as he struck down man after man, his blade slicing cleanly into already-dead flesh. Soon he was covered in black blood, some his own, his face contorted into a mask of rage as he flung down the body and charged the warriors. Some were missing, Whisper noted, either having retreated or killed by her army. But her men were dwindling as well, and soon they would be outnumbered in this ambush.

Whisper spun around when she heard the sneak attack, throwing a dagger without looking and smirking when she saw the blade find its mark deep in the throat of her enemy—not a Circle member, not one of Splinter Foot Girl's fathers, but a soul lost in the Land of the Dead. Creator had turned even some of her own people against her.

"Clever spirit," she whispered, then grimaced when she took a step only to stumble. Her dagger hadn't been the only one thrown, and she looked down to see a knife protruding from her left knee. Furious, she grabbed the hilt with a bloody hand and pulled it from her leg, wincing and biting back a cry of pain. She may have been the half-breed, but she wasn't immune to that kind of agony.

Throwing the mangled knife to the ground, the blade bent from impact with bone, she turned slowly and faced down Splinter Foot Girl. The spirit was fighting Hunting Hawk, but not well. He was well trained, a former War Chief who could hold his own, although it was only a matter of time before her fathers came to her aid. Whisper wanted Splinter Foot Girl for herself, to defeat her before anyone else could send her spirit into its second death. And she would defeat her with the army feared by all.

The air was thick with the scent of blood, the earth covered in black, sticky rivers, ashes of the dead blowing in a wind that continued to send icy shudders up their backs. On the ground, fallen snow had mixed with the blood and ash to make a sickening gray that clung to their boots as they raced to fight their next enemy.

Whisper could end this now, and knew how. The Army of the Dead, though not yet complete, served her now, and once they had risen Splinter Foot Girl and the council men would go running, and never return. No one faced down the army that had once served the Raven-Eater.

She had to get to the Barren Plains and find a way to burrow down through the ice and snow. Leaving Hunting Hawk to hold his own, Whisper ignored the searing pain in her knee and arm and started for the Barren Plains.

An urgent murmur spoken on the vines of wind swept through Whisper's head without warning, and she heeded the alert just as a huge, solid, spear-tipped chunk of ice thrust forth from the ground directly in front of her, sending her stumbling. Without that message, the ice would have cut straight through her.

Her back slammed into another icicle that pierced through the earth, and she fell to her knees and knocked her head against the ground when a third arced out and sliced through her right calf. Momentarily stunned, Whisper braced herself on her knees and elbows, struggling to listen carefully as the voices spoke to her.

It strikes from the north, the whispers shouted, and she launched herself to the right just as a razor-sharp icicle broke through, aiming for her stomach.

From the south, it comes. Whisper rolled across the earth, dodging the second attack, but not quite fast enough. The tip of the ice chunk grazed her side, cutting easily through skin. Over and over she rolled, listening to the whispers, letting them guide her from one safe spot to another. The sound of breaking earth and grating ice deafened her to all but the voices, the pain of hitting head and knee and elbow against the hard ground making her forget about the battle around her.

Finally the whispers stopped, along with the ice attack. Crawling to her knees, Whisper turned her head slightly to watch the bloodshed. She heard nothing but a roaring in her ears, saw nothing but a haze of red that filtered her vision, felt nothing but a jolt of rage and pain when she saw the spear graze Hunting Hawk's shoulder and slice through flesh.

Then she heard a war cry from behind and a rumbling in the earth, and knew help had come at the right moment. As she pulled herself to her feet, a horse leapt high over her head and landed solidly on the ground before her, its rider sending a single glance back over her shoulder before charging into the horde of enemies. Brave Woman was true to her name, stabbing the spirits without thought as she forced her way in, knocking Hunting Hawk to the side and dismembering the man who had cut open his shoulder just moments ago. She was magnificent in battle, long black hair flowing out behind her, movements elegant and precise, her face a visage of courage and deadly might.

When the earth rumbled again and she realized what was happening, Whisper nearly laughed. She felt the power swell and surge within her, strengthening her aching limbs, taking away her pain. Her focus turned back to the Barren Plains, and she plucked her dagger up from the ground and sent it through one of the ice mounds, shattering it into tiny pieces.

As she ran, more ice shot up at her feet. But she was made of this land, and this land was true to her. The particles of dirt, the tiniest blades of grass, even the creatures that lived beneath the ground that were nearly invisible to the naked eye, told her where to step and where to expect the next attack, whispering to her above the winds to ensure her safety.

Then, as she reached the edges of the Barren Plains, he appeared.

Adagatiya burst through the rock in a torrent of stone and fire, soaring into the sky to the sound of terrified shouts and screams. With each pump of his wings, the dragon sent down waves of heat, turning the snowfall into rain that evaporated before ever touching the dirt. Then he turned his head and opened his mouth wide, sending a blaze of fire in Whisper's path as she ran to the center of the Barren Plains. He lit her way, melting the snow until she reached her mark. The dragon turned, satisfied, and went back to help the others.

Rushing to her chosen place of sacrifice as fast as her bloody, injured legs would allow, Whisper slid to the ground on her knees, raised the dagger high above her head, and with a scream of rage and war slammed the blade into the earth.

Chapter 34

Hunting Hawk was tired, but he was determined to see this battle through to the bitter end. Some of his men had fallen, but more of the enemy were down. And yet, they kept coming. Somehow, Creator had recruited spirits from their own land to fight against them, and they fought fiercely. Some had only their bare hands, but they used them well.

Just when he thought it might be best to retreat and take refuge in the Fire Tower, he heard Whisper scream what he could only describe as a soul-shattering howl that terrified him to the core. Not because she was injured, not because she was in pain, but because she was filled with such anger that she was about to unleash an evil the Land of the Dead had not seen for nearly twenty years. And then he felt the rush of stale, hot air from the Barren Plains, blowing his tangled black hair around his face, his clothes flapping in the wind.

One by one, the warriors turned, facing the most frightening sight of all. The Army of the Dead had risen, disturbed from their graves and standing atop broken mounds of cracked, dry earth. Some were stripped near to the bone, decaying flesh hanging off tendon and muscle; others were dressed in full battle gear, gripping solid weapons meant to destroy. And in their center was Whisper, her hair whipping around her in a halo of fury, her black eyes nearly glowing with the power it took to resurrect the ones who once served the evil that ruled the Land of the Dead.

They stood in place, staring down the intruders, almost daring the enemy to make the first move. Hunting Hawk had to give Whisper credit for restraining herself in the attack. She didn't have to move. All she needed to do was to show who and what was backing her. Now that the show had been made, Splinter Foot Girl saw what she was up against and knew she would not win this fight.

Signaling to her men, Splinter Foot Girl took a step back and sheathed her dagger. "Until next time, half-breed."

Only when the last of the invaders had faded into the distance did Whisper move from her stance. She left the Army of the Dead where they were, and where they would remain until she gave them the command to move. She walked over to Hunting Hawk, lifting a hand to his injured shoulder and pressing her palm into the wound. He winced as blood seeped over her fingers. He felt the heat from her hand, and from the dullness in her eyes saw that she was draining what energy she had left after summoning the army to heal him.

"I am fine," he insisted, taking her hand in his. "War Chiefs prefer scars." Whisper nearly smiled, but maintained her stoic expression as she turned to what was left of her guards.

"You fought well," she complimented, appreciating the fact that they were all caught by surprise and still battled hard. "Go and rest." The men nodded and headed back to the Fire Tower, and Whisper turned back to Hunting Hawk. "You as well. I must go."

"Wait." Hunting Hawk grabbed her arm, his grip slipping slightly, his hand wet with blood. "You cannot follow them."

Whisper huffed and pulled her arm free. "I am not following them. I must go to *Owenvsv*. I need my sanctuary."

He would let her go, because he knew what her place of retreat meant—somewhere to reflect, relax, and heal. And so Hunting Hawk nodded, and Whisper whistled sharply. Moments later, Eagle appeared and swept down, and Whisper leapt on his back.

Together they soared high to sanctuary, Whisper relaxing on Eagle's back as she thought about the attack. She should have been prepared, should have expected that Creator would send an army her way after the Circle's deaths. The amount of energy it took to keep her men alive and raise the army was more than she had predicted, and she allowed herself a moment to be happy that Eagle had forgiven her for her act of betrayal so that she could rest upon his back.

That moment was all she had, for just as she was lifting herself to a sitting position she heard the roar behind her. Before she could turn, something slammed into her and she felt the cold bite of metal slide through her gut, twist, and shove deeper as she cried out in pain. Whisper struggled to free herself, her teeth clenching together as blood seeped from her mouth, but the figure had strong arms wrapped around her and not even Eagle's frantic, high-pitched squeals could send the stranger away.

As the pain in her stomach grew to agony, and as black blood began to pour from the wound, Whisper did the only thing she could think to do. She grabbed hold of the stranger's wrists and took him with her as she tumbled off Eagle's back.

The shock of freefalling startled the man into releasing his victim. When they parted, Whisper managed to turn her head to see who she was fighting, and the shadow of a winged beast flying off into the distance. She recognized the man as a member of the Circle. Tall Bear, her grandfather had called him. Together they rocketed toward the river, Whisper's face contorted in a mask of pain and ire, Tall Bear reaching for her throat with a second knife as he fought to finish the kill before his body met the earth.

She managed to arch her body away from him enough to avoid the blade, the effort sending her stomach into spasms.

Whisper hit the water first, and although she had been expecting the impact, it still stole her breath and sent her in a spiral as the current sucked her under. She felt Tall Bear's hands grasp for her ankle as he too was taken in, but unlike Whisper, fear overtook him as he struggled to discover where he was and what was happening.

As she tumbled in the dark water, Whisper saw a flash of sliver dart through the water, so large and thick that she knew they were being watched by the beast that stalked the waters of her sanctuary. The part of her that loved the taste of war longed to go after the creature even in her wounded state, but the beast would not bother them in this fight, as that was a battle for another day.

Her back slammed into a rock, sending stabs of pain up her wounded spine, and soon Whisper felt the familiar cold water that signified her entry into *Owenvsv*. Despite her injuries, she splashed her way to the shore as soon as she surfaced, fighting off the sharp biting teeth that dug into her arms and legs, eager to attack now that she was defenseless. Before long she collapsed on the edge of the stone shore, pulling her feet out of the water enough to have the razor-mouthed creatures giving up and turning at the arrival of the second intruder.

Rolling onto her back, coughing up mouthfuls of blood and water, Whisper watched with both satisfaction and horror as Tall Bear rose from the water, eager to complete his mission. His expression changed to panic when he felt the first bite. Before he could take a step, his blood coated the surface of the water and he collapsed, gasping for help. His arms flailed, sending black water splashing, but it was over in only moments and soon Whisper was alone in her sanctuary.

A second ambush, and one that had injured her severely. She couldn't be killed, it was true, but she could be hurt, and it would take time to heal. But more than that, if she was weak enough then others could do to her what she had threatened to Splinter Foot Girl—tear her apart and force her soul to wander restlessly without a body as its host.

If she used up too much of her power at once, too much of her energy, her enemies would strike and tear down what she valued most—the Land of the Dead.

She had to get back to the Fire Tower and make that show of strength, let Creator see that he had lost this battle. But when she tried to rise, the pain in her stomach clenched down in a jagged bite that sucked the breath out of her. She collapsed back on the hard stone, breathing heavily, one hand covering the knife wound while blood slowly pumped from the lesion. She vaguely felt bites on her legs from her entry into *Owenvsv*, but they were trivial to the fact that her fingers were starting to tingle and a black haze was clouding her vision.

How had she gotten to this point?

Before she could figure out what had happened, how Splinter Foot Girl and her men got past her guards, Whisper heard scratching on the stone. She turned her head slowly, half in a daze, mouth parting in a rare show of shock and confusion. Slowly, painfully, she lifted herself to her elbows and watched as the first gray-scaled fish heaved itself out of the water.

Then the others followed, one toothed beast after the other, crawling from the murky waters on shaky legs that ended in four webbed toes, jaws snapping as they circled around Whisper, already tasting the scent of fresh blood in the air. Some of them gasped in the new air, others dragged scaly stomachs on the stone, leaving behind thick, mucus-like trails in their wake. They watched her curiously, ravenously, beady gray eyes glinting and long narrow teeth clicking together eagerly.

Whisper eyed the creatures back, still half on her back, covered in blood and smudged with mud. Part of her was filled with the slightest twinges of fear, the other was amused at Creator's last little gift to her. First Blue Corn Maiden, then Splinter Foot Girl. Now, he had forced evolution on creatures belonging in the Land of the Dead so that they could feast on her flesh.

"You will not have me," she whispered, reaching for her knife. As soon as she moved, they launched into attack.

Pure will and spite brought Whisper to her feet, kicking and stomping as she lashed out with the blade. Her arrows were gone, but she still had her knife and hands, and that was all she needed. She felt the bites on her ankles, another on her shoulder, and she screamed in rage as she slammed her back against the stone wall, flattening the fish between her body and rock. But still more came from the water, and she was draining fast. When dozens upon dozens of beasts cornered her at the wall, racing toward her in a skittering mass and leaping as high as their new legs would allow, Whisper reached up and yanked the golden feather from her wet, dirt-caked hair. She held it just before her, breathing in shuddering breaths. Use it when needed most, Sun Woman had said.

Channeling what power she had left, Whisper conjured up a fire in the palm of her hand and the feather burst into flames, searing the surface of her eyes in a flash of pain.

Seconds later, she disappeared.

Chapter 35

As he returned to his brothers in the Forgotten Lands, Dark Water couldn't shake the guilt in leaving Whisper behind. With each step he felt the weight of his decision pushing down on his shoulders, his mind racing with horrible images of what might be happening.

But he wouldn't let himself turn around. The half-breed had to know that she couldn't treat people in such a way, dangling their greatest desires right in front of them only to snatch it all away in the end. He could have blamed himself for allowing her to deceive him, but that wouldn't change the truth that she was a deceiver, a merciless dictator.

And he wanted her for himself.

Dark Water craved the feel of that power, yearned for her touch, to know what it was like to have those black eyes locked on his and searching every part of his soul. He wanted to grab hold of her long, thick hair, taste every part of her, make her want more.

Before he could have everything he wanted, she had to respect him, and the only way he could demand that respect was by refusing his service. She would come to understand what she had done, and would suffer the consequences for it. After that, Dark Water was convinced she would return to him.

It was only a matter of time.

* * *

Splinter Foot Girl faced the Great Spirit with her head hung low, hands gripping one another tightly. "I apologize, Great Spirit. I have failed you. I did not destroy the half-breed." She wiped at a tear, hating this feeling of failure, then frowned when she felt the gentle hand on her chin tip her head up until she was looking into his eyes.

"You did not fail me, Splinter Foot Girl," Creator said softly, offering her a smile. "This battle was not meant to destroy her. The half-breed cannot be destroyed, only weakened. I was able to keep the council members from passing into their second deaths for one last fight, and they did the Spirit World proud by fighting to their last breaths. The half-breed is weak, and the Land of the Dead is vulnerable. Can you not feel it?"

Taking a moment to reflect, Splinter Foot Girl realized that she could, in fact, feel a change in the air. It was slight, but it was there nonetheless, a sense of foreboding and fear, a taste of blood on the breeze. "So what happens now?"

"Now," the Great Spirit put an arm around the young woman, leading her to a window, where they looked out over the land lit with the fires of a thousand torches, "we gather our forces, and prepare to make the Land of the Dead our own. We use our influence to weaken the minds of the people, until they see the half-breed as their enemy, not their leader."

As they discussed plans for their next battle, working on ways they would improve the Land of the Dead and help the child make it a place of her own, with Splinter Foot Girl by her side to be that helpful counselor and confidant, their voices traveled down the corridor and into Smoke Speaker's room.

The last remaining member of the Circle, the Elder had earned the Great Spirit's trust and was determined to remain loyal to the one who believed in him most. He had told Creator everything he could remember about the Land of the Dead and about his granddaughter, and his spies had told him the rest, including details about the place the half-breed called sanctuary. The Great Spirit said Whisper had declared this war, Whisper had brought his wrath upon her and her land, Whisper must face the consequences of her actions. Her refusal to submit and her determination to continue this fight only proved that she was not ready to rule, and that the Land of the Dead needed to be in the hands of one chosen by Creator himself.

While Smoke Speaker couldn't help but feel that the Great Spirit was right, that Whisper was not ready to rule in many regards and had brought the battle upon herself, he nonetheless ached for her. He missed those days living with her in Howling Vines, watching her grow from a beautiful child into a strong, fearless woman ready to walk the Red Road set by her ancestors. He missed their long talks at the fire, skinning and cooking their kills together while sharing the stories of their people. And most of all, he missed that feeling of family, and for the first time wondered if he had made a mistake by forsaking eternity in the Land of the Dead with his daughter and granddaughter for what he had thought to be a higher calling.

A sudden pain in his gut had the Elder gasping and rising to his feet. He clutched at the area with shaky, bony hands, closing his eyes as he searched his thoughts for the source. This was not a pain experienced by his own body, but by the one still connected to him in so many ways.

"*Kanegv*," Smoke Speaker whispered, lowering himself to his knees. He could feel what she felt, that sudden bite of metal, the tearing of flesh and muscle, the pulse of blood pumping from an open wound. She was hurt and she was frightened, and now he could no longer be there to see her through the darkest of times.

But there was one thing he could do, one thing he would do not for the half-breed, but for his granddaughter.

Crawling to the middle of the floor, the Elder built a fire. He allowed the flames a moment to burn, then added a special sage that grew only in the Spirit World. White smoke poured from the fire, and in those smoky strands, he reached out to the one spirit who would never forgive him for his betrayal.

* * *

Sun Woman brought him to that place where forgotten spirits reside, where only memories of what once was and what could be again lived. He resisted the entire way, making talk of the love he left behind and the child he would never have the chance to meet. She let him talk, let him grieve over the loss of life and come to terms with the fact that he would never see them again, even if he was yet to accept it. It didn't matter to her how much he needed to talk about them, as it was only a matter of time before those memories were lost.

As she expected, by the time they arrived, Cole Daivya was almost gone, and rising in his place was another she was yet to identify. Soon she would know who was stronger, the lost brother of the Little Men, or the son once accepted by the Raven-Eater.

Together, they entered the forest clearing to the sound of beating drums and the sight of a blazing orange fire. The dance still continued, the same dance Whisper had witnessed, and once they were in sight of the people Sun Woman took a step back and left the rest to Cole. She saw her daughter on the other side of the fire, twisting and turning on the arm of another man. Her breath hitched in her throat at the vision, eyes watering when her daughter's beautiful face came into view. It had been so long since she had seen that wonderful face, so soft in the firelight, so young and innocent. Sun Woman hadn't seen her daughter since her death, as she could not enter this place of memory without the one person who could bring her back.

Second Son had been the first to see her daughter dancing at the fire before his brothers, the first to fall in love with the face that lit up the sky. Second Son had been the one to open the box and allow her daughter to escape in the form of a redbird, unable to bear her distressed pleas. And he had run after her desperately, trying to get her back both for Sun Woman and for himself. Now, only Second Son could recognize that face as the one meant for him and speak her true name to let her daughter know this man was safe, this man meant home.

Second Son's spirit resided in the body of Cole Daivya, whether the man knew it or not. The second born of the Little Men had sought this body in the Land of the Living in order to have that second chance with Sun Woman's daughter, waiting for the day he would be summoned again for this very purpose. He had been dormant within Cole while in the living body, but now he could rise to the surface to greet the woman he loved. Sun Woman assumed Cole to be Fighting Fox when he first crossed over the Bridge of the Dead, but now it was clear that the Raven-Eater's accepted son was nowhere near as powerful as the lost brother of the Little Men.

Sun Woman watched as Cole's mind slowly began to slip away, and knew the very moment when Second Son took his place.

The fire dancers moved in unison from one side of the hearth to the other, and the man formerly known as Cole took a step forward when the woman came into sight. She was beautiful, tumbling black hair accented with braids and blue feathers, a softly defined face, full mouth set in a gentle smile, and dark chocolate eyes framed by thick lashes. She moved gracefully, interlocking her arms with the other men, feet kicking up hot dirt as she danced. All around her, men and women beat their hands against buckskin drums, their own feet bouncing to the sound of the music.

"Blue Cloud."

The name was whispered, but she heard it as clearly as though the words were spoken directly into her ear. Sun Woman's daughter stopped dancing, a single solitary figure in a midst of writhing, moving bodies, and looked around to see who had called her name.

As the figures danced around her, swirling in a blur of color, the curtain of bodies parted just enough so she could see the man waiting for her. Slowly, she stepped out of the circle, a strange sensation passing through her. It had been so long since she hadn't danced that it felt wrong to keep her feet placed firmly on the ground. But there she stood as she took in the sight, a man with bright blue eyes, sandy blonde hair, and a strong build. She didn't know his face, but he knew her name, and the way he said it...

Then she took a closer look, and recognized the spirit in front of her. The eyes and hair were different, but the facial structure, the body, the stance, even the big, rough hands, they all belonged to one person, the man she had seen for only the briefest of moments when she escaped what she had perceived to be her makeshift prison. That brief moment had been all she needed, though, to know that in her escape she was leaving behind the man she was meant to be with forever.

"Second Son."

The moment she said his name, it felt as though the weight of the world lifted off her shoulders. She looked behind her and no longer felt the longing to be part of the dance, no longer craved the warmth of the fire. When the man reached out, she took his hand, and he led her away from the clearing.

A woman was waiting for them at the edge, a striking figure with tears glistening in her eyes. Her hands were clutched at her waist, but she opened her arms when she saw the pair.

"Blue Cloud."

"Mother."

Mother and daughter embraced, bridging what seemed like an eternity of being apart. Forever could have passed without them noticing, but it was only moments before they released one another.

Sun Woman dabbed at her eyes gracefully, then looked at the man before her, noting that nearly all traces of Cole Daivya were gone. "I would like to ask that you stay with Blue Cloud, and with me. I have many great plans for our people, and as my daughter's husband you are promised a place of high standing." She smiled even when Second Son frowned, taken aback by her strange offer. "Whatever you choose, Second Son, know that you have fulfilled your oath to me. You and your brothers are free."

Chapter 36

She parted ways with them happily, peace filling her being. Her daughter was back, in the arms of the one who would love her for all of eternity, and they had all the time in the realm to be with one another. Sun Woman would give them this time to be together, to let her daughter adjust to existence outside of that place of memory, and then the pair would return to her to complete the vision she had for them all.

Before she entered the Sky Vault, Sun Woman felt the intruding presence. She had sensed the disturbance earlier, but was so involved with Second Son and Blue Cloud that she disregarded the feeling. But now there was no mistaking that creeping sensation up her spine, that scent of blood mixed with dirt and smoke.

The half-breed was in the Sky Vault, and she was injured.

Sun Woman quickened her pace and reentered her realm to find Whisper lying just outside her longhouse, hands clutching her stomach. Rivers of black pooled around her, soaking the soft earth.

"*Kanegv*," Sun Woman whispered, kneeling down at the woman's side. "What has happened?"

Whisper opened her eyes, eyes that were red and raw, focusing on Sun Woman with such intensity that the other spirit nearly drew back in fear. "Creator," she answered, her voice weak. "Ambush...attack at...sanctuary."

Sun Woman understood the message clearly enough. The half-breed was all-powerful, but she was also young and yet to realize her full potential. Until she knew and accepted all that she could do, she was vulnerable to surprise attacks and even injury. And the Great Spirit knew that just as well as Sun Woman did.

While she didn't trust the ruler of the Land of the Dead and would not invite her to her home for a simple meal and chat, Sun Woman nonetheless felt indebted to Whisper and would help this one time. "Come, child." She gently moved Whisper inside her hut, placing her on a pile of straw mats and covering her to the waist with a warm blanket.

First she gently touched the flesh at Whisper's temples, which was blistered and already starting to peel. Her eyes were burned as well, which told Sun Woman that the girl must have sent her call for help in a moment of panic, not bothering to distance her face from the flames. The eyes would heal, as she could clearly see that they were already reconstructing the parts destroyed by fire, so Sun Woman didn't need to exert any energy on her face.

Then she pried Whisper's hands away from the wound.

"*Unelanvhi,*" she prayed to the Sky Vault's Creator, staring down at the injury. It was clean, but it went straight through. It needed to be healed fast, and there was only one way to do it. "*Kanegv,*" she said again, putting a hand to the woman's forehead. "I must warn you. I need to cauterize this wound, and it will be painful."

"Do...do what you must," Whisper wheezed out, blood dripping from the corner of her mouth. She squeezed her eyes shut, then bit down hard on the thick wad of buckskin Sun Woman placed between her teeth.

Balancing herself, centering her souls, Sun Woman kneeled at the bed and placed her hands over the wound. She closed her eyes, feeling the heat of the blood on her skin, the pulse of the woman's spirit shuddering between realms. Closing her eyes and whispering a chant, Sun Woman let the power flow through her.

Whisper bit down harder when the first wave of warmth coursed through her, then curled her hands into fists when that warmth turned into burning heat. Her fingers gripped the straw, piercing the makeshift mattress as she struggled against the fiery pain. A guttural, animal sound escaped from deep in her throat and her back arched up against Sun Woman's hands, but the older spirit held her down without breaking the chant.

Smoke and steam hissed up from the wound, and as an orange glow began to light from beneath Sun Woman's fingers, the skin around the lesion turned black and closed over itself. Whisper felt the fire stab through her stomach, grabbing hold of the bloody bits of torn flesh and searing them shut. She couldn't concentrate on anything but the pain, her throat raw from struggling to hold back the howls of agony, her hands aching from their tight grip on the straw and blanket.

When the wound was fully closed, Sun Woman leaned back, fatigued by the effort. Whisper had collapsed back on the bed, also exhausted. The sun spirit brushed back the hair from Whisper's eyes, then murmured to her in a soft, soothing voice.

"Sleep, child. Your body must heal. You are safe here."

Trusting that voice, knowing it was true, Whisper allowed herself the time her body needed to regenerate.

Her body was weak, but her spirit was strong. Sometime between healing and rest, Whisper felt herself detach from that which held her grounded. She was weightless, free, not at all constrained by the physical boundaries of the body.

And yet, she found herself staring down at her pale, lifeless self, angered by the fact that she was so weak. The body had too many limitations, while this spirit held so much power. It would take many more moons for the body to catch up, and she was impatient. Only in time would she come to realize and fully grasp everything she was capable of, and until that time, she was forced to exist with limits.

"*Ulisi ageyutsa.*"

The word startled her from her thoughts, and she looked away from her resting body to find the man who matched the voice. Only one person would call her that, only one man would dare to give her the title of Granddaughter. She saw him sitting at the hearth, a shadowy, misty apparition that could only be formed by exerting an intense amount of energy.

"*Galonuhesgi,*" she replied.

Smoke Speaker sighed, saddened at being considered a traitor. His granddaughter would never forgive him, but he had hoped this meeting would leave them at peace with one another. "I did not come to fight with you, *Kanegv.*"

"Then why are you here?"

"Because you are injured. Because I miss what we had together. And because despite everything, I still love and care about you."

Whisper hesitated, unsure. She believed his earnestness, but that didn't erase his betrayal. Still, the Elder had raised her, taken her from the Land of the Dead as a child and protected her, trained her until the day she was ready to rule. For that, and because he was likely risking his place in the Spirit World to speak with her, she would listen to what he had to say.

She sat across the fire from him, staring through the gray smoke at him. "What do you want?"

"To apologize," Smoke Speaker answered, clasping his hands together. "I have failed you, *Kanegv,* in many ways. I spent so much time in your youth trying to destroy every trace of the Raven-Eater in your blood that I never taught you how to use what gifts you did have. I thought you were ready to lead the Land of the Dead, but I see now that I should have told you who and what you were sooner, taught you to use your gifts more before your death. You never belonged with me, or in Howling Vines, but your mother and I did what we had to do to keep you safe. I was selfish in your training, and for that I am sorry."

Whisper felt a strange sense of regret somewhere deep inside her, a feeling she wasn't used to. "You did what you thought best," she said, her voice soft, training her eyes on the fire. "No one could have known what traces of the Raven-Eater were in me, or what would happen after my death."

"I should have known," Smoke Speaker insisted. "I knew what the Raven-Eater was capable of, and should have predicted his bloodline would have burned out our own. I supposed I wanted you to enjoy what time you had in the Land of the Living."

"I did."

"Perhaps…and yet I still did not prepare you to fight your greatest enemy."

Whisper nearly rolled her eyes, but stopped herself. This one time she would show the Elder the respect she wasn't sure he deserved. "I will accept your apology for your regrets, Smoke Speaker. But it does not change the fact that you broke your word, and left your family for the Spirit World. I do not need your explanation," she cut him off when he started to defend his reasoning.

"…Perhaps it was an oversight on my part," he said after a few moments. "I did not think you would have taken it so personally. I never thought you would care as much as you did."

"Because I come from the Raven-Eater? Because a child born of evil is unable to love?"

The word *love* threw him off. "I…I never said you could not love, *Kanegv*. But tell me, did you want me back because you feel love for me, because you feel it is the human thing to do, or because you were angry at Creator, or at me?"

She took a moment to respond in order to reign in her anger. She didn't want this meeting to be one of hate. "Smoke Speaker…even the half-breed can feel loyalty, and be hurt by betrayal." The look on the Elder's face of surprise had her huffing, insulted. "What does it matter, Smoke Speaker? We all must face the consequences of our decisions."

"As you have." Smoke Speaker gestured to the hut, where her sleeping body lay. "How much longer must this war go on?"

"Until my demands have been met."

"Are your desires more important than the well-being of all the dead in both spirit realms?" When Whisper didn't answer, but merely stared through the smoke with those deeply black eyes, the Elder sighed again and lifted a hand. "As I said, I did not come to argue. I came to apologize, and to see you. I also wanted to tell you a story, one I never got to tell you during your training, and I hope you will allow me to speak it now."

Whisper shifted, but didn't respond. The Elder took her silence as permission to speak. "As you know, in the beginning, Man lived in the Sky Vault, and only when the Great Buzzard made land for our people did he moved down to the earth. But it was not until later that Man discovered how and why he came to be."

"A tale of water to wine?" Whisper asked sarcastically.

Smoke Speaker ignored the dig. "One day, Man was walking with Woman and came upon a lodge. An old woman greeted them, calling herself Basket Woman, Mother of the Stars. She invited Man and Woman inside, and introduced them to her guests, Wind, Cloud, Lightning, and Thunder, as well as her many beautiful daughters. Her daughters taught Man and Woman the sacred dances of their people, then the sacred ceremonies that we have come to know today.

"But it was Evening Star, who dances to the Western Sun, who brought them the basket of the moon. Made of the earth, the basket represented our sacred directions and carried the gifts that would help Man and Woman when they returned to their people. Basket Woman then showed them a game, planting seeds that represented the moon and using thirteen sticks as counters, as thirteen is a sacred number." Whisper was aware of that, but managed not to respond with disdain as the Elder continued.

"When they had learned everything they needed to teach their people, Basket Woman and her guests returned back to their homes, leaving Man and Woman to continue their legacy." Finishing his story, Smoke Speaker sat back and waited for his words to register with his granddaughter.

It was a far different version from the creation story of their own people, and Whisper suspected it was one from another tribe told for the Elder's own purpose. "And what is the lesson you hope for me to learn, Elder?"

"First Man and Woman were given the gifts of our people for a reason, *Kanegv*. They were to teach us how to live in harmony with the earth, and how to carry on the traditions of our heritage. We are nothing without the ways of our ancestors." He leaned forward then, intensity spread across his wavering face. He was getting weak, and needed to give Whisper this one last message.

"You must walk the Red Road, *Kanegv*," he said urgently. "You must remember who you are, and why you fought for your place in the Land of the Dead. You must heed your training, or else everything we have worked toward is for nothing. Do not let hate and anger blind you from yourself. Do not let the Raven-Eater win."

Whisper started to respond, but just as she opened her mouth Smoke Speaker's image flickered. Within seconds he was gone, wisps of gray joining the fire's smoke that drifted up in the clouds.

Chapter 37

Second Son returned to his brothers with excitement in his heart. He hadn't seen them since the day of their exile into the Forgotten Lands, since he decided he could not live in that place of darkness and wanted the chance to be reborn. And now he was back, with the woman he loved at his side. They were destined to be together, and would follow one another to the ends of the Spirit World, the Land of the Dead, or wherever else the Red Road brought them.

As they walked through the Forgotten Lands, Second Son noticed the changes with each step. The air was lighter, didn't taste like death and despair. The trees even seemed to respond, wilted leaves lifting, branches not as saggy, starting to reach up to the sky as dark clouds began to part. The forest was coming back to life the closer they got to the clearing.

When they reached the Little Men's home, Second Son stepped across the barrier happily, Blue Cloud holding onto his arm. It was just as he'd remembered it from his one day in exile. Nothing had changed, and he hadn't expected it too. His brothers were creatures of habit.

He stopped in the center of the clearing, waiting. It wasn't long before the huts rustled and six small figures stepped out carrying war weapons. They grew to their full height and stalked forward, causing Blue Cloud to hide behind the man who was to become her husband.

Dark Water took the lead, narrowing his eyes at the intruder and wondering who would dare to enter the Forgotten Lands. There was something familiar about this stranger though, enough that he stopped short and took in the face.

"Second Son," he whispered, recognizing his brother in the body of Cole Daivya. He looked different since the time he walked across the Bridge of the Dead. His hair had grown to his shoulders already and his blue eyes were the color of the earth. His shoulders were broader as well, the skin at least two shades darker. This was not Cole, not Fighting Fox, but the second coming of his once-lost brother.

"Second Son," Dark Water said again, lowering his weapon and grabbing the man into a hug. "It has been too long."

Second Son accepted the embrace, welcoming his brothers as they gathered around him. He answered their questions, introduced them to Blue Cloud, and shared with them some of his adventures hopping from body to body in the Land of the Living. The more they talked around the bright, blazing fire, the more the Forgotten Lands transformed, and soon the clearing was a lush landscape filled with the scents of flowers and the sounds of chirping birds.

"It was Sun Woman," he said in response to his brothers' baffled expressions as they looked around them. "All she ever wanted was her daughter returned to her. Now Blue Cloud is safe, and so she has lifted the curse. We are free, my brothers."

Free. It was a word Dark Water never thought would be his own. He had trouble believing it even now, but the more he took in his home, the more he realized that his lost brother spoke the truth. There was no trapping sensation binding him to the Forgotten Lands, and the forest opened up new pathways leading them to new homes among their people.

The half-breed had kept her word, he thought with some amusement, in her own way. It hadn't happened the way he'd envisioned, but Second Son was back, and they were free. Which meant, he concluded, that he had turned his back on Whisper in the one moment when his loyalty would have mattered the most. He may be free, but he was still indebted to the half-breed.

"We can start over," Earth Dancer said, dropping his spear. "Move anywhere we desire, away from these forsaken lands."

"Perhaps we should let our lost brother decide where to move our home," Star Seer suggested, and the others agreed. Only Second Son was hesitant.

"My brothers...Sun Woman has given us the freedom to live where we wish, it is true. And...and I have chosen to live in the Sky Vault with Blue Cloud. It is where we belong," he said quickly when they began to protest.

Dark Water stepped forward. "This is Sun Woman's doing," he snapped, pointing at Blue Cloud. "She has clouded your mind, taken advantage of your bond to her daughter."

"No, brother. My heart has always been with Blue Cloud. I wish to be with her. It is why I chose to be reborn." He frowned sympathetically when Dark Water threw his arms out to his sides in frustration. His fear at losing his brother yet again was written clearly across his face. "Brother, you too can go and find the one who calls to your heart...Perhaps, the half-breed."

It was said quietly so that only he could hear, but at the name, Dark Water's eyes widened. How the man could see down to his very core he did not know, but it shook him, especially since he didn't want the others aware of his affections. Challenging his brother could lead to just that.

Nodding and swallowing hard, he stepped back. "Very well, brother. You are free just as we are. Today begins a new day for us all."

As they began discussing what their new lives would behold, and where freedom would take them in the Land of the Dead, Dark Water reflected on his brother's words. Yes, there was one who called to his heart, one place meant for him to spend his eternity. The only problem was that in order to get it, he would have to take the place of the one who called himself the half-breed's mate.

* * *

Waking slowly, Whisper was momentarily confused and disoriented by her surroundings. It was bright, a harsh light glaring into her black eyes that were so used to darkness and shadows. She felt as though a spotlight had been turned on only inches from her face, blinding her from the truth of where she lay. Then she tried to sit up and the pain in her stomach made her falter and wince, and she suddenly remembered what had happened.

They invaded as an enemy militia in the night, creeping into her land with a stealth she would not have imagined possible. It angered her to know they had gotten past her defenses, and even more so to accept that one of them, Tall Bear, had succeeded in bringing her down. If she'd been more prepared, if she'd allowed herself to give in to the power her body craved, let her body take in the gifts granted to her by her bloodline, then it could have been avoided.

Her sigh was tinged with pain when she rose from the straw bed, holding a hand to her stomach. Her eyes, damaged by the sudden blaze of the golden feather, began to adjust to the light, rebuilding their strong, thick filters that allowed her to see all as she looked down. Her top was nearly destroyed, torn to pieces up to her chest and coated with dried blood. There was no bottom, as it had been ripped off to get to the wound, which, she noticed, was a foul black color with crusted, charred edges. She felt her lip curl back in disgust as she lightly ran her fingers over the burned flesh.

"It was that, or bleed to your second death," a voice said from the doorway of the small hut. Whisper looked up, startled to see Sun Woman standing in the frame, silhouetted by her own light.

"I cannot die a second death."

"Perhaps, but you can be weakened enough that others may think you have, and decide to take over your land." Sun Woman entered, setting fresh clothes on the foot of the bed. "I attempted to remove your clothing, but you fought me even in your sleep. I did not wish to combat against the half-breed."

Whisper heard amusement mixed with sarcasm, and ignored it. "How long have I been here?"

"I have risen and fallen seven times in the Land of the Dead," the sun spirit answered. "You arrived some time before me with the golden feather, I do not know when. I was away, with Second Son."

Whisper looked up at the name. "So he has returned. And your daughter?"

Sun Woman smiled brightly. "She has returned as well, and has gone to meet Second Son's brothers in the Forgotten Lands. They will return soon. You held up your end of the bargain, and so have I. Consider this a gesture of my appreciation for all you have done."

"But we are still not allies."

"Nor are we enemies," Sun Woman agreed. Then she watched as Whisper inspected her wounds. Her stomach was covered with cauterized flesh, and the black seemed to eerily blend in with the inkings swirling from her ribcage. Her face showed only a few shallow lacerations across the cheekbone and chin in addition to the burns around her eyes, but her legs still were healing from the gouges taken out by the creatures at her sanctuary.

Not shy in her wounded state, Whisper stripped off her destroyed, blood-soaked clothing and turned to grab the new set. When she did, Sun Woman saw the tattoos spread across her back, and nearly gasped in wonder. She'd heard stories of those markings, how they depicted a path through the Land of the Dead, how they pulsed with activity when the half-breed needed to know something about her kingdom. It was a beautiful map, an incredible representation of one woman's dedication to follow her destiny.

The tattoo, if it could be considered that, seemed to shift and alter itself, and yet never move at all. Sun Woman saw the symbol of the sky lit up with a dark red outline, and what she guessed to be the Fire Tower faded and shadowed. But then, within seconds the image returned to its original state and she was left wondering if she'd even seen anything else at all.

"You are the true heir," Sun Woman found herself saying. Whisper turned slowly, wrapping a piece of buckskin around a cut on her wrist. Her expression was quizzical. "The Land of the Dead…your markings…it is true what they say."

"What do they say?"

"That only you can truly lead the realm of the forgotten dead. That you and the Land of the Dead are one, and cannot be parted."

It was something she had known since she was a child, but it flattered her to have the spirit of the sun confirm what her grandfather always said. "Perhaps you should send that message to Creator. He seems to have forgotten who rules the Land of the Dead, and believes it belongs to him."

"*Kanegv*." A motherly tone crept into Sun Woman's voice. "You take this matter far too personally. The child was never about you." That familiar darkness crept back into her eyes, but Sun Woman held her ground.

"Not about me?" Whisper repeated, finishing her wound dressage and lightly touching her temples. She held back a wince when her fingers grazed against tender flesh. "Creator wishes for the child to replace me, yet it is not about me?"

"Creator has been searching for a ruler to lead the Land of the Dead long before you took the Fire Tower, and long before the Raven-Eater assumed authority." It was time for Whisper to hear the truth about her war, regardless of the consequences. "But it is not as simple as choosing any child from the Land of the Living. The child must be one born of our bloodline, the bloodline of the Great Spirit. Even you come from him, *Kanegv*, as do I. As does your grandfather. The reign of the Raven-Eater complicated matters. He soiled the Land of the Dead, made it a dark place. And so only a child born of his blood could restore it back to what it once was."

"I *am* born of his blood. As you just said."

"But you are the half-breed." Sun Woman shifted when Whisper huffed and stalked out of the hut. She began to circle the fire slowly, but still she listened. "You were born of two equal halves, with a stake in both the living and dead realms. The Great Spirit needs a child born only of life, for only a child of the light can see the Land of the Dead for what it could be."

Whisper let the words sink in. It was true, she had never known the Land of the Dead before her father's reign. And it was true, she was not born entirely of the light. But she was insulted by the suggestion that she could not rule her land in a way fit for the Great Spirit or any other. "And Creator believes that a child born of the boy could rule my land better?"

"The boy," Sun Woman repeated. Whisper had spoken the words with such contempt that the spirit believed she had nearly gotten down to the root of the true problem. "The boy has a name."

"The boy does not deserve a name."

"Is this what fuels your war, *Kanegv*?" Sun Woman asked, genuinely curious. She prided herself on knowing all about both the living and spirit realms, but the half-breed baffled her. "The Raven-Eater never accepted you, but he did accept the young Cole Daivya as his own, gave him his mark and his former son's name. It is jealousy that fills you with such hate and rage?"

Now she was irritated, and the anger that filled her helped take away some of the pain in her gut. Whisper felt herself restoring, as though accepting her true identity gave her body the strength it needed to be whole again. "Jealousy? I do not even know the boy, and I have never desired to sit at the Raven-Eater's hearth."

"Then why can you not call him by his name?"

"He does not *deserve* his name!" Whisper shouted, throwing out an arm. In the distance, thunder rolled, causing Sun Woman to take a step back. Never before had another creature or spirit been able to establish any kind of control in the Sky Vault. It was her realm, not to be broken by another. She held up a hand in peace, but Whisper wasn't finished.

"The boy was stolen from his life, and I will admit that his death was unjust. But I died so that he could live. I walked the path destiny set before me, and gave up what life I had in the Land of the Living for him, for his family, and for the sake of the Land of the Dead. The boy was granted a new life here, and a name. Then he left, and he forgot what was given to him. He turned his back on his name, on what was once his. He never allowed himself to look past the visions that haunted him at night to see what could have been. No, Sun Woman, the boy is not worthy of a name."

"Then what of the girl? His child? Does the child of the unworthy deserve a name, or a place in the Land of the Dead?"

"The child is untainted. She could be granted everything. But I will not allow Creator to take away what I died and fought for."

They stood facing one another silently for awhile, Sun Woman giving Whisper a chance to calm down and Whisper gathering her strength while refusing to admit to the burning in her stomach. Finally Sun Woman took a seat on an ornately carved chair and folded her hands in her lap.

"What do you want, *Kanegv*? What do you hope to accomplish with this war? You cannot destroy the Great Spirit, and he cannot destroy you. All you can do is weaken one another, and meanwhile, all dead souls must suffer for it."

"He took Smoke Speaker from me."

"The Elder chose to go, and chose to stay."

"He plans to replace me in the Land of the Dead."

That one she could not argue. All she could do was offer insight. "*Kanegv*, the Great Spirit is not your enemy. You and Creator will always stand on opposite sides of the battlefield. It is your very nature. You are not enemies, but leaders of opposing armies. It is neither right nor wrong, but is simply what must be. You must find a way to be at peace with one another."

She wanted to be furious, she wanted to destroy Sun Woman. But, she also knew deep down that the sky spirit was right. And it interested her, being counseled by the spirit who had her own plans of war, however close to the chest she thought those plans may be. Whisper knew what Sun Woman wanted, as she had spies everywhere who knew how to obtain information in the most discreet and dishonest of ways, and what she desired made her no better than the half-breed.

"I must go," Whisper said suddenly, walking back to the hut and grabbing her weapons. She secured the belt at her waist. "I thank you for your hospitality, and you will be rewarded, ruler of the Sky Vault."

Before Sun Woman could protest, Whisper stepped into the center of the hearth and vanished back to her land, leaving the spirit sitting in shock at the cunning delivery of a title she had not yet earned.

Chapter 38

Brave Woman stood guard at the top of the Fire Tower, hands clasped behind her back as she stared out at the vast land before her. It was quite a view, one she had never seen before. Back during her living times, she had lived on open stretches of land sometimes broken up by deep craters in the earth. She had never known mountains or caverns, or hilly plains spotted with villages.

All seemed at peace eight days after the Great Spirit's attack. Blue Corn Maiden and Splinter Foot Girl had retreated, the snow was gone, the air was warm, the morning sun was rising. And yet, something was wrong.

No one had seen Whisper since the attack. Eagle brought Hunting Hawk to *Owenvsv*, but all the War Chief found there were scraps of tattered clothing and gnawed bones, angry evolved creatures, and a lot of dried blood. Now, he was holed up in the Fire Tower with Blue Feather, consoling the mother as she grieved for her lost daughter.

Brave Heart knew better. The half-breed was alive, but she was in hiding. She had been injured and retreated somewhere safe where her enemies couldn't find her. Now it was just a matter of time until she came back. But the Land of the Dead sensed her absence, and responded in kind. The sky was cloudy gray, the tree trunks wilted, even the villagers seemed listless despite the strange interruption in the realm that encouraged celebration. It seemed that with every passing day, the land lost more of the half-breed's scent and self, as though losing its own identity and opening itself up to new influences.

Whisper was connected to this land in more ways than one, and Brave Woman would do what she must to make sure the true heir to the Fire Tower remained in place.

Brave Woman had made a pact with the half-breed, and she was a woman of her word. But more than that, she wanted what was owed to her at the end of this war. She did not consider herself a violent person, and in fact preferred the peace and solitude of a village life away from the battlefield. But Whisper's promise filled her spirit with hope that she could live the life stolen from her by war. Was she willing to fight the Great Spirit for that chance? Was it worth angering her very Creator for the opportunity of love? Brave Woman wasn't sure, but she knew she had to try. The thought of Little Eagle returning to her had overcome her senses, and she longed to be in his arms.

She turned when the door to the rooftop opened behind her, brow furrowing when she saw the man who stepped out. "Why have you returned?"

Dark Water stopped short. He'd heard of Brave Woman Counts Coup, a spirit who defied the odds and become one of the most renowned warriors of her people. Now she was staring at him suspiciously, as though he'd done something wrong. "I have come to fight for the half-breed," he answered.

"How did you get in the Fire Tower?"

He smirked at that. "I am one of the Little Men. I go where I please in the form I so choose."

"Does Hunting Hawk know that you are here?"

"He does now."

Both spirits spun around to see Hunting Hawk at the doorway, thick arms crossed. He was glaring at Dark Water with hate in his dark eyes. "You have no place here, Dark Water. You walked away from the battlefield."

"And now I have returned. *Kanegv* held up her word, and so I will uphold mine. The Little Men will fight with her, as we fought with Sun Woman." Then he looked around and noticed the missing figure. "Where is she?"

Hunting Hawk sighed and unfolded his arms. A Little Men brother was not to be trusted, but the man had already proved himself more than once. "She has been missing since the attack. We do not know what happened to her."

Before Dark Water could respond, a sharp cry pierced in the distance. They trio ran to the edge of the Fire Tower to see Eagle flying straight for them, and on his back was a tired and irritated-looking Whisper. They were silent when she landed, feet connecting solidly with the stone, but Hunting Hawk stepped forward when she winced upon impact and stumbled slightly.

"You are injured." He grabbed for her, but she brushed him off while scanning the rooftop and taking in her visitors.

"Sun Woman healed me. I am fine." Whisper allowed him to examine the wound, and to take her face in his hands as he inspected her tender eyes, but not to help her walk. She looked first at Brave Woman, nodding her approval, then glared at Dark Water. "What do you want?"

"Only to pledge my loyalty."

Whisper scoffed, sarcasm in the sound. She returned her stare to Brave Woman and lifted a brow as though incredulous over his words. "Dispose of him."

Dark Water jerked at that, holding up a hand. "You need me for this war, half-breed."

She turned slowly, bracing herself against Hunting Hawk. "What war?"

Hunting Hawk led his ruler and wife to their chambers, guiding her by the elbow. They had left Brave Woman and Dark Water on the roof, staring with shock in their eyes at Whisper's parting retort. Neither spoke as they retreated to their private quarters, feet echoing hollowly off the stone walls. Hunting Hawk stood back while Whisper stripped off the shirt given to her by Sun Woman and inspected her wound in a pane of glass. He noted the other lacerations on her arms and shoulders, and wondered if there were any on her legs as well. She would always have a scar on her gut, one that told of the great war between spirit worlds, but he silently hoped her face would heal completely. The redness and peeling flesh that surrounded her eyes was hard to stomach, and infuriated him even after she revealed that she was to blame for lighting the golden feather. Seeing Whisper in pain was not something Hunting Hawk could easily get over.

"I went to *Owenvsv*," he said quietly, looking at the floor and studying the cracks in the stone. "I found the bones of a man, and the blood of a woman...You were missing."

"I was forced to escape. Sun Woman cared for me."

"And you could not send a message?"

"I was not conscious, Hunting Hawk," Whisper snapped, pulling a decorated shawl over her shoulders. "It is of no concern—" she stopped, seeing the worry spread across his face when he lifted his head to meet her gaze. In his eyes she saw love and fear, not anger or annoyance.

He had been worried about her, she realized, terrified that she would never return. His concern touched her, bringing forth emotions that were both unfamiliar and welcomed. Guided by some strange sense of wonder, Whisper swallowed her words and instead walked over to Hunting Hawk and didn't resist when he lifted a hand to her hair. Hunting Hawk took a moment to simply be with her, wrapping his arms around her shoulders and drawing her close, breathing in her scent, memorizing every curve of her body. And for once, she let him do just that.

He'd thought he lost her. Despite how much he believed in his mate, his queen, and her strengths, for seven nights he suffered visions of what may have happened to her. Even after eighteen years, Hunting Hawk never realized just how powerful his connection to Whisper was. It was that same connection she was begin-ning to realize as well, his fears reaching the part of her that had once longed for someone to call her own.

"What did you mean, *Kanegv*, about what you said to Dark Water? Have you called off this war?"

At the question, Whisper sighed and turned away, taking a seat on the edge of the bed. Sun Woman's questions and words were burning on her mind, as was Smoke Speaker's visit. She wasn't used to this sense of confusion and hesitance, and resented the spirits who brought upon the feelings.

"What do you believe, Hunting Hawk?" she asked genuinely, wrapping the shawl tighter around herself. "Is it a war worth fighting?"

He thought carefully, sitting down next to her. "It does not matter what I think, *Kanegv*. Your war is my war. I will follow you into battle no matter the cause."

"Why?"

"Because I believe in you, and what you stand for." He shifted so that he was kneeling in front of Whisper. "We are all tasked to walk the Red Road, as your people call it. I may only have been a simple War Chief in my time, but even I understood that we must follow the path set before us. Our paths are connected, *Kanegv*, and where you go, I follow."

She studied him for a long time, a thoughtful expression settled in her nor-mally furious eyes. "I will get what I want. The Red Road does not end in retreat."

"Then tomorrow, we fight." Hunting Hawk smiled and rose. "But tonight, we rest, and thank our ancestors for another night together."

Without protest, Whisper gave in to his request, sending a silent prayer those who would lead her into victory. Tomorrow they would plan their attack, but tonight was just for them.

Chapter 39

The woman once promised to Cole Daivya made the decision to move on, to hold her head up high and take the first step on the path to a new tomorrow. Her heart still ached, her thoughts still drifted back to the days of laughter and joy once shared with the man she would never stop loving, but her baby, their baby, deserved to be brought into a world of happiness. Part of her was angry that Cole had chosen to leave this life of his own free will, but the other refused to believe it. She would hold on to the whispers that said he was taken by a higher power, and not because he wished to leave his future wife and unborn child behind.

Moving on, though, meant getting rid of the things Cole once held closely guarded, sorting through old files and books and gifts that were no longer needed. She enlisted the help of his parents, Ian and Julia, but only Ian was willing to look through and discard the items of his dead son's past.

Ian worked on the garage while she focused on the office. Cole kept the room in almost impeccable order, with all papers categorized and everything in its proper place. For the most part, she knew what to expect from each cabinet and drawer, as she often helped him with the finances and other business aspects when he had taken on part ownership of his father's landscaping company. The only area she rarely went to was the closet, so she started there.

She began by pulling out random pieces of the life that had been collected over the years—beach chairs, serving trays, extra picture frames. Then she took down a few of the boxes that lined the top of the closet. They were topped with a thick layer of dust, causing her to sneeze as she slowly opened the first one. Inside she found a few children's books on dinosaurs that made her smile, old model cars he had put together as a kid, and a box of baseball cards she'd never known he had. Something about the innocence of the box's contents made her tear up, thinking of all the things Cole could have shared with their child, but she brushed the tears aside determinedly and reached for the second box.

The blue baby blanket had the tears forming again, as did the picture of Cole as a boy with his grandfather at what looked like a campsite. Then her hands found a leather-bound journal, and she frowned when removing it from the box, as her late fiancé was not an artist and had never kept any kind of portfolio.

Curious, she untied the hemp strings that bound the leather together and opened the journal to the first page. The portrait of a woman stared back at her, and she found herself completely mesmerized by the image. The woman was young, with eyes so black and deep that they seemed to contain all the life and death the world had ever known. Her hair was blowing in an invisible breeze, and her mouth was set in a hard line that told the story of a long and difficult journey. Everything about her face was hard, she realized, as though the woman was no stranger to trouble and was used to a life filled with burdens forced upon her shoulders.

Turning the page, she saw the woman at a river, head tilted ever so slightly as though listening to something in the distance. Who was this woman, she wondered, a slight surge of jealousy running through her. And why did Cole have drawings of her?

The next image had her frowning again, one of the woman leaning over a much younger Ian, appearing to tend to wounds on his back. They were in a cave or stone shelter of sorts, a fire burning behind them. The more she turned the pages, the more she saw of a journey she could not understand, and then she reached an image of Cole as a child, dressed elegantly in Native American finery.

"I don't understand," she whispered, running her fingers over the picture. Her baby kicked at that moment, startling her out of her thoughts. "Yes, I agree," she said to her stomach. "We need answers."

She found Ian knee-deep in boxes in the corner of the garage. Wordlessly, she handed him the journal.

Ian took the book from the woman he would always consider to be his daughter-in-law. He didn't know what it was, but the first drawing had him sucking in a deep breath that he hoped wasn't too obvious. When he looked up, he saw that apparently it was. "Where did you get this?"

"In a box in the office closet. What are the drawings of? Who is that woman? Why are you injured and why is Cole dressed like that?"

He shook his head at the barrage of questions. "These aren't easy answers. It's better that you forget you saw this."

"Forget?" Her voice was incredulous. "I just want to understand. Cole couldn't draw to save his life, not even landscape plans. So who drew him as a kid, and why? And why are you in the pictures? It's like a sketch for a book or something."

Memories flooded through him, pictures of places he had tried so hard to forget. He closed the book, holding it tightly to his chest. "You don't need to understand everything. Cole had a past, just as you do. It doesn't matter now."

"Doesn't matter?" she repeated, angry now. "For as long as I knew him Cole suffered from terrible nightmares. He was haunted by something but would never tell me what, and I respected his privacy. But if something was truly wrong, then I deserve to know! His *child* deserves to know, if it's something that might affect her!"

"This conversation is over." Ian ended the talk by setting the book down on a box and stalking out of the garage. She watched him leave, not bothering to stop him. When the taillights of his car had disappeared around the corner, she sank down to the garage floor cradling the book. There, she spent the rest of the afternoon studying each picture carefully and wondering what is was that terrified the Daivya family for so many years.

That night, she dreamed of a place that terrified her to the core. In her dream, she awoke in a world of gray surrounded by lost figures with drooping shoulders and dark eyes that never left the ground. Something drove her forward, and she wandered slowly, pushing back dead and thorny branches with one hand while keeping the other on her growing belly for comfort. Overhead, the sky was dark with threatening clouds, while a light breeze carried the smell of rain and loneliness in the air.

Soon she came to a river stretching far beyond what her eyes could see. A hazy mist hung just above the surface, and to her right was a small, rickety raft made for only two. A few feet from that raft sat an old man on the shore, a fire burning in a stone hearth. He was thin and frail, long white hair resting on bony shoulders. He had a thin buckskin shawl wrapped around him, the same material that covered his legs, and his feet were bare. The man looked up when she approached, smiling a welcoming smile and gesturing to the fire.

"Will you join me?" he asked, watching her with those solid, sympathetic eyes until she relented and took a seat across from him. "It has been far too long since I have seen a woman of the living."

"What…what does that mean?" Her voice was nervous, but she fought to keep her expression serious and confident.

The old man smiled again. "Just that you are a fresh sight for these old eyes." He reached out and stoked the fire, sending white embers up into the sky. She watched the smoke as it twisted and tumbled in gray puffs, eyes widening when she thought she saw a face appear, then dissipate just as quickly. She looked again, and there, in the smoke, she saw the silhouette of a woman. The figure was somehow familiar, but frightened her nonetheless for a reason she could not explain.

"She is the one you seek," the old man said quietly, firmly.

She broke herself out of the trance. "She...she who?"

"The woman with the black eyes."

When the man said nothing more, she threw her arms out to the side and shook her head. "What does that even mean?" she asked again. "Who are you, and who is this woman with the black eyes?"

"Seek out the woman with the black eyes. She will have the answers to your questions."

With that, the man waved a hand in the fire, sending a curtain of smoke between them. When it cleared, she opened her eyes to a bright new morning.

Chapter 40

Brave Woman followed her orders and saw Dark Water to the outskirts of the Barren Plains. She didn't say a word as they walked, but knew they were both thinking the same thing. It seemed that the half-breed had called off her war, or was considering it, which worried them both.

For Dark Water, it meant that he had lost his chance to prove himself to Whisper. Before, he had considered their partnership to be nothing more than a business deal. He wanted his brother back, and would do what it took, even if that meant working for the half-breed. As it turned out, that partnership grew to mean something more to him. Now, not only was Second Son back, but they were all free to live out their lives in the way they so choose to do.

He owed Whisper his freedom, and with it, his heart. But the war ending before it even began meant he would never get that chance to prove his worth.

For Brave Woman, it meant her dream of being with Little Eagle was fading from her vision, slipping between her fingers no matter how hard she struggled to hold on. Her bargain was not fulfilled until she fought in the half-breed's war. No war meant she was not needed, and if she was no longer needed, she would be dismissed. And then, she would be alone for the rest of her existence in the Land of the Dead. Having that hope ripped away from her was almost too much to bear. Each step leading Dark Water away from the Fire Tower was another step away from Little Eagle.

Her sorrow and anxiety were evident in her rigid shoulders and strained expression. Dark Water waited until they were on the other side of the Barren Plains until he spoke, using the time to carefully observe the woman and calculate his offer based on her body language. She was disappointed that he was being sent away, that much he could read on her face. She was also upset about not being able to fight, that he could read in her tense shoulders and clenched hands. But why?

"You made a deal with the half-breed," he said when they reached the outskirts. It was a statement more than a question, and Brave Woman stopped short.

"It does not matter now."

"But it does. You bargained with the half-breed, and cannot get what you want until the fight is finished. I can help you."

She turned at that. "How?"

Dark Water took a step closer, his back to the Fire Tower in the distance. "We both want this war, Brave Woman, for our own reasons. And so does the half-breed. She has been corrupted by someone, and my guess is Sun Woman. Sun Woman is conniving, and works only for herself."

"As does the half-breed."

"Yes, and as do we. The half-breed wants this war, and we must show her why."

The look of deception and bloodlust frightened Brave Woman, but at the same time made her see exactly what he saw—the two of them riding into battle, claiming glory for their own. And at the end, Whisper praising them for their bravery and loyalty, giving them everything they wished for in return.

Closing the gap between them, Brave Woman glanced at the quiet, dark Fire Tower in the distance before turning her gaze to Dark Water. "What do you propose?"

* * *

The effort it took to communicate with the Land of the Living exhausted the Elder, even in an eternal body that dwelled in the Spirit World. But he had done what he set out to do, and his job was nearly complete. Ever since Cole Daivya had been taken from his world and placed at the Raven-Eater's side, he had kept watch over the boy. He had to make sure the child didn't grow up to be a replica of his adopted father, didn't bring the darkness of the Land of the Dead into the lives of those whose hearts still beat. And save for nightmares of a place he did not understand, Cole seemed relatively unaffected by a time he could not remember.

It disturbed Smoke Speaker that Ian, who had shown such promise after his return from the Land of the Dead, refused to speak about the event, that he never offered his son words of advice or guidance when the boy spoke of the night terrors. He left his son to sort out his troubles on his own, and so as an adult the man who once went by the name Fighting Fox was torn between the normal life he craved and the spirit existence he did not understand. And the rebirth of Second Son, a spirit hiding in the shadows of his mind until he could return to his brothers, only made Cole's existence that much more troubling. These things the Elder saw in his smoke readings and in the messages brought to him by his kindred helpers.

When Smoke Speaker felt his time was coming, he had his journal sent to Cole's home in hopes that they would bring some peace to the man. He felt Cole's troubles were partly his own fault, as he had used his magic on his memories to keep the boy from being held back in his future by visions of the past. Perhaps his spell had been too strong, or perhaps it never should have been woven into the boy's mind at all. No matter the reason, Cole was a changed boy since he returned from the Land of the Dead, and the things he did not know had led to his death.

That was why the Elder felt it was his duty to watch out for the woman Cole had chosen to love, and the child not yet brought into the world. The woman sought answers only one person held, and it was his job to lead her in the right direction.

With a tired sigh, Smoke Speaker dressed for the day and stepped outside into the clearing, shrouded in the lack of light despite it being morning time. It was an empty place without the council, a lonely place, and now the responsibility was upon his shoulders to watch after the child and see to it that she walked the Red Road. But then he saw that the clearing was not empty, and that one lone figure sat at the end of the farthest bench. It was a white-robed figure, a man the Elder feared and loved at the same time.

Smoke Speaker slowly approached the Great Spirit, wrapping his beautifully decorated shawl around his broad but bony shoulders. "Good morning," he greeted, taking a seat next to Creator. "It is going to be a fine day. I can feel it in my souls." Creator didn't answer, but instead kept his gaze straight ahead on the stone wall. Smoke Speaker followed his stare and saw nothing but white rock. "Great Spirit? Are you alright?"

The regal figure sighed at the question, clasping his large hands together and resting them in his lap. "I have done a lot of thinking, Elder," he answered, his deep voice tired. "I have come to the conclusion that I made a mistake."

Smoke Speaker frowned, looking long and hard at his leader. "The Great Spirit makes no mistakes. He merely takes a new path on the Red Road."

The other man smiled at that. "That is kind of you to say, Elder, but not true. The only beings who do not make mistakes are those who cannot admit when they have made one." He was quiet for a moment while Smoke Speaker mulled over his words. Then he turned to the other man and asked, "Elder, do you know why I brought you here?"

"To act as a council to the child, to help her follow the Red Road so that she may help you lead the spirit lands."

"Yes...but why did I choose you, specifically?" At that, Smoke Speaker could only shrug. The Great Spirit placed a comforting hand on his arm. "You are a powerful Speaker, one with talent that is to be admired and respected. But more than a Speaker, you are also the one who raised the half-breed, the man who was able to tame the wild parts of the child and raise a woman who understood all parts of the medicine wheel."

"You choose me because I am *Kanegv's* grandfather."

"Because of much more than just that, Elder. You are her grandfather, but you are also her guide, the one she once looked to for reassurance and acceptance. And now, she sees you not as her equal, but as someone she must fight against."

Smoke Speaker shifted uncomfortably. "I. . .I am not sure what you are saying, Great Spirit."

"My mistake was in making you part of the child's Circle. I see now that I should have made a second council with you as its leader, a Circle for the half-breed."

"To. . .do what?"

"To gather information on her, learn how she thinks and acts, what parts of the Raven-Eater still make up her blood. To gain her trust, and show her that we are not her enemies, and must instead work together to avoid bloodshed and war. And when the time comes, to lead her back to the Red Road when she veers off-course."

Smoke Speaker listened to the proposal silently, and when the Creator was finished, he addressed the one issue he saw with his plan. "And who are we to decide when she veers off-course, Great Spirit? If it is her Red Road to walk, then it is her path to decide."

The Great Spirit smiled again. "That is where you come in, Elder. With your guidance, she will stay on the right path."

"And how do we gain such information on her?"

"You are not the only one with connections in more than one world, Elder." The Great Spirit raised a hand, and a third figure entered the clearing. Smoke Speaker's eyes widened when he recognized the face.

"Earth Keeper," he whispered. "I heard you had been captured."

"He had been," Creator answered for the man, who was standing tall with his hands behind his back. He looked the part of a loyal soldier, just as Smoke Speaker knew him to be. "Earth Keeper is my closest ally, and an exceptional spy. He has also made his own friends in the Land of the Dead, and they will act as your insiders for information during council. Even now we know that the half-breed went missing after the attack, and reappeared a changed being, but how much has changed is yet to be determined. If she is planning to continue this war, then you must lead your council and help them along the way."

"Will we meet here?"

"No, you will never meet as a group. I cannot risk losing your Circle as I lost the other. Their deaths haunt me, and their murders will forever stain the Spirit World. For that, I am heartbroken. But you are a Speaker, Elder, and it is time to use your gifts for the Spirit World. I will worry about the child for now, and you must focus on the half-breed. You will speak with your council in your own ways, and always in private. No meeting should ever be anything less than secret."

Smoke Speaker blew out a breath, considering his options. If Whisper ever found out he was conspiring against her, working for Creator in an effort to forge her own Red Road, she would strike him down on the spot. But on the other hand, she was alone, and her recent actions proved that she was in need of guidance by those who truly cared about her, by those who saw her as more than just the half-breed.

And so he nodded, and faced the Great Spirit squarely. "I agree. Who else shall make up the Circle?"

* * *

That night, the woman dreamed of a different kind of forest. This one was dark and frightening, with thick, thorny branches that ate at her flesh and sticky, black, tar-like rain that dripped from fat leaves. Only this time, there was no river of salvation, no old man to offer words of kindness and advice. She was alone.

When she woke, she was drenched in sweat and tears. Why she was crying, she did not know. She grazed a hand across her swollen belly when she felt the baby, her baby Anya, kick, and for the hundredth time that day wished her child could have known her father, even if for only a short while.

Sitting up, she realized the book of drawings was next to her. Once again, she had fallen asleep to the haunting images drawn by charcoal of her late fiancé, his father, and the mystery woman. No, she thought, not a mystery. She was the woman the old man had spoken of, the woman with the black eyes, of that much she was sure. What she wasn't sure of was how, or why, to find her.

Slowly, and with some difficulty, she rose from the bed and padded into the living room, chilled by the cold air. Within moments she had a warm fire going, and settled before it with a hot mug of tea, adding in a sprinkling of her favorite herbs. There, she spent the rest of the night thinking of the stranger, the old man, Cole, and the journal, struggling to tie them all together. She could find no connection, no common bond, and that frustrated her more than she could express.

When the fire died down, reduced to golden ashes that simmered and sparkled in the night, she decided to go back to bed for a few hours. On impulse, she tossed the rest of the tea herbs into the fire, conjuring up a brief but bright blaze. Somewhat sadly, and with a hint of defeat, she whispered, "Help me, woman with the black eyes."

Chapter 41

A voice whispered through her thoughts, invading her dreams. Whisper's eyes opened to the sound of a plea, but when she rose she found that the room was empty. She shook her head to clear her mind of the strange voice, only giving a moment's thought to who was searching for the woman with black eyes. She couldn't concern herself with the troubles of the living unless that living being was the child.

Dressing lightly in the early morning heat provided by *Adagatiya*, Whisper wrapped her weapons belt around her waist and slipped her feet into unstrung boots, not bothering to lace them as she headed into the bedroom's alcove. There she found Hunting Hawk standing at the window. He turned when he heard her come in but didn't say a word. Instead, he stared at her with a half-smile on his face, as though he knew something she didn't.

"What?" Whisper asked when he simply held his gaze. Confused, she looked around, and only then did she see what awaited her in the center of the room. Her lips parted in shock, her breath passing out of her as she edged closer to what she prayed was not a mere vision or mirage. "Hunting Hawk…" she whispered, kneeling down and reaching out to touch the edges of the new stones. "You did this?"

"I had help," he answered, gesturing behind her. Whisper looked over her shoulder to see her mother standing in the doorway with a wide smile. "We knew how much it meant to you, so we rebuilt it while you were away."

"How did you know I would return?"

"I had faith that you would come back to me, *Kanegv*."

Barely able to hold back her own grin of amazement, Whisper rose and stepped inside the medicine wheel. It was not an exact replica of the one she had built with her own two hands, but it was beautiful nonetheless. It rippled with power as soon as she placed her foot on the stones, vibrating within her.

Her eyes closed, she said a prayer to the blue, North; the white, South; the red, East; the black, West; the yellow, Above; the brown, Below; and finally, to the green, Center. When her offering was complete, she opened her eyes and found herself looking directly into Hunting Hawk's.

"The feel of this is different," she told him, opening her hands wide at her sides. Her palms faced inward, fingers pointing to the floor.

"The first wheel was made for *Kanegv*," he responded, stepping inside the circle. Whisper felt the punch of power in her gut, wrapping around her like a weave of protection against the intruder. "This one was made for the half-breed." He closed the gap between them, taking her face in his hands. "You have walked the Red Road of your grandfather's ancestors. Now it is time to walk the Red Road of your father's bloodline. Only when you accept both halves of your souls will you be at peace with who and what you are."

She felt something dark trickle inside her, something foreign and yet, familiar. "You are the one who told me not to let the Raven-Eater win. Now you wish me to embrace him."

"No, I wish for you to gain control over him. Creator tried to destroy you, take you away from me and replace you in the Land of the Dead. His plan nearly worked because you were unprepared, unable to control what gifts are lurking inside you. This wheel is meant to draw those gifts out, and help you master them."

A dark spark of light shot out from the center of the wheel, connecting at her fingertips. Whisper breathed in deeply, a strange sound of rushing wind passing through the air as her pupils deepened. "And are you prepared for the half-breed's return?"

Hunting Hawk smiled at that, a look of both amusement and wickedness passing across his face. "I look forward to it."

From the doorway, Blue Feather watched the exchange. It made her nervous, seeing such passion in Hunting Hawk's eyes for what Whisper was doing and such a display of power as soon as her daughter entered the wheel. It was true, they had built the new medicine wheel as a way for Whisper to gain control of who and what she was, but so that she could better understand her lineage and make smarter choices about the future, both her own and the Land of the Dead's. But the way Hunting Hawk was talking, it sounded as though he wanted the half-breed to take over completely.

"*Kanegv*," she said quietly, holding out a pleading hand, "this wheel is meant for your own good, for you to fight your true enemy and emerge a victor. You must use it as a way to lead you back to the path of the Red Road."

"And I will," the other woman answered, her black-eyed stare never leaving that of her mate. Whisper reached up and locked an arm around Hunting Hawk's neck as the air in the alcove rippled. "Leave us."

"*Kanegv*—"

"*Adanvsdi!*" The deep-throated shout echoed off the stone walls and nearly knocked Blue Feather Heart off her feet. Frightened, the young mother stumbled out of the room and closed the door behind her, falling back against the wall with her heart racing.

The transformation, the takeover, had begun. Now, she could only hope that the small bit of magic she was capable of producing, and had woven into the wheel when Hunting Hawk wasn't looking, was strong enough to reign in the Raven-Eater's wrath.

Inside the wheel, Hunting Hawk wrapped one arm around Whisper's waist and grabbed her thick black hair with the other hand. She snarled at him in a way he read as inviting, and so he pulled her head to the side and lowered his own to her neck. Her eyes closed, she tightened an arm around him while the other hand fisted in his shirt just as a whirl of gray air spun up from the outer circle of the wheel. Green mist swirled at their feet, yellow and brown wisps wrapping around their locked bodies.

Whisper felt a dozen sensations at once—Hunting Hawk's lips on her throat, his fingers tugging at her hair, the smoke brushing over her skin, the rumbling of stone beneath her feet, the power that swelled within her core, inviting her to a new side of her very self, encouraging her to let go of the barriers she had placed around her souls.

Hunting Hawk was right. This was not a time to reign herself in. This was a time to embrace who she was, what she was capable of doing, a time for passion and lust, a new era of regime where *she* forged the Red Road's path, not destiny.

"*Tohi adedi,*" she whispered in a breath. Freedom to be whoever she so chose to be, freedom to rule with her own hand and mind.

"*Tsatsiyohisdi,*" she whispered again. A release from the chains that bound her in the Land of the Living, a release from the woman she was forced to be by the Elder, by the Great Spirit.

Her teeth clenched as rage battled with compassion within her, whispers in the wind passing by her ears in a welcoming dance of her new reign.

"*Ulanigvgv.*" Power to control the forces within her, power to take back the life stolen from her by the Raven-Eater and lead as a ruler her people could fear, admire, and respect.

"*Owasv,*" Whisper growled as blue and white mist rose up from the stone. An invitation into the Self, bringing that power and freedom within her, within the Self to join both halves of her souls together.

The stones rippled in a sudden blast of power, sending the pair tumbling to the hard floor. Hunting Hawk landed on top of Whisper, still holding her by the hair as he nipped at her upper lip.

"*Aquatseli*," he said in her own native tongue, his voice low and rough. An angry breath hissed out of him when Whisper reached up and took him by the throat.

"I belong to no man." Her gravelly tone matched his, with a hint of darkness that had Hunting Hawk lifting himself up onto his elbows. But she merely locked her legs around his and pulled him back down, tempting him to do as he pleased. His lips found her own and feasted there before moving to her chin, her throat, her shoulders. Again Whisper's lips parted, and when they did, red smoke rose from the eastern side of the wheel, crawling up her arms and chest, slipping past her mouth to be breathed in with each deep breath she took. It filled her blood, giving life to the parts of her she had forced to stay dormant for so long.

When all was awoken within her, her eyes flew open.

Hunting Hawk felt the sudden shift in the air, a coldness that frosted his skin mixed with a burning heat that came from the woman beneath him. He looked into Whisper's face, seeing those black pits that reminded him so much of the Raven-Eater darkening with widening pupils that seemed to swallow him whole. A wicked smile tugged at the corners of her mouth, a noise coming from deep in her throat that sounded too much like a growl for murder.

"*Kanegv*," he whispered, kissing her forehead, her cheeks, her lips as the colored winds spun around them, shaking the stone walls. "Come back to me." He looked again to see her eyes begin to clear, and felt the heat begin to subside. But still she held that look of darkness, and he realized who and what she had become. Not evil, not good, but two parts equally fused together to form one supreme being.

"Welcome home, half-breed," he grinned, pressing his body firmly against hers. "Allow me to be of service to you."

"And only me, War Chief." Whisper, *Kanegv*, the half-breed, all three seemed to grab him at once, laughter echoing in the whirling wind, completing the circle as one Red Road came to an end, and another revealed itself to them both.

Chapter 42

They met in secret, away from the watchful eye of the half-breed, out of sight's distance from the Fire Tower. Dark Water and his brothers sat around the fire with Brave Woman, and before them were the men and women gathered for their army. They were a small gathering of soldiers, but their size did not worry them. They were merely the front lines, and more forces would come once news of their courage and valor had reached the right ears.

When his army had gathered, eagerly awaiting his words, Dark Water rose and stepped in front of the fire. He faced the men and women sitting on the dirt, names he had collected over the years should the Raven-Eater ever declare war on his kind, spirits who hoped for an eternity greater than what the Land of the Dead had to offer. They were not all of his people, some were white of skin, others more he did not know, races that were foreign to him. But here, in this army, it did not matter. They were all brothers and sisters fighting for one cause.

"We ride for the place of crossing at the next rising sun," he addressed his army. He was not interested in pleasantries and words of encouragement. They already knew what they fought for, and what was at stake. "The half-breed thinks her war won't make a difference in the Land of the Dead. We are here to prove otherwise. With our courage, and our commitment, and our blood, we will prove our places here and burn the path to our freedom. You will fight, and she will realize what she has forgotten."

"Do we ride to our second deaths?" one woman asked, and Dark Water searched for her in the crowd. She was an older woman with short yellow hair and a dark scar across her throat. "The half-breed has given up, so why should we risk our eternities for it?"

"You will risk your eternity for *her*," Dark Water answered, emphasizing Whisper's spiritual being not without a breath of vehemence, "because if you do not, Creator will send another to rule the Land of the Dead, a being with no stake in our realm, a mere child who will rule according to the way he sees fit. And that way is not kind to our people. There must always be casualties of war. If you are too cowardly to fight, then you may leave this army now." The woman hung her head low, refusing to meet Dark Water's eyes.

He turned then and gestured to Brave Woman, who rose and crossed her arms, staring out at the sea of strange faces. "Brave Woman and I will lead you into battle, and we will have our glory." A thunderous cheer rose up from the crowd, shaking the trees that surrounded the clearing.

Now there was but one step left, a message to send to the half-breed that she would not get until they were already on the battlefield. With this message, she would know that there were those who believed in her even when she did not believe in herself, and come to see her followers as more than simply men to make deals with.

With this message, the half-breed would be his.

* * *

It was the first time he had attempted to contact the spirit named part of his council. The Great Spirit had chosen his members wisely, and Smoke Speaker was confident that with these men and women, his granddaughter would be shown the right path and put an end to this war before both their worlds were destroyed forever.

Carefully, he stacked wood and tinder then struck a fire, waiting until the flames were tall and hot before opening a leather pouch filled with white sage. He performed his traditional cleansing ritual, praying to all seven sacred directions for a safe and strong connection. Pinching a bit of sage between his fingers, he bent over the fire only to be knocked back by a rumble that echoed throughout the Spirit World. The air thickened, the trees bent in a fierce wind, and dark clouds covered the sky. Yet within seconds, all was right again.

"Something has happened," the Elder murmured, and, with no time to waste, tossed the offering into the fire while speaking the name of the one he sought. Soon he heard a whisper on a tendril of smoke, and then a stronger voice speaking to him through the fire.

"Smoke Speaker," the being greeted. The voice was thin and airy, as though being spoken in a breeze. "Will we be meeting with the rest of the Circle?"

"Just us for this evening." The Elder shifted into a comfortable position, sitting cross-legged before the fire. "I wanted to speak with you in private about *Kanegv* and gain your own insight into her as a leader, as a woman."

"You know as much as I about her character, Elder. *Kanegv* is a born ruler. Her blood runs thick with power. There is no other to do this task but her, no other to lead the spirits in the Land of the Dead. As a leader, she is strong, capable, just. Not always fair and sometimes rash, but such is her nature and it should not be changed."

"Should her acts of evil be forgiven because they are of her nature?"

"What is evil to you, Elder, is just to her. Who are we to decide who is right?"

The question made Smoke Speaker stop and think. His council companion was wise beyond his years, but even that did not mean he was always right. "The boundaries of good and evil are clear. The Spirit World is of the light. She has declared war against the Great Spirit, and we should not call her evil? She has taken on a battle she cannot win."

"Can she not?"

"How could she? *Kanegv* was raised to be a ruler in the Raven-Eater's stead, but she does not yet have the training or experience to lead an army, nor the bloodlust."

"Perhaps not, but the half-breed does." At Smoke Speaker's confused frown, the being laughed. "Did you not feel the tremble that worked its way through the spirit realms? *Kanegv* has finally embraced both halves of her souls. The half-breed has risen. Do not fear, Elder," he said at the man's look of shock. "This does not mean the Raven-Eater has returned, only that she has finally embraced her bloodlines in order to become the being she must in order to be a fit ruler for the Land of the Dead. Now, she is whole."

Smoke Speaker swallowed hard. "Then what do you suggest we do?"

The being sighed then, and the Elder could hear disappointment in the air as it passed through the smoke. "You are her grandfather and guide, Smoke Speaker. You reached out to her in a vision. She spoke to you of loyalty and betrayal, of hurt, and most importantly, of love. Oh yes, I know of what happens in all realms, Elder. Are you so blind that you cannot see what this is about?"

"It is about revenge," Smoke Speaker answered. "It always has been. She trained with me, slit her own wrists, and defeated the Raven-Eater for revenge against what he did to her mother. And now she battles the Great Spirit for what I have done to her."

"You give yourself too much credit, Elder." Through the flames, Smoke Speaker saw the spirit shift closer to the fire, staring intently at the Circle leader. "It is true, that in taking your place in the Spirit World, you denied the half-breed what she had hoped for her entire life, both in the living and spirit worlds. Just as it is true that it was Hunting Hawk who led her to the Red Road to be walked only by the half-breed. The child, Elder, is her second chance."

Smoke Speaker shook his head, thoroughly confused and now annoyed. "Her second chance at what?"

"To have a family."

It was so simple, so serene a vision, that he couldn't believe it. "*Kanegv* has never expressed desire for family. She rarely even lets Hunting Hawk touch her. No, the desire for this child is one of revenge. And it is revenge we must fight to force out of her thoughts."

"If we work against the half-breed in this Circle, then we all will lose."

"I know what is best for my granddaughter. I respect your guidance and council, but I feel that in order to end this war, we must find a way cast out any traces of the Raven-Eater. I once believed her to be a strong and capable ruler, one that the Land of the Dead needed to survive. But now I see that she clearly cannot handle that much power. It has made her feel invincible, and entitled. I must bind her, and her gifts, until she is ready to truly use them, for good."

Defeated, the being sighed again and stepped back, nearly breaking the connection. "Then, Smoke Speaker, you have failed her."

Chapter 43

Whisper sat watching Hunting Hawk sleep for awhile, letting the vision of his resting body fill her mind. She took in every aspect of him, her expression contemplative, her hand casually placed at her chin as she observed his every feature thoughtfully. His chiseled, tanned face marked by the scars of battlefields; his full mouth that only hours ago had savagely taken her own; his broad, bare shoulders inked in the fashions of his people; his muscled chest scarred by war, deeply bronzed and accented by black tattoos; his narrow yet sturdy hips that she nearly longed to grab hold of. The thick blanket covered the rest of him, but she knew his body by heart already.

And now, that body was exhausted. It had been a long, grueling, gratifying night, and they both felt the impact. The medicine wheel was a powerful thing, and had served its purpose well. She could feel the change within her, and it was not a subtle change. And yet, for all the differences she sensed in her body, for all the whispers she could hear that she never had before, and for all the sensations she had never known in life, she felt as though she was finally in control. That need to wrestle with her emotions, that fear of losing control of a power she did not understand, was gone. In its place were dark thoughts swarming in her mind, visions of what she could only guess were the evils committed by her father, but there was also good, ideas for what the future could hold and so much more.

She knew she was capable of terrible things and great things alike, and already she felt the pull of the dark. But she was not afraid of that pull anymore, not afraid to go against her urges or to give in to them, and she had Hunting Hawk to thank for her new self.

He didn't know how much he had risked by taking that step inside the medicine wheel with her, or staying with her while her body resisted and rejected itself, then finally accepted the blood that burned fresh and powerful. She could have led him to his second death during her transformation, but still he remained, steadfast in his loyalty and love.

She had images of him throughout the night, Hunting Hawk grabbing hold of her hair when her body jerked, holding her wrists back when she tried to strike at him, pressing her shoulders to the stone when she cursed and snarled, cradling her against his chest and gently stroking her back when exhaustion overcame her, but they were fuzzy, the memories of a broken spirit not yet whole. What had happened the previous night was a puzzle, her mind struggling to fit the pieces together as her body adjusted to a new existence. She remembered the craving to kill, the fear of hurting Hunting Hawk, the deep aching pain in losing her grandfather, the scent of her own blood. But where that blood came from, she was yet to discover.

As the morning sun rose, a dusky orange haze filled the stone room. Her time of watching was up, and so Whisper rose from the fur-lined seat next to the bed and stood over her husband. Hunting Hawk had been willing to give up his life for her, and his resting body now paid the price for that action. He was weary, perhaps even weak, and she did not wish to worry about his safety while in combat. So she would do this one thing for him, and prove that even the half-breed understood what his actions meant for the realm, and for her.

The white feather in her hair lifted as an airy breeze drifted in through the open window behind her. Her long black locks floated gently around her head, framing her slender yet sculpted face in a dark halo. Her eyes narrowed and her breath deepened; this was what she had opened herself up to, this force of power bestowed upon her by her lineage. She could use it for good, for evil, for the ways she saw fit. And Hunting Hawk was her first choice.

Goosebumps formed along Hunting Hawk's chest and shoulders as she lifted her arms out to her sides, then lowered them to his body, palms grazing over his flesh. She had never done this kind of magic before, but something inside guided her, formed the words, brought forth new visions of what she was capable of doing. She felt a pounding in her chest, a burning in her blood, as a swarm of images passed through her thoughts and a rush of whispers invaded her senses. They told her where to put her hands, where to touch Hunting Hawk, what to say as power pulsed out of her.

Whisper's eyes followed the long scar down his left cheek, neck, and shoulder, the wound that had been his end, then ran a finger along the center of his stomach, moving her hand in a circle and in curves along the tip to form what looked like horns. Everywhere her finger touched, a bright yellow glow blazed before fading into the flesh. Then she traced a second design above his heart, a round pattern with four points at the sacred directions, sun-like in appearance.

"*Vlenidohv ganetliyvsdi vlenidohv,*" she whispered, the words forming before her in a curl of ashy smoke. The mist curled and twisted, floating downward and sinking into Hunting Hawk's skin where her finger had touched.

To complete the spell, Whisper clutched a hand to her chest when a searing sensation gripped her heart. It was an intense pain, one that calmed her at the same time. She threw her head back just as a white light exploded from beneath her hand, rays of color shimmering between her fingers as the hand-drawn marks on the man's chest glowed lightly before disappearing again.

Hunting Hawk woke from a sleepy, seemingly drug-induced haze at the flashing colors. He couldn't comprehend what he was seeing, what looked like wings of light emerging from Whisper's hand. He could see only the profile of her face, her eyes closed and shimmering beneath their lids, her mouth relaxed in a serene expression he had never known her to have. She seemed to be wrapped in a cocoon of power; he could feel its vibrations deep in his own bones. Then that power and light faded, and they were left alone in the stone room silhouetted by early morning light.

Hunting Hawk lifted himself to a sitting position just as Whisper raised her head and opened her eyes. For a moment she looked lost, then the familiar darkness settled in her face. When she turned her gaze to Hunting Hawk he nearly shivered, as he now looked into the eyes of the half-breed.

"What did you do?" he asked, brushing a hand over his chest when he felt a strange tingling.

"What had to be done."

There was something different about her voice, something heavier. It brought him back to the night before, when she had said things that frightened him to his core, when she had shouted for the deaths of those she loved most, when she had pleaded for an end to her pain. One day they would have to talk about what had happened on the night of her transformation, the words that had been spoken, the strange sounds and visions that erupted from the center of the medicine wheel. Now was not that time, not when Whisper's mind was still struggling to make sense of recent events, when he couldn't be sure that she was fully healed both on the inside and out, ready to take the first steps on the new Red Road.

But when she settled down next to him with a soft sigh and leaned onto his shoulder, Hunting Hawk cast aside any fears and instead rested his head on her own. Whatever she had done to him, he would trust that it was *Kanegv* who held onto the power, and had gained control of the half-breed.

* * *

Blue Cloud was home now, back where she belonged, with family. She had her mother, she had Second Son, and all was right in her world. Sun Woman smiled from the moment she rose to the moment she lay down to rest, and she felt a peace she had not known since her daughter's death so long ago.

Now she was back, sharing the Sky Vault as they had in the past. There was a new member to their family, but Sun Woman didn't mind Second Son's presence. She was wary about him still, but kept such reservations to herself and was willing to reserve judgment until she saw what the future held. Until the half-breed won or lost her war, and until Sun Woman could determine if he was useful in her own battle, the Little Man would be kept at arm's length.

Already she could sense the change in him. When he arrived on the other side of the Bridge of the Dead, he was a spirit wrestling with the souls of three men. Cole Daivya fought to hold on the memories of his former life. Fighting Fox struggled to break free when he realized he was home. And Second Son recognized the land of his brothers and longed for the woman who held his heart.

For any other being, it would have been too much to endure. But for this body it was a rebirth, and in that rebirth, the life and memories of Cole Daivya had been burned out by the more powerful spirits. Sun Woman couldn't detect any traces of the boy, and instead only felt Fighting Fox's presence buried deep beneath Second Son. She was sure Cole was still in there somewhere, trapped behind the more command-ing forces, but so long as Fighting Fox remained buried as well she would not concern herself with the triple identities.

She watched as her daughter and Second Son set up their new home. Together they had built a strong, sturdy longhouse made of wood that grew only in the Sky Vault—tall slender trees that provided shade and sanctuary from the vast openness of the realm. The longhouse had large open windows with thick curtains, and an opening in the center of the roof that allowed smoke to escape.

While Blue Cloud decorated the inside with what few trinkets Sun Woman had to offer, Second Son stepped outside and walked over to where Sun Woman waited. They stood observing the new dwelling for a moment before he spoke. "It is a strong home," he stated, his deep voice carrying across the clearing.

Sun Woman frowned. "And yet you sound dissatisfied."

His voice lowered then, and he sounded somewhat ashamed. "I spent many years lurking in the shadows of Cole's mind. I saw what he saw, felt what he felt. I never intended to stay in that body, but the Raven-Eater finally caught up with me. Being reborn with the boy, I felt almost whole again, and could not wait to return home to my brothers. But I was trapped in the body, and eventually accepted that I would never return home." Then he sighed, frowning as he stared at his new home. "I have been thinking about the half-breed," he admitted. "She rescued me from banishment, led the boy to his death so that I could live again in the spirit realms."

"She did so as part of our agreement."

"Yes. I know that I was merely a bargaining chip, but that does not change how I feel."

Worry started to creep up in her gut. "And how do you feel?"

Now he looked at her. "That I owe the half-breed my loyalty, if only for her war. She is the reason I was set free."

"*I* am the reason you were set free, Second Son. You owe your loyalty to *me*." The words came out harsher than she had intended, but her worry was bringing forth anger. He seemed to know, though, that she would not do anything to harm him. He was, after all, her daughter's chosen husband.

"Sun Woman, I know my brothers, and I know that Dark Water will be taking them to the forefront of the war despite what he may have said before. We are stronger together, and we can defeat the enemy. I will return to you and Blue Cloud, but I must go and fight for the half-breed so my own soul can rest in peace."

"The half-breed does not expect you to fight, nor does she need you. She has her followers, her counselors, and does not look to any others."

He wondered how she knew so much about the leader of the Land of the Dead. Sun Woman's voice was tinged with hate, and yet there was a hint of something else, perhaps fear. "Is this personal, Sun Woman? Do you not wish me to go because of Blue Cloud, or because of your own feelings toward the half-breed?"

Sun Woman turned and took hold of the man's arm. Her eyes were grave, her mouth in a thin line. "Second Son, the half-breed cannot be trusted. She will use you, and bargain with you, but her words often deceive those who do not listen carefully enough. You are part of the Sky Vault now. You belong to neither the Land of the Dead nor the Spirit World. You are needed here, for tasks far greater than what the half-breed has planned. Taking sides could mean your very eternity should one ruler decide to strike you down. Yes, I worry about my daughter and her happiness is my first concern. But I do not hate the half-breed. In fact, I nursed her back to health. But this is not our war."

Second Son pulled his arm back just as Blue Cloud exited the longhouse and started their way. "It is not our war," he agreed quietly, "but it is my own internal battle that I must fight."

He smiled when his future wife came to a stop before him, ending the conversation before Sun Woman could refute his words.

Chapter 44

In only a matter of days Smoke Speaker had met with everyone in his Circle, at times privately, other times as a group. Some feared they had gathered too late, as Whisper and the half-breed had already become one, while the rest thought it a good thing. Now, she could move beyond the struggle and become the leader she was born to be, and they would be there to guide her along the way.

The Elder, however, feared there was more to his council than even the Great Spirit had hoped for. This was not a Circle meant to guide; it was one meant to bind, to protect the Spirit World against the wrath of the Raven-Eater and his offspring. It was designed to control the half-breed, and only he and his council members knew how to do that. They knew *Kanegv*, had studied her moves, how she thought, how she acted and reacted. With this information, they could defeat her on the battlefield.

Smoke Speaker had done all he could for his granddaughter. He had raised her as a child, taught her about her people, helped her take her first step on the Red Road, and ultimately, watched as the blood ran from her open veins so that she could take her rightful place in the Land of the Dead. He was supposed to help her rule that land upon his own death, as had been the talk throughout her training, but he choose to forsake those plans for a higher calling and now was forced to suffer the consequences.

There was nothing left to be done for Whisper. They had taken action and put their own plans into motion, and what happened next was up to her.

* * *

The moon was rising as Whisper stood on the cliff-top overlooking the Barren Plains, hands clasped behind her back as she stared out at her land. Night was her favorite time in the Land of the Dead, when shadows settled over the realm and glittering stars lit up the earth. She saw village fires in the distance, some closer than others, heard laughter and voices carried in the wind, listened to the words of her people as they settled in for the evening. To her left a fire burned, flames reaching up from the crevices below and licking up toward the sky. *Adagatiya* was awake, and while she didn't care what the beast did in his lair, part of her did wonder what went on at night that required such fires.

Before she could contemplate the matter further, something stirred in the Barren Plains. Whisper recognized the familiar pattern tracing its way beneath the earth, and heard the tiny voice that called for her as it neared.

Utlav was coming with a message.

She made her way down to the Barren Plains quickly, keeping her eyes on the mound of dirt as it edged its way closer. Whisper stopped a few steps into the Plains, making *Utlav* come to her. Only when the brown head had popped out of the ground did she lower herself to the ground, balancing on the balls of her feet.

My queen.

She heard the voice though the creature's mouth never moved. Her eyes narrowed suspiciously, as they always did when *Utlav* came to see her. "You have a message?"

Suddenly she noticed something she never had perceived before as the beast stared at her, a tug in her mind and gentle prying of invisible fingers as though he was attempting to read her thoughts. Then as quickly as she felt it, a part of her mind snapped to attention and the sensation stopped. *Utlav* drew back and its claws curled inward, forming small fists.

"You have been intruding," she whispered, her head cocked to the side. "How many thoughts have you stolen, beast? How many secrets have you given to the enemy?" She lifted a brow when a shudder ran through the creature. "The thoughts of the half-breed are not so easily taken, are they?"

Utlav shifted, bowing its furry head though they both knew it was insincere. *I am but a humble servant to all*, was his reply, and despite herself, Whisper believed it to be true. The creature didn't serve any one being but itself. She could not fault the beast for being what it was created to be. It did explain certain events in the recent past, perhaps even how Splinter Foot Girl was able to sneak up on the Fire Tower so easily, and Whisper was pleased to know that in accepting who she was she could no longer be fooled by such tricks.

"What do you want?"

He noted the change in her voice, a darker kind of tinge that frightened him. She sounded more confident, less uncertain in her words, indifferent in her subject and yet not missing so much as a single breath of wind. What she couldn't hear before was now clear, what she didn't know before was now in the forefront of her mind. He would have to tread carefully in his messages from now on.

I bring a message, my queen, from your dear friend.

Whisper frowned. A dear friend could easily mean a deepest enemy. *Utlav* liked to twist words, pit ally against ally, brother against brother. He was not the most intelligent of creatures though, which is why he didn't realize that many were on to his tricks and used them to their own advantage. "Go on."

Dark Water and his army hung up their swords this very evening, my queen. They will not fight in your war.

"Why not?"

He desires to show himself as your most hated enemy, my queen. In being a coward, you will come to despise him as well.

"Hate?" she repeated, confused. "I do not..." Slowly the words came together. *Utlav* deceived in ways different than her. Whereas Whisper was able to twist words and lead thoughts in her desired direction without speaking mistruths, this creature was more inclined to lie and turn words around altogether.

Dark Water hung up his sword this evening, refusing to fight in the war. If she surmised correctly, he and an unknown army were marching toward the Spirit World to fight in her war. And why? To show himself as a true enemy, which could be the truth, or, she guessed, it could mean he was attempting to show some kind of affection. Again, she had to wonder why. So she would fall in love? Whisper didn't think the eldest of the Little Men was so jaded as to believe he was worthy of her kingdom.

"Thank you for the message," she said to *Utlav*, who gave another bow before disappearing all too quickly back into the earth, relieved to escape the half-breed's presence. Then she turned and faced the Fire Tower, glancing over at the rising red flames before starting the hike back up the mountainside.

If Dark Water was fighting the war, then she would wager Brave Woman was with him leading the front lines. After all, their agreement was not complete until she played her part on the battlefield. Whisper couldn't fault the spirit for taking part in Dark Water's plan. She only wanted her time with Little Eagle, as was promised. She did, however, fault Dark Water for planning a battle behind her back.

She had no choice but to fight now, and fight hard. Lately she'd been questioning the war and her own abilities, fighting a strange feeling of apathy toward the Spirit World, an intruding sensation she couldn't explain but seemed to be taking over her senses. Part of her wished to give up the war, to hang up her weapons and retreat.

And yet, Dark Water and his army were risking their eternal lives for her, and while she questioned his motives, his actions also inspired bloodlust and vengeance in her heart. She would let Dark Water and Brave Woman fight, would let them suffer the consequences of their rash actions, and would arrive with her own army to bring down her greatest enemy.

* * *

The woman woke in the early morning hours, before the sun had risen to grace the day with its warm orange glow. At first she felt sick, then damp with sweat, then the pain set in and she found herself doubled up in bed.

Not just any pain though, she realized. Contractions. She was in labor.

Luckily, she had prepared for this moment. Her friend was on call, and so in just moments she was ready to go. Nerves and excitement were building when she hurried to the car, and as she cast a look over her shoulder at the home she had been creating with her fiancé, just a hint of sadness crept through her. But she pushed that feeling out of her mind and focused on the happiness instead. Her child, their child, was about to be brought into the world.

Just before walking into the hospital, she extended a kindness she didn't really feel by sending her late fiancé's parents a message. She was sure they would come, for the face of their granddaughter was more powerful than any distrust between her and Ian.

With a soft sigh, she slipped her phone into her bag and stepped out of the car. The sun was just beginning to rise, and the sky was still filled with beautiful reds and purples that had a soothing affect that calmed her nerves.

"It's time to meet our daughter," she whispered to the sky, picturing Cole in her thoughts. A single tear slipped down her cheek. "I'll tell baby Anya how much you love her."

Chapter 45

Before she could go to war, Whisper had to prepare.

Her first task had been to contact Grandmother Spider, asking the spirit to return the sun to the Spirit World. The ancient spirit had been reluctant to give up her claim, demanding payment in return. It was a steep price, one Whisper would later be forced to pay with her own blood, but they came to an agreement at last. Within moments after settling their contract she watched from her mind's eye as Grandmother Spider unraveled her web, the sun peeking back into the Spirit World one spin at a time. The people rejoiced, happily hugging one another while praying to the Great Spirit in gratitude, as though *he* had been the one to rescue them from eternal darkness.

Although Whisper felt a bit disgusted with herself in restoring light to Creator, and silently cursed the beings of the Spirit World for their ignorance, she nonetheless allowed Grandmother Spider to continue her unwrapping. She did not want those fighting for her to battle in darkness, or pass into their second deaths never having seen the light one last time, if it came to that.

Her second task was a stop to the one who always understood her. It wasn't guidance or support she sought so much as it was a friendly face, one that would never cast judgment despite any feelings of concern or disagreement. She may have been the half-breed, but even she could not foresee who would emerge the victor on the battlefield. She could not be killed, but others could, and she would not be pleased to lose any spirit that resided in the Land of the Dead.

She stalked through the cave quickly, making turns in the dark that she knew by heart. Soon she came to the cavern, which, as always, was filled with orange light radiating from the fire. And at that fire, *Kamama* was waiting for her.

"I have been expecting you."

Whisper sat on the hard ground, crossing her legs and staring up at the creature. "You know why I have come?"

Kamama smiled and fluffed out his brilliant blue wings. "I know everything about this land, my child. Dark Water and Brave Woman have crossed through to the Spirit World to fight your war. They fight for their own purposes, as do you. And you intend to follow, as soon as you leave this cave I imagine, as you are dressed for battle."

Whisper cast a look down at her clothes. *Kamama* was right, as she had on her finest war gear. She hadn't bothered to remove all her weapons for this visit. Thin yet strong metal was strapped across her chest, the breastplate tying at the shoulders and along her sides. She wore a light shirt beneath the shield that protected her skin from chafing, while her pants were thicker and covered with solid black hide that allowed for agility but still kept her limbs safe from blades and arrows. In place of her usual shoes were boots that laced up past her ankles with hard, thick soles and jagged pieces of metal at the top and sides. Around her waist was a wide-strapped belt, from which hung four sheathed daggers and her own special medicine bag.

Her long, toned arms were bare but for the straps around her elbows and wrists that protected her from the sharp feathers attached to each arrow. And though she rarely went hand-to-hand in combat, leather was wrapped around and in between each finger for protection. To complete the war gear, Whisper had tied back her hair in a tight braid, a band around her forehead to keep her eyes free of any potential loose strands, and black beads—the color of death—accented each blue feather that hung from the braid.

Anyone who turned their gaze upon her would be instantly intimidated, and take large steps back for their own protection. She looked every bit the part of a fierce and merciless warrior, lean muscles lining her limbs and broad shoulders ready to carry the weight of the world. She was a woman who could not be defeated, but welcomed anyone to try.

"I know you do not agree with this war, *Kamama*, but it is something I must do. I hope that we can still have these times when I return."

Kamama edged closer to the fire and settled down on a bundle of furs. "It has been an honor, my child, to watch you grow into your souls and embrace your blood. Now I will watch as you follow the Red Road, wherever it may take you."

There was something in his voice that had her frowning. "You believe I am making a mistake."

"I believe you are following your heart, and that is never wrong." *Kamama* fluttered a wing, sending embers racing up from the flames. In those flames, Whisper saw Dark Water and his army about to advance. Both armies had formed on either side of the battle line. "The Great Spirit's army is strong."

"As is mine," she replied quietly. Only she knew just how many were ready to fight for her. The Raven-Eater had built an impressive army, but she was stronger than he had ever been.

When she appeared lost in thought, *Kamama* stoked the fire and cast the images back into the embers. "I know what it is you seek, *Kanegv*, and I pray you find it."

"And what is it I seek?"

"The defeat of your greatest enemy," he answered, a knowing glimmer in his opaque eyes. "Find peace in this war, *Kanegv*, and when you face the Great Spirit, remember this. The death of one enemy only allows for another to take its place. You must decide who you would rather be fighting."

Hunting Hawk was waiting for Whisper when she exited the cave. He held out her bow, and after she had strapped it to her back, gestured behind her. "We have a visitor. Arrived just after you went inside."

Whisper turned to see Second Son standing tall with his hands gripping a set of double-tipped spears. He was struggling not to shiver, as the Land of the Dead was still chilled with Blue Corn Maiden's curse and *Adagatiya* was not able to heat the earth with the impending war. He was needed elsewhere.

With a hand on the hilt of her dagger she approached the newcomer. "Second Son," she greeted cautiously, frowning. "Why are you here?"

The question was sincere, but it still made him nervous. "I have come to fight with you and my brothers."

"...Why?"

"You returned my spirit, whether by contract or kindness, and so I have sworn my loyalty to you until this war has ended. After that I will return to Blue Cloud in the Sky Vault. But for now, I wish to fight."

Whisper analyzed him for a moment, using her new gifts to probe his mind, finding his thoughts honest and pure. He was a rare find, this brother to the Little Men, one of honor and courage, one who understood the contracts of war and yet abided by his own sense of nobility nonetheless. She could tell by the unspoken words that whispered from his thoughts that he would fight until the end for her, and no other, and wished to fight at his brothers' sides.

"You may fight, Second Son. And that fight begins now."

The trio began the march to the place of crossing. Whisper's army was already there, as she had sent them ahead under the leadership of her head guard, and she had her newest recruit walk ahead of them so she could see him in case he attempted a move.

"You believe we can trust him?"

Hunting Hawk lifted a shoulder. "No more than we can trust anyone on our side or another's. He seems sincere enough, but it does not matter. You are the half-breed. You will know when one crosses sides."

She hoped he was right, and deep down knew that he was. She was still adjusting to the new sensations within her, still coming into her own as he claimed, but there was a certainty in her mind that told her she was making the right decision. Just as it had been the right decision to leave her mother behind at the Fire Tower. She wanted to fight, Blue Feather had argued, to help her daughter through this war, but Whisper wouldn't relent. She wanted her mother safe.

They met up with their army at the place of crossover, where *Adagatiya* was waiting for her. She could not ride Eagle into this battle, as the winged creature was a noble beast that would not fight against the Great Spirit or any other leader of the spirit realms. Eagle was loyal to his queen, but also to the Creator, who had bestowed upon him the task of aiding all lost souls to peace in the Land of the Dead. Though it annoyed her to be without her familiar companion, Whisper would not ask Eagle to break that trust or the bond that connected them.

So instead she would ride the dragon, and incinerate any who crossed her path.

* * *

When the morning sun touched the horizon, Dark Water stood on the front lines prepped for battle. His feet were wrapped in thick hides coated with the spikes of a creature found only in the Land of the Dead, the same spikes that adorned the shoulders of his fur-lined tunic. That tunic was covered with hard-plated armor that not even the sharpest of blades could penetrate, and a newly fashioned sword was strapped across his back along with a quiver of arrows. His head was hooded by thick black fur, which he pushed back when the Great Spirit's army came into sight.

Next to him, Brave Woman sat confidently atop a black horse painted with green and brown inked designs. The horse was protected in the same plated armor along its head, legs, and flank. The armor matched Brave Woman's own shields, which she wore proudly, thrilled to be back in battle. Her long black hair was secured in twine, and a thick leather band decorated in the symbols of her people circled her head. In one hand she carried a thin spear tipped with a strong flint blade, in the other was a battle ax with a curved blade and bone handle. She stared straight ahead into the horde of soldiers, fingers tapping on the spear as she waited patiently for the right man to appear.

And soon, he did.

She heard the army at her back murmur in trepidation, then a hush settled among them. But still she kept her gaze forward, narrowing her eyes at the spirit. Brave Woman had never known the man personally, but the half-breed had mentioned him, expressing interest in his abilities to elude certain death and fury in her guards' inability to track him down. He was the only one to ever escape the wrath of the half-breed, the spirit who found a way out of the Fire Tower and outsmarted *Kanegv*.

And today, to avenge the half-breed and earn her respect, Brave Woman would claim Earth Keeper's honor for herself.

Both sides stood perfectly still, only hair, feathers, and loose clothing lifting in the heavy wind. They were waiting to see who would make the first move, and Earth Keeper had ordered his army to not draw first blood. Instead, they had watched as the army from the Land of the Dead marched closer and closer in a rising dawn tinted with white, the first light the Spirit World had seen in weeks, coming from the south as the sound of their stomping feet carried across the open plains. It was a large army, but nothing compared to the masses that made up Creator's forces.

Brave Woman could see the scorn and derision spread across Earth Keeper's face, which no longer bore the suffering of Blue Corn Maiden's eternal winter. He thought them meager, a pathetic attempt for battle. The very thought burned her blood, bringing back memories of when she was once looked at as weak, inept, unworthy. And so with a sharp kick to the horse's sides, she raced forward to show everyone why she was forever known as Brave Woman Counts Coup.

The look of bored amusement on Earth Keeper's face changed to one of confusion when he saw the woman on the horse start trotting in his direction. He lifted a hand to signal his army to stand down, instead deciding to see what she wanted. From the pace, he could clearly see she was not leading her army into attack. This was a solo mission, and he was curious.

His interest only heightened when she headed straight for him, that look of intent and determination deepening as she neared. She slowed just a step when they were within speaking distance, and Earth Keeper started to ask of her intentions when she struck out with a speed he would not have thought possible of a woman.

Brave Woman smacked the butt of the ax handle across Earth Keeper's cheek, counting coup on the War Chief. Before he could retaliate, she let out a fierce war cry that matched the shouts coming from the men and women behind her, then turned back and raced for Dark Water.

Spitting a mouthful of blood, Earth Keeper watched Brave Woman ride back, incredulous by her attack. "So you draw first blood," he said to himself, furious he had been struck but satisfied that the enemy had advanced first. He lifted an arm, hand gripping the hilt of a sword. It wasn't a weapon he had used during his living years, but was one he found useful now.

With a single shout, Earth Keeper lowered his arm and moved his army forward. At the same time, Dark Water signaled his troop. The two sides ran for one another, slamming body against body, clashing weapon against weapon, spilling blood in the first war the Spirit World had ever seen.

Chapter 46

From high up in his sanctuary in *Oway*, the Great Spirit watched as the battled raged on below. The wind carried the sounds of gasping breaths, clanging metal, feet stomping against blood-soaked earth to his ears, but he stood still and steadfast, deep brown eyes stoically taking in the sights of war. Spirits on both sides were vanishing into their second deaths, while injured bodies littered the battlefield. Dark Water and the Little Men had made good footing into the Spirit World, but Creator's army was strong, and would defeat them before they could reach his home.

"This is madness," Smoke Speaker said from behind, approaching the window. "They will be destroyed."

"Such are the ways of war, Elder. We did not invite them to fight, and we did not draw first blood. What happens now is for the Red Road to decide."

Smoke Speaker didn't need to ask where the Red Road led. He could see, just as plainly as the Great Spirit, what was happening on the battlefield.

Fighting true to her name on the open plains, Brave Woman struck out left and right as enemies battled against her. She cried out in pain when a blade sliced through her lower leg, dropping to the ground on one knee. She felt warm blood flowing down her shin, soaking through her gear. The blade had pierced right through her armor.

Refusing to show her pain, Brave Woman looked up at the figure masked in black, sneering at the smile spread across his face. He wanted her to scream and beg for her life, but she wouldn't give him the pleasure.

"You will die for the half-breed," the man snarled, raising his dagger.

Before he could lower his arm, Brave Woman kicked a foot out, connecting with his ankle. The spirit tumbled to the ground, and as he fell she reared up, sending her spear through his chest. The soldier disappeared in a burst of gray ash.

Brave Woman rose to her feet, favoring her injured leg only slightly. "I will die for the half-breed," she whispered to the empty air. "But not today."

Then she turned, and desperation sank in her gut. Her warriors were dropping quickly; they were no match for the Great Spirit's army. More and more came from *Oway*, huge beasts carrying armed fighters who sent down arrow after arrow, hordes of warriors carrying weapons that far outweighed their own. Soon they would be overrun, defeated, sent to their second deaths.

And then, just when she thought all hope was lost, she heard Dark Water shout to his brothers. She didn't understand the words, but the tone was crystal clear—he was excited about something. Spinning around, her black hair loose in her braid and wet with blood as it clung to her scratched and dirt-stained face, Brave Woman saw what made the Little Men celebrate.

There, on the horizon, stood the Army of the Half-Breed.

* * *

She approached from the south, the first warrior in line as they reached the outskirts of the war field. The sounds of battle hit her first, beginning as mere whispers that trekked across the mountainous landscape then becoming thunderous roars that slammed into her mind and echoed through her head. It only took a few seconds to control the rushes of noise, but they were enough to tell her what to expect.

When they came up over the hill, the sounds met the vision.

As much as Whisper thought she was prepared, as often as she had envisioned it in her mind as a living woman, as many times as she had killed without flinching, the fact remained that she had never seen war in person. She had never witnessed a battlefield with her own eyes, never taken in the vast open field scattered with broken and bloody bodies, never smelled the ashy scent of hundreds as they passed on to their second deaths all at once or heard the pain-stricken screams of the fallen. This was so much more than she could have ever imagined, a depiction of death as it struck down spirit after spirit right in front of her.

To her right, battles raged with swords and scythes, men and women screaming at one another. To her left, archers aimed for their marks, releasing flame and poison-tipped arrows that struck down the enemy. Her eyes, red and scabbed but healing nonetheless, could barely take everything in.

For the briefest of moments, something that may have been fear passed through her.

With a shake of her head, Whisper unclenched her hands and took in a deep breath, still a holdover from her living years. She faced Hunting Hawk and Second Son. "We will lead them to the battlefield, and we will strike down every last soldier that fights for Creator."

"Every last one," Second Son agreed, while Hunting Hawk silently pulled his dagger from its sheath and secured a shield on his shoulder and arm. He had been waiting for this moment, his time to get back into the fight. Being a War Chief was in his blood; war was what he did best.

She saw the warring fighters closest to her stop when they sensed her presence. Half the battle seemed to freeze, while the other half continued the slaughter. Eager to take down her enemies, Whisper took the first step onto the battlefield.

Silence met her ears.

But this was a strange kind of silence, one foreign to her, filled with noise but not the kind she was accustomed to. For a moment she thought she had gone deaf, for what she saw did not match what she heard—and what she heard was nothing but the sound of fighting. There were no whispers in the air, no spirited voices echoing off the earth to aid in her fight, no inner speeches calling to her souls. Her thoughts were empty, abandoned. She could feel the loss every bit as she could hear it, as though some part of her had been ripped out of her and crushed.

Startled, she stumbled back a step, and as soon as her foot crossed the invisible barrier the whispers and pounding screams began again.

"What magic is this..." she murmured, furious and slightly concerned. As a test she moved forward, then back, fury building with the change in sound.

"*Kanegv?*" Hunting Hawk asked, touching her arm. "What is it?"

Whisper shook her head, huffing in disbelief. "Creator's magic is strong," she replied quietly. "He has taken away what he believes to be my greatest advantage."

He watched her for a moment, trying to understand as the look of confusion on her face only deepened. That confusion turned to frustration, then anger. When she cocked her head to the side in the position he recognized as listening to the wind, brow furrowed as though struggling to hear, then sigh and stomp at the ground, he knew what had happened.

Creator had deafened her on the battlefield, Hunting Hawk realized. How he accomplished such a feat was beyond his ability to comprehend, but the magic was strong, and his curse was clever. He had made her unable to detect attacks in advance, made her just like the rest of them. Or so he believed. "Then perhaps it is time to show Creator what the half-breed can truly do."

As the words coursed through her, the corners of Whisper's mouth turned up into a knowing leer. She unsheathed her blade with one hand and grabbed her shield from Second Son with the other, preparing herself for battle. Then she turned and faced her army, confidence and courage spread across her strongly sculpted face. Her soldiers were rocking with the excitement to fight, yelling her name, calling for blood.

She felt the heat of the battle at her back, heard the change in the air the closer she stepped to that barrier. But before she crossed over, she would hear and feel the steadfast creed her warriors had for her. They weren't interested in long, inspiring speeches that encouraged them onto the battlefield. They weren't waiting for their leader to show her courage through thundering orations that filled the other army with fear. They wanted only to fight, and to know that they fought for strength, leadership, sanctuary, loyalty, righteousness.

Whisper took her place at the head of the army, her face dark and her eyes flickering with the promise of bloodshed. As her blood began to heat within her, as her mind raced with images of victory, she used the power of the half-breed to give this one message to her army.

"*Alasdi!*" she shouted, her declaration carrying over the spirits. *Fight.*

"*Adahisdi!*" she screamed, her voice nearly breaking by force. *Kill.*

Then she lifted an arm above her head, blade fisted in her hand. "*Adasegogisdi!*" she made her final command, and with roars of warfare thundering across the earth, the army surged forward with her last word in their souls.

Conquer.

Smoke Speaker had seen many things in his long living life, and even more when joining the Spirit World. But never before had he seen anything quite like this. He'd watched as the Army of the Half-Breed marched to the battlefield, witnessed his granddaughter's confusion when she discovered her sudden deafness, heard the thunder of shouts as she and her soldiers fueled their thirst for blood and vengeance.

But what he hadn't initially seen, and what he certainly hadn't been expecting, was *Adagatiya.*

At Whisper's last shout, the beast rose from back and soared over the army, a magnificent visage of red-hot fire and fury. He barely slowed as he arced toward the ground at Whisper's feet, and she leapt onto the creature's back. She was...riding the dragon, he realized with dread, sitting atop the scaled back as though she owned the beast and had trained with him her entire life. He'd heard stories of the dragon who gave life to the sacred waters as a child, but never before had he believed he would see the creature that inspired the legend. And now, the half-breed had teamed up with *Adagatiya* to conquer the Spirit World.

Before he could wonder what the dragon was capable of, the beast lifted to the sky and showed them all what he was worth.

A blaze of fire erupted from the dragon's breath, scorching the earth, somehow only igniting the enemy in fiery orange ashes. Black smoke tumbled up toward the blue sky, creating a gray haze that settled above them ominously as the flames licked closer to *Oway*. Riding tall, Whisper's face was alit in the flames, a portrait of inferno that brought forth death and destruction. She didn't need to hear the whispers that traveled the wind. No, the Elder realized, she traveled something far better, something more than magic or beast.

She traveled the Red Road.

Chapter 47

It was a strange sensation, not hearing anything but the sounds mere men and women heard every day. She was one of them, and yet, something very different. Whisper sent down arrow after arrow, slicing flint through flesh and bone as she cast her enemies into the darkness. She reveled in their screams, laughed internally at their feeble attempts to bring her down. They shot at *Adagatiya*, aiming for the wings, but he was a well-armored beast. Only one spot was truly vulnerable to such small weapons, and that happened to be the spot she was straddling atop his back.

It was thrilling knowing they were both nearly invincible, if not slightly boring. Before the Raven-Eater had sent her to her own second death, Whisper had felt the fear of a fight, terrified she would die before her time. It made her stronger, faster, more aware. Now, she didn't have that fear, and in its place was the time to question what she was even doing in this realm.

As it had during her living years, her mind began to wander. She killed the enemy mindlessly, guiding the dragon to new areas where Creator's army was thickest. All the while, she wondered how much more it would take to convince the leader of the Spirit World to give up his claim on the child. Sending every soldier within the spirit realms to their second deaths would accomplish nothing for her, and everything for the Great Spirit. So why was she here?

An arrow pierced her shoulder, the stone tip burying itself deep in the skin. With a snarl, she yanked it out, barely wincing when bits of blood and flesh came with it. A second grazed her cheek, and fury built as her concentration broke just long enough to let herself get wounded. She could handle the pain, the injuries, but she would not let the fighters believe themselves to have gotten the better of her.
Directing the dragon toward the ground, she lifted herself gracefully and leapt from his back after a quiet yet stern command—burn *Oway*, and return to safety.

It was a quick fall, and she landed solidly on her feet. As soon as she hit the ground the two warriors who shot her nocked their second arrows. An entire fleet of men behind them did the same. Within seconds she had close to sixty arrows pointed her way, and nearly half that in swords and daggers.

"The war ends now, half-breed," one of the lead fighters snarled, spitting out the word *half-breed* like it was acid on his tongue.

In response, Whisper merely took a single step back, her mouth curling into a sneer as her black eyes narrowed. Slowly, she lowered herself to one knee while holding her bow out in front of her with one hand, and her prized bone-handled dagger in the other. Never breaking her stare with the spirit whose arrow had pierced her shoulder, she brought the dagger down, touching the tip of the blade to the earth.

Loose dirt lifted from the ground, lightly at first, then thicker as it swirled around Whisper in a tornado of earth and stone. Faster it whirled, surrounding the half-breed in a cocoon of power and protection. She rose to her feet, her glare even and threatening, readying an arrow in her bow and releasing it just as the men before her sent an onslaught her way. The arrows struck the cloud burst and bounced off, piercing into the spirits coming up around her. Enraged, the warriors rushed forward, fighting to get through her shield, but their weapons were not strong enough to break the barrier.

Whisper's, however, were far stronger than that.

She slashed through the barrage of dirt, feeling her blade slice through flesh, smelling the scent of blood in the air. She didn't need to hear the whispers on the wind to know when each spirit died its second death, although she was blinded to those who tried to attack from behind. Still she pushed forward, screaming in rage with each release of the arrow, feet stomping hard on the ground as she speared the enemies straight through the heart. Black blood splattered her face, coating her hair, sticking to her gear. Her eyes saw only the faces of pain, her vision blurring until she was driven by vengeance and fury alone, letting her senses take over and guide her in her battle. She may have been deafened to the whispers, but that didn't mean she was immune to her own gifts. Her blood was alive with sensation; she could feel each pulse and quiver through her veins as she lashed out.

When those senses faded and her sight cleared, Whisper stood still long enough to see that she was on the battlefield, her enemies destroyed. All around her the war continued, but in her small battle circle, she was the victor. Only the injured lay at her feet, squirming and moaning in pain, begging for mercy.

She should have felt victorious, satisfied, but instead she felt only anger. Her fight was not with these men and women, it was with Creator and the Elder. These spirits were not meant to die at her hand, just as her own soldiers were not meant to be destroyed at the order of the Great Spirit.

That familiar sense of wrath building, Whisper looked to her sides, taking in the fight all around her. And there, only steps away, was Dark Water. He fought with his brothers, Second Son included, their foreign armor coated with blood and their faces twisted in expressions of glorious murder. Her fury only grew when she watched Dark Water pierce an enemy's throat and laugh, the sound strangely flat to her ears, which were accustomed to echoes that revealed a spirit's true thoughts.

In that deafness she found the answer to the question that had been forming since she first climbed on the dragons' back.

A low sound formed in the back of her throat, growing into a snarl as she stalked over to her prey. Dark Water turned when he sensed her presence, and began to smile only to be cut off as she grabbed him by the throat.

"*You*," she growled, squeezing tighter. Although she could not kill him by suffocation, she could still inflict pain and disfigure him for the rest of his own eternity. "This is your doing."

"*Kanegv*," Dark Water gasped, gripping at her hand. Crushing pain seared through him. "We fight...for your honor."

"There is no honor in betrayal," she replied, her voice low and her teeth clenched. "This is *my* war, and your fighters dared to shed first blood without me."

The Little Men surrounded them, weapons poised. But they could not fight for Dark Water, as the invisible barrier of air and shadows fought against them when they tried to break through. Whisper and her prey were alone in their circle.

Dark Water gasped again, feet kicking as she lifted him off the ground with a strength he never would have imagined of her. "*Kanegv*...we fight for you."

"For me?" she scoffed, eyes narrowing, hair blowing back as the wind began to pick up. "Or for your own purposes, to prove yourself worthy, to take another's place." Her fingers tightened, digging hard into flesh and bone. His eyes widened, realizing that she knew his motives. Then she dropped Dark Water at her feet, watching him collapse. "You are banished, Dark Water. You are *adehohisdi*."

Stepping out of the circle, Whisper left the eldest brother of the Little Men staring after her with desperation and despair in his eyes.

* * *

From the Sky Vault, Sun Woman watched as the battle raged on. It was a wondrous sight, one of bloodshed and torment, one that revealed the true powers of both spirit realms. She saw the half-breed in the midst of the war, staying true to herself by leading her army straight into battle, slicing down her enemies one by one. She saw the Great Spirit watching from *Oway*, somber and silent though his eyes showed the sorrow he felt for the losses on both sides.

This was a senseless war, Sun Woman thought, to all but the two who would not give up their stubborn ways. And yet, it was those two who were yet to fight one another. Hundreds had already died their second deaths, but the leaders of both armies stood strong.

Sun Woman gasped when she saw Whisper grab Dark Water by the throat. *She turns against her own*, the spirit thought, a hand lifting to her own neck. *So it has come to that.*

In another time, Sun Woman thought that she and the half-breed may have been of some use to one another. The sky being had her own plans for the future, her own ideas of revenge against the ones who could never look at her without screwing up their faces and squinting their eyes, yet looked upon Father Moon so lovingly. Now that Blue Cloud was back, they could pool their gifts together and turn on their other half, and with the addition of Second Son, a powerful brother to the Little Men, it would be even easier. Bringing Whisper into her mission would make them unstoppable, and Sun Woman was sure she could convince the half-breed to do her bidding. After all, she had been far more loyal and offered far more assistance than the moon spirit ever had.

But this display before her, Whisper attacking Dark Water for leading a small army into the front lines of her own war, it made no sense. Sun Woman prided herself on knowing all in the Land of the Dead and Spirit World, and wondered if she had missed an exchange somewhere along the lines. There was more prying to do, she thought, more spies to interrogate, more of the story to unravel.

For now the spirit of the Sky Vault could do nothing but watch, but when this war ended, she too would have to question her loyalties.

Chapter 48

*A*dagatiya had his orders, and he planned on fulfilling them. His loyalty was to the half-breed now, and he would destroy whatever she asked in return for his freedom. And so after she leapt off his back and tumbled onto the battlefield, he changed direction and flew straight for *Oway*.

As he neared, he saw two figures in an upper-story window. One watched him calmly, the other had panic written across his face. If he could have smiled, the dragon would have done so happily.

He would burn the palace down, giving his ruler the upper hand in this war, ensuring her victory. With a low growl he opened his mouth wide and shot out a stream of liquid fire at the earth. A fiery red trail blazed across the grass and began to surround *Oway*, viscous black smoke curling up toward the sky. Quickly, the flames licked closer until they were brushing at the stone.

Making a second pass, an ear-shattering roar echoing around the land, *Adagatiya* released a second burst of flames, blackening the towers at the top and crisscrossing the eastern walls. But before the dragon could wonder why Creator wasn't fighting back, he saw the change in the stone.

Ice slicked up from the ground and down from the sky, coating the palace from corner to corner. When it touched the fire, the flames were doused in hissing steam, though remnants of their burns remained beneath the ice. A heavy snow began to fall and sleet poured down as the dragon circled *Oway*, searching for the source of the sudden winter.

He found her standing along the northern wall, one hand on *Oway*. From her fingers, ice cracked and formed, spreading to protect the Great Spirit's home from further ruin. *Adagatiya* landed only yards away, growling and scratching at the earth with his talon-tipped feet.

Blue Corn Maiden relinquished her hold, stepping forward. "Your presence is not welcome here, beast. Return to the Land of the Dead, or perish."

Suddenly furious, the dragon launched a burst of flames at the spirit, who merely held up a hand. Fire met ice in a flash of white light, knocking them both back a few steps.

You will burn for your loyalties, the dragon sneered as Blue Corn Maiden straightened and readied herself for a fight.

"And you will return to your cage."

They fought with every bit of power they had, Blue Corn Maiden sending up sharp shards of ice through the earth, piercing the dragon's feet and slicing open his sides. *Adagatiya* responded in kind, burning a circle around them and spitting out spheres of flames that scorched her skin. The air all around them smoked and sizzled, surrounding them in hazy mist like a world all their own. They stepped around one another carefully, Blue Corn Maiden lashing out and throwing jagged ice picks at the dragon, who howled when they sliced through his face. She took advantage of his moment's hesitation, casing him in a cold wind, making him shiver as the snow started to build around his aching limbs.

But *Adagatiya* was stronger than that, and would not allow a snow spirit to defeat him. *Your ice is no match for fire,* he told her, shaking snow off his scales.

"I am more than ice, beast. I am winter. I am snow. I am the frozen parts of your spirit begging to be free." As she spoke, Blue Corn Maiden cupped her hands, white light glowing through her fingers. "My winds will suffocate your flames, and send them back upon yourself. You will perish for being what you are." She thrust her hands forward, releasing an enormous wave of wind and ice.

At the same time, *Adagatiya* summoned all the power within him, everything that had been locked away deep inside him during the Raven-Eater's reign. He channeled the flames waiting to be freed from every corner of his being and sent them straight at Blue Corn Maiden.

Their forces collided halfway, crashing into one another and tumbling around, fighting for a break. The strain showed on both their faces, the dragon's jaw trembling and Blue Corn Maiden's arms shuddering from the force. She clamped her jaw together, biting down hard in an effort to maintain her hold, but soon recognized exactly what she was up against.

This was more than just a dragon held captive under the Fire Mountains, she realized. This was an old magic, older than the half-breed, older than the Raven-Eater, and even older than her. *Adagatiya* was stronger, more powerful, and that showed in the sudden burst that he pushed toward her. The flames broke through her force, shattering her control, and searing the palms of her hands.

With a cry, Blue Corn Maiden dropped to the snow, cradling her hands to her chest. The dragon remained, watching her cautiously, curiously. Dreading what she would see, the snow spirit observed her hands, lips parting in shock when she saw the black, charred flesh and heard the hissing of open wounds. Her hands shook from the shock of the attack. In time, they would heal, but not quickly enough to defend *Oway* and certainly not quickly enough to protect her own self.

As much as it shamed her, she had to retreat. Her energy was weakened not only by her battle with the dragon, but also from sending winter to the Land of the Dead. "Forgive me, Great Spirit," she whispered, then disappeared in a flurry of snowflakes.

Satisfied, *Adagaliyu* launched himself in the air, leaving the palace behind in a torrent of flames.

* * *

Her child was healthy, ready to be born into the world. Nurses and doctors were happy, smiling with each visit. Friends called to wish her well, and the parents of the man once known as Cole Daivya had come, eager to welcome their grandchild into the world.

She rested in bed, looking through a photo album. Cole smiled up at her, playfully hugging a friend's puppy. In another, he was kissing her on the cheek as she grinned at the camera. It was from his first birthday they celebrated together, at the surprise party she had planned with his parents. That had been a happy day, she remembered, one of the few where he wasn't tormented by nightmares.

The thought of nightmares had her frowning. Closing the album, she looked over at Ian, who was watching a sports game on the hospital television. "Have you met the woman with the black eyes?"

Startled from his own thoughts, Ian looked over at the woman he would always consider family. "I beg your pardon?"

"The woman with the black eyes," she repeated. "Have you met her?"

She saw the dread fill his face, and the hard swallow when he tried to hide it. "That's...that's not much information to go by."

"And yet you know exactly who I'm talking about. Whatever Cole was running from in his dreams, you are too. Only you know exactly what it is to be afraid of, and he never did."

Ian sighed, rubbing his hands over his tired face. "There are some things that do not concern you. This is one of them."

"It concerns me when I start seeing the same thing in my dreams," she snapped, a hand on her swollen stomach. "I deserve to know."

Ian rose to his feet quickly, the chair scraping harshly against the tile floor. A scowl crossed his face. "Don't pretend to know things you know nothing about. Just leave it alone."

"Or what?" she called after him, just as he reached the door.

Ian turned slowly, barely looking over his shoulder. "Or she just might find you, and steal your soul for herself."

Chapter 49

Humiliated into retreat, infuriated by the disrespect, horrified by the command, Dark Water stumbled away from the battlefield. He was shamed, *adehohisdi*, banished, trading one exile for another. And for what purpose?

He had done nothing but follow the half-breed into war, show her that he, above all others, believed in her fight and was by her side until the end. He was the one to shed first blood, to prove to Creator that none of them could be controlled. He began the war to end all wars, knowing they would have won, that the half-breed *would* win, all because of him.

And now she had taken that honor away from him.

Stumbling over a rock, Dark Water fell to a knee, grimacing and punching the earth with an angry hand. He kneeled there for a moment, pitying himself while imaging the feel of Whisper's blood running through his fingers as he slit her throat. Any affection he may have ever felt for her had curdled and left a bad taste in his mouth, and now he wanted nothing more than to cut that smirk off her face. To dishonor him, his brothers, was unforgivable, even if disgracing and turning against her people was in the half-breed's nature.

But the half-breed couldn't be destroyed, and if harmed her body would heal itself. Alone, Dark Water couldn't end the war or even help the Great Spirit win. One spirit, or seven, weren't powerful enough for that kind of battle. Shouting his frustration, he lifted himself to his feet, and saw Hunting Hawk on the edges of the battle.

No, he realized, there were other ways to bring down the half-breed.

Driven by a blind fury, Dark Water shadowed his head in the fur of his cloaked armor, stalking his prey. With each step, his hate for Whisper and the War Chief grew. Hunting Hawk had honor in life and in death, having died in battle defending his people, and now he fought to defend the woman who held his heart. He was a man of great stature, thick muscles now slicked with blood that would frighten off nearly any enemy, a strong face that told stories of a fierce yet noble life. And he had won the affection of the untamable, of the merciless, of the half-breed.

Hunting Hawk was her only weakness.

Enemy after enemy the War Chief cut down, reveling in each kill, eyes flashing with the thrill of war. In his fight he never saw the figure slinking up behind him, never sensed the attack. When Dark Water was within arm's reach, he released a guttural scream and drove his blade deep into Hunting Hawk's heart.

She was fighting knife to spear when she felt it, a sharp, hot stab of agonizing pain in the center of her chest. The excruciating feeling brought her to her knees, crying out as grief and unbearable hurt swept through her.

Gathering her wits, using the power of her bloodline to heal what parts of her were broken, Whisper got to her feet shakily and desperately searched for Hunting Hawk. She was connected to only one spirit, and only his pain could she suffer. A thousand gruesome images pulsed through her mind, pictures of what could be, what she prayed wasn't possible.

Then she saw him on the edge of the field, fallen. Dark Water stood over him, dagger dripping black blood. He was watching the body menacingly, waiting for it to disappear into its second death. Still throbbing from the attack, Whisper ran to her mate's side, shoving Dark Water out of the way hard enough to make the man stumble.

"Perhaps you should remember your loyalties, half-breed," he said with glee, sheathing his knife as Whisper rolled Hunting Hawk onto his back. His eyes were closed, his body lifeless. "What will you do without your precious War Chief?"

Whisper said a silent prayer, running trembling fingers over the wound, which went straight through his chest. Her brow furrowed as her eyes narrowed and burned at the thought of eternity without Hunting Hawk. A single tear escaped down her dirt-smudged cheek, leaving behind a smudged trail. She pressed her lips together tightly, fighting back a sob, swallowing hard when blood seeped through her fingers. A feeling she didn't recognize, one she thought may have been grief, surged through her, nearly overcoming her as she stroked his pale, still face with a trembling hand. Her touch was tender, loving.

"I have not lost my War Chief," she replied suddenly, her throat tight, running a hand down Hunting Hawk's rigid face again before straightening to face Dark Water. He prepared himself for a fight, but she only stood there.

"Are you a coward now, half-breed?" Dark Water sneered. "Will you not fight the man who has slain your mate? Or was your love only for show, as the half-breed cannot love?"

Every part of her ached to fight, but she controlled the urge to shed more blood. Not for this fight, or this spirit. He would face the consequences of his actions, but not by her weapons. "I have no need to fight you, Dark Water. You have not slain Hunting Hawk, but you will soon see what happens to those who cross the half-breed."

Before he could respond, Dark Water felt the stab in his back. He turned, but no weapon had pierced his flesh. Then the stab deepened, spreading slowly, agonizingly, through his chest. He fell, his eyes full of questions. Just as his lips parted to ask what was happening, a shimmer caught his eye. Hunting Hawk's chest had begun to glow, two symbols drawn in light.

"*Nvdo iga ehi*, Mother Sun. Everlasting life," Whisper said quietly, lowering herself down to her mate once again. She traced the pattern with a finger. "*Uyona*, the horns, for protection." She observed Dark Water, satisfaction in her face. "*Vlenidohv ganetliyvsdi vlenidohv*. Life exchanges life, Dark Water."

The eldest of the Little Men collapsed onto his back, feeling his spirit fade slowly. Whisper crouched over him, scorn and a hint of pity in her eyes. "Did you believe me so foolish that I would allow Hunting Hawk into battle without my protection?" She shook her head when the spirit could only stare up at her incredulously, gasping pleas for salvation. "*Didayolihv dvgalenisgv*, Dark Water. Until we meet again."

Just as Dark Water passed into another world and Hunting Hawk's eyes opened, Second Son appeared. "Brother!" he yelled, grasping for Dark Water's body, but it was too late. He disappeared in a cloud of gray dust. Stunned, the man looked up at Whisper. "What have you done?"

"He did this to himself, Second Son. He attacked Hunting Hawk. No one, not even Dark Water, is protected against that."

"He believed in you!" Second Son leapt to his feet, voice breaking with grief. "He—" Suddenly he was speechless, and found that he was nearly unable to remember even his own name. "What...what is happening to me?"

Whisper's eyes were sad when she answered. "The contract I made was with Dark Water, and Dark Water alone. I am bound by our agreement only while he is alive. In his second death, our contract is void. It is unfortunate, but it was our agreement. In his betrayal, you must suffer the consequences. Your spirit must return to the Land of the Living, in exile from your brothers until another offers you mercy."

She felt the slightest bit of sadness for the spirit as she watched Second Son leave Cole's body. She didn't think it fair for him to be forced back into exile because of Dark Water's crimes, but she had meant what she said. Her contract was not with Second Son, and she would not make another agreement with the Little Men unless her land depended on it. And even then, she wasn't sure it would be worth the risk.

As soon as Second Son's spirit departed, a hard look took over the man's face. Whisper had been expecting Cole to return, but this was not the man she had lured to the Land of the Dead. This spirit before her was cold, unforgiving, unafraid of anything, not even the war around him. This was the spirit of a boy all grown up, the boy accepted into the Raven-Eater's hearth who knew only how to be fierce and tough, unbreakable.

"Hello, Fighting Fox." As soon as she said his name, a rumble went through the earth, shaking at their feet. Whisper cast a scornful look down. "He calls for you."

"He calls for his son. He calls for his true heir." Fighting Fox's voice was hard and familiar, the voice of the Raven-Eater.

"Then go to him. My fight is not with you."

"It will be soon, half-breed. We will return for our vengeance." And with his promise, Fighting Fox faded away. Whisper stared at the empty air until she heard Hunting Hawk speak behind her.

"You were right. There is a land of second deaths." He ran a hand down her arm when she knelt at his side. "The Raven-Eater lives."

"And he will die, again. But that is another battle for another time. Can you fight?" She helped him to his feet, inspecting the wound on his back.

"Yes, thanks to you." He retrieved his weapon. There was no time to marvel over what Whisper had done, how she had saved him. That would be a conversation for another time. "We have wasted enough time. Let us end this war."

Chapter 50

Blue Cloud knew the moment she lost Second Son. The young sky spirit fell to her knees, gasping at the horrible sensation of loss in her chest. Sun Woman could only hold her daughter and offer soothing words that she knew meant nothing. Just as there was nothing to be done.

Dark Water was to blame for Second Son's exile, and not even Sun Woman could bring him back from that. She could not fault Whisper for the eldest Little Man's actions, as he had confused bravery with stupidity and attempted to murder the half-breed's partner and companion. No other spirit could have saved him from Whisper's wrath, and none would have dared to try.

But while she couldn't fault the half-breed, Sun Woman could hate her for what she had done to her daughter. Dark Water was gone, but Whisper was still alive and able to experience what wrath the leader of the Sky Vault was ready to cast down upon her.

Sun Woman could only thank her good fortune that Blue Cloud was part of her contract with Whisper, and not Dark Water's. She would keep her daughter so long as she was part of the Sky Vault, and she would be one with that Sky Vault forever. No one, not even the Great Spirit himself, would take Blue Cloud away from her ever again. Sun Woman would see to that no matter what it took.

"I hate her, mother," Blue Cloud sniffled, burying her head in her mother's shoulder. "She took him away from me. She took everything away. I want revenge."

Sun Woman pulled her daughter back, staring her straight in the eye. "Watch your tongue when speaking of the half-breed," she said sternly. "She has eyes and ears everywhere. The Sky Vault does not need a war like the one battling below us."

"So then she gets away with it? All because of who she is?"

"No." Sun Woman hugged her daughter again, remembering the shockwave that ran through the ground felt even beneath her own feet. "New spirits are being born, Blue Cloud, and old spirits are returning. There will soon come a time when new contracts must be made."

And then, she said within her own mind, channeling her thoughts to her daughter, *we will both have our revenge.*

* * *

Safe in his own home, having conjured up enough rain to douse the flames that threatened *Oway* after the dragon departed, the Great Spirit could watch the fight no longer. Both armies had made their points, and fought honorably. No more needed to die. He turned to Earth Keeper, who had come to report on their losses only moments ago.

"Let us end this," he said softly, and Earth Keeper nodded. He turned sharply and exited, never looking at Smoke Speaker, who sat at a small wooden table with his head in his hands. It didn't take long to hurry through the stone corridors, exiting out into the harsh light clouded by ash and smoke. Fires still burned all around him, parts of *Oway* blackened in soot. The ground was scorched, smelling of blood and decay as they stomped over fallen bodies and thickened blood.

When he reached the battlefield, Earth Keeper drew his weapons and shouted as far as his voice would carry. "*Kanegv!*"

Fighting on both sides stopped. Weapons fell to the spirits' sides as they stared at the man who had shouted for the half-breed. It was an invitation to fight, they all knew, one man seeking to take on the leader of the Land of the Dead alone.

And soon she appeared, Hunting Hawk at her side. She had a look in her eye that frightened any who dared to look her way, a look of death that matched her very appearance. Disheveled from combat, bloodied and wounded, and yet stronger than ever, she exuded a strength and confidence they would never know, and certainly never challenge.

"He lives," she said sarcastically when she reached Earth Keeper. "Tell me, how did you escape the Fire Tower?"

She didn't want an answer, and he knew it. But just to taunt her, he held up the dagger he knew she would recognize, the same one she had slammed into the stone just out of reach. She looked at the blade, but didn't show any signs of recognition, not giving him the satisfaction. "This war ends with us."

"You wish to fight me? You cannot kill me."

"No," he agreed, "but I can rip you apart, piece by piece."

The threat meant to frighten her only made her grin her malicious smirk. "You may try."

The other spirits, Hunting Hawk included, backed up as Earth Keeper stepped forward, entering into an invisible barrier that would mark their fighting circle. Whisper held a black shield made of the metals that forged the Fire Tower; Earth

Keeper's was light yet built of a Spirit World steel that no weapon could penetrate. In his other hand he held a double-edged sword, Whisper a long dagger with her bow and quiver strapped across her back.

They circled one another, sizing up their opponent. Silence fell around them, all eyes watching fearfully. Only Hunting Hawk was unafraid for his leader, as no spirit could defeat her.

Whisper placed her feet carefully, for once having to fight without the direction of the voices, her helpers, guiding her actions into victory. Earth Keeper mimicked her every move, to the point that it annoyed her. "Do you always wait for the enemy to draw first blood, Earth Keeper?" she asked scornfully. "Are you such a coward as that?"

Enraged, the man rushed forward, slaughter in his snarl. He lashed out at Whisper, who ducked easily and slammed a hand on his back that sent him tumbling to the ground. A cheer from her army rose up, and another from his own when he leapt to his feet.

The battle had begun.

Metal glinted beneath the afternoon sun as they lunged for one another, aiming for bone and flesh. Earth Keeper released a furious scream as her knife pierced his shoulder, matching her wound. Whisper clenched her teeth and refused to show pain when the tip of his sword sliced through her shin, nearly sending her to the ground. If she so chose, she could have crushed him on the spot, using the blood of the half-breed to destroy him with ease, but there would have been no honor in that fight. Instead, she chose to bleed and hurt, to fight like a true warrior.

She was a trained fighter, as was he—true soldiers who understood the art of war and relished in its triumph. But Earth Keeper fought for glory, while Whisper fought for something far deeper. She had more to lose, more to gain, more emotion strengthening her every move that had the man exhausted in defending himself.

Dirt kicked up as they charged one another, blood splashed outside the circle as Earth Keeper's fist connected with Whisper's mouth, gasps sounded when she responded by sending her dagger straight into his thigh. Nearly defeated, Earth Keeper fell onto his back and Whisper followed, straddling her enemy with her knife poised above his heart.

"*Stop!*"

It wasn't the command that made Whisper hesitate, but the voice, a voice so familiar that at first she thought she was imagining it. But then the speaker appeared, pushing her way through the sea of soldiers, dropping to Earth Keeper's side as though protecting him from his second death.

"Please, *Kanegv*, don't do this."

Confused, Whisper stood and stepped away from Earth Keeper, her face a portrait of bewilderment. "Blue Feather?" she asked her mother, who looked up at her fearfully. "What are you doing here? How did you get here?"

Blue Feather didn't answer, but Earth Keeper did. He laughed, drawing himself up to his feet and bracing himself against her. "You asked how I escaped the Fire Tower, half-breed. Here is your answer."

Her confusion only grew as she attempted to understand. Whisper looked at her mother, seeing truth in her eyes. "You...you freed him? How? Why?"

"*Kanegv*." Blue Feather took a step forward, holding out a hand in an attempt to comfort her daughter. As she did, Earth Keeper and his army reformed in a straight line, a barrier between the half-breed and *Oway*. "It is not as it seems."

"It seems as though you have betrayed me."

"Never." Blue Feather shook her head insistently. "I only met Earth Keeper when you brought him to the Fire Tower. I went to see him while you were away, and we spoke. He explained his mission, what the Great Spirit wished, and it was not to harm you. He only wished to end the war before it began, to bring peace to both lands by settling a truce."

"And you believed his lies."

"He did not lie to me, *Kanegv*. I feared that at first, and worried that after releasing him he would return to the Spirit World and I would never see him again. But then my father reached out to me, and I knew he was keeping his promise."

"Smoke Speaker?" Each part of the story was only confusing her more. "You have spoken to the Elder?"

Blue Feather worried she was saying too much, but it was too late to turn back now. She cast a nervous look backwards to see Earth Keeper holding Smoke Speaker back. Both looked at her anxiously.

"It...it was for your own good." Her voice shook when Whisper stepped forward, her black eyes flickering. "I promise you, *Kanegv*, it was for your own good."

"*What* was for my own good?"

"The...the Circle. We only wanted to help lead you down the Red Road."

"You...took up council against me?" Incredulity filled her question.

"*For* you, *Kanegv*."

"*Against* me!" she shouted, her words echoing across the open land. Soldiers on both sides flinched and braced themselves to take cover. "Is your council to blame for the ambush at the Fire Tower? Are you the reason why I hear nothing on the battlefield?"

Blue Feather hesitated before answering. "...Yes."

"How?"

The question came out as a low growl that terrified Blue Feather to the core. "It was...magic. What little bit I have, mixed with that of the Circle. I wove it into your medicine wheel." In a fury, Whisper reeled around to face Hunting Hawk. His expression of shock matched her own, but she could not extinguish her suspicion. Seeing what was about to happen, Blue Feather grabbed Whisper's arm. "No, *Kanegv*! Hunting Hawk was not part of this. This, I did on my own while he slept."

Yanking her arm from her mother's grasp, Whisper shoved Blue Feather back a few steps. "And are you also to blame for my medicine wheel's destruction? Was it you, and not Creator?" Her mother's tearful silence told Whisper she was right. "You—"

The sound of fluttering wings cut her off. Momentarily forgetting Blue Feather, Hunting Hawk, the army around her, Whisper watched as the winged spirit landed beside her. As stoic and peaceful as ever, *Kamama* regarded her.

"Do not blame your mother for this council, *Kanegv*. What she speaks is the truth, we gathered for your own good, not to harm you."

"You too?" she whispered, taken aback. "And who else? Smoke Speaker? Creator?"

"Do not be angry, child," *Kamama* soothed, a wing grazing her arm. "The Red Road can be a treacherous place. We only wish to guide you along the way."

"I do not need *guidance!*" Whisper shouted, any hurt and despair she felt turning into blind rage. Then she turned on Blue Feather, shoving the woman to the ground and nocking an arrow at her throat. "Perhaps I kill you now, woman, and your magic along with you."

"Kill her, and suffer the consequences."

Whisper looked up to see Earth Keeper with an arrow aimed at *Kamama*. The butterfly looked both scared and sad. Then she understood. "I see," she said slowly to Blue Feather, drawing the arrow back further. "So you found yourself a lover in your treachery. And in doing so, made yourself an enemy."

"She is not your enemy, *Kanegv*," *Kamama* said, ignoring Earth Keeper. "I have told you many times, your fight is with your greatest enemy, and you have yet to discover just who that is."

"Then who is it?"

Kamama sighed, wings drooping. But before he could answer, someone else did for him.

"Yourself."

Chapter 51

Whisper searched for the speaker, refusing to respond when she saw the Great Spirit appear at the Elder's side. It was no surprise that he would be in partnership with Smoke Speaker, or his Circle, but she was curious as to why he would dare to speak to her.

Creator clasped his hands in front of him, looking somber and deathly serious. "You have demanded vengeance since you were a child, half-breed. You have taken what you desired, and given nothing in return. You are driven by hate and anger, and are not satisfied until blood is spilt in your name. And yet, the one spirit you refuse to battle is the one causing all your pain. That spirit, is yourself."

Dread crept through him when Whisper lowered the arrow closer to Blue Feather's throat as though to prove a point. "Then perhaps walking the Red Road means embracing the enemy, Creator."

Desperation clung to his next question. "Do you know the legend of the Blackfoot, of a young warrior and Chief Mountain?" When Whisper merely glared at him, Creator took that as a negative and an invitation to continue. He moved forward, stepping in front of his army.

"The warrior was brave and won many victories, so many that he was named War Chief. As War Chief, he took a wife, a woman he loved dearly, and they lived happily along with their new baby. But soon, war broke out between his tribe and another, and the enemy cut down his war party.

"Swearing vengeance, the War Chief gathered his men and planned a hunt on the enemy. His wife begged to join the war party, but he refused, ordering her to stay home and care for the children and elderly of their tribe, which rested at the base of a mountain."

Creator regarded Whisper with a stern expression, which made her narrow her eyes and aim the arrow at Blue Feather's forehead. "The War Chief died on his raid, and his wife's grief drove her mad. She would never again be the happy, strong woman and mother of a War Chief. She was broken, and lost in the confusion of her own mind.

"Then came the day the villagers could not find her, and after a search they found her high up on the mountainside, clutching her child to her breast. They begged for her to come down but she refused, and before they could rescue her, she leapt from the mountain onto the rocks below."

He paused to let the imagery sink in, hearing murmurs work their way throughout the crowd. Only Whisper appeared unaffected. She had turned her head slightly and was watching him from the corner of her eye.

"They buried her there, in the rocks, and buried their War Chief next to her. To this day, the people worship that burial place, and respect Chief Mountain for its sacrifices. They say that in that mountain you can see a woman holding a child in her arms, along with the man sworn to love her."

Creator finished his story, edging his way to the half-breed, stopping when he got only as close as he dared. "Do you know why I told you this story?"

Flexing the hand that gripped the bow, Whisper never took her eyes off her mother when she answered. "You wish to warn me of what I may lose in this war. You think me weak, a woman who will break, a foolish girl who makes sacrifices she does not understand."

The Great Spirit sighed, and behind him, Smoke Speaker worried he was about to say or do something foolish. Even Hunting Hawk placed a hand on his knife, which only made Earth Keeper press the tip of his arrow into *Kamama's* throat. "War brings out parts of us we never knew dwelled within our souls. Strength turns to weakness, bravery to cowardice, despair to rashness. If you are not careful, you too will fall over the edge of the mountain. While we will never be allies, I do not wish for you to end up like your father."

Indecision tore at her. She wanted Blue Feather to die for her treachery, and yet, this was her mother staring up at her with fear in her eyes. The half-breed lusted for the smell of blood, for vengeance; Whisper lusted for an end to this war. She may have been whole now, but that didn't take away the pain and confusion of betrayal.

Time seemed to stand still as she battled with the two parts of herself. The arrow shook ever so slightly. To lower it would mean defeat, surrender. To release it would mean they were right, that she was the hopeless offspring of the Raven-Eater. Pride waged war with truth within her, and truth with honor. Her eyes never left Blue Feather as she considered her options and fought the internal war. Only paces away, Earth Keeper's gaze never left Whisper, waiting for the moment she released her arrow so he could fire his own.

Knowing what fight Whisper faced, Hunting Hawk came to her side, touching her elbow gently so as not to disturb her aim. She didn't look at him, but he sensed a change in her that told him she was listening.

"*Kanegv*, they want you to do this. They want you to give in to the Raven-Eater's blood, so they do not look like the enemy. Do not let them win." He ran a hand across the small of her back. "*Kanegv*...come back to me."

The words snapped her out of her daze. Slowly, nearly painfully, she lowered the arrow, then tossed it aside. Hunting Hawk breathed a sigh of relief, as did Creator and Smoke Speaker. Only Blue Feather panicked, her eyes wide with terror as she screamed.

"Earth Keeper, *no!*"

The arrow pierced *Kamama* straight through the heart, the blue spirit vanishing in a cloud of dust before a sound could be made. A sneer crossed Earth Keeper's face as the color drained from Whisper's. The power that had been swarming around her faded, leaving her standing in a space empty of magic or emotion.

For a moment, it seemed like she too was about to fade away. Whisper's lips parted as though she had seen something terrifying, her eyes stared into vacant air, and she stumbled back a step like she could no longer comprehend how to walk. Hunting Hawk braced her as the world around them exploded into chaos, turning solider against soldier.

She felt the loss deeper than any other, a part of her ripped from her souls and cast down into the land where spirits died again. The arrow had pierced more than *Kamama*; it had pierced straight into her core, tearing through her very being, attempting to destroy what had once made her human. More than just her name, more than her life, but her spirit, that which connected her to both worlds.

The confusion settled in her mind, masking her senses. But something greater lurked, the part of her that longed to be free. The thought of freedom clouded her judgment, filled her mind. They wanted to murder her spirit, trap her soul. The very idea of it had her gripping a hand firmly around her dagger.

Somewhere far off in the distance, Whisper heard Hunting Hawk calling her name. She heard Blue Feather shouting curses at Earth Keeper, and Smoke Speaker fighting against another spirit's hold as he rushed forward.

Whisper cast their voices out of her head as wrath and anguish screamed out of her, pushing her forward. Her dagger lifted high, shimmering in the sun, then raced downward. She saw only Blue Feather's frightened face as the knife aimed for her heart, but when Smoke Speaker leapt to her defense, it was too late to stop the attack.

Her blade buried itself deep in the Elder's back. She felt it slice through, felt it destroy him. With a sob, Smoke Speaker stumbled, grabbing hold of his daughter. He tried to speak, but his mouth couldn't form the words. Blue Feather cried out and clutched at her father, her hands shaking as they slid over blood-soaked clothes. A horrible choking sound escaping the Elder's throat, he could only offer her one final look of love before he disappeared into his second death. It was over so fast that even Whisper had to take a moment to comprehend what just happened.

Hunting Hawk caught her as she fell back, holding her tightly when she simply looked down at her hands in shock over the black blood that now coated them. Silence surrounded them; not even the Great Spirit could speak. Whisper had just killed Smoke Speaker, her own grandfather, in an attempt to murder her mother. The tides had turned on the war, and the half-breed had revealed herself to them all.

Whisper sent out a silent call before the Great Spirit's army could react, and *Adagatiya* appeared before them. Hunting Hawk lifted her onto the beast's back and followed suit, never looking back.

As they rode off, Whisper lifted a hand, palm facing her warriors. Just as the Great Spirit's army rushed forward to defeat them, they vanished back into the Land of the Dead.

* * *

The time had come for her child to be brought into the world. Already the nurses had prepped her, and were in the final stages of delivery. Ian had come back to her room only moments before, and there was no time now to discuss what he had meant by the woman with the black eyes finding her.

Pain raced through her belly with each contraction, one she welcomed as it brought her closer to meeting her daughter. *Baby Anya,* she whispered in her mind, imagining herself speaking to the child within her. *You are my light and my life.*

Ian and Julia were at her sides, comforting her, encouraging her with each breath. Julia placed a gentle hand on her shoulder, telling her of what wonderful things awaited her in motherhood.

Soon the pain became unbearable, and tears streamed down her cheeks as she pushed, harder and harder. Her stomach burned, and she gripped their hands as hard as she could. Something didn't feel right inside, or in the way the nurses called her name.

Let it be over, she prayed. *Let my child be safe.*

Chapter 52

W hisper sent Hunting Hawk away, promising she would return to the Fire Tower soon. But for now, she needed to be alone. She needed sanctuary. She needed to understand what she had done and how she could make it right again. The river welcomed her, washing away the blood on her trembling hands and pulling her beneath the cold water to her secret place, which was empty of the newly evolved creatures. They had found their own way out, she guessed, exploring new parts of the world.

On the shore, she searched the sacred pool for answers, gripping the sides of the stone cauldron hard. "Show him to me," she whispered, commanding the visions to come to her. "*Show him to me!*"

But the water remained clear, revealing to her only the depths of the shallow bowl. Smoke Speaker was in a place not even the fates could find. A new idea came to thought.

"Show me the Raven-Eater."

The water rippled, a black shadow clouding the surface. It formed the outline of a man, a man without face or definition, a man not wholly formed. The figure stood on the edge of a cliff, looking over a burning river very much like her own private sanctuary. It turned her direction, and the water bubbled then cleared as though afraid to show any more.

"He lives," she said quietly. "But where?" For that, the water had no answer. "How do I find him?"

Whisper's eyes narrowed when the water revealed the beast to her, the creature that dwelled within her sanctuary's river, the one even she was afraid to hunt. The stories told of that creature, the legends that had haunted her dreams as a child, warned of a power far beyond her understanding. To fight it would be to walk the road of death.

But she would fight, for the Elder. He had taken council against her, betrayed her despite his promises, but he was her grandfather, the man who had saved her from the Raven-Eater and raised her as his own. He was a kind man, who sacrificed his own life for his daughter's. He deserved better than that place of second deaths.

But fighting the beast, traveling to that forsaken land, meant a quest to end all quests, a journey deep into the last spirit realm where lived mankind's darkest fears and demons.

"I will find you, Smoke Speaker," she promised, hoping that wherever he was, he could hear her on the whispers of the wind. "I will make you proud."

To take that journey meant sacrifice on her part as well. She knew what she had to do.

* * *

It devastated her to be left out of battle, sent away where she could have no part in the fight. Splinter Foot Girl couldn't help but feel that she was being punished for her failed ambush, for not destroying the half-breed while she had the chance.

No, instead of fighting, Creator told her to go home. He said she had lost enough family for this lifetime in eternity, that she had sacrificed enough. He could not ask her to give up any more for his cause. It didn't matter that she wanted to fight, that she begged to avenge her fathers in war against the half-breed. Her words were met with silence and sadness, and the Great Spirit refused to relent.

She departed *Oway* with a heavy heart, fighting back tears. Splinter Foot Girl traveled alone to the place where she would rise up to meet her family, but as she was departing the Spirit World she felt a shift in the air and her vision went white. When it cleared, she discovered she was standing in what she could only guess to be the Sky Vault.

A regal figure stood before her, waiting patiently with a soft smile on her elegant, if not aged, face. Splinter Foot Girl approached slowly, gripping her knife. She looked around quickly, taking in the vast open stretches of white, the oasis of tropics just off to the east, the sounds of waterfalls and babbling brooks and springtime in the air. There was peace here, along with a foreboding sense of danger.

"Sun Woman?" she asked, wondering what the sky spirit could possibly want with her.

Sun Woman nodded, reaching out and taking the younger woman by the arm. "Welcome, Splinter Foot Girl. You must be curious as to why I called you."

"…A bit."

"It seems we have both been discarded, Splinter Foot Girl." Sun Woman led her to the hearth, where a savory sharing of meat was cooking over the fire. "Creator sent you away just when you needed him the most, as the half-breed stole from me the spirit I needed for my own purposes."

"I asked to fight," Splinter Foot Girl whispered, staring down at her hands. "I pleaded to avenge my fathers' deaths. But I had already failed him. He no longer needed me."

"I need you."

Splinter Foot Girl looked up at that. Her brow furrowed. "For what purpose?"

Sun Woman leaned forward, pale yellow robes grazing the earth. "The half-breed may have retreated, but this war is not yet over. My daughter has returned to me, and together, we are stronger than those older than us. Stronger even than Father Moon."

She felt like she should have known what the sky spirit was saying, but Splinter Foot Girl couldn't put the pieces together. "And where do I come in?"

"You want revenge for your fathers' deaths. You want to prove to the Great Spirit that you are worthy. I want to help you."

It was true. Splinter Foot Girl did want those things. She longed to show the half-breed what she was capable of, to be the one who earned the glorious title of stripping the leader of her strength, to prove to Creator that he made a mistake in casting her from his army. But, she wondered, at what cost? Just as the half-breed was a deceiver, she was not so naïve to believe Sun Woman to be completely honest.

"And what do you ask for in return, Sun Woman?"

At that, the sky spirit smiled and rose to her feet. She stretched out her arms, gesturing to the paradise all around her. "The spirit realms are weakened, and will be for many moons. Their leaders have been revealed for who they truly are. New boundaries are being drawn, new loyalties being sworn. Old powers are rising, and with them, chaos. I ask that you serve in my war, Splinter Foot Girl, and in return, you and your family will have your place in the Sky Vault."

It was tempting. Too tempting, and so she gave in to her dreams of a place where she and her fathers could look down on every realm with joy. But still she had one last lingering thought.

"Who are you going to war with, Sun Woman? Who must I fight?"

Her eyes shone with vengeance and anticipation when she answered. "We will own the sky, Splinter Foot Girl. And with it, everything the eye can see."

Chapter 53

He was waiting for her when she arrived, arms folded across his chest, a single solitary figure set against a dark backdrop unbecoming of Creator's character. The white of his robes clashed against the black of the night, the wavering portal in the air next to him threatening to swallow him whole. The stoic expression on his face didn't change as she neared, but she did note the suspicion in his eyes.

"You came."

The Great Spirit lowered his arms and took a step forward, wondering about the slightly surprised tone in her voice. "You expected I would not."

It wasn't a question, but she answered anyway. "I expected you to ignore me, or come with an army of men."

"You destroyed most of my army, as I am sure you remember."

"I did what was necessary for The Land of the Dead."

"You did what was necessary for yourself." Creator sighed then, and lifted a hand. "I did not come here to argue with you. You asked me to meet you at the place of crossing, and I have. What do you want?"

Whisper took a moment to collect herself, mouth pressed in a tight line as she bit back the flash of anger brought forth by the battle of words. She forced herself to remember that Creator was not the enemy, and that although they would always stand on opposite sides of the battlefield, they must work together.

"It is time that we end this," she told the other spirit, laying down her dagger to make a point.

Creator regarded her suspiciously. "You seek truce in a war you started?"

"I am not the only one to pick up an arrow, Creator. You knew what would happen in stealing Smoke Speaker from me. You are not innocent in this war."

The statement amused him, but he would not engage in another argument. He was here to make peace, if such a notion was possible. "I suppose you want retribution for the Elder, although he died his second death by your own hand."

Whisper shook her head, eyes sad. "No," she replied quietly, looking at the dry earth. "His death was of my own doing, and for that I will do what I must to get him back. I will find the land of the second deaths," she said when the Great Spirit's expression changed to one of derision.

"It is a suicide mission." But he would not try to talk her out of it, and they both knew it. Instead he merely shook his head and glanced over at the barrier between worlds as though bored. "If it is not retribution you want, then how do you propose your truce?"

This she had thought long and hard about. Gesturing to a spot only steps away from the barrier, Whisper sat on a small fallen tree while Creator rested on a rock across from her. "Blue Feather will stay in the Spirit World with you. She is not meant for the Land of the Dead. She is too kind-hearted and generous. This realm will ultimately only destroy her."

He had already planned on keeping the woman upon her consent, for Earth Keeper. "Agreed."

"You will accept Brave Woman into the Spirit World, so that she may live out her days with Little Eagle. It is true that she fought against you, but only so that her contract would be fulfilled."

"Little Eagle may cross over into the Land of the Dead."

Whisper shook her head. "They are both good spirits, and deserve to live in the light."

The Great Spirit considered for a moment silently, deciding that it would do him well to have both in the Spirit World, as they were renowned warriors and loyal to the one they served. "Agreed."

"You agree to never hold council against me again. No Elder, spiritual leader, or any other being will use his or her power against mine, or strip away my own. Counsel will never be taken against Hunting Hawk either." It burned her to know just how many were conspiring against her, and hurt to hear just who those spirits were. And while she understood that it was not done out of hate or spite, it did not erase the sense of betrayal.

Creator saw that hurt in the tight lines of her face, heard the slight hint of desperation masked by anger in her voice. And despite himself, he felt pity for the woman.

She was alone, he realized. Despite having Hunting Hawk, despite having an entire realm at her disposal, she was forever alone in who and what she was. No spirit living or dead would ever understand the half-breed, but would instead try to control her, target her as something different to be feared, as he had done himself. To know what you are, and to know there would never be a soul to share that power with, had the power to devastate.

For that reason, and that reason alone, he nodded. "Agreed." When Whisper looked up and faced him with that steely gaze, he knew more was coming. "You have another demand?"

"I want the child."

At that, the Great Spirit laughed. It was a deep chuckle, and nearly heartfelt at the absurdity and, what he considered to be, naivety of the question. Whisper merely let him laugh, as she had known he would not agree in the beginning. Finally, he stopped and leaned forward, a hint of a grin still on his face, "This I will not agree to."

"It is my final demand for a truce with the Spirit World."

Creator sat up straight, hands gripping his knees. "So you demand that I take on two spirits previously living in the Land of the Dead, that I never take council against you or your War Chief, and that I give up the child meant for my own purposes, all for a war you declared?"

"Yes."

The seriousness in her voice silenced him out of sheer amazement. He had always known the half-breed to be rash, demanding, selfish, and at times merciless. But never before had he known her to be foolish. "Has your reign made you so unwise, half-breed, that you would believe yourself worthy of such a demand?" He rose when she merely lifted a brow and continued her deep, haunting stare. "You insult me, half-breed, to force your spirits into my realm while attempting to steal one out of it. And you think yourself far more valuable than the Spirit World considers you to be."

Whisper rose along with him, not letting her anger over their gathering cloud her judgment. This was something that had to be done, not for the truce, not for the Great Spirit, not for the child, but for the plans she had for her own future. "Without the child, we will not have peace."

With a shake of his head, Creator turned and nearly passed through the crossing. Something held him back, a sense of curiosity and dread. Slowly, he faced Whisper again. "Tell me, half-breed, what would I get out of this?"

It hurt her to speak the words, both physically and spiritually. Her hands flexed at her sides, and she swallowed hard before answering. For a moment she wasn't sure she could say anything at all.

"I will give up the Land of the Dead."

Now she had his curiosity peaked. The Great Spirit abandoned his retreat and walked over to where Whisper stood, crossing his arms. All around them, the sky began to fade into early morning light. Sun Woman would be in their presence soon, and Creator did not wish to be trapped in the Land of the Dead for another day, as crossing was only possible when Father Moon hung in the sky. In that early light he saw traces of plant and animal in the distance, reminding him that they were never truly alone.

"You declared this war because the child was meant to take your place. And now you wish to give up you reign? Why?"

"No spirit can rule forever, Creator. You know this." Whisper lifted a shoulder as though dismissing the thought, one he found terrifying but could not deny. "I know that even if I sought a truce, you would always plan for the girl to take my place. But a child raised by the Great Spirit cannot rule the Land of the Dead. She must live here, and learn our ways, not yours. This realm cannot be guided by a child of the light."

He knew there was more to her reasoning. There was always more when the half-breed spoke, hidden meanings behind her words, deceit veiled by agreement. "You would never give up this realm. The Land of the Dead is your very being, half-breed."

"The Land of the Dead does not define me, Creator. But what I do in the Land of the Dead, does." At that, Whisper looked out in the hazy dawn light and sighed. "This is my land, Creator. It was born to me, and I was born to it. But to end this war, and replace what was lost, I will do as I promise."

"And when would this heir take her reign?"

"When the time is right." When Creator looked at her doubtfully, Whisper simply returned the smirk. "She would need training, and education. The Land of the Dead's ways are not so easily learned. When she came of the right age, this land will be hers."

"Who decides when she comes of age? How do I know you would not simply kill her when her time to rule had come?"

Offended, Whisper put her hand on the bone handle of her blade. The Great Spirit noted the action, setting his face into a hard, unforgiving expression. "Do not insult me, Creator. I will not harm this child in any way. She will be my own. My... *uwetsi ageyv.*"

My own. My...uwetsi ageyv. Suddenly the Great Spirit understood. What he had taken away from her in calling on the Elder, he would be giving back to her with the child, the daughter of the light. Life exchanges life, and with that exchange, came peace.

He would be giving up his own vision for the Land of the Dead's future, but would also be gaining the promise that the darker spirit realm would be free from the blood of the half-breed, of the Raven-Eater. If he agreed, then he would be giving his people the chance they needed to restore their traditions, their beliefs. Accepting a contract with the half-breed, he realized, was sometimes necessary for the greater good.

"Morning comes, Creator. Do we have an agreement?"

Torn between refusal and consent, battling between his head and his heart, the Great Spirit sorted out his thoughts as quickly as possible. Whisper waited patiently. For her, there was no rush for time. She could see his torment, and reveled in it.

Finally, Creator lifted his head and faced her squarely. "I have my own demands, if this child were placed in your care. She will follow the training I set for her, although you may incorporate your own if I agree. She is never to make sacrifices of any kind, and she will not accompany you on your quest to find Smoke Speaker. She will keep her given name and not one of your own, and she will take the husband chosen for her by the Circle I create. She will never be harmed by your hand or that of your servicemen, but she will be taught to defend herself when necessary. You are never to hold her back from training, and will teach her anything she desires when it is asked of you.

"In this exchange, you will end all plans of retributions against the Spirit World and its inhabitants, and vow never to enter my realm again or send your own spirits in your stead. You will not contact any spirits in the Spirit World, your mother included, and you will send any messengers assigned by my hand back unharmed, if I so choose to contact you."

"Is that all?" Whisper asked, somewhat snidely.

"No." Creator shook his head. "You will close the crossing behind me, to guarantee you or your kind never enter the Spirit World again. If we must communicate, it will be through the sacred waters. Do we have an agreement?"

She didn't need to think it over, but she hesitated long enough to make the Great Spirit uncomfortable. "Agreed."

"Good. I pray you take this task seriously, and guard the child as though she were your own."

"I will."

The Great Spirit eyed Whisper cautiously, wondering if he was making the biggest mistake either spirit realm had ever seen. There was hesitation in his eyes, and something else she couldn't identify. "Perhaps I was wrong about you, half-breed. Perhaps you understand more than simply hate and war. But make no mistake, should you break our agreement, you will suffer me." He turned to the portal in the air, pausing to glance over his shoulder. "And *Kanegv*, if you were to seek my advice, I would tell you to mourn Elder Smoke Speaker, and move on. If you search for him, you may find more than you bargained for."

Then he stepped through the crossing, and disappeared. Whisper stared after him for a moment as the morning sun washed over her. It was a harsh, angry light, telling her that Sun Woman was displeased, as she should be. But that was a battle for another day.

With a regretful sigh, Whisper raised a hand and placed it on the strip of cold, solid air. It vibrated beneath her fingers as she channeled her power into it. With a flash of light and the sound of breaking glass, the portal shattered, sealing off her world from Creator's forever.

* * *

It hurt more than it should have, and at first she tried to tell herself that everything was alright. But it was the look on the nurses' faces that told her she was wrong. This delivery wasn't going the way they had planned. Julia kept her calm, wiping the sweat from her brow, while Ian simply let her hold on as tightly as she needed to.

The moment her child entered the world, she knew. Not by the sound of a crying baby, but by her own mother's intuition. Anya was here with her, but she was silent, as was the doctor. Something wasn't right.

It seemed like ages before anyone would speak to her, although everyone rushed around her while machines beeped and nurses shouted. Julia was pushed away, Ian lost his grip, and she fought them in a frenzied panic. Out of the corner of her eye she saw the blood, so much of it, all over the bed, all over her. She smelled it next, knowing it came from her.

Then there was a sense of peace, but whether she dreamed it or not she didn't know. She asked to see her child, and baby Anya was placed in her arms, quiet and still and innocent. A tear slipped down her cheek, and she wanted to apologize, wanted to tell her child it would all be alright, but hardly had the strength to do anything more than kiss her beautiful little girl on the top of her head.

She closed her eyes then, hugging her baby close to her heart. "Your daddy loves you so much," she whispered, the sights and sounds of her hospital room fading. "My baby Anya."

Just before slipping into a dreamless sleep, just before the sun slipped below the horizon to welcome a warm summer night, she felt Ian once again take her hand, his fingers pushing her sweaty hair away from her face. Then she heard him whisper in her ear, his voice choked and mournful.

"Let you walk in beauty, and may your eyes ever behold the red and purple sunset."

Chapter 54

Earth Keeper paced the room angrily in long strides, freshly scrubbed from the long battle but still showing marks of war days after the attacks. Blue Feather watched him from her seat at the stone table, twisting a bone bracelet in her hands.

"How could you give up the child?" he asked in an accusatory tone. "After everything we went through, after everything the Circle sacrificed, you just *gave* her to the half-breed!"

The Great Spirit turned from his place at the window, where he had been looking over his sunny, peaceful land with a warm smile. He would accept his War Chief's anger, because he knew it came from a place of genuine concern.

"I did not give up the child, Earth Keeper. I made a bargain with the half-breed."

"With the enemy."

"The half-breed is our enemy only when there cannot be peace between us. This child offers us peace, and more than that, she offers us hope." He crossed the room and took the other man by the arms. "The half-breed has taken it upon herself to find the land of the second deaths, and when she leaves on that quest, the child will take her place."

"There is no land of the second deaths. Everyone knows that."

"The half-breed does not." Creator released Earth Keeper and went back to the window, offering Blue Feather a comforting squeeze on the shoulder as he passed. "The child will be raised as an heir to the Land of the Dead's throne. She will be educated, trained, protected, and instructed in a way that will ready her for her rule. And she will rule as a child of the light, for while she will be raised as a child of the half-breed, the Circle already did their work with her."

At Earth Keeper's confused frown, the Great Spirit laughed. "You did not think the Circle had failed, did you? Smoke Speaker and his men were guiding the child even in the womb. Already she is instilled with the values of our kind. We have won, Earth Keeper. There is nothing left to be fearful or angry about."

"How can you be so sure? How can you know that the child will be safe with the half-breed?"

"Because," the Great Spirit said, his eyes flashing threateningly, "the child was meant to be with the half-breed all along."

At that, Earth Keeper was speechless, but Blue Feather suddenly found her voice. "What are you saying?"

Creator took a moment before answering to look out over his land, saddened by the blackness that tainted the Spirit World. It would take time, and a lot of it, for the earth to heal itself. "The half-breed was right, Blue Feather. A child raised in the Spirit World could never rule the Land of the Dead. Its darkness would destroy any traces of the light. But the light must also be there to rule, which means the child must come of my realm. This has always been the problem, as it is contradictory in its demands. When the Raven-Eater stole the boy and the half-breed saved him, I knew the time had finally come for the new ruler to be found. We only had to wait for the boy to grow, and produce a child of his own. A child we could guide in the light, yet was born of the Raven-Eater's blood."

"Why didn't you just tell *Kanegv* this?"

"The half-breed never would have accepted the child had she of been a gift."

"You tricked her."

"No. I allowed her to believe what she chose, and let her come to her decision on her own. This is the way it must be, Blue Feather, for the sake of both our spirit realms."

Having said his piece, the Great Spirit left the window and headed for the door, his long white robes flowing behind him. Just before leaving, he looked back at the two he had become fond of. "Be at peace, Earth Keeper. Wed the woman you love, and be happy." He gestured to Blue Feather, who was peering back at him with a slightly horrified expression, and smiled. "The half-breed is no longer a concern to us. I must go now to personally collect a spirit. I leave you both in peace."

After Creator had departed, Earth Keeper stopped pacing and let the words sink in. In his own way, the Great Spirit had brought about his own victory without ever actually taking an innocent life. He had blinded the half-breed to her future just as he had deafened her on the battlefield, and now all they had to do was wait.

In a way, the deceit amazed him. Creator had fooled the half-breed, something no one ever would have thought possible. But in doing so, he had also fooled Earth Keeper, and the spirit wasn't sure how he felt about being blindly sent to the Land of the Dead. He supposed that had he of known about the plan, the half-breed may have broken him and made him confess, and so Creator was only protecting himself, and his realm, in his secrecy.

Extending a hand, he grinned down at his future wife and lifted her to her feet. He made all the promises to Blue Feather he had never been able to make to a woman in his living life, and he meant them all. She would be his wife, and he her husband, and they would be happy together.

He kissed her long and hard, then swept her into a hug. As he held on to his savior and companion, he spoke of all the wonderful things they had to look forward to in their eternity among the Spirit World. Her face buried in his shoulder, Blue Feather could only pretend to be happy.

She had sacrificed her daughter's love and her father's life for Earth Keeper, and could only pray that the Red Road would one day bring them back together again.

* * *

It didn't seem possible to Brave Woman that this moment was actually happening. Nerves she didn't think were possible in the spirit realm tingled in her stomach and she clutched her hands open and closed in excitement. Having been summoned by the Great Spirit himself just days after Whisper fled the battlefield, Brave Woman could only pray that he called upon her for a greater purpose, though she feared she was soon to be punished for her loyalty to the half-breed.

She had done her part, and battled fiercely, leading warriors into war bravely, fighting for the half-breed's honor. And in return, she got nothing. She was forced to return to her village, forever cursed with the knowledge of what could have been, had Whisper not let rage get the better of her and murder the Elder. Despair ate at her, growing into hate the more she pictured the war.

Then, just when she was contemplating traveling back to the Fire Tower to demand retribution for her service, Creator sent his message.

He requested that she meet him at the Western Sun, a place she hadn't seen since she first passed into the Land of the Dead. Brave Woman wasted no time in traveling to the Sun, and when she arrived, the Great Spirit was waiting for her.

Suddenly shy, Brave Woman offered a nervous smile and stopped just before Creator. "Greetings, Great Spirit."

Creator regarded the woman cautiously. She was a beautiful spirit, strong and capable, gentle yet tough, anxious but struggling not to show fear. Yes, she would do nicely in the Spirit World. "Hello, my child. I am pleased you received my message, and decided to meet with me."

Brave Woman smiled and shook her head. "Who would refuse a message from Creator?" Her smile faded when he didn't answer. "Why have you called upon me?"

He clasped his hands behind his back casually, looking up at the spinning red and purple sun. It truly was a beauty on this side, he thought, a side he rarely ever saw. "You made a deal with the half-breed," he said, noting the alarm that crossed her face, "an agreement in exchange for your loyalty."

Her response was hesitant. "Yes, I did." She sighed, lowering her head. "Not that it matters. The half-breed ran from war, and in doing so our contract is broken. I agreed to help her win, and only then would she hold up her end of the agreement. The stories about her are true. She serves only herself."

The Great Spirit reached out and gently took her chin in his hand. "The half-breed is many things, but even I must admit that she never goes back on her word." Hope fluttered in Brave Woman's eyes. "She asked that I make this offer to you, and give you what you deserve."

For a moment, Brave Woman feared Creator was going to send her to her second death. Surely that was all Whisper thought she deserved for leading an army into the Spirit World without her permission. But the gentleness in his face told her otherwise. "And...what is that?"

The Great Spirit swept out an arm. "A place in the Spirit World, Brave Woman. A home with Little Eagle."

At the name, a man stepped through the Western Sun. Brave Woman's eyes widened, tears filling as joy warmed her. "Little Eagle," she whispered as he approached, adoration written across his face. For only a moment she allowed her gaze to drift back to the Great Spirit. "*Kanegv* asked this of you?"

Creator only nodded, allowing the half-breed this one moment of honor as Brave Woman approached the man she longed for, the one destined to be her mate in eternity. Whisper stayed true to her word, she realized, and gave her something so much more. Silently, unable to form the words that stuck in her throat as emotion overcame her, Brave Woman closed the gap between Little Eagle and herself, letting him take her face in his hands.

"My love," he said quietly, his voice awakening pleasant memories from so long ago. "I have come to bring you home, if you will still have me."

She took his hands in her own, a single tear escaping down her cheek. "My home has always been with you."

Together, they turned and followed the Great Spirit. Brave Woman left the Land of the Dead behind carrying nothing but the clothes on her back, eager to experience all that the Spirit World had waiting for her.

Chapter 55

Peace had settled in the Land of the Dead, the threat of war vanquished along with Blue Corn Maiden and her eternal winter. Father Moon hung high in the sky, sending white light down over the land in a picturesque portrait that softened the scent of death that still hung in the air. It even softened the half-breed as she sat atop the cliff that dropped down into the river, Hunting Hawk at her side.

Together, they peered out over the cliff, watching the water as it rippled. It seemed too short a time ago that they had stood over the Fire Tower cliffs after battling the Raven-Eater, fighting for their rightful places. Now, they rested after another fight, Whisper grazing her fingers over the scar on Hunting Hawk's back, Hunting Hawk relishing the waves of power that radiated from her.

She was different now, but somehow the same. She still was the face of youth, a young adult once on the verge of becoming a strong and beautiful woman, and yet it was not a face that told tales of childhood and youthful antics. It was a face hardened by time and battle, with haunting black eyes that saw down to one's very core. It was a face that revealed power that no one would ever comprehend, but Hunting Hawk did understand that the power was what made her what she was, what he loved and feared and respected.

For too long he and everyone else had feared her becoming the half-breed, letting go of her human side and giving in to the blood of the Raven-Eater. For too long they had tried to suppress that magic and the power that filled it. What had once given her a hardened look of evil was now becoming of her, made her look more like the royal leader that she was meant to be.

They had been wrong to fear this part of her. The half-breed wasn't what should have frightened them, but rather, the effort it took for Whisper to hold back the power within. It was that struggle that carried her rage, burning through her souls to wreak havoc on the spirit realms. But as the half-breed she was calm, ever-powerful in her newfound body, and even rational. Hunting Hawk didn't have to test her to know that she was still fiercely dangerous and able to split him in half if she so chose, but now she had control.

She had walked the Red Road, and discovered the place where fate led.

"Do you think it will work?" Hunting Hawk asked suddenly, staring down at the dark water so far below.

Whisper followed his gaze, the scabbed skin around her eyes nearly healed, noting the ripples in the water. Moonlight glinted off scales as the beast churned in the waves. "It will work," she answered softly, confidence in her statement. "It has to."

And she meant it. She'd started weaving the plans for finding the Elder, trepidation already filling her when she thought of what she must do. But it was making those plans that kept her going, gave her hope, helped her forget the pain and self-hate swarming within her at what she had done.

It would take many years to undo her actions. *Ukenta* was not easily caught, and Whisper would need to gather all the power within her to not only capture him, but also to see through his veiled promises and threats to get what she wanted from his mind. And even when she caught him, the journey to the land of second deaths would not be so simple. She didn't know how long it would take to map out her course, gather loyal followers willing to risk their souls, and prepare for the quest no spirit had ever embarked upon before, but she had an eternity to make it happen.

And while planning this journey, she had the child to train. Whisper couldn't leave the girl alone in the Land of the Dead, and nor could she bring her along. Creator would never agree to such an undertaking, which meant the search for Smoke Speaker had to wait until the child was old enough to be left in the care of another. But Whisper would wait for as many years as it took, and could only pray that by the time she found him, the Elder had not succumbed to whatever emptiness had entered his soul after its second death. For now, she would plan from the Fire Tower, until the day came for her to set off on what would be both a search for her lost grandfather and a battle to the final death between Whisper and the Raven-Eater.

Killing Smoke Speaker was an accident, but that didn't take away his passing. Nor did it make it any better that it was supposed to be Blue Feather on the other end of the blade. She had attempted to kill her own mother, blinded by grief and loss, and now they all knew the half-breed as she truly was.

Except, Whisper knew that wasn't her true self, as did Hunting Hawk. Although she didn't feel what most daughters felt for their mothers, there was love and respect there nonetheless. And she once would have given up her own life for the Elder. In fact, she had.

Now, she was torn between sensations of loss, defeat curdling in her gut and souring her vision of the world. There was a tangible emptiness in her souls due to

Smoke Speaker's death, and an even larger void in losing *Kamama*. The winged spirit had been her guide, her companion, her constant friend, and having that ripped away from her was like having a part of her own spirit brutally torn away and discarded. Whisper could only hope that in time, something else filled the hollowness that had settled deep within her before the nothingness overcame her altogether. Losing *Kamama* and the Elder was hard enough. She didn't know if she'd have the strength to fight what took their places should her fractured souls be invaded by the darker parts of her realm.

"The child and her mother have entered the spirit realm," she said then, staring out over the land from her spot on the edge of the cliff. "We must greet them at the Bridge of the Dead. And then, we go hunting."

Together, they rose and walked through the moonlight. The Land of the Dead welcomed them, and with each step, Whisper, *Kanegv*, the half-breed, forged a new path down the Red Road.

Epilogue

She was afraid of this dark place, this world of gray where lost figures roamed around with their heads hung low, shuffling their feet as they wandered. At first she tried to ask them where she was, what was happening, but their angry snarls scared her away. So now she wandered as well, letting the pull of an unknown force be her guide. In her arms, her child squirmed and fussed, tiny hands clutching at her hair.

After what seemed like an eternity, she came to a river, and there the old, decrepit man showed her the way across. At the Western Sun, he said, she would find salvation. She had asked about the woman with the black eyes, one of the few things she could remember from her old life, but the old man had refused to speak anymore. He was afraid of something, she could tell, which only frightened her more.

She kept the Western Sun in her sights, letting it lead her to the Bridge of the Dead. She remembered this place from the drawings, the ghouls that surrounded a bone-and-flesh gate, the tattered strips that held the bridge together, the disheveled hut that housed two phantom spirits of evil. She faced them bravely, staring them squarely in what she guessed to be their faces. And they let her pass, with just three words whispered in an echoed, whispery sound.

"*She. . .awaits. . .you.*"

The promise lured her forward, holding her crying baby girl close, braving the Bridge of the Dead with courage. And there, on the other side, stood the woman with the black eyes.

"They. . .they said you were waiting for me."

"They were right."

The voice was low and rough, yet gentle at the same time. It didn't scare her, but rather, it filled her with wonder as she looked into those eyes, so haunting and deep. "Where am I?"

Whisper smiled, holding out her arms and gesturing to the land all around them. "In the place you dreamed of."

Had she of known this woman with the black eyes, she would have recognized that smile as cunning and deceitful. In her ignorance, she thought the woman was kind and genuine, and that her glance down at baby Anya was one of fondness, and not cunning eagerness. "What's your name?"

"*Kanegv*. This is Hunting Hawk." Whisper nodded in his direction. "Come, and we will show you the way home."

She allowed them to show her the way, the Western Sun looming in the distance. She looked over her shoulder, a bit afraid, but they only smiled again and gestured the path home. These spirits were here to help, and she felt reassured that such friends had come for her and her child. So she turned and faced the sun bravely, eager for the adventure that awaited them.

When the woman's back had turned, Hunting Hawk spoke, his voice low. "So what happens next?"

"We welcome her to the Land of the Dead," Whisper replied, her eyes on the woman. "The child's spirit was taken just before passing into the spirit realm, and so she will grow into her matured body here. But the mother died in the living realm, and unexpectedly, so her spirit belongs to us." The mother arriving in the Land of the Dead had been a surprise to Whisper, as the contract had been for the child only. Unless she had misunderstood the Great Spirit, the mother's death was purely coincidental, and unfortunately so. Now, Whisper was faced with the decision of what to do next. The woman should have gone to the Spirit World, but Whisper had taken her from that eternity, just as Creator had taken the Elder from his. Having the mother with the Great Spirit was a risk she was not willing to take.

Whisper and Hunting Hawk followed the woman as she headed toward the Western Sun, keeping in her wake. "We will continue with our plans as already discussed. The child will live with us," she said contemplatively, pondering over the spirit before her, "in the Fire Tower."

"And the mother?"

Whisper narrowed her eyes as they reached the outer edges of the Western Sun, feeling the familiar strain and burn. The woman stopped as well, frightened by the sensation as the child began to wail. When she answered, her voice was quiet.

"Destroy her."

The look on Hunting Hawk's face revealed his surprise. "Is that truly necessary?"

"The child belongs to us, Hunting Hawk," Whisper answered. "We are her family now. The woman is not supposed to be here, and we cannot have her searching for her daughter from the Spirit World. Destroy the woman, and we will create a new lineage, one that not even Creator would dare to challenge."

A rumble made its way under their feet, shaking the land of Waiting and nearly sending them all to their knees. Something dark and sinister was waking beneath them, and the child's presence only made it stronger. Hunting Hawk grabbed hold of the woman before she and the baby could fall, but Whisper held her ground, sending a scornful look down at the earth, lips pulled back into a sneer.

"And then, Raven-Eater," she snarled, power sending her promise down to the deepest depths of the land she would one day find, "I am coming after you."

Acknowledgements

Walk the Red Road was made possible by the generous efforts of many amazing people. Without the incredible support and enthusiasm shown for Beyond the Western Sun, Walk the Red Road would be just a dream. I am so appreciative of the many opportunities provided to me after the publication of the first novel in The Whisper Legacy, and look forward to working with more schools that are implementing, or planning to use, my book in the classroom.

As always, I must take the time to thank my family. Those closest to me know how special writing is; they understand my passion for it, and never stop believing in me. The support shown by my parents, brother, grandparents, aunts and uncles, and everyone else is remarkable and what inspires me to write more. It also helps tremendously that I have a loving and awesome husband who never lets me lose sight of my dreams, and is always there to offer words of support and motivation that keep me on my own Red Road.

In addition to my family, my friends have been an extraordinary support system. The SB/E girls have given me a newfound inspiration to write, and their friendships mean the world to me. Along with this, I must thank those who have provided their own time and energy to fuel the creation of Walk the Red Road, including Mackenzy Dodds, my trusted young reader; Kate Knapp and Roger Grondin for being the most excellent of editors; Kristi Strong, my best writing friend who shares in my passion for the written word; Melissa DeSimone for giving me the courage to market my novels; Nicole VanNienwenhove for helping with the text on my cover; Steph Williams for advice on my synopsis; and Kelly Hall, an unbelievable artist who created the cover art for this book.

Kelly brought her own vision to The Whisper Legacy while breathing life into a character close to my heart, and it has been an immeasurable joy working with her on this project.

Sources & Inspirations

As with <u>Beyond the Western Sun</u>, my inspirations for the legends and lore in <u>Walk the Red Road</u> came from years and years of reading, researching, and listening to storytellers speak about their Native American culture. To ensure accuracy of my memories, I used the following to verify accounts of certain stories:

Blue Corn Maiden: First People Website. http://www.firstpeople.us/FP-Html-Legends/BlueCornMaidenandtheComingofWinter-Acoma.html.

Splinter Foot Girl: First People Website. http://www.firstpeople.us/FP-Html-Legends/SplinterFootGirl-Arapaho.html.

Various Stories: Native American Lore. http://home.online.no/~arnfin/native/lore/index0.htm.

Stay Tuned for Book Three in The Whisper Legacy

www.ingramcontent.com/pod-product-compliance
Lightning Source LLC
Chambersburg PA
CBHW020341180626
46812CB00001B/298